Catherine Jones was in
husband for twenty-five. ...
life in civvie street in Oxf...
She is the author of one p...
available from Piatkus, an...
army wife under the name A...

Sisters In Arms

Catherine Jones

PIATKUS

First published in Great Britain in 1998 by
Judy Piatkus (Publishers) Ltd of
5 Windmill Street, London W1P 1HF

This edition published in 1999

The moral right of the author has been asserted

A catalogue record for this book is available from the British Library

ISBN 0 7499 3088 8

Set in Times by
Phoenix Photosetting, Chatham, Kent
Printed and bound in Great Britain by
Mackays of Chatham PLC, Chatham, Kent

Acknowledgements

While I was writing this book I was constantly amazed by the kindness and enthusiasm of the people who helped me. In particular I would like to thank: Colonel Jackie Smith, Colonel Nigel Williams, Lieutenant Colonel Stewart Walker, Major Alison Forster-Knight, Major Sheila Johncey, Lynn Curtis of Piatkus Books, Ann de Gale, Nigel de Lee, James and Caroline Good, Abigail Kirby-Harris, Sarah Leigh of Peters, Fraser and Dunlop Group Ltd, Diana McLeod, Jayne Owen, James O'Donoghue of the Serious Fraud Office, Don Short of the Solo Literary Agency Ltd and Sheridan Stevens JP.

I must also emphasise that all the characters in this book are entirely fictitious and no one is responsible for my interpretation of any facts or information that I was given.

This book is for Penny, Victoria and Tim, with my love.
They were ignored too much while I was writing it.

Westbury, July 1987

Amanda Hardwick, blonde, statuesque and in the latter half of her twenties, alighted from the Paddington train at Westbury station and immediately began assessing her fellow candidates for the Army Regular Commissions Board. Her first thought was that she was the oldest in the group by a long way. Beside her the others all looked like schoolchildren, and then she realised that most of them would be exactly that, albeit sixth-formers. Since she had been teaching French in a state secondary school in Northampton for nearly five years, she used the skills she had acquired sizing up new classes to take stock of her fellow candidates. Mostly what she saw was entirely predictable, like in a new tutor group of Year Sevens: a gaggle of kids who wanted to do their best, not stand out from the others, and get a decent result at the end of the day. However, the tall, slim girl with the wild fluorescent-orange hair – surely she couldn't have chosen that colour deliberately? – dressed in a scruffy calf-length dress like an overlong T-shirt, and an outsized leather jacket, made Amanda do a double-take. She looked as if she should be travelling around with a New Age commune, not wanting to become a future member of HM Forces. Amanda glanced at the man in uniform who had been sent to pick them up and was amused to see that even he was staring in amazement at this apparition. She hid her smile as she watched him shake his head incredulously.

Amanda climbed on the bus last of all and sat at the back. She saw that Miss Misfit was sitting next to a poor kid who looked terrified out of her wits. Whether this was at the prospect of the Commissions Board or whether the red hair was the cause, Amanda couldn't tell. She caught the eye of the soldier in his rear-view mirror and grinned at him. As if he understood, he raised one eyebrow and shook his head. Amanda nearly laughed out loud. She suspected he'd never seen the like either. As Amanda watched, the two girls got into conversation.

Edwina Austin, the red-head, was acutely aware of how out of place she looked. She had known she'd made a ghastly mistake with her choice of clothes as soon as she had got off the train and seen the half-dozen other hopefuls. She had noticed their glances and realised that whereas her hair and clothes had been almost conservative at art college, they were distinctly out of place here. As she had boarded the bus she'd heard one of the boys – one whom she had rapidly summed up as a trainspotting wimp – snigger and mutter, 'No chance.' Well, fuck you, thought Edwina, squaring her shoulders and preparing to brazen her mistake out. The girl next to her on the bus looked very young but she had a pleasant face. Edwina didn't think it would do any harm to try and make a friend.

'Hi,' she said. 'I'm Edwina Austin.'

'Lizzie Armstrong,' came the reply in a cultured, almost posh voice, so different from her own harsh, north-country one. Lizzie shifted round in her seat slightly so she could offer her hand to Edwina. It was obvious to Edwina, from the expression on Lizzie's face, that the other girl was wary of her. It's my hair, she thought morosely. But she was grateful, all the same, that this schoolgirl was taking a chance on being friendly towards her. Edwina thought that it was probably because after these few days they were unlikely to meet again – if first impressions counted for anything, Edwina knew she'd already blown her chances of being selected. Conversely Lizzie looked, and sounded, exactly the sort the Army was probably looking for.

'I'm really nervous about this, aren't you?' Lizzie said.

'Yes. Shit scared. God knows what I'll do if I fail. I tried art college but it didn't work out, and I don't want to go back to living with my mum.' Edwina paused, then added, 'Anyway, I just really like the idea of joining up.'

'Me, too.'

'Do you know what's involved at the Board?'

'Not really. My father told me what he did when he joined up, but that was donkey's years ago and I expect everything's different now.'

'Oh. You come from an Army family then?' Unfair advantage or what?

'Only partly. My mother was in the Wrens.'

2

Christ, thought Edwina, this gets worse and worse. I don't stand an earthly against the likes of her. I bet she knows stacks more than I do. Although, Edwina reasoned, the pressure is worse for her; if she fails her dad will want to know why, whereas if I fail my mum won't give a toss.

The conversation dried up, partly because both girls were engrossed in their own thoughts, and partly because it was apparent that, apart from a shared wish to become Army officers, they had little in common. Edwina sensed that Lizzie had sized her up and dismissed her chances, which made her all the more determined to prove to these toffee-nosed public-school types that she was just as good as them. Still, no point in alienating Lizzie. She obviously had some good gen on what was going to happen over the next few days and she might be persuaded to share the info.

They stared out of the windows at the small town of Westbury. Then they were through the town centre, such as it was, and the minibus prepared to turn off the road.

'Look, we're here,' said Lizzie. Edwina followed the direction of the other girl's gaze and saw a pair of stone pillars with a wrought-iron archway over the top.

'*Arbeit macht frei*,' she muttered to herself as they passed underneath.

'Sorry,' said Lizzie, not quite catching what had been said.

'Nothing,' replied Edwina, realising that her comment might well be construed as tasteless in anyone's book. Now was no time to make enemies. She told herself to watch out that her quick tongue didn't let her down. She felt a frisson of apprehension as the bus came to a halt. She wished that she'd worn a skirt and jersey. But stuff it – it was too late to go home and get some more suitable clothes. Nothing for it but to front it out.

At the back of the minibus Amanda was still riveted by Edwina's appearance. If her hair wasn't such a mess she could be quite attractive – although she was so thin as to be verging on scrawny. A teaching friend had once described one of their sixth-formers as 'built like a racing snake'. Looking at Edwina this phrase popped into Amanda's mind. The other girl was certainly pretty in an immature way, although Amanda suspected that her mother still dictated how her hair should be cut and what clothes she should wear. On the other

3

hand, the red-head, who was obviously in need of large quantities of guidance, couldn't have received any at all. What on earth had possessed her to come on something like the Regular Commissions Board so incredibly badly prepared? Surely someone had briefed her about what to expect? And anyway, even a complete idiot would realise that if you wanted to join something as traditional and conventional as the Army then it would be a bright idea to look as though you were capable of conforming. Amanda shook her head and sighed. Well, if nothing else it would be interesting to see what other gaffes this strange female would no doubt make over the next few days.

The bus pulled to a halt and Amanda gathered her bits and pieces together and got off. A woman in a blue housecoat asked them to gather round her and then, looking at a mill-board in her hand, asked them to follow her to their accommodation block.

'If you could unpack and then go over to the candidates' mess' – she pointed to the large building they could see across the lawn – 'for lunch and a briefing. Lunch is at twelve-thirty, so you've plenty of time.'

'It's like being back at boarding school,' Lizzie said to Edwina.

'I wouldn't know. My local comp didn't encourage us to stay on the premises after hours.'

Amanda saw Lizzie redden. Poor little scrap, she thought, that was mean of the red-head. Just because she's already made a balls-up of her own chances, there's no need to take it out on anyone else. They were escorted to a low brick building surrounded by immaculate rose beds and even neater lawns.

'OK, Miss Austin and' – there was a pause while the woman consulted her board again – 'Miss Armstrong?' The two girls answered their names. 'First room on the right.'

Poor Miss Armstrong, getting stuck with the weirdo as a roommate, thought Amanda. She hoped that the schoolgirl was tougher than she looked, because she was probably going to need it if the red-head went on being a prize bitch.

'Mr Brown?' An affirmative from one of the boys in cords and sports jacket. 'The single room at the end.' The list continued and the rooms were allocated until finally, 'Mr Wetherall and Mr Hardwick?'

'I think there's a mistake,' said Amanda. 'I'm *Ms* Hardwick.'

'Oh dear. That's my fault, I should have double-checked. Still, no harm done. There's a spare bed in the room on the right.' And she ushered Amanda into the same room as Lizzie and Edwina.

4

Bugger, thought Amanda. She was not best pleased at the idea of sharing a room with anyone – she was a bit long in the tooth for this sort of girls' dorm treatment – and she was certainly unhappy at the prospect of being cooped up with the red-head. But what the hell? And if she wanted to escape from the tedium of teaching and into something more fulfilling then she'd just have to knuckle down and get on with it.

Edwina had already thrown a scruffy old holdall on to her bed and was sitting beside it. She had let her mask of hard indifference slip and on her face was an expression of abject despair. She looked sadly at Lizzie, who had taken the bed-space next to her.

'Oh, Lizzie! How could I have been such a fool? I can see I've got this all wrong. My clothes are awful and I don't stand a chance. What am I going to do?'

Lizzie looked at Edwina and stopped unpacking.

'Well, I think we wear some sort of Army coverall quite a lot of the time. And perhaps if we made your hair a bit less visible – tied it back or something?'

Amanda, across the room, had to restrain herself from suggesting that the only think that would make Edwina's hair less visible would be a brown paper bag over it.

'God, it's a fright, isn't it? I wanted just to perk up the colour a bit – it's auburn really – and I didn't read the instructions on the bottle properly.' That wasn't quite the truth; she hadn't read the instructions at all. For all her openness, even Edwina couldn't bring herself to admit publicly that she'd been so utterly foolish.

'Look,' said Lizzie kindly, 'I've got a couple of blouses I could lend you, if that would help. I'd let you borrow a pair of cords but they'd only come down to your knees.' There was a good six-inch height difference between the two girls.

Edwina sniffed miserably. 'Why do I always bugger up my life?' she moaned. 'I screwed up at school and got crap A-level grades. I went to art college thinking it would be brilliant and wild and exciting but I was bored fartless. None of the other students had any oomph about them at all, or else they were into illegal substances.' Lizzie's eyes widened at this and Edwina wondered if she'd ever known anyone who'd smoked dope, let alone taken heroin. She continued, 'Then when I left I couldn't get a job for months and when I finally did, in a publishing company, they got taken over by some American outfit and I was out on my ear.'

'Well, that's hardly your fault,' said Lizzie.

'No, but now I've finally decided which direction I really want to go in, and it looks as though I'm going to make a complete balls of it.'

'You don't know that,' Lizzie said.

'Get real,' retorted Edwina.

Amanda felt she had to join in. If she was going to be sharing a room with these two for a few days she couldn't ignore them. 'Come on. It's not as bad as that. We none of us know quite what's involved. Besides which, it's your *potential* as an Army officer they're after. There's no way they're expecting any of us to be perfect. They want people they can train.' She realised she hadn't introduced herself and held out her hand. 'I'm Amanda, by the way.'

Lizzie and Edwina introduced themselves and the three girls continued to chat as they unpacked and put away their clothes, and then got down to the business of tying back Edwina's hair. After fifteen minutes they all knew that Lizzie had gone to boarding school at the age of eight, that her father was a lieutenant colonel and that she had lived in more houses than she could remember – school seemed to have been the only constant in her life. Edwina told them about her scrapes at art school, that she had an odd mother and that she'd represented Yorkshire Schools at cross-country and had successfully completed two marathons. And Amanda revealed that she'd discovered she hated teaching and that she'd thought of joining the Army after meeting a recruiting officer who had come to talk to the sixth form. They even broached the subject of their reasons for joining up: Lizzie admitted that it was because every relation she'd ever known had had a career in uniform and she couldn't think of anything else to do; Edwina was drawn by the promise of all the opportunities for sport; and Amanda said she was after travel and a chance to get away from children and work exclusively with adults who had a sense of discipline.

As they walked over to the mess for lunch and the promised briefing, Edwina moaned yet again about her hair, although it was now in a tight French plait and, as Lizzie had predicted, slightly less visible.

'Why the hell didn't you dye it back to its right colour before you came here?' asked Amanda.

'It didn't seem so out of place in Leeds,' said Edwina, not the least bit thrown by Amanda's directness. 'I didn't realise what a backwater I was coming to. And I didn't realise just how' – she paused, not quite knowing how to carry on, but couldn't think of a better way of phrasing it – 'middle class everyone here would be.'

Amanda snorted. 'Christ, Edwina, you're priceless. Do you really know what you're planning to join? Who on earth did you expect to find here if it wasn't a whole bunch of middle-class, ex-public-school, middle-of-the-road, dyed-in-the-wool ordinary people?' As she said this, they walked into the main anteroom of the candidates' mess to be confronted by about sixty other hopefuls, all members of the socio-economic groups that she had just described. Edwina reddened as everyone in the room stared at her – and her hair. She squared her shoulders and led her two companions to a group of chairs on the far side of the room, ignoring the whispered comments. Edwina had never been lacking in courage.

'Let me buy you two a drink before lunch,' she offered.

'A tonic water for me, please,' said Amanda.

'And me,' said Lizzie. 'I wouldn't mind a gin it it but I've got a feeling that arriving at one's first test smelling of drink mightn't be too bright an idea.'

Edwina, who'd been about to order a Bacardi and Coke for herself, changed her mind. There was a minute possibility of her clothes and hair being overlooked, but Lizzie was right about the booze.

After lunch they received the promised briefing from the SO1, a title he obligingly translated for them as Staff Officer Grade One, which meant he was the training officer there. It obviously made sense to Lizzie, coming as she did from a military background, but Edwina and Amanda were still none the wiser. Having been told what their programme would be for the remainder of the week, laughed at the couple of jokes, and been assured that the Board did not have microphones and cameras installed to monitor the candidates when they were not being tested (a claim none of them was sure they believed), they were then split into syndicates. Before they left for the first series of tests, the syndicates were photographed with each candidate wearing a numbered bib, which they would continue to wear for the remainder of the week, because, as the SO1 explained, the Board could not be expected to remember everyone's name and this prevented mix-ups.

From then until dinner they had almost no time to call their own. There were IQ tests, tests on their knowledge of the Services, their general knowledge and current affairs and their grasp of the English language. By the time they had finished that lot, they were all feeling

shattered. The three young women straggled back to their accommodation lacking the energy to do more than exchange a few words.
Amanda said that she was going to have a bath and then go over to
the mess to watch the news.

'Too much making my brain ache and sitting around,' said
Edwina, 'If I don't go for a run I'll go spare.'

'You don't think you should watch the news?' said Amanda.
'They seem shit-hot on current affairs here.'

'I've got a Walkman. I'll listen as I run; that's if I can find Radio 4
on it. I don't even know if it can get it.'

Amanda didn't say anything but wondered how anyone could
exist without Radio 4. When, after several minutes, Edwina had
failed to tune into the station, she found it for her in a matter of seconds. Edwina thanked her.

'I'll be back in about an hour or so. Save me a place at dinner.'

'Tell you what. We'll meet you in the bar at seven o'clock.'

'See you then.' And Edwina loped out of the door wearing shorts,
a singlet and a pair of training shoes that were dropping to bits.

'I wonder how far she's running?' said Amanda, who was adequately fit but certainly no athlete.

'Goodness knows,' said Lizzie, 'but she mentioned at lunch that
her best time for the London Marathon was three hours fifteen.'

'Jesus. That's fit!'

Amanda went off to have a soak in the bath and to collect her
thoughts. As she lay in the almost scalding scented water she wondered if she really would fit into the disciplined world of the Armed
Forces. She compared herself to Lizzie, who was obviously a cer-
tainty for selection, and felt quite despondent. She wondered if she
was too old for this sort of regime, but twenty-eight wasn't over the
hill, was it? Surely, if she had the right qualities her maturity might
be considered a bonus rather than a drawback. Amanda sank lower in
the water, closed her eyes and hoped against hope that the Army
would find her acceptable.

The truth of the matter was that she wasn't a natural loner, she
hated living on her own and she thought that the camaraderie of the
Army would fill an impending void in her life. When she had first
started in teaching there had been no shortage of other single women
with whom to share a flat, but now she was nearing thirty, all her
friends had married and she found herself becoming increasingly
isolated. She'd rowed with her parents – a matter she hated thinking

about – and had drifted from one unsatisfactory relationship to another. She had envisaged a future of teaching with decreasing enthusiasm by day, followed by lonely nights. The Army recruiting literature, given to her by the visiting schools liaison officer, had promised so many of the things her life seemed to be missing. Once she had checked that her age wouldn't be a bar, she had looked with increasing eagerness into the possibility of joining up. And best of all, living in an officers' mess would mean that she would have the privacy of a room of her own while enjoying the comforting knowledge that there were plenty of people in the same building. Yes, the Army could be the answer to a maiden's prayer, she thought hopefully.

The water was growing cold. Amanda got out and towelled herself vigorously. It crossed her mind that she'd lived in that sort of environment before; at teacher-training college. But then, although the girls on the course had been in the majority, the boys had all seemed to have one objective – to screw as many of the female residents as possible in the shortest possible time. Amanda thought that the sort of code of conduct the Army would insist on would prevent that sort of harassment. Or at least she hoped so; she felt too old to fight off unwanted attentions all the time.

After dinner a few of the more energetic candidates, and those possessing cars, ventured out to discover the local pubs near Westbury. Edwina had considered the idea but decided that she wasn't going to jeopardise her chances more than she had done already. She'd be better off staying in and mugging up further on the day's events around the world. If she passed RCB she could go and get blitzed with her mates in Leeds any day. It also meant that she had the chance to quiz Lizzie further about what she could expect over the next few days. It soon became apparent from Lizzie's answers that there was no way to 'bone up' – either she had the right stuff or she hadn't, and if she hadn't she wouldn't fit into the organisation anyway. The trouble was, now that Edwina had met some of the people with whom she might be sharing a career, now that she had seen the Army close to – albeit just this one establishment – and now that she knew more about the sort of jobs she might find herself doing, she was even more eager to pass. She was grateful for Lizzie's input and for lending her a few more suitable bits of clothing. Amanda had come up with a pair of slacks which fitted reasonably well, despite being too big round the waist, and Edwina knew that both she and Lizzie were warming towards her, now they had got over their first impressions. They'd even swapped phone numbers and addresses and promises of keeping in touch if one – or all – should fail.

The next day was taken up with yet more interviews and further tests of their mental powers, their logic processes, their physical abilities, their leadership qualities, their sense of humour, their confidence and any other characteristic which the Army could find a way of examining and evaluating. Naturally, the candidates were unaware of the whole gamut which was being scrutinised: when they were required to do the assault course they could all see that the Commissions Board was taking a close interest in their strength, agility and general fitness levels, but what they couldn't see was that their determination to clear an obstacle which defeated them was of greater interest. Anyone could be made fit enough to scale a twelve-foot wall – not everyone had the strength of character to keep trying to overcome an obstacle despite being wet, cold, bruised and battered. When it was time for group discussions, it wasn't just the candidates' input which the Board wanted to hear; they were also looking for those who listened to the points of view of others and could recognise an idea of merit, even if it opposed their own.

Edwina could see that Lizzie had the whole process buttoned up, and although she was confident that her natural physical ability was easily the best in their group, she wasn't convinced that she'd managed the other tests at all well. For a start, telling one overweight and dim-witted candidate what she thought of her when she clouted Edwina with a plank in the leaderless test (accidentally, but it still hurt) was probably going to count against her. She wasn't hopeful that her immediate apology negated her outburst, but it was too late by then.

Later, at lunch, Lizzie had consoled her. 'You only said what we all thought, you know, Edwina. It's just that *fuckwit* was probably a teensy bit strong, even if it was awfully funny.'

'I know,' groaned Edwina, 'I shouldn't have said that. But the cretin should've looked where she was going. And then to look like she was going to cry . . . I ask you!'

'Well, your apology sounded sincere.'

'That's a relief, because it bloody wasn't.'

Lizzie giggled. 'Oh, Edwina, I do hope we both pass. Sandhurst will be fun to be at, but you'll put a bomb under it – I just know.'

Edwina grinned ruefully. 'Well, here's hoping. You must be a dead cert – but me . . .? I cocked up arriving here with those clothes, and that's that. I told them at the interview that I'd like to have a chance to rerun that bit of my life. The nice colonel – you know, the dishy one' – Lizzie nodded – 'well, he said it was to my credit that I recognised that, but even so I think I stuffed my chances.'

'But you were brilliant round the obstacle course, and in the planning exercise you seemed to have the whole thing sorted. I got completely side-tracked by all the red herrings they threw in.'

'Never mind. We'll see.' But Edwina was anything but hopeful about her chances. 'You're so lucky; having the right background must be an advantage.'

'But they're not looking for stereotypes,' said Lizzie, trying to sound reassuring.

'That's as may be, but my home life can't be standard for potential officers.'

'It can't be that different, surely?' said Amanda.

'I wouldn't bet on it. My mum is completely scatty and disorganised. Her excuse is that she's a painter. Oil paintings,' she added quickly, 'not home decorating.'

'Gosh, really?' Lizzie was impressed. 'Is she famous?'

'Well, she sells her stuff, but we couldn't live on it. Luckily she had a loaded relation who left her some money in trust, otherwise God knows how we'd survive.'

'Handy,' observed Amanda.

'Especially as my dad doesn't contribute. He buggered off when I was about seven – couldn't stand my mother's total lack of organisation. We haven't heard from him in years.' Lizzie and Amanda didn't know what to say. 'Anyway, enough about me. Even if they're not after stereotypes, you can probably get your dad to pull a few strings, can't you, Lizzie?'

'He's only a lieutenant colonel.'

'Sounds pretty senior to me,' said Edwina, who had learnt the order of Army ranks in an effort to look prepared for her possible future career.

'Yes, but only in the RCT.'

Edwina knew that this was the Royal Corps of Transport, but she was at a loss to see why that should make him less important than any other lieutenant colonel. Christ, the Army was complicated!

'Even so, you've had the advantage of living around the military all your life, so don't you know someone with some clout?' asked Amanda.

'Not really. I was away at boarding school for a lot of it. I've never had that much to do with it, to be honest. Every time I came home my parents seemed to be living in a new house, and by the time I made any friends on the patch they would have moved again. I knew the families of friends at school much better than any of my parents' neighbours.'

Edwina thought this sounded rather sad.

'What about you, Amanda?'

'My father is a full-time history teacher and a part-time Methodist lay preacher.' She could have added that he was also a bully and a tyrant, but that would have been owing up to too much.

'Seriously, what does he really do?' said Edwina, not believing a word of it.

'He really is.'

Edwina opened and shut her mouth. Then she said, 'But you drink.'

'I do lots of things he doesn't approve of.' To the extent that he called me an 'abomination' and threw me out of his house, she thought bitterly.

'Does he approve of you changing career?'

Amanda shrugged by way of an answer. Possibly, possibly not, but then he mightn't know. They hadn't spoken for years. He'd forbidden her mother to have any contact with her, and although Amanda still wrote, she never had a reply, so she didn't know if they read her letters or not.

Each of the three girls looked at the other two and thought how odd their childhoods had been in comparison with her own.

When the result arrived, with amazing military efficiency only twenty-four hours after her return home, Edwina was both delighted and amazed at her pass. Her emotions were only surpassed by the indifference of her mother, who hardly paused in the painting of a large canvas to acknowledge the fact. Gwenda Austin made it plain to her daughter that she couldn't understand where she'd got this idea that a career in the Army was for her. Apart from the fact that the IRA seemed hell-bent on bombing and machine-gunning the British Army into oblivion, she just couldn't see her wild and ill-

12

disciplined daughter taking orders from anyone. Even Edwina's protestations about all the sporting opportunities, the adventurous training and the chance to take up things like skiing and sub-aqua failed to convince her mother that this was the right career move.

'Well, I'm not going to get excited about it,' she said, mixing cobalt blue and white on her palette. 'You probably won't last five minutes in the Army. You'll either flounce out or get kicked out. It isn't just sport, it's discipline too.'

'Thanks for the vote of confidence, Mum. By the way, the perspective of that house is all wrong.' It wasn't, but it would panic her mother for hours, and Edwina wanted to get her own back for Mum's lack of enthusiasm. She fished Lizzie's number out of her jeans pocket and rang her – ignoring her mother's exhortations about waiting for the cheap rate.

'Brilliant,' shrieked Lizzie down the line.

'It's good, isn't it? And I'm really pleased that you passed too. But I knew you would, so it can't have come as a surprise to you either.'

'No, but Daddy would have been dreadfully cross if I'd made a mess of it, and I really didn't want to let him down.'

'I wonder if Amanda passed?'

'No idea. I haven't had a chance to phone her yet. Do you want to, or shall I?'

'I don't mind. Why don't I give her a ring, then if it's good news I'll tell her to ring you. If you don't hear from her, you'll know the answer.'

'OK. I'll see you in September then, when our intake starts, unless you want to meet in London beforehand.'

'That's an idea. I'll be in touch about that.'

'OK. Well, until then goodbye, and well done.'

Intake, thought Edwina. Trust Lizzie to have the jargon off pat already. 'Just one thing before you go, Lizzie – '

'What's that?'

'I'm going shopping right away for a skirt and jersey, and I'm going to get my bloody hair fixed.'

13

The Royal Military Academy, Sandhurst, September 1987

Edwina was completely stunned by her first sight of the Royal Military Academy. Even her mother, who was difficult to faze, stopped the car and stared in amazement when they arrived at the head of the long rhododendron-lined drive which led from the A30 and which suddenly broadened out to present a vista of the three colleges, all imposingly grand, fronted by acres of sports pitches and lawns. Immediately facing them, and most beautiful, was the pale and elegant Old College. In front of it were ancient cannons and stands of even older trees.

'Good God, Edwina. I thought you'd be training in an army camp – this is like a stately home.' There was a pause as they looked across at the view.

'Bloody hell,' whispered Edwina, awe-struck.

'I suppose I ought to have listened to you about my clothes,' said her mother suddenly. Then she added accusingly, 'Why didn't you tell me what it would be like?'

'Because I didn't know, not really. I mean, I had a glossy brochure about becoming an officer, but it was mostly about the sort of jobs I could do. There was a picture of that bit,' Edwina waved a hand in the direction of the Grand Entrance to Old College, 'but I thought it was quite small.' The photo Edwina had seen had given no clue as to the vast frontage of the wonderfully proportioned neo-classical building, with its portico and wings and graceful colonnades. Edwina suddenly wished her mum were more conventional. At home, flowing skirts, gypsy blouses and shawls seemed normal, but here . . . Oh God, it was like RCB again, when she herself had turned up in the wrong stuff. At least this time Edwina was certain that her own neat wool skirt and co-ordinating jacket were perfectly OK –

14

she had Lizzie's advice on a joint shopping trip to London to thank for that – but she was worried about what impression her mother would make and whether it would matter.

'Stop fussing,' Gwenda had said to Edwina when she'd suggested that her mother should wear something less outré. 'It's you that's joining up, not me.'

'But Mum, I know this sort of thing matters. I know what the other people will be like. And please don't wear your shawl, you look like some sort of ageing hippie.' As Edwina said this she knew she'd made a mistake. She'd inherited her own wilfulness from her mother, and nothing was more likely to make her mother dig in her heels than a comment like that.

'Don't you care?' said Edwina quietly, in desperation.

'I am who I am and I'll wear what I like, thank you.'

No wonder her dad had walked out, thought Edwina. Her mother was the pits!

Edwina resigned herself to the inevitable, and remembered that when she'd wanted a place at art college she'd been jolly grateful to have a mother who was an artist, albeit only a moderately successful one. It was a shame that now she'd chosen a completely different career, her mother seemed such a flaming liability. Edwina sighed deeply.

'And what about that place?' asked her mother, looking at the massive Edwardian red-brick building to their right, topped with a large domed clock tower.

'I don't think that was in the booklet at all. I don't know what all these buildings are, Mum,' said Edwina, feeling exasperated with her own ignorance. 'That's what I'm here to learn about. And if we don't hurry up we're going to give that soldier over there apoplexy.' Edwina grinned at the man in green camouflage who was frantically waving his arms to direct them to the parking spaces allocated to the new cadets and their parents. He looked relieved when Gwenda slipped their battered Volkswagen into gear and drove up to the side of Old College as he'd directed them. She parked it behind a large Mercedes and a Volvo estate, where it looked more ramshackle than ever. As they got out of the car another soldier directed them to the front entrance, where several frighteningly smart female soldiers met them; all stared hard at Gwenda.

Once Edwina had booked in, she was advised to take the car round the back of the College, as it would be nearer to their lines and so easier for them to move the mass of luggage which filled the little boot.

'What the hell are "lines"?' asked Gwenda when they got back to the car.

Edwina shrugged, and said that she hoped Lizzie would arrive soon to translate. Her ignorance was beginning to make her feel miserable, despite her fantastic new surroundings. They followed the directions given to them until they reached Chapel Square, where they had been told they could park while they unloaded Edwina's kit. There were several cars there already, with parents and students busy toing and froing laden with a variety of paraphernalia such as cases, duvets, ironing boards and posters. Edwina got out of the car and gazed at the Memorial Chapel, which dominated the quiet, tree-filled square. She wondered to whom it was a memorial.

With a slight feeling of apprehension, Edwina walked up the steps and through the door into the back of Old College. The corridor was dim and cool and smelled strongly of floor polish, which was unsurprising when you looked at the shine on it. Edwina's heels clacked loudly as she walked along, wondering where to go. A smart young female soldier with several stripes and a crown on her sleeve appeared and showed her which room had been allocated to her.

'I'll come and collect you at three o'clock to take you up to the anteroom. You'll be able to meet the DS and the other students and have a cup of tea.'

'Thanks,' said Edwina as she put her case on the bed, although she only understood the bit about meeting the students and tea. DS? Anteroom? Heigh-ho, she thought, I'll learn.

Her mother, following with a duvet clasped in her arms, looked impressed when she saw the room, which was bigger than Edwina's room at home and boasted the advantage of a large sash window looking out on to the square.

'Well, it's a sight better than your digs at college, I'll say that.'

Edwina forbore to mention that the standard would not have to be very high to be an improvement – in fact anywhere not running with damp or with a mainline railway yards from the bedroom window would be luxury in comparison. She looked around her. The room seemed more than adequately furnished with a bed, armchair, bureau, wardrobe and dressing table, and in the corner a basin. Edwina had never had a basin in her bedroom before, unless you counted the couple of nights she had once had in a B&B in the Dales.

Her mother, who had busied herself opening cupboards and testing the light switches, revised her opinion to 'very nice' in a tone faintly tinged with disapproval, as if Edwina didn't deserve these conditions. Edwina didn't reply. She was gazing out of the window at the chapel and trying to come to terms with her feelings of pride and awe; that she was a part of this amazing establishment and her home was going to be in this fabulous building for the next seven and a half months.

She was over the moon to discover that the Army, delighting in order, had allocated the rooms for the female students alphabetically, and thus Lizzie Armstrong was to be next door to her. As she ferried her stuff in from the car she kept her eyes peeled for the arrival of her friend. The shriek she let out echoed loudly when she saw Lizzie struggling along the corridor hefting a suitcase, and several heads appeared round doors to see what had caused the commotion.

'Lizzie! Great news; they've put us next to each other,' yelled Edwina along the length of the corridor.

'Brill,' replied Lizzie, panting slightly. 'Hey, the hair's better,' she added as she got closer.

'Thanks. This is how it should be,' said Edwina, pulling a lock across her face to look at it as she spoke. She wrinkled her nose. 'That orange was gross, wasn't it?'

'I don't think *gross* quite captures how bad it was.'

'No. You're right there. The officers at RCB must have all been colour blind.'

'Or perverted.'

Edwina laughed. 'I've heard that's what uniforms do to you.'

At that point Edwina's mother appeared in the door, just as Lizzie's parents came along the corridor carrying a battered old trunk between them – a legacy from Lizzie's boarding-school days. Lizzie, tactfully trying not to stare at Mrs Austin's appearance – it explained everything about Edwina's clothes at RCB – made the introductions to her own parents. She had just finished when Amanda appeared.

'Hi, you guys,' she boomed. Both Edwina and Lizzie ran along the corridor to greet her. 'Hey, Edwina, what an improvement in the hair colour!' she said after they'd exchanged hugs.

'I know. It really was dreadful before.'

'I can't think why you tampered with it. It's such a stunning colour – Titian.'

'Bless you,' said Edwina.

Amanda snorted with laughter. 'God, I'm glad you're here, Edwina. I met someone in the summer who had a cousin at Sandhurst a few years back. I was warned that the first few weeks are killers. I was told that if you don't have a sense of humour it's grim, so we're going to need all the laughs you can give us. Now, does anyone know where my room is?'

'It's alphabetical,' said Lizzie. 'Edwina and I have ended up next to each other, but we haven't had a chance to look for yours yet. I've only just got here myself.'

The staff sergeant who had obligingly shown Edwina to her room was not in evidence, so Amanda took the initiative and began to walk down the length of the corridor, examining the names on the doors, then back up the other side. 'Frobisher, Goldsmith, Goudge . . .' She was back opposite Edwina and Lizzie when she exclaimed, 'Hardwick! I don't believe it.'

'Great,' said Lizzie. 'It couldn't have worked out better for us if it had been planned.'

'I think we'd better get our rooms straight now,' said Edwina. 'In half an hour we've got to be in the anteroom – whatever that is.'

Lizzie, with her superior military knowledge, explained that it was the equivalent of the lounge in a large hotel.

'Are your parents here?' she asked Amanda, not seeing anyone with her.

'No. I've got my own car so there was no point in dragging them along. I'm a bit long in the tooth to want my hand held.' She had meant it as an off-the-cuff remark to explain why she appeared to be the only cadet without parental support, but then she saw Lizzie look at her own parents and reddened. 'Oh hell, I didn't mean it the way it came out. Sorry . . .' There was an awkward pause of a few seconds, then Amanda said, 'If you've finished moving all your kit I could do with a hand. That's the drawback with having been on my own for so long and being independent.'

It seemed only a few minutes until the efficient staff sergeant came to fetch the students and their parents and show them the way to the anteroom. They were led back through the main hall and up the stairs, past vast paintings of valorous deeds in bygone battles – there to inspire future cadets in such acts of selfless bravery. The anteroom was already comfortably full with a number of men and women in uniform when the crocodile following the staff sergeant arrived.

After the Grand Entrance and the exterior of the building, this room seemed disappointingly low-key; a few rather dull military prints hung on the wall and thirty or so armchairs, covered in non-descript material, were pushed against the wall. The décor, once away from the public gaze, was definitely subfusc. Tea was offered to everyone, and soon little groups of parents and students, each with an officer to answer any questions and keep the conversation going, were chatting about the Academy, their journey there or other such inconsequential matters. Lizzie, Edwina and Amanda stuck together in a corner, checking out the other students and keeping a low profile. Edwina was also trying to keep as much distance as she could between herself and her mother in the hope that no one would connect them. Lizzie's parents, on the other hand, had obviously met up with some old friends amongst the people in uniform. Not for the first time Edwina felt a twinge of jealousy about the advantages conferred on Lizzie through her background.

'Chopper Armstrong, you old reprobate,' boomed a tall, distinguished man in khaki uniform as Lizzie's father walked over to where the tea things were laid out to get a refill for himself and his wife.

'Richard! Can't shake hands, sorry,' he guffawed as he nodded towards the cups in his hands. 'What are you doing here?'

'About to take charge of your daughter, I should think.'

'Good luck to you, I say. And you'll need it.'

Lizzie, standing with Amanda and Edwina, groaned. 'Oh, God. I don't need this.'

'Look,' said Edwina rather tensely through clenched teeth, 'what you don't need is *that*.' And she pointed to her mother, who had just flicked her shawl over her shoulder and managed to spill an officer's cup of tea. 'Your father knowing the teachers isn't going to queer your pitch like my mother is hell-bent on queering mine!' Edwina looked in horror as her mother made matters worse by insisting on dabbing at the aggrieved officer's uniform with a distinctly grubby and paint-stained hankie. Even Lizzie, embarrassed as she was by her father's loud conversation, could see that whatever her problem was, it wasn't as bad as Edwina's.

Later, when the parents had gone, and after they'd eaten dinner and their rooms were straight, the three women gathered in Edwina's room.

'Not so bad, all things considered,' said Edwina, summing up all their thoughts.

'I expected to get marched around the place the moment we arrived,' said Amanda.

'No. I knew they'd get rid of the parents before they begin to be horrible to us. I've no doubt that things are going to be different tomorrow,' said Lizzie. And since she seemed to know about military matters, Edwina and Amanda went to bed worrying about their immediate future.

'No jeans in the mess,' said Edwina in dismay as they returned to their lines after a briefing the next morning. 'What am I supposed to wear?'

'Skirts and blouses, like Captain Roberts said.'

'I know, but . . .' Edwina wasn't happy.

'You must have had some idea about how we're supposed to dress from the kit list. I mean, what with the "long black skirt for formal wear" and "skirts and dresses for casual wear", it hardly implies that scruffy clothes will be allowed within a mile of this place. Apart from what you're wearing you did bring some other suitable stuff with you, didn't you?' asked Amanda, only too aware of Edwina's shortcomings.

'Yeah, yeah. After my monumental cock-up at RCB I wasn't going to risk going my own way again. But no jeans . . . I ask you. Still, I suppose I now know that we don't have teachers but Directing Staff and that the other two colleges are called Victory and New.'

'I imagine by the end of the week we'll know no end of jargon,' said Amanda, whose knowledge of matters military was broader than Edwina's but still pretty scanty.

'I'll be glad when I understand what our timetable means. What the hell is "stand to bed" when it's at home?'

They found out that apart from anything else, 'stand to bed' would involve getting up at about six every morning to be ready for the room inspection that it entailed, and that the matter of jeans was the least of their worries. In fact they would have been grateful for the free time to change into casual clothes. They were shooting, running, signalling, climbing, marching and drilling throughout their waking hours, and as each activity required a different form of dress or uniform, they spent the remainder of their time washing, ironing,

20

polishing and bulling. The only times they seemed to be stationary were when they were standing to attention while their rooms were inspected, and when they were formed up on the square after breakfast while their uniforms were inspected. The students got into the habit of checking each other's rooms and appearance for the least trace of an imperfection before the arrival of the sergeant major, but it seemed to all of them that however hard they tried, however careful they were, the sergeant major's eagle eyes could spot a speck of dust on a mirror or the merest hint of a smear on a bulled toecap from twenty paces. Edwina came in for particular attention on the parade square because of her unruly hair.

'I give up,' she said after yet another dressing-down. 'It doesn't matter how much spray I use, how hard I whack in the hair pins, it just doesn't want to stay put. I really think I'm going to go the hairdresser and have the whole lot chopped off.'

Lizzie was aghast. 'Edwina, you can't do that. Your hair is fabulous. I'm sure that once we've all passed off the square things will ease up a little. The lads in the senior intake all say that it doesn't matter what any of us do in these first five weeks, it's always going to be wrong. It's just the DS's way of mucking us about to start with.'

What with the pressures of the inspections, coupled with the phenomenal amount of reading that was required to prepare themselves for the theory classes, not to mention homework and essays to complete, it was no wonder that at the end of two weeks the fresh-faced girls who had joined up were reduced to exhausted automata.

'It's hopeless,' said Amanda.

'What is?' asked Lizzie. It was almost midnight but the three of them were gathered together in Lizzie's room, bulling boots and shoes – their nightly ritual.

'I'm not going to manage the endurance run. I'm not fit enough, I'm too heavy and I run like a duck.'

Edwina couldn't stop herself smiling at Amanda's accurate self-description.

'Well, I do,' said Amanda, seeing the smile.

'You need to do more training,' said Edwina.

'That's easy for you to say. You run like the wind and do ten miles for pleasure. So far I've never run further than a mile, and even that kills me.'

'I could help you,' offered Edwina.

21

'But when? We never have a minute of the day to call our own, and by the time we've done everything there's no time left for you to drag me round the playing fields a couple of times.'

'There could be,' said Lizzie. Edwina looked disbelieving. 'No, seriously. Look, I'm tons better than either of you at bulling shoes – I've been helping my father do his since I was a nipper. So why don't I do all your bulling and that should free up an hour for you to take Amanda out. What do you say?'

Edwina, who loathed bulling and was anyway pretty hopeless at it, jumped at the offer.

'But Lizzie, it's too much for you to take on,' said Amanda, who wasn't sure that she really relished being trained by Edwina but could hardly refuse in the face of her friends' combined generosity.

'No it isn't,' said Lizzie. 'I'm only doing my share. And I'm sure that as things go on we'll both need your help on the academic side.'

'Yup, what goes around comes around,' said Edwina cheerfully, thinking that she'd got far and away the best deal out of the three of them.

'Edwina, I can't go on. My lungs are bursting,' panted Amanda.

'Oh yes you can,' said Edwina heartlessly, jogging backwards to watch the progress of her protégée.

'I can't.'

'Oh yes you bloody can. Now, match my stride and concentrate on your breathing; in, two, three, four, out, two, three, four. That's it, two, three, four, out, two, three, four. Right, keep that up.'

Amanda pressed on, her legs and ribs aching, envious of Edwina's effortless running.

'How far have we come?' she said, the words hardly audible over her agonised breathing.

'Not far enough if you've still got enough breath left for conversation,' countered Edwina cheerfully.

'Cow!'

'You're running twice round the rugby pitches today, and each day we'll go a little further until you can do three miles. Then we'll up the ante a bit.'

Amanda didn't reply. She didn't have the breath. And if she felt this bad now, after only one circuit, what the hell was she going to be like at the end of the second?

Edwina, noticing her discomfort, said, 'No gain without pain, Amanda. Such a cheering thought.'

'I'll kill you,' mumbled Amanda. 'So help me I'll kill you.'

'How did you get on?' asked Lizzie when Edwina bounded into her room twenty minutes later.

'Me? Fine. Don't know about Amanda though. I left her crawling up the steps complaining of being tired.'

'You are heartless. How far did you take her?'

'Only about a mile.' She caught sight of the shoes lines up neatly by Lizzie's bed. 'Cor, shiny or what! You are a wonder, Lizzie. I've never managed a shine like that on mine yet. The sergeant major is always muttering about them at inspection.'

'Thanks, but don't worry. It really is a knack. Once you get it, bulling is easy.'

'I believe you, millions wouldn't.'

Amanda appeared in the doorway, her face brick red. She leant against the doorpost, shoulders heaving, perspiring profusely.

'God, you look dreadful, Amanda. Come and sit down.' Lizzie dragged a chair across to her.

'Thanks.' The word came out between heaving sobs and gulps of air. Amanda bent forward to put her head between her knees.

'Shit, you're not going to be sick, are you?' exclaimed Edwina, moving to a safe distance. Amanda didn't answer, just shook her head. After a few minutes she had recovered sufficiently to sit up in the chair, her face slightly paler but still an interesting shade of red.

'I think I'm going to die,' she announced between puffs.

'No chance,' said Lizzie. 'Only the good die young.'

'So I hope your life insurance payments are up to date,' said Edwina to Lizzie.

'That was a tasteless thing to say, Edwina. Even for you,' said Amanda, not in the best of tempers after her gruelling run.

Edwina shrugged and said a little sulkily, 'Only a joke.' There was silence; the joke had obviously fallen flat.

'I hate you for what you've just put me through,' said Amanda with a wry smile, trying to lighten the atmosphere.

'Oh, you don't mean it,' said Edwina.

'I flipping do. I've never hurt so much in my life.'

'Ah, must have done you good then.'

'Don't you have any feelings?'

Edwina thought for a second. 'No, don't think I do.' She carefully picked up her shoes so as not to spoil the fantastic finish. 'Right, well, I'm off to get my kit ready for inspection tomorrow. Then I think I'll go out for a proper run.'

Amanda picked up a magazine from Lizzie's bed and hurled it at Edwina, who side-stepped neatly, waved and left.

'God, I wish I was as fit as her.'

'Don't we all?' said Lizzie admiringly. 'If anyone can train you up for the endurance run, it'll be her.' Amanda agreed and then, still tottering with exhaustion, took her leave of Lizzie.

'I've still got a mass of things to do. There's my uniform to press, that précis to read on *Mapco*, and my military law exercise to complete. I'm going to be working till midnight again.'

'Me too. How I long for a decent night's kip.'

Back in her own room, Edwina rapidly squared away her uniform, then thought about looking at her Manual of Military Law but decided to set her alarm half an hour early and do her homework in the morning. She left the lines and loped up the road behind New College which led past the Faraday Hall and then towards Barossa, the pine-, birch- and scrub-covered training area behind the RMA. She thought about running out that way, but it was pretty dark and Edwina wasn't fool enough to risk injury – that could mean being back-termed. Instead she turned right off the road and ran down past Victory College and over the Wish Stream, then turned again towards the Staff College, which shared the same grounds as the RMA. As she jogged along with her easy, effortless stride, she saw a figure running towards her; obviously someone from Sandhurst but she didn't know his name. At the start she'd tried to make an effort to meet the other cadets and learn their names but after the first week she'd been too tired to bother any more. Once she'd got these first weeks under her belt Edwina planned on joining a few clubs and societies in order to broaden her social life, but it wasn't top of her list of things to do yet. She recognised the runner approaching her. She'd seen him out jogging round the RMA on more than one occasion, and their paths had even crossed a couple of times. They nodded to each other in greeting as they passed.

Quite why Edwina called out, 'Fancy some company on your run tomorrow evening?' she didn't know. There were plenty of female cadets who would have been glad to have someone to train with, but perhaps Edwina, super-fit as she was, sensed that this man might provide the sort of challenge that her peers would not.

'OK,' the runner called over his shoulder. 'Outside the NAAFI. Eight o'clock.'

Edwina turned and jogged backwards for a couple of paces and shouted, 'It's a date.' She only hoped that her heavy workload would allow her to keep it. And she'd have to beast Amanda around the playing fields again. Bugger. There just weren't enough hours in the day.

The next day, when the sergeant major carried out the early-morning inspection, Edwina was complimented on the standard of her shoes.

'There, Miss Austin. I said you could do it if you applied yourself.'

'Yes, Ma'am,' replied Edwina meekly, wondering if she ought to own up to the fact that they were entirely Lizzie's handiwork. She told Lizzie about it later when they met in the dining room for breakfast.

'I'm pleased to know my efforts were appreciated,' said Lizzie, slightly smugly, as she helped herself to scrambled eggs and toast. Edwina was piling her plate high with eggs, bacon and beans when Amanda joined them at the self-service counter. Breakfast was the one meal of the day no one missed. Fainting on the parade square was a chargeable offence if it was discovered the miscreant had skipped breakfast.

'Really, Austin, you make me so envious,' said Amanda. 'How come you can eat all this greasy stuff and not put on any weight?' Amanda was breakfasting on a piece of toast and a cup of black coffee.

'Because I shall burn it all off pushing you round the sports pitch this evening. And that reminds me; you'll have to be ready to run at five this evening. We can go out instead of having tea. I've arranged to go for a proper run this evening and I won't be able to fit it in if I'm hampered with you.'

'Hampered?' said Amanda in mock disgust. 'You really know how to make a girl feel wanted.'

'I know. All this and charm too; gosh, you lot are lucky to have me around.'

Neither Lizzie nor Amanda could stop themselves from smiling. But Edwina's good humour was tried to breaking point when she was told to do her military law exercise again and present it to the instructor first thing the next morning.

25

'It simply isn't good enough,' Captain Roberts informed her crossly. 'There's nothing difficult about it, you just have to take your time looking up the references in the manual. And I suspect, from looking at the work you have given me, that you tried to rush it.'

Edwina reddened with shame. That was precisely what she'd done – the half-hour she'd given herself that morning had been nowhere near enough time.

'I want to see the work – done properly, mind – on my desk first thing tomorrow.'

'But ma'am, I've arranged to go out for a run this evening,' she moaned.

'From what I've heard you don't need the fitness training. Missing one evening's run won't hurt you.'

'No, ma'am,' said Edwina dejectedly. She wondered whether, if she skipped lunch, she might have time to do most of the exercise then. She wasn't going to get tea because of her arrangement with Amanda. She didn't fancy missing too many meals. Perhaps she could grab a sandwich and jog and eat at the same time. She knew that her iron constitution would allow her to make it up to herself at dinner, and go out for a good long run half an hour later. She would just have to hope that nothing prevented her from getting to dinner bang on time.

'You're late,' was the austere greeting of Edwina's new running partner when she arrived at the NAAFI at ten past eight.

'I know,' puffed Edwina, who had sprinted there. 'I had a mountain of stuff to do before dinner and I got delayed. I'm Edwina, by the way.' She held out her hand.

The man, tall and lean with Aryan good looks, hesitated momentarily before taking it. If she had 'dinner' and not 'tea' then it meant she was a cadet. He'd assumed the woman was the new admin clerk, whom he'd heard was a tasty red-head. As a platoon colour-sergeant, it might not be too wise to associate with her – fraternising between officers and other ranks was heavily frowned on. Besides which, if she knew that he wasn't officer material she might not want to be seen with him. Which would be a shame, because she was easy on the eye.

'Call me Ulysses.' If he kept his rank out of it for the time being, then Edwina wouldn't be any the wiser. He hardly had anything to do with training the girls.

'Come on then,' said Edwina. 'We'd better get going before it gets too dark. I fancy doing about ten miles tonight – where do you suggest we go?'

'Follow me,' said Ulysses, cynically wondering if she had said that just to impress. 'If it's all the same to you, I suggest we run on the roads where the lighting will be half-decent.' Already they were jogging at a good pace, their long strides matching exactly, along the road that would lead them around Old College, past the lake and New College, past Victory College and then down the long rhodo-dendron-bordered drive to the guardroom at the Staff College entrance.

After a mile or so Edwina said, 'Is Ulysses your real name?'

'No. It's Andrew Lees, but everyone calls me Ulysses.' In fact the nickname had nothing to do with the legendary Greek hero, but with a drill-sergeant's taste for invective, tempered by barrack-room humour. As a recruit in the Parachute Regiment at Aldershot, Andrew had taken longer than was acceptable to his tyrannical company sergeant major to master the intricacies of an about-turn on the march. When, for the third time that morning, he had stepped off on the wrong foot after completing the manoeuvre, the warrant officer yelled across the entire width of the parade square, to the amusement of all within earshot, 'You're fucking useless, Lees.' His fellow recruits had, within the space of a day, transformed the sobriquet of 'Useless Lees' into Ulysses. Andy rather hoped that Edwina would make the heroic connection and not ask further questions. He was sorry that he was debarred from getting to know her better by reason of rank – she was one hell of a looker and undeniably fit. He wouldn't mind giving her a good seeing-to ... Shame she was a cadet and out of reach. Never mind. He decided to take his mind off screwing.

'How are you enjoying Sandhurst?' he enquired.

'Bloody hard work. I mean, the physical stuff's no problem, but all these inspections . . .' Edwina made a gesture of disbelief.

'It'll get easier,' sympathised Ulysses.

'Yeah. And pigs fly.'

'It does. Take my word for it.'

'So how come you're the great expert?'

Damn, thought Ulysses. I can't pretend I'm a student. 'I'm on the staff – a colour-sergeant.'

'Oh.' She didn't sound impressed, but then cadets at this stage in their careers rarely understood the cachet that being selected for that job bestowed on an NCO. Only the very best were chosen to train future officers, and Ulysses was one of the youngest there.

They concentrated on their running for a while and the conversation ceased. They ran on in silence, arms pumping, legs pounding, their trainers slapping on the asphalt in perfect unison as they covered the miles. They reached Frimley in about thirty minutes and then turned towards Deepcut and the long pine-fringed road that led past the Ordnance Corps Depot, back over the motorway and, ultimately, to Camberley. Ulysses had been expecting Edwina to be flagging by now. He had set a deliberately fast pace in order to test her and was now rather wishing he hadn't. Had he been running with a man he might have throttled back slightly, but to admit to a girl that he was finding things a bit tough when she apparently wasn't – no way. He gritted his teeth and concentrated on the rhythm of his breathing. He glanced across at Edwina. Her running seemed easy and effortless although her singlet was drenched with sweat. For some reason Ulysses wanted her admiration.

'I'm trying for SAS selection in a few months, so I need to put in lots of extra training.' But he hadn't reckoned with Edwina's military ignorance.

'Why's that then?'

'Huh?' Ulysses couldn't believe she didn't know the reputation of the selection process for the toughest part of the British Army. 'Come on, you must have heard about the SAS and what's involved for selection: days spend tabbing miles across Welsh mountains, map-reading exercises, endurance runs.'

'Oh, not for wimps then?' She still sounded unimpressed, and worse than that, she was still barely panting.

Ulysses wondered what it took to get a reaction from Edwina, but he didn't analyse why it mattered to him. He'd never been short of girlfriends; in fact, his looks, coupled with the glamour of a smart uniform, had meant he'd been able to pick and chose. But this bird was different from the women he usually dated, who tended to be pretty but not overly bright; this one undoubtedly had brains as well as beauty. And he'd never met a girl who could match him at running. Edwina was something else entirely and he wanted to see more of her.

They ran on until they reached the end of the Maultway and then raced down the undulating road from the Jolly Farmer roundabout to the Staff College gate of the RMA, about a mile away. Ulysses had to use every last ounce of energy to beat Edwina, which made him wonder momentarily whether he was as fit as he thought he was. But he knew in his heart that Edwina was a supreme athlete and it wouldn't be completely dishonourable to be beaten by her – well, apart from the fact that she was a woman. When they parted they arranged, to his delight, to meet again the next evening.

'So who's this running partner you've found yourself?' asked Amanda when for the fifth time Edwina told her that their run would have to be fitted in instead of tea.

'I don't really know much about him except that he's a colour-sergeant.'

'Ho-hum. You want to be careful there,' said Lizzie.

'Why on earth?' said Edwina.

'Because, stupid, the Army doesn't like officers and other ranks getting too friendly. Bad for discipline.'

'I can't see why that should be, and we're hardly "friendly". We just like running and it's nice to have some company. Besides which, he said he's a member of the Academy orienteering team and thinks that I should try out for a place too. If it's OK with Captain Roberts I'm going along to a competition next weekend to see how I do.'

'Brilliantly I should think,' said Amanda.

'Well, the running side of it won't be a problem, but I'm not so confident about the map-reading.'

'It'll certainly go down well with Colonel O'Brien if one of her cadets gets selected.'

Edwina sighed. 'I could do with that. I've been on the carpet yet again over room inspection.'

Amanda and Lizzie grimaced.

'But you know what's required.' Lizzie tried to keep her exasperation out of her voice.

'I know. It's just that as soon as I get one bit of it up to snuff, I seem to get something else wrong.'

'What was it this time?' asked Lizzie.

'Dusty mirror. And it's not fair, because I did dust it.'

'You know what you need to do,' said Lizzie.

'What?'

'Move your dressing table so it's against the window. That way the light won't shine on it and the dust won't be so easy to spot.'

29

'Do you think it'll work?'

'If it doesn't you're no worse off.'

It said much for the others on the course that they were all so fond of Edwina, her ready humour frequently lightening a bad day, that no one had blamed her directly for the fact that they were still subjected to a daily room inspection. Once everyone's room passed muster every day for a week then it would be reduced to a weekly inspection. Edwina's room was proving to be the stumbling block.

'Edwina?' Amanda's voice had a slight wheedling tone.

'Yes. What are you after?'

'A couple of the others want to come out for a run with us. Would you take them too?'

Edwina raised her eyes skywards. She really didn't want this sort of hassle; training Amanda was bad enough. But she knew that it was her fault that they still had to get up at a ridiculously early hour to get their rooms ready. She was over a barrel and she knew it.

'A couple. How many's a couple?' she said warily.

'Well, Lorna Barclay is definitely one, and Jane Goudge was keen, and I think Linda Hough is interested. Maybe a few others.'

'OK.' Edwina wasn't happy but how could she refuse? 'Spread the word, but you can also tell everyone that I won't hang around for latecomers. I haven't time.'

Early the next evening Captain Cathy Roberts stood at the window of her office and watched with interest as Edwina beasted most of her platoon down the King's Walk, the long drive which led up to the Grand Entrance of the Old College. It was hard not be impressed by Edwina's energy as she sprinted up and down the squad like a sheepdog, encouraging the ones at the front, bullying the ones at the back, physically pushing the slowest and all the time having enough breath to shout instructions to them all. Cathy Roberts, who had joined the WRAC in the days when the training had been far less physical, wondered if she herself could pass the course as it was now. She doubted it. She found the annual basic fitness test tough enough. She'd long since decided that she'd been built for comfort not speed, but that didn't matter to the Army – now it was a case of pass your BFT or get out. She heard a knock at the door.

'Come in,' she called, expecting one of her fellow platoon

commanders. She was surprised to see Lieutenant Colonel O'Brien walk in – their company commander. She braced to attention.

'Ah, I see you've been watching Edwina,' said Colonel O'Brien in her soft Irish brogue.

'Yes, ma'am. She's very fit, isn't she?'

'Extremely.'

'How is she getting on, apart from the physical side?'

'Frankly, ma'am, she's hopeless. She's scruffy, her work is mediocre, and as for her attitude . . .' Here words failed Cathy Roberts.

Denise O'Brien stared thoughtfully at Cathy. 'But her platoon adores her.'

'Yes, but –' Cathy shrugged. So what if they did? It didn't make Edwina any better as a cadet. Frankly, Cathy was going to recommend that Edwina should be given a one-way ticket home at the end of the term.

'And she is the one out there getting them fit for their endurance run,' continued the company commander.

'Which is very good of her,' said Cathy, loath to acknowledge anything of the sort and failing to pick up the unspoken criticism that it was Edwina doing this rather than their platoon commander.

'So you don't think you've been a bit unfair on her, a bit hard?'

Cathy shook her head.

'I've noticed how you never give her the benefit of the doubt, like you do Lizzie Armstrong, for example,' said Colonel O'Brien. She sometimes sat in on lectures to see, first-hand, how the cadets were doing.

'But ma'am, Miss Armstrong is a completely different kettle of fish,' protested Cathy.

'You mean she has the right background?'

'No, it's not that.'

Denise said nothing; she wanted to hear Cathy justify her attitude to Edwina, which she was beginning to think was unnecessarily and unjustifiably vindictive.

'It's her spirit. She always seems to maintain the upper hand. She never seems to accept that she might have to change to fit in with the system. It's as though she thinks the Army ought to change to suit her.'

'Hmm,' said Colonel O'Brien to encourage Cathy to carry on.

'And she never loses her sense of humour,' said Cathy finally. This was what rankled most with Cathy, who always felt that Edwina was somehow secretly taking the piss out of everything.

'So you think that if you're really hard on her you might bring her to heel? Get her to conform to the "system"?'

'Something needs to be done to curb her, certainly.'

'She's an officer cadet, not a mustang,' said Colonel O'Brien. 'You don't think that her spirit might not be one of her greatest assets?'

'I'm afraid I have to disagree with you there, ma'am.'

'I see. I'm sorry about that, because I think it's an error of judge-ment on your part.' Denise O'Brien did not raise her voice or speak in an unpleasant manner, but Cathy was acutely aware that she was being severely criticised by her superior officer and she resented it bitterly. All the more because it was Miss Edwina Bloody Austin who was the cause of it.

'I think you should ease up a little on Miss Austin until the end of term and see how she responds. There are other qualities that make successful officers apart from knowing how to indent for stores or write a semi-official letter.'

'Thank you for your advice, ma'am,' said Cathy stiffly.

When Colonel O'Brien had gone, Cathy went over to the officers' mess in New College and ordered herself a large gin, which she swigged in one gulp. She'd ease up on Miss Austin all right. Given enough rope, Edwina would be sure to hang herself in the end. There was no way she was going to see that lippy red-head commissioned now, she thought.

Over the next few weeks things suddenly seemed to be easier for Edwina. She, however, was completely unaware that, for example, it wasn't the wheeze of moving her dressing table that got the platoon off daily inspections. Nor that the less frequent comments about her hair were due to Cathy's enforced leniency rather than her own ability to pin it up properly. Equally she was blissfully unaware of the simmering resentment which now seethed in her platoon com-mander's entire being.

But life still had its drawbacks. Even with one fewer inspection to prepare for each day, she longed to rid herself of the extra hassle the daily runs with her peers imposed on her scant free time, especially as the runs gradually become longer with the platoon's increased fit-ness. Soon they could run one and a half miles, then two miles, two and a half miles without collapsing. One day they managed to pass the three-mile barrier. Now that everyone could run that distance without throwing up or falling out, Edwina knew they would be able to get to five miles relatively rapidly and then she could call it a day. She was impatient for that moment to come. Finding time to fit in serious runs of her own was getting harder and harder, and having been promised a place in the Academy orienteering team she was determined to keep it. Competition was stiff.

Their free time was becoming ever more scarce as they now had lectures in the evenings, plus formal and informal social occasions, parties and, on top of it all, yet more work. Edwina, Amanda and Lizzie, who had all thought that they had been tired at the end of the first fortnight, now knew what it felt like to be truly exhausted; they couldn't even sit down to watch the evening news, timetable permitting, without dropping off to sleep. Worst of all were the lectures for the whole Academy, which took place in the Churchill Hall – a vast charcoal-grey bunker-like theatre which would have fitted in better on the South Bank than at a military academy, for in the upholstered comfort of the tip-up seats, with the lights dimmed for the benefit of slide projectors, it was virtually impossible not to feel drowsy. The Directing Staff watched from the back of the hall for the tell-tale woodpecker nodding of heads, so the cadets found that often they were paying more attention to maintaining their consciousness than to the words of the lecturer. To be caught sleeping in a lecture, especially one given by a guest speaker, was a heinous crime, ranking alongside slovenliness, sloth and unpunctuality.

Lizzie, right school, right accent, right family, was a natural as far as the Army was concerned. And Amanda had discovered that once she had mastered both running long distances and getting by on only five or six hours sleep a night, the course wasn't too difficult. It was obvious to all that she had a good brain, and the DS only had to explain things to her once for her to get to grips with them. Her written work was exemplary, she was habitually smart in appearance and it came as no surprise to anyone that she was a natural shot too.

'But I've got the bloody confidence area to get round,' she moaned to Edwina who, unlike her two friends, was finding just about everything to do with the training very heavy going.

'Yes, but you've only got to face it the once. You can't expect much sympathy from me – every day is a struggle for me. I'm always in trouble, Captain Roberts seems to have it in for me again, and if anyone is going to get things wrong it's always me.'

'I thought you said she'd laid off you,' said Lizzie.

'She did for a bit, but it was too good to last. It's just like it was before, only worse if anything.'

'I know,' said Amanda, full of sympathy for Edwina. 'I think if I had Captain Roberts to battle against as well as everything else on this course, I'd have sacked it by now.'

'Yeah, but you know what I'm like. The more she tries to see the back of me the more determined I am to hang on and prove her wrong.'

'Still, you'll shine on the assault course competition. There's nothing she'll be able do to take the gloss off your performance there.'

The thought cheered Edwina up a little. She grinned and said, 'And after that it'll be the end-of-term treat.'

'Huh?'

'The confidence area.'

'Some treat!' Amanda signed heavily, and tried to put the thought from her mind.

Edwina's way of taking her mind off her troubles was either to go for a run or to go to a party, both activities officially encouraged by the staff at Sandhurst. Luckily there was a party scheduled for that evening, as there frequently was on a Saturday night. The runs she could take at any time, but Edwina had to wait until the weekends to let her hair down on the dance floor. For although the lines were completely out of bounds to members of the opposite sex – on pain of instant dismissal should the rule be broken – the development of social skills was considered to be an important part of the cadets' training. To this end each Company was expected to organise at least one party a term, so there was no shortage of social occasions and they were generally good fun. Edwina and Lizzie positively looked forward to these events, but not Amanda.

'You never come to the dances. Why aren't you coming to the Inkerman Company bash? It's bound to be a good do, they've got a professional DJ for the evening,' said Edwina later that evening, standing in the doorway of Amanda's room, dressed in a figure-hugging black dress which did nothing to hide her physical attributes and emphasised the colour of her hair. She looked stunning and she knew it.

'I've got someone back home,' Amanda fibbed.

'You are good to be so faithful. Most of the other girls seem to have ditched their men in favour of what's on offer here.'

'I'm not being loyal, really, it's more a case that I'm not into cradle-snatching.' Since Amanda was on the way to being nearly ten years senior to most of the cadets, male and female, Edwina found this a more than credible explanation. Amanda, feeling guilty about her lie, turned back to her books.

'Well, don't work too hard while I'm not here to keep an eye on you,' said Edwina as she skipped off to the party.

After she'd gone Amanda realised that she wouldn't be able to keep her distance from dances indefinitely. If nothing else, there was her own commissioning ball to think about – always assuming that she got that far. Not only would she have to put in an appearance at that event, but she'd also be expected to go accompanied by some suitable consort. Lizzie and Edwina had organised themselves with regard to that particular issue – they both had any number of hopefuls waiting to escort them – but Amanda still had no one lined up. The 'someone back home' was definitely *not* an option, and she certainly didn't want to risk partnering one of the male cadets. Amanda knew that many of them would assume that taking her to the ball equated to a licence to take liberties too. God, the last thing she wanted was to spend the evening fighting off unwelcome amorous advances. She wondered if she would be able to persuade her second cousin to partner her; he was respectable even if he was a crashing bore. Well, it was worth a try. At least her cousin could be relied on to keep his hands to himself.

The first term at Sandhurst was drawing to a close and all the cadets were involved in rehearsals for Sovereign's Parade for the senior term – all male this time, because there were only two intakes of women a year to the men's three, though the women were expected to make up the honour guard with the men. They all found these rehearsals inspirational, as they could imagine that it would soon be their own turn to march through the doors of Old College.

As well as the parade rehearsals, all the cadets had interviews to discover how they were doing. For Amanda and Lizzie these only amounted to a formality. They had done well in all the tests and exams, their rooms and kit had always been presented for inspection at a consistently high standard, and even though Amanda, as she had feared, had had to be brought down by a PTI from the top of the system of forty-foot-high rope walkways and death slides known as the confidence area, it had been forgiven because it had been obvious to everyone that she had been genuinely frozen with fear.

The company commander, not their platoon commander, had summoned Edwina for her interview, which did not augur well for her prospects. She waited outside the Colonel's office with a fair degree of trepidation, for she had a pretty good idea that she was about to be told she would have to do better. She knew she was the best female cadet in all matters involving fitness, and was possibly better in that area than ninety per cent of the men; she had been selected to try for the Army orienteering team in the New Year and had done well in the skill-at-arms competition. She was good at tactics, she understood basic signals procedure and, thanks to her runs with Ulysses across the training area, she had acquired a first-class eye for ground use from a military point of view; where would be a safe lying-up point, good spots for an OP and dead ground useful for concealing a complete platoon. But in every other area she was not up to scratch, and she knew it. Her problems with bulling her boots and getting her room ready for inspection had been the least of her shortcomings; her hair, wild and curly, still refused to stay in place no matter how much lacquer she used, so on parade and during drill lessons long wisps always escaped, to the annoyance of the sergeant major. Her essays on military history were adequate but no more, and she hadn't helped herself when she'd flippantly suggested in one lecture that Wellington could have had the Battle of Waterloo squared away in no time at all if only he'd had access to a couple of tactical nuclear weapons. She couldn't motivate herself to spend more than a bare minimum of time on military law, service writing or Army organisation, and it showed. The bottom line was that if what she had to learn didn't involve modern battlefield techniques and related subjects, then she couldn't raise any interest. The male DS were mostly impressed by Edwina, but not so the WRAC, least of all Cathy Roberts. At a meeting of all the DS the previous week, Cathy had been adamant.

'She's hopeless on much of the theoretical side. She just won't put the hours in that are required.'

Colonel O'Brien had raised an eyebrow, but Cathy had refused to change her position.

'I'm sorry, ma'am, I've given her every opportunity, every encouragement, but she consistently fails to meet the grade I demand.'

Since her dressing-down, Cathy had been careful not to pick on

Edwina when the colonel was present. In fact she'd gone out of her way to demonstrate in public, at any rate, how much she was being fair to Miss Austin, because she was not going to be accused of being vindictive again. She was ambitious and had plans to get to the top of her corps, but she wasn't going to let some bloody inefficient cadet screw up her chances, so whenever the colonel was safely out of the way, Edwina was left in no doubt that her performance was way below par. The last thing Cathy wanted was for Edwina to dispute the matter when she got thrown out – which was what Cathy planned for her. Her input at the DS's meeting was all part of her long-term scheme to spike Edwina's guns.

Of course the details of the meeting were highly confidential, but the outcome of the DS's decision on Edwina had to be relayed to her.

'I'm putting you on a three-month warning, Edwina,' said Colonel O'Brien sadly. 'Do you understand what that means?'

'Yes, ma'am.' Edwina felt suddenly physically sick. She'd been expecting to be informed that her written work wasn't perfect – Cathy Roberts had told her often enough, for fuck's sake – but this . . . If she didn't make a significant improvement in the next three months, she would be off the course.

'It really *is* only your written work, Edwina,' said the colonel, who had not enjoyed telling Edwina this and wished to soften the blow. She went on, 'No one can fault your enthusiasm for the rest of the course. If only you could apply some of that to the classroom.'

Edwina nodded miserably. She knew the colonel was right, and now was not the moment to say that she found all the theoretical stuff so pointless. 'I promise I'll try harder, ma'am.' Her voice was hardly a whisper.

'Just see that you do, Edwina. I really don't want to lose you.'

Edwina was nearly in tears when she returned to her room. Lizzie was waiting for her.

'I'm on a warning.'

'Oh, poor you. Was Colonel O'Brien awful?'

'No, that's the worst bit, she was really nice. And anyway, there was no reason for her to be horrid. It's only me I'm letting down. Oh God, Lizzie, what am I going to do?'

Edwina knew the answer, as did Lizzie, who kindly didn't spell out the obvious and thus make Edwina feel worse. Instead she put her arm round her and gave her a hug.

'You know, I really want to make it to the end. Not just to prove everyone wrong, but because . . .' Edwina, not given to any sort of sentiment, paused. 'Well, I'd just love to.' She reddened slightly.

'We all do,' said Lizzie. 'Everyone may have joined for different reasons, but I think we all feel the same way about the Army now. I think we're supposed to – it's part of what this course is all about.'

Amanda, when she heard the news, was just as sympathetic as Lizzie and promised Edwina that she'd help her as much as she could. After all, she would only be returning a favour; without Edwina's efforts she would never have got through the endurance run. She felt deeply sorry for Edwina, who looked so miserable and pale.

Lizzie got up from her chair and sat beside Edwina on the bed. She put her arm round her and said, 'We'll get you through, whatever happens. I'll help you with your kit and in any other way I can. Promise.'

Edwina, tired and miserable, couldn't help the tears rolling silently down her cheeks. She couldn't find her handkerchief, and Amanda produced a clean tissue.

'You're a hopeless case, Austin. You can't even organise a hankie for yourself.'

Edwina smiled sadly and nodded in agreement.

Edwina's spirits stayed low as the end of term rapidly approached. Despite the parties and the prospect of two weeks' leave, her morale was at rock bottom. Lizzie and Amanda were at a loss as to how to cheer her up.

'Are you doing anything nice over Christmas?' said Amanda as they sat in Edwina's room on a Sunday afternoon. Outside, the cold winter rain was hammering down, but the three girls were sitting on the floor, snuggled up against the radiator with Edwina's duvet over their knees, clasping cups of coffee. They looked cosy despite the draught through the ill-fitting sash window.

'No, nothing much. Mum will probably have some of her weird relations to stay.' She sighed heavily. 'Being surrounded by a whole load of bohemian vegans isn't my idea of a good time.'

'You're exaggerating about your relations,' said Lizzie, laughing, trying to lighten the conversation.

'Not really,' replied Edwina flatly. There was another silence.

Edwina stared out of the window at the falling rain. 'I'd go for a run if it wasn't so horrible.'

'Still running with Ulysses?' asked Lizzie.

'No. He's been allowed some leave to train seriously for his SAS selection. If he passes he won't be coming back here.'

'Are you going to keep in touch?'

'Not much point really, is there? If we get too friendly the Army'll just put a stop to it.' Edwina sounded thoroughly cheesed off. She stared at the rain again. Then suddenly she said, 'What I need is a shag. That'd cheer me up.'

Lizzie squawked with laughter. 'It's not so bad being celibate, is it? I mean, Amanda's managing without complaining.'

'How do you know I'm not getting my oats?' asked Amanda.

'Well, stands to reason, doesn't it?' replied Lizzie. 'We all know you've got this faithful hunk stashed somewhere. Are you seeing him over Christmas?'

Amanda dodged the issue. 'Oh, I haven't really made any plans yet. I've got a friend who's got a cottage in Dorset. I thought I might go there for a bit.'

'So you're not going home to see your folks?' Lizzie was aghast. She couldn't imagine spending Christmas without her family.

'I don't think so. We don't really get on.' Talk about an understatement, she thought.

It suddenly occurred to Lizzie and Edwina that they knew surprisingly little about their friend. Amanda had told them all sorts of superficial stuff – that she had been a teacher, had gone to an ordinary grammar school in the Midlands, enjoyed classical music and listened to Radio 4 – but beyond that she had disclosed virtually nothing. They knew lots of unimportant things about her, but there were some yawning gaps – her relationship with her parents appeared to be yet another one of these holes.

Edwina, curious, said, 'What did you do to upset them?'

'We had a big row about my choice of friends and we've never really made up.'

'Some row,' said Edwina, who had had countless arguments with her own mother but had always made up – eventually. 'Christ, who were your friends? The Kray twins?'

Despite Amanda's low spirits, she couldn't help smiling at Edwina's throwaway remark.

'Yeah, well, it's all pretty unpleasant.'

Edwina got the hint that this wasn't something Amanda wanted to elaborate about, and even she had enough tact to drop the subject. She watched the rain streaming steadily down from a grubby grey sky and wondered what Amanda and her parents had really fallen out over.

Lizzie stretched a hand out to Amanda. Amanda took it and gave a small smile.

'Don't worry, Lizzie. It happened quite a few years ago now and I've got used to not having them around for me.' She let go of Lizzie's hand and took a gulp of her coffee. She hoped that neither of her friends would want any further details, because she wasn't prepared to let them have any.

Edwina's morale took a definite turn for the better the following day when it was discovered that the white horse ridden by the Academy adjutant at the Sovereign's Parade, which was due to take place in two days, had been dyed green. As soon as they could, the three friends went to view the spectacle for themselves.

'Do they know who did it yet?' Edwina asked Amanda, who usually knew the answer to most questions.

'No. And I suppose we can only hope they don't find out, because it's bound to be a sacking offence.'

'Contrary to section sixty-nine of the Army Act 1955,' intoned Edwina.

'Being prejudicial to good order and military discipline,' added Lizzie.

'In that Officer Cadet Bloggins, on the seventeenth of December, painted the Academy adjutant's horse green,' finished Amanda, giggling. Her laughter was infectious and all three were soon chortling helplessly.

'Surely they can wash it off?' said Lizzie as they regained control. They stared at the defaced nag. It did look most peculiar.

'If they could I think they'd have done it by now,' said Edwina, her laughter bubbling just below the surface. The horse whickered indignantly.

'What will they do?' asked Amanda.

'I suppose they could blanco it,' offered Edwina.

'Or get another horse.'

'They can't do that, Lizzie. It wouldn't be trained to go up the steps.'

As they watched, a groom appeared with a bucket of warm

soapy water and began to wash the horse. As far as the three women were concerned, it didn't seem to make an appreciable difference. Still, as they commented later, it gave Sovereign's Parade an extra dimension, with everyone trying to spot any telltale remains of the practical joke as they marched around the square. The horse gleamed pristinely but whether as the result of plain soap and water or more drastic measures, the authorities wouldn't say.

The following day, still suffering faintly from the effects of their seniors' commissioning ball the night before, the three women piled into Amanda's car, their suitcases crammed into the boot, all of them looking forward to the holiday, if nothing else. Amanda had obligingly offered to give them a lift, although Edwina was only going as far as Reading station, where she could catch a train heading north. Lizzie was bound for Winchester and her parents' latest quarter and was right on Amanda's route to the south-west.

'I can't wait to get up at lunchtime, put on a pair of really scruffy jeans and go down the pub for a pint of Guinness,' Edwina said, sounding more cheerful than she had done for some days. She was lounging across the back seat of Amanda's Mini Metro, in a remarkably unladylike pose.

'You don't seriously drink Guinness, do you?' said Lizzie, who was almost more horrified at the thought of a woman drinking pints than anything else.

'Only when I'm out of uniform. You don't *really* like dry sherry, do you? I mean, I know we all pretend to, but it's only part of the act, isn't it?'

Lizzie didn't like to admit that she did, she'd virtually been weaned on it. She deflected the enquiry from herself. 'What are you looking forward to most this leave, Amanda?'

'I'm not sure. A lie-in certainly, and cheese on toast while watching some rubbish on the TV.'

'And wearing slippers outside my bedroom,' added Lizzie.

'And getting laid,' from Edwina.

'God, you're not still feeling randy?' said Amanda.

'Constantly. More bromide in the tea, that's what's required.'

'Only for you,' said Lizzie.

'Hear, hear,' agreed Amanda.

From the back of the car Edwina gave her a long look. Not for the first time, she couldn't believe that Amanda was as uninterested in sex as she made out.

When their second term started after Christmas they had the novelty of a junior term to look after. When they saw the new intake struggling with their uniforms and the military way of doing things, they suddenly realised how much they had learnt since September. It even boosted Edwina's flagging self-confidence to discover that she could help the new girls and that they valued her opinion. She felt a real sense of achievement and renewed her determination to complete the course. Amanda, as she had promised, took upon herself the role of Edwina's personal tutor, and as things began to improve, so Edwina's sense of humour returned. They still had the stress of the final exercise to face, they still had to take their final exams in various subjects, but the end was definitely in sight. They were measured for a variety of uniforms, all of which added to their sense of security. After all, if the Army was giving them hundreds of pounds of allowances to spend on individually tailored uniforms, which could not be passed on to others if the intended owner failed the course, then failure seemed less of a threat.

Edwina had another interview with Colonel O'Brien and was told that her work had made considerable improvements and that if she maintained her standards she would be off her warning in a few weeks.

'But I don't want you slacking now I've told you this news.' Colonel O'Brien, sitting very erect behind her tidy desk, smiled at Edwina. Edwina had to make an effort not to sag with the relief that swept over her.

'Thank you, ma'am. I won't, I promise, I've learnt my lesson.'

'OK, well, that's all.'

Edwina stood up, saluted, about-turned and marched smartly from her company commander's office. Once outside, she relaxed and almost skipped down the austere corridor and back to the lines.

Cathy Roberts watched her go with a look of pure venom. It had irritated her more deeply than she thought possible that Edwina's friends had rallied round to help her so much with her written work. She couldn't prove that some of Edwina's best efforts were more the product of Miss Hardwick's brain than Miss Austin's, and she was still determined that Edwina was the last person who should be commissioned off this course. She was certain, as she watched Edwina walk down the long, echoing corridor, that she would find a way of ridding the Army of this loose cannon. Miss Austin wasn't that clever, and she was bound to slip up before the end of the course.

Edwina maintained her improvement in her work and was the outstanding performer on an adventurous training exercise in North Yorkshire, and everyone was certain that she would be marching with the rest of her company at Sovereign's Parade. So it was with a great deal of shock that the course heard, less than a fortnight later, the news that Edwina was in deep trouble and had been summoned to Colonel O'Brien's office yet again.

'What has she done now?' Lizzie whispered to Amanda in the classroom.

Amanda shrugged by way of reply. None of the other cadets knew either. As soon as they could escape back to their lines, Lizzie and Amanda rushed to Edwina's room to see what was up. They found her prostrate on her bed, sobbing her eyes out, a half-packed suitcase beside her.

'Edwina, what on earth's the matter?' said Lizzie, rushing to her side.

'I've been s-s-sacked,' sobbed Edwina, her eyes red and puffy, her face blotchy.

'Sacked? But why?' said Lizzie and Amanda simultaneously.

'Captain Roberts s-s-saw a m-m-man coming out of my room last n-n-night.'

'Huh?'

'B-b-but she can't have done.'

Lizzie and Amanda realised that they would have to get Edwina calmed down before they had a chance of getting the story out of her. They all knew that if Edwina really had had a man in her room then there would be no clemency; the rules had been made perfectly plain at the start of the course, as had the consequences of any such breach. A dozen soggy tissues, two cups of hot sweet tea and masses of sympathy later, Edwina finally became coherent enough to tell the story. It seemed that Captain Roberts had been out for the evening with her fiancé and had been returning late, sometime after midnight. As she entered Old College she was aware of loud music coming from within the WRAC lines. She was on her way to investigate when the music suddenly stopped and a few moments later she saw a figure creep out of Edwina's room.

'But who was it she saw?' asked Amanda.

'I don't know,' said Edwina miserably.

'Didn't you ask her?'

'Yes, and all she said was that I should know. Which is ridiculous, because I didn't have a man in my room last night or any night.'

'Why didn't she challenge him?'

'I don't know that either. I'm sorry, I was confronted with this accusation and I was so stunned I stopped thinking straight. It's all so unfair.'

'Well, I'm going to find out who it was,' said Lizzie. 'I believe you, even if the DS don't.'

She immediately left the room and went to confront the male cadets in their own anteroom. She stormed in as they were all just about to leave after their morning coffee break.

'OK,' she shouted at the top of her voice, 'which one of you shysters was hanging around our lines last night?' There followed total, amazed silence, partly because of the nature of the accusation and partly because it was Lizzie, renowned for being shy, who was making it. She took a deep breath and continued, 'One of you was, and Edwina is going to be thrown off because of it. I don't care if it was some sort of mistake or a practical joke, but whatever it was, it's backfired.' Silence. Lizzie wasn't sure what to do next. Her small supply of courage was failing. She crossed her arms and tried to look defiant, but inside she was quaking at the thought that she'd just made a dreadful fool of herself and, worse, alienated all the people who might be able to help Edwina. She was about to flee when a voice came from the back of the room.

'It was me. I couldn't stand her damned music any more.' Junior Under Officer Jeremy Moore, candidate for the Sword of Honour and future officer in the Argyle and Sutherland Highlanders, stepped forward. 'It was obvious that she'd either gone out or fallen asleep with her bloody radio on, and I couldn't sleep with the racket going on. I came down to your lines to get her to switch it off. I hammered on her door but I didn't get a reply. I assumed she'd gone out so I went in and there she was fast asleep. I was so surprised I just switched it off and legged it before she woke up and cried rape or something. I didn't realise anyone had seen me.'

'Thank you,' said Lizzie, feeling a shattering sense of relief. 'Will you come with me to see Colonel O'Brien?' She knew that Jeremy's career now hung in the balance and dismissal was on the cards for him too, but he was a true gentleman and honourable behaviour came as naturally to him as breathing – lying simply was not an option.

'Yes, I suppose I must.'

It came as quite a surprise to them both to find that a deputation consisting of Edwina's entire platoon was waiting outside Colonel O'Brien's office in order to protest Edwina's innocence. Amanda, who had been dubious that Lizzie would have any success, had rounded them up – there was nothing to lose after all. Lizzie quickly explained to the waiting platoon Jeremy's part in the misunderstanding, and they followed her into the colonel's office as Jeremy explained his presence in the female lines.

Colonel O'Brien was amazed by the efforts that Edwina's platoon had gone to in order to clear her name. She listened in silence to the explanation from Jeremy and the protestation from Lizzie that this was the truth. Whatever else, Edwina could certainly command loyalty and love from her fellow students. This wasn't the first course that had been entrusted to Colonel O'Brien's command, nor was Edwina the first student she had had to sack. In previous instances of dismissal, no one had protested; in fact in one case the other students had seemed to welcome the departure of a particular individual, who had been deemed a complete liability by almost everyone. Obviously Edwina had something special. The colonel listened carefully until Jeremy and Lizzie had finished their explanation. Then she spoke.

'Thank you. I shall not make any decision until I have spoken to Captain Roberts and the college commander. Ask the CSM to come and see me.' Colonel O'Brien wanted to tell the sergeant major to stop Edwina leaving the Academy until the whole matter had been thoroughly investigated as a result of this new information. 'Now please return to your lectures.'

They saluted and left, still unsure of what awaited Edwina – and now Jeremy.

Edwina sat in her room, racked with apprehension and bitterness. It was all so bloody unfair, she said to herself for the hundredth time. She wouldn't have minded if she had been caught in bed with this man, whoever he was – God only knew, she'd felt desperate for a bonk – but she'd been as good as gold throughout the whole course and even she wouldn't have been so stupid as to jeopardise things at this stage. She'd almost finished her packing and was folding up the last of her issue kit ready to hand back to the quartermaster. A wave of rage swept over her and she scrunched up the green Army jersey in her hands and threw it across the room. Her tears had long since dried as her anger had grown. If she found out who had come to her room last night, if indeed anyone had, she vowed she would get her own back somehow – she'd have his balls, to start with, and decide what to do with the rest of him later.

Edwina wasn't the only person feeling anger. Colonel O'Brien was incandescent with rage, and she was focusing it on Cathy Roberts.

'Apart from the fact that I have been made to look foolish, I have put a young lady through a dreadful and completely unnecessary ordeal,' she said icily.

'I'm sorry, ma'am,' stuttered Cathy. 'I really did see him leave.'

'But why didn't you challenge Mr Moore there and then?'

'I couldn't.'

'Why not.'

'I wasn't in a fit state to.'

Colonel O'Brien stared at her. 'Had you been drinking?' she said, horrified at the enormity of her own suggestion. No female officer at Sandhurst would ever allow herself to drink too much.

'My fiancé had just broken off our engagement.' Cathy dodged the question of the drinking.

'So, because of your own personal unhappiness, you were prepared to jump to conclusions without checking out the facts?'

'Yes,' said Cathy, almost in a whisper.

'When you reported this incident to me, you made it sound as though you'd caught the two of them *in flagrante delicto* but the young man fled before you could recognise him.'

'Yes.' Cathy had to agree.

'Yet it wasn't like that at all.'

'No.'

There was a long pause while Colonel O'Brien thought about what she should do.

'I shall have to tell the college commander everything, of course.' Cathy nodded unhappily. 'This incident will probably be reflected in the grading of your next confidential report. This was a serious error of judgement.'

'Yes, ma'am,' said Cathy meekly, although inside she was raging against Edwina, Lizzie and Amanda. The three of them were all in this. Why did the other two have to meddle in Edwina's business? It was their fault she was on the carpet. God help any of them if they ever crossed her path again, because next time there would be no Colonel O'Brien to protect them; next time she'd sort them out once and for all.

It had been an hour since the company sergeant major had knocked on Edwina's door and told her that she was not to leave the College but hadn't explained why.

Edwina was unaware of Lizzie's actions and of Jeremy's honesty, and she didn't know that her case was being reviewed. She assumed that there was some hitch with the paperwork to get rid of her. Frankly, she thought, she didn't need this kind of hassle. She would rather have gone quickly, got it over and done with. If she'd left when she'd been supposed to, she would be halfway to London and the train to Leeds and her mother saying 'I said you wouldn't last.' In her irritation at being kept waiting, she kicked one of the suitcases lying at her feet.

There was a knock on the door. Edwina froze and her heart rate doubled as she realised that this was probably the moment she'd been dreading. She cleared her throat and said nervously, 'Come in.'

It was Colonel O'Brien. Edwina leapt out of her chair and stood to attention, her training making her act automatically despite her nerves. What now? she wondered. A final dressing-down? Her throat was dry and she felt quite dizzy with fear, but she stood straight, determined not to let it show.

'Edwina, please sit down.'

Edwina perched on the edge of her bed while Colonel O'Brien removed her hat and sat in the armchair opposite.

'Before I go into any explanations, I would like to tell you that I have decided to reverse my earlier decision to remove you from the course.' Edwina's jaw dropped open, then she shook her head in disbelief.

'I'm sorry, ma'am, I don't understand.' She shook her head again.

'It appears that a man did leave your room last night, Captain Roberts wasn't mistaken on that count.'

'May I ask who it was?'

'It isn't a secret, your entire platoon now knows. It was Junior Under Officer Jeremy Moore.'

'But I've never even spoken to the man.' Edwina stopped herself

47

from adding that as a general rule she liked to be on first-name terms, at the very least, with anyone who shared her bed.

'Well, I gather that last night he did no more than walk into your room, switch off your hi-fi and then leave again, and both the college commander and I are inclined to believe him. Furthermore we're satisfied that nothing untoward happened and that you were unaware of his presence.'

Again Edwina held her tongue at the thought that no one had been inclined to believe her when the affair had first been reported. But then she didn't hold any cadet rank, nor was she in contention for any prize. Jeremy had made no secret of the fact that he wanted the Sword of Honour and didn't mind that as a consequence he was referred to as a 'blade-runner' by his peers.

'But why didn't Captain Roberts say anything to him when she saw him last night?'

Colonel O'Brien had hoped that Edwina wouldn't ask this. Edwina looked at her company commander, still waiting to find out why Captain Roberts hadn't dealt with the matter then and there.

'Captain Roberts has given me an explanation which has satisfied me; however, I don't think it's appropriate for me to repeat what was said.'

Edwina shrugged. Colonel O'Brien obviously wasn't going to elaborate and Edwina wondered why. There had to be a good reason why Captain Roberts had only observed the incident and not intervened and the only one which sprang to mind was the she'd been in no state to. Edwina wondered for a second if perhaps her platoon commander had been on the booze but then dismissed the idea as too unlikely.

'Anyway, I would like you to put this unfortunate incident behind you,' said Colonel O'Brien. 'I don't think it'll matter if you miss the rest of this morning's lectures. I'm sorry you'll have to unpack again, but under the circumstances I imagine you don't mind too much.' She rose to go and Edwina leapt to her feet and went to open the door for her.

'Thank you, ma'am. I can't tell you how pleased I am this has been cleared up.' Edwina didn't really have to speak. The look on her face said it all.

'You've got your friends to thank really. It was Miss Armstrong who found Mr Moore. And even if she hadn't done that, Miss Hardwick had already got the whole platoon together to try to convince me to keep you.'

48

After the colonel had gone, Edwina wondered how she was ever going to be able to make it up to Lizzie and Amanda. God, how she valued their friendship. Lizzie had been her safety net since that first day at the RCB, and Amanda had got her through this term by making her sit down and work. What wonderful friends! She only hoped that one day she'd be able to help them as they'd helped her.

With only a week to the end of term, the rehearsals for Sovereign's Parade dominated everything. The girls' uniforms had all been delivered from Moss Bros, their shoes bulled to a flawless shine and their drill perfected. Amanda and Lizzie had both been promoted to the rank of Junior Under Officer, as had a girl from their sister platoon. One of these three would be the Sash of Honour winner and would also have the responsibility of commanding the WRAC company in the actual parade. On this occasion the DS would take a back seat and, apart from the Academy adjutant on his white charger, no one other than the cadets themselves would be on parade. Lizzie and Edwina were both equally delighted when Amanda was further promoted to Senior Under Officer and told that she had been awarded the Sash. Amanda was concerned that Lizzie might feel disappointed but was reassured by her friend.

'Honestly, Amanda, you did miles better than me in the exams. I really wasn't expecting it. I was amazed when it was even suggested that I might be in contention.' Lizzie had later confessed to Edwina that standing out on the parade square bawling orders would have been an ordeal, not a privilege. As for Edwina, she was grateful just to pass, and certainly hadn't been looking for anything other than her commission.

The day of the parade dawned overcast but dry, much to everyone's relief. The weather forecast promised sunshine later. Reveille was at the normal time but there was little to do before the parade began except have breakfast and check over already immaculate uniforms. Amanda could hardly eat she was so nervous, but she knew that she would be on the square for almost two hours and forced down scrambled eggs and toast. She hoped against hope she wouldn't see them again. It was almost a relief when the moment came to march the company on to the square and the proceedings got underway. Amanda knew that all the women on the parade were so well drilled it wouldn't matter what words of command she gave, they would all do the right thing regardless. There was also some comfort in the fact that they formed the last company on the parade, so for all of them it was just a case of follow-my-leader. Even so, she was shaking so much she knew that the hem of her skirt was oscillating in sympathy with her kneecaps.

Behind her, standing rigidly to attention like all the other cadets in the warm spring sunshine which had broken through the thin cloud as promised, were Edwina and Lizzie, both feeling vicariously proud for their friend and both thankful that it wasn't them. Drilled by the academy sergeant major to Guardsman perfection, they were not only immaculate in their turn-out and bearing, but they also exuded a pride and happiness which was tangible to the enthralled parents and friends watching from the stands. The band played softly as the inspecting officer, Her Majesty The Queen, walked between the ranks of the senior term, exchanging a comment here and a pleasantry there with the cadets who were to be officially commissioned into the Army on the stroke of midnight that night. Then, her inspection finished, she returned to the saluting base, and the elegant and imposing façade of Old College rang with the shouts of command. Five hundred cadets were brought to attention; each bulled boot hit the ground simultaneously, every white-gloved hand slapped the butt of each rifle at exactly the same moment. The company of girls on parade had no weapons, but in all other respects they were equal with the men. At the front of the parade, and indifferent to the robotic movements of the cadets, the Academy adjutant's grey horse fidgeted because of the flies pestering it. The occasional stamping of its hooves and the swishing of its tail were out of place with the precision of the other movements. Another volley of manic shouts and the cadets were formed into close order ready to march past. Round the square they marched, swinging along to the jaunty music, snapping their heads right as they passed the saluting base and looking *not* into Her Majesty's eyes, as they had been told countless times, but over her shoulder, although a number of those on parade couldn't resist a second or two's disobedience. Then the slow march past as 'Auld Lang Syne' played, the climax of a parade which had lasted over an hour, and mothers (and some fathers) in the audience surreptitiously dabbed their eyes with tissues as their offspring went up the steps and through the Grand Entrance, followed by the Academy adjutant, still astride his grey horse.

'Yes!' said Edwina under her breath, as she passed through the doors. The 'Yes!' came again louder, as she heard the doors slam behind her. She'd made it. Around her disorder broke out; hats were thrown in delight, whoops of joy resounded through the cavernous hall, back-slapping, hand-shaking – all the manifestations of a major ambition achieved. In a corner by the stairs a small group of three drew away from the rest.

'We've done it,' said Amanda.

'I can't believe it,' replied Lizzie, hugging her and leaving a smear of lipstick on her cheek.

'Oh, don't. I think I'm going to cry. Oh God, I am. Look, my mascara's going all over the place,' sniffed Edwina as she fished in vain for a tissue. She resorted to wiping her tears away with the back of her hand, leaving grubby smears on her white gloves.

'I don't believe it, you still haven't got a hankie. You've got to brace up now,' said Amanda with a giggle. 'You're an officer and a lady, not some grubby little oik cadet.'

'Not until midnight, so I'll still pick and flick if I want to,' said Edwina in mock defiance, although her nose wrinkled in disgust at the thought.

'What is the world coming to?' said Amanda.

Edwina struck her forehead dramatically with the palm of her hand in a gesture they all recognised as one belonging to Colonel O'Brien, and, affecting a strong Irish brogue, said, 'B'Jaysus, I don't believe your behaviour, Miss Austin.' It was a near-perfect, if over-the-top, imitation.

'Neither do I – and I've never said "b'Jaysus" in my life,' replied an identical brogue.

The three friends froze in horror. Edwina, with her back to Lieutenant Colonel O'Brien, mouthed, 'Oh, shit!' Then she fixed a rueful smile and turned to face her company commander.

'I'm sorry, ma'am. Oh God, what can I say?' Edwina had gone pale in embarrassment despite the normal healthy colour of her skin.

'Well, that's something I thought I'd never see,' said Denise O'Brien, 'Miss Austin flummoxed.'

'I'm sorry. I didn't see you there.'

'Well, I didn't think that even you would be stupid enough to make fun of me to my face. Besides which, did you think I was going to put you on a charge at this stage in the day? And with me wanting to get away from you lot and take my own leave.'

Edwina, relieved, shook her head, and her hair, disturbed by the earlier removal of her hat, took the chance to effect further escape from the pins used to try and tame it. In exasperation Edwina shoved the most obvious tendrils behind her ear and grinned wider.

Around them the shouts and laughter of the other cadets, predominantly male, had changed to a frantic flurry as the call went up to return their weapons to the armoury as soon as possible. This was something that the girls were spared. The crescendo of shouts and running boot-clad feet forced Colonel O'Brien to raise her voice to be heard.

'But don't push your luck too far, Miss Austin – some sacrifices might be worthwhile.'

Edwina laughed, and almost despite herself so did the Colonel. Amanda and Lizzie looked at Edwina with undisguised admiration – she really was frightened of nothing and no one.

'Are you looking forward to the ball tonight, ma'am?' Lizzie, always the diplomat, said to change the subject.

'Naturally. Despite what you lot might think, it'll give me great pleasure to see you all with pips on your shoulders.'

'Yes, ma'am. It means we're out of your hair once and for all,' said Edwina.

'There is that, to be sure. But to be honest, Miss Austin, I really didn't think you were going to make it at one stage, even though you'll probably make a first-rate officer. I'd have been sad if we'd lost you.' The colonel smiled at them. The three girls sensed that she was fond of them, although they also knew she had to maintain outward impartiality. They knew she'd pushed them hard to make them achieve their absolute best, and despite the exhausting inevitability and annoyance of being told that, if they really tried, they could gain an extra half-mark, or run half a mile further, or bull their shoes to a yet deeper shine, they were grateful. Although sometimes they felt they were being picked on or asked the impossible, they understood her reasons and respected her for them, and her affection for them was returned.

'Now, you've got guests for lunch to look after, and you, Miss Austin, need to do something about your dreadful hair.' But even as she admonished Edwina, Colonel O'Brien was still smiling.

The three girls braced to attention as she departed.

'I'll miss her when we go,' said Lizzie.

'Bollocks,' said Edwina, no more ladylike than she had been when she'd first come to the Academy over seven months previously.

'Don't give me that,' said Amanda. 'If it hadn't been for her sense of fairness, you'd have been off this course.'

'OK, I concede.' Edwina saw her reflection in the glass door of a display case. 'My bloody hair,' she groaned. 'Why won't it do as I bloody want it to and stay pinned up?'

'I suppose,' said Lizzie, 'it's because it's like you – you never seem to do what anyone wants you to do either.' She shrieked as she ducked a mock punch thrown by Edwina and fled down the corridor to the ladies' loo. There the three friends jostled their way through the press of the other dozen or so female cadets who were jockeying for places in front of the mirrors. Edwina, putting her weight behind her shoulder, managed to squeeze through into a corner. Amanda and Lizzie followed her. Once there, knowing that Colonel O'Brien had gone to her flat upstairs in order to tidy herself up, and the coast was therefore clear, Edwina resumed her shameless mimicry of her company commander.

'How can you expect the highest standards from your troops if your own hair is untidy and your uniform is creased? You know what we expect, Miss Austin, so please produce the standard.' Amanda and Lizzie, giggling, joined in the last sentence, one they'd heard on countless occasions. Edwina, despite the chattering press of women around her, found the elbow room to drag a comb through her hair with the finesse of a farmer raking hay, then she pulled the whole mass into a ponytail at the back of her head before winding it excruciatingly tightly prior to skewering it with a dozen pins. Although she sprayed her head thickly with lacquer – enough to glue anything together, commented Lizzie – the instant she replaced her hat on her head, a curl sprang free. Edwina mouthed an expletive at her reflection in the mirror while Amanda and Lizzie, immaculate as always, dusted her shoulders to remove any fallen hairs or, God forbid, dandruff. She grimaced and said, 'Right, let's go. I'll never get tidier.' It would have to do. The crowd of cadets had thinned somewhat in the time it had taken Edwina to sort herself out, so her muscle power was not required, which was just as well if her hair was to remain within the limits of acceptability.

The three young women walked back into the main entrance hall of Old College looking jaunty and relaxed. But underneath, despite the excitement of the day and the achievement that it represented, they were all faintly apprehensive about their futures. From here on they would no longer be taking orders but giving them. In a couple of weeks they would be reporting to their new units, where they would be judged not just by other officers, but by the soldiers and NCOs in their platoons, who would have years more experience than them and who could make life difficult or unpleasant. The RMA had done its best to prepare them; the rest was up to them.

Amanda identified that as well as apprehension she was feeling sad too. Being commissioned also meant being separated, each of them off to different posting. She wondered how their friendship, not yet a year old but welded in the intense heat of the RMA, would fare. One of their contemporaries had once wondered how three such opposites got on so well together. Edwina had retorted that only a mental defective would suggest that three of anything could be opposites, but they all knew what had been meant by the remark. And even though they knew the old saw about opposites attracting, Amanda couldn't help wondering if they would now drift apart. She hoped not.

The next morning, after their commissioning ball, Edwina went out for a run to clear her head. Far too much champagne was definitely no good for a girl, she decided, her temples pounding in unison with her feet as she jogged steadily round the Academy grounds, trying to remember every last detail of the beautiful place that had been the centre of her world for just under eight short months. She sucked in lungfuls of the clear April air and wished that the rhododendrons were out – she adored their vibrant colours. As she ran past the lake and along the main road towards the Staff College, her mind wandered from admiring her surroundings and she began to wonder instead how Lizzie and Amanda were going to get on in their new postings. In some respects Edwina felt lucky that she was going to continue with her training for a few months. She was going on a troop commanders' course at the School of Signals in Dorset. It would give her a chance to find her feet as a commissioned officer before being given real responsibility. Poor old Amanda, though, was going to Guildford to train WRAC recruits.

'But I joined the Army to get away from bloody teaching,' she'd exploded when she got Lizzie and Edwina alone later. 'How often do you have to tell the Army something before they take it in! I mean, I had to repeat myself about three times when I was joining up that I didn't want to join the Education Corps and the stupid woman who

interviewed me kept telling me the benefits if I did.' They sympathised with her objections to going to Guildford, and Edwina said
that if she got posted to an all-female unit she'd go spare. Lizzie said
that she didn't think that training recruits would be anything like
being a schoolteacher but Amanda had just give her a withering look
by way of reply. Amanda was jealous of Lizzie's posting; she was
going to be the assistant adjutant of a smart artillery regiment based
in Aldershot. OK, the location wasn't the best, but the unit had a
reputation for going on exercise throughout the world, it had first-
class sports teams and, as Amanda had put it, it was in the heart of
the military world so the social life would be excellent. It certainly
sounded attractive to Lizzie, who tried not to look too excited
about it in deference to Amanda's obvious disappointment over her
posting.

'Oh well, it's only for two years,' sighed Amanda. 'I'll just have to
hope I get something more exciting next.'

Guildford, May 1988

Amanda drew up at the guardroom of the WRAC Centre and wound down her window.

'Can I see some ID please?' said a smart young private whose appearance was marred by galloping acne. The engine of her little car purred quietly as Amanda removed her ID card from her purse and proffered it. The female soldier looked at the details and instantly stood to attention, saluting smartly. As Amanda was dressed in civilian clothes she hadn't realised whom she'd been addressing.

'Thank you,' said Amanda as her card was handed back to her. 'Can you direct me to the officers' mess, please?'

'Of course, ma'am.' The instructions were simple and succinct and Amanda passed under the red and white striped pole and into the barracks that was to be her home for the next two years. She wasn't looking forward to it. Being closeted with several hundred women didn't sound as though it would be much fun. Also, she'd heard that the workload at Guildford could be pretty punishing, to say nothing of being under the scrutiny of any number of sexless, humourless senior female officers for all one's waking hours. Training establishments were notorious for their pernickety attention to the most trivial of rules, and as Amanda had only just escaped from one, the idea of being at another was grim. Still, she wasn't the sort of woman who let situations get her down. It was only for two years, and there was always the hope that she might get posted early. Besides which, she had her car, so it would be easy for her to get away from the place at weekends, duties permitting. She drove through the barracks, built at the height of sixties unimaginativeness; flat-roofed, square-sided, uniform and unremarkable buildings, surrounding a monstrous parade square where a platoon of some thirty young women were being drilled in the art of saluting to the left and the right. Everywhere was immaculately tidy; the grass neatly cut, paths swept, direction signs gleaming with fresh red and white paint, all the normal hallmarks of any training establishment.

She drew up in an enclosed courtyard outside the front entrance to the mess, by a notice that forbade parking. She planned to unload her cases on the steps, drive the car to the mess car park and return to carry everything in. But she'd barely got the boot open when a figure hurried out of the front door.

'Hello, ma'am, I'm Staff Barry, the mess manager. You must be Miss Hardwick. We've been expecting you. You leave your cases to me. I'll get them taken to your room if you'd like to find a parking space.' Amanda had had no chance to do more than smile and nod as Staff Barry took control of her belongings. 'Off you go, before one of the majors sees your car here. Follow the road back the way you came and you'll see the signs to the car park. I'll meet you back in the anteroom.'

'OK, thanks.' Amanda started up her car and drove to the car park. On her return to the mess, a tea tray, complete with a plate of biscuits, was waiting for her, and her cases had been whisked away to her room. She suddenly realised the difference between her arrival at Sandhurst and here. Now she was an officer, and Staff Barry and her team of mess stewardesses were there to look after her and make her life off duty as comfortable as possible. Amanda thought she could get used to this.

When she'd finished her second cup of tea, Staff Barry reappeared to escort her to her room.

'The other officers will be back about five-ish. Tea and toast will available in the anteroom then, and dinner is from seven thirty till eight,' said Staff as they walked up the few steps that led to the long corridor that housed the junior officers' bedrooms. Beside them a flight of steps led downwards. 'The majors and the senior officers live down there,' Staff informed her as they passed. They walked along the corridor. 'Here's yours,' and Staff threw open the door to reveal a room of larger dimensions to Amanda's one at the RMA, but furnished identically. The room was light and airy and a big aluminium-framed window looked across some shrubbery and grass – pleasant but uninspiring. Amanda's packing cases had already been delivered and were sitting in the middle of the floor. Her cases were on the bed, which was made up and covered by a clean, but dreary, cotton bedspread.

'Thank you, Staff,' she said.

'While I'm up here I'll just show you where the baths and everything are. Oh, and one other thing: as I pointed out, the majors live below you. They get really ratty if you subalterns make too much noise, so please don't run along the corridor or play your music loud. When you meet the others they'll tell you I'm not exaggerating.' Amanda didn't doubt for a moment that she was.

It didn't take Amanda long to move the furniture in her room so that she would be able to see out of the window while she was lying in bed. Then she unpacked her clothes and hung them in the spacious wardrobes. Her packing cases could wait until later. She glanced at her watch – four forty-five. Everyone would soon be arriving for tea. Perhaps now would be as good a moment as any to meet them. She was quite looking forward to encountering the other subbies, but she wasn't so sure about the majors. Senior WRAC officers could be absolutely terrifying, especially *en masse*.

Amanda wandered back into the anteroom, decorated in the same dreary way that most of the rooms at Sandhurst had been: oatmeal-coloured curtains, pale-gold stretch covers on the arm-chairs and a beige carpet. Hardly eye-catching or memorable, but safe. On the walls were hung a series of the ubiquitous Joan Wanklyn paintings. These ones, naturally, showed members of the Corps undertaking various duties around the world. There was one of them performing search duties in Northern Ireland, all looking coolly efficient. Another showed the girls manning a communications centre in Germany, looking coolly efficient, and yet another depicted some lucky ones stationed out in Hong Kong, wearing tropical dress and, despite the heat, looking coolly efficient. Amanda began to feel a fit of giggles coming on. She thought she'd better move away from these pictures and turned around, only to be faced with a massive portrait of the Duchess of Kent, looking – oh God! – coolly efficient. Amanda, laughter bubbling up in her throat, fled back to her room until she'd brought herself under control. After about five minutes she felt able to return to the anteroom. Just as she entered it she heard voices approaching from the other direction, and half a dozen subalterns poured in, chattering nineteen to the dozen. They were all in full number-two dress but each had a different-coloured flash on her epaulettes. Amanda knew that this denoted the company to which each belonged but couldn't remember which was which. She'd soon learn, she thought. As the group neared the table where the tea things were set out, one young woman, a vivacious-looking brunette with short bubbly curls, caught sight of her.

'Hi, you must be Amanda Hardwick. Welcome to the mess. I'm Bella de Fresne.' Amanda felt drawn to her immediately; her voice was cheerful and her smile genuine.

'Hello. It's nice to meet you.'

'Have a seat and I'll put some toast on for you.'

'Great, thanks.' Another self-assured young woman sat next to her.

'I'm Caroline, and I'll introduce you to everyone else in a minute. Your room OK?'

'Yes, fine.'

'If you want anything,' said Caroline, 'just ask Staff Barry. If it's legal she'll get it, believe me.'

'I do, I've already met her.' Amanda began to feel much happier. She'd heard a lot about Guildford, mostly hearsay and rumour, and some of it hadn't sounded too good. But no one had mentioned what a nice bunch the other subalterns seemed to be. She felt that despite the down side, Guildford might prove to be fun. If nothing else, the company of like-minded people would no doubt be stimulating, and she certainly wouldn't be lonely. Perhaps her initial disappointment over her posting would prove to be ill-founded.

She was just about to return to her room to finish her unpacking when a booming voice in the lobby called for Staff Barry.

'Oh God, Major Blenkinsop,' explained Bella to Amanda. Then, 'Tell you all about her later,' *sotto voce*, as a large woman with an improbable bust stamped into the room. She glowered at the gang of lieutenants and went and sat as far from them as she could. She picked up a copy of *The Times*, shook it open noisily and began to read, rattling the pages and snorting loudly when she came across a story she disapproved of.

'I'd better get going,' said Bella. 'It's "In Night" tonight so I've got to go back over to the barrack block before dinner. Tell you what, Amanda, as you're in my training company, why don't you come over too? You'll be able to meet some of the NCOs and see what the recruits get up to. It'll give you a feel for the raw material that you'll be working with in future.'

'OK,' agreed Amanda. 'I'll just go and press my uniform.'

59

As the two women left the anteroom so did the other lieutenants, leaving the irascible Major Blenkinsop behind on her own.

Amanda returned to her room, where she changed out of her civilian clothes and into regulation tights, shirt and green tie. She grabbed her uniform jacket and skirt and took the lovat-green suit along to the ironing room to get rid of the few creases it had acquired on the back seat of her car. As she stood there, half dressed, she listened to the cheerful voices of her fellow subalterns drifting along the corridor to the ironing room. They certainly sounded happy enough, she thought. She wondered if Guildford's reputation for being grim was exaggerated.

She had just arranged her skirt on the board when she heard footsteps approaching and Bella entered the room. She cast her eyes over Amanda's figure and then looked directly into Amanda's eyes and smiled. The gaze was cool and appraising, then she blinked slowly and laughed. Amanda smiled back at her, glad of the company while she carried out this boring task, and wondered whether the other girl was this friendly with everyone. She reckoned that Bella was probably much the same age as Lizzie – hardly older than most of the recruits she was training – but for all that she came across as incredibly self-assured.

Bella moved across the room, perched on the windowsill and said, 'So, shall I fill you in on the major personalities here – the emphasis being on *major*, although one or two of the captains are a bit iffy?'

'Oh, do,' said Amanda who was never averse to hearing a bit of gossip or scandal. 'What were you going to tell me about Major Blenkinsop, for starters?'

'Well,' Bella was obviously relishing the telling of the tale, the *on dit* is that she and the QM, that's Major Green – who I'll take you to meet tomorrow, because you'll need to draw some kit from her – anyway, the rumour is that they have had a lovers' tiff and neither of them is on speaking terms, which is a bit tricky when you consider that Major B is the adjutant here.' She grinned wickedly.

'Good heavens. And after all we've been told about there being absolutely no lesbians in the WRAC,' said Amanda, half riveted by the news and half shocked at the revelation.

'Come on, you don't believe *that*, do you?' Bella looked thoughtfully at Amanda. 'You don't strike me as the sort of woman who would have done.'

Amanda stared back at her, halting her ironing. 'No,' she said, 'no, I didn't, for a minute.' There was a silence for a second or two as Amanda held Bella's gaze, then the older woman dropped her eyes and continued concentrating on pressing out a small crease.

'Good.' There was something about Bella's tone of voice that made Amanda flick a glance at her again. Bella stared coolly at her and then continued, 'Anyway, no one knows if it's true or not, but they haven't been seen within fifty yards of each other for a month or so, and until then they were as thick as thieves.'

'But surely no one knew for certain they were . . .'

'Jumping all over each other?' said Bella, raising her eyebrows archly.

'Well, yes, I suppose so.' Amanda couldn't imagine the large, forty-ish Major Blenkinsop in any sort of sexual relationship – certainly 'jumping' seemed an athletic improbability.

'Well, of course, we didn't know for sure, but it spices things up a lot to indulge in a little speculation.'

Amanda noticed how the top of Bella's nose wrinkled when she smiled or spoke. She finished pressing her skirt and slipped it on; hopping on one foot momentarily in an effort to avert it dragging on the floor and any creases reappearing. Then she got to grips with her jacket.

'So what else should I know about?'

'Staff Barry, as you have probably already guessed, does her best to protect us subbies from the worst of living here. She'll always warn us in advance, if she can, if the majors are about to get on the warpath about the noise level in our corridor. She'll also make sure that you get something to eat if duties here mean you miss a meal.' Amanda nodded, taking in what was being said while she concentrated on the sleeve.

'Now, most of the captains are quite nice. Don't, for heaven's sake, make the mistake that I made when I arrived here of calling them ma'am. I got so brain-washed at Sandhurst that I was almost calling other subbies ma'am, but they're junior officers just like you and me, so it's definitely Christian names only.'

'I'll make a point of it,' said Amanda as she unplugged the iron and put on her jacket.

'But beware of Gina Danby – she's a two-faced cow who'll drop you in it before you can say Jack Robinson. She's mess secretary, and if she discovers anyone breaching any of the mess rules she goes running to the president of the mess committee as fast as her fat legs will carry her.' Bella stood up and walked over to Amanda. She smoothed Amanda's jacket across her shoulders and made sure the free ends of her epaulettes were properly buttoned and tucked under the edge of her collar. She moved back half a pace to look Amanda over. 'That's it. You suit this uniform better than most people do. It must be your figure.' Again that cool stare.

'So what did you do to upset her?' Amanda deliberately brought the conversation back to Gina Danby. She suspected that she was being sent certain signals and she wasn't sure she was receiving them correctly. It could be dangerous if she was mistaken, for she had only known Bella de Fresne twenty minutes. But she had the feeling that Bella had uncovered something in her character that she thought she had buried deep out of sight. She felt quite unnerved, yet also, if she was completely honest with herself, excited. She hoped that Bella didn't notice her apprehension.

Apparently she hadn't, because she carried on with her story about Gina. 'I took a bottle of wine from the bar, meaning to sign for it the next day, and I forgot. I got two weeks' extra duties for that. Then she caught me making a personal telephone call on the duty officer's phone – another two weeks of extras. None of the other captains would have said anything, let alone reported it.' Amanda knew that both peccadilloes were minor and a rifting on the spot would have been more than sufficient. 'And on the subject of the duty phone – it really is only for duty calls. If you want to chat to chums using the military phone network, do it in your office in office hours and when the sergeant major or the OC aren't in earshot. Right, ready for your first "In Night"? Come on, then.'

It turned out to be a fair walk across the barracks to the three-storey block which accommodated the recruits under training. Bella led Amanda round the building while she cheerfully checked up that her training platoon were all cleaning their rooms properly ready for room inspection the next day. She exchanged pleasantries with the young women, asked after their boyfriends, admired their choice of posters on the walls, and the range of soft toys that swamped their bed spaces. Amanda couldn't help admiring her easy style, which made her seem eminently approachable whilst still commanding respect. She hoped that, with experience, she would become like Bella. She didn't think she'd go far wrong if she took Bella as a role model.

The remainder of Amanda's first week at Guildford quickly became a whirl of introductions, initial interviews, guided tours and files of hand-over/take-over notes to read and inwardly digest. She sat in on lectures on military law, personal hygiene and Army traditions. She learned where and how to make up slides to use as teaching aids and was given a list of duties she would be expected to take on in addition to that of teaching the recruits. Being the mess entertainment officer didn't seem too onerous but she was horrified to discover she was NBC training officer too.

'But I know nothing about nuclear, biological and chemical warfare,' she complained to Bella.

'Don't worry, you're down to attend a course in Wiltshire in your first break. You'll learn everything you need to know at a fun-packed week at the Defence NBC Centre.'

'Bugger, I don't fancy that at all.'

'You'll survive it. People do, you know.'

'Heartless witch.'

Bella just grinned and blew her a kiss.

During these first few days Amanda was reminded of her first weeks at Sandhurst; it was all early mornings, late nights and a constant pressure of work in between. She longed to contact Lizzie and Edwina to find out how they were getting on, but there was no time for chatty phone calls.

It wasn't until the following Monday, when her predecessor finished handing over her platoon and Amanda finally had her new office to herself, that she was able to rifle through the green loose-leaf book which was the Army's internal telephone directory. It only took her a few minutes to find the number for the assistant adjutant at Lille Barracks in Aldershot. She checked the code and dialled the number, hoping that Lizzie was at her desk and the adjutant wouldn't take the call. She had no idea how he would react to one of Lizzie's friends ringing up for a chat.

'Hello, Miss Armstrong speaking,' came almost before the phone had rung once.

'Hi. It's Amanda. Can you speak or is your boss breathing down your neck?'

'Amanda!' Lizzie sounded really pleased to hear from her. 'How great to hear from you. How's Guildford?'

'OK. I have to be honest, it's much better than I imagined.'

'I *am* pleased.'

63

'And what about your job?'

'Amanda, I can't lie. I'd love to tell you that it's the best thing ever. But I feel as though I've been cast adrift. The girl I took over from left on Friday night, and I don't seem to have a clue about anything. It all seemed clear when she was here, but now . . . The adjutant is nice enough – I can talk about him as he and the CO have gone down to the gun sheds – but I hate having to ask how to deal with every last thing that I get in my in-tray.'

'Yes, but there must be some compensations. What about all those hunky Gunner officers?'

'Well, yes, I suppose so. But it would be nice to have another woman to talk to. Actually I feel rather lonely.'

'That's one thing I don't have to contend with. There's so many of us living in the mess, and since all the subalterns are doing the same basic job, there are loads of lieutenants I can go to for advice and not worry about looking a prat.'

'Lucky you. But you've got so much self-confidence I don't think you could look a prat if you tried,' said Lizzie with feeling. 'I've felt a complete fool most of the time since I got here. I don't seem to be able to get anything right. Anyway,' she changed the subject, 'have you heard how Edwina is getting on?'

'Not a word. I don't think I'll be able to ring her during working hours because she'll be in lectures, won't she? And the only military phone in our mess is the duty one – use it for private calls at your peril.'

'At least here there's a phone on the bar for anyone to use.' It was about the only advantage that Lizzie seemed to have over Amanda. 'I'll try and get hold of her if you like.'

They exchanged a few more details of their first impressions of their jobs, and agreed how delightful it was to live in an officers' mess and be waited on hand and foot, then Lizzie promised to phone Amanda as soon as she'd heard from Edwina.

'I'd better go now,' she said. 'I expect the CO and the adjutant will be back in a minute. I'm glad Guildford isn't all bad.'

'Thanks. Speak to you soon, 'bye.' Amanda put the phone down feeling really sorry for Lizzie. The poor kid had sounded quite fed up. It probably didn't help that she was such a shy, quiet little mouse. Obviously the job wasn't as good in reality as it had seemed on paper. Amanda thanked her lucky stars that things had gone the opposite way for her.

Aldershot, May 1988

Lizzie put the phone down and gazed at her in-tray, trying to keep her growing feeling of bewilderment under control. She looked at the thick pile of files and wondered why everything was now such a mystery when only a week ago, with Jilly, the departing assistant adjutant, there to show her what to do, it had all seemed so straight-forward. Simon, her immediate boss, had said brusquely that, rather than making a balls-up which he would have to sort out later, would Lizzie please ask him what she should do if she wasn't absolutely sure. But Lizzie had got the impression that he expected her to be able to cope. If only she had someone other than Simon to ask, she thought. Simon was obviously up to his eyes in work – Lizzie knew he never finished in the office until at least seven o'clock at night because she could see the light from her room in the mess – and she really hated breaking into his concentration to ask him questions, which always seemed so stupid once he'd curtly given her the answer. It didn't help either that the commanding officer had told her, during her initial interview, how wonderful Jilly had been as an assistant adjutant.

'You've got a hard act to follow if you are going to match her standards. She gave her all to this regiment, which, to be honest, is the least I expect from my officers.' He stared at Lizzie unsmilingly and she got the distinct impression that she wasn't really welcome and that, if the colonel had had his way, Jilly would have stayed put in her job. 'Do you play hockey?' he shot at her suddenly.

'A bit. Not very well.'

'Pity. Jilly played for the regiment.'

Well, bully for her, thought Lizzie dejectedly. The colonel then revealed that Jilly had been 'one of the boys' in the mess and had also won the CO's prize for the best essay written by a junior officer. Lizzie left his office feeling decidedly second-rate.

The funny thing was, she thought, she hadn't liked Jilly that much during their week together. She'd seemed friendly enough and had given her some good advice on how to do her new job, but now Lizzie felt as though it had all been a little perfunctory, that there were things she ought to have been told about and hadn't been. It was true that Jilly had tried to make Lizzie feel at home in the mess; she'd shown her where there were some nice pubs around Aldershot, she'd made sure that Lizzie hadn't been ribbed by the other subalterns and had warned her about the sort of practical jokes she might expect. But looking back, Jilly's answer to rather a lot of questions had been 'You'll get the hang of it' or 'You'll pick it up as you go along.' Not very informative.

Lizzie pulled a file off the pile and opened it. What the hell was this all about? she thought as she read the top folio. None of it seemed to make sense to her, not even the title of the memo. She hurriedly shut it and tried the next one. This was better; Simon had scrawled a message to her on the most recent letter on it: 'L. Copy this and send to BCs with covering letter asking for returns by Monday. Nil returns are required.' Lizzie felt a surge of relief that at last here was something she could tackle on her own. Swiftly she drew a sheet of scrap paper out of her drawer and drafted a letter to all battery commanders asking them to read the attached letter and let her know the figures required, even if the answer was none, by the following Monday. She then made a careful note in her desk diary for that day to check that all the replies were received. She wrote some instructions to the clerks on the file, attached her draft letter to the cover and dropped it in her out-tray. She was reaching for the next file when the CO and the adjutant returned. She got to her feet.

'Do sit down, Lizzie,' said Colonel Tilling. 'I'd like some coffee if you can arrange it, and ask Richard Airdrie-Stow to come and see me.'

'Certainly, sir.' Lizzie spoke to his back as he walked across the room and through the door which connected his office to theirs. He shut the door behind him.

'Lizzie,' said Simon, 'don't stand up each time the boss comes into our office. Just first thing in the morning will do.' He sounded exasperated.

'Sorry,' said Lizzie quietly. He had mentioned it before but she was still suffering from the brainwashing of Sandhurst where you stood up every time a senior officer entered the room. She sidled from behind her desk to go to the little pantry to make the coffee. 'Do you want one, Simon?'

'Yes, milk no sugar.' *Please* would be nice, thought Lizzie. She busied herself with the granules of instant and the kettle. Her feeling of achievement that she'd dealt successfully with the file had evaporated with the brusqueness of the CO and the adjutant. She knew that others at Sandhurst had thought that her posting had been one of the most desirable, but right now she felt miserable and useless and her self-confidence had never been lower. While she was waiting for the kettle to boil, she rang Richard Airdrie-Stow, a battery captain, and passed on the CO's message.

'Did he say what it was about?'

'Sorry, I've no idea.'

'Well, did he sound angry or happy?'

'I don't know, just ordinary, I think.'

'Oh, never mind then. I'm on my way.'

Lizzie replaced the receiver and felt that she'd even got passing on the message wrong. Probably Jilly-the-wonder-woman was a mind-reader along with all her other talents, and could warn the junior officers when trouble was afoot. Lizzie returned to the pantry and slopped boiling water into two mugs, added milk and sugar and flung the teaspoon back on to the tray, feeling thoroughly despondent. Carrying the hot drink carefully she knocked on the CO's door.

'Come.' She went in, put the coffee on the little coaster with its smart Gunner crest embossed in gold, and went out. The CO didn't even look up. Lizzie didn't particularly want thanks for carrying out this small errand, but in her low state she felt that the snub from the CO was deliberate. She returned to the pantry and collected Simon's coffee. She was just about to carry it across the corridor and through to their office when a figure hurrying past knocked it out of her hand and down her front. The shock of the scalding coffee soaking through her brand-new uniform shirt made her cry out with pain and anger, then, to her embarrassment, she burst into tears.

'You'd better go and sort yourself out,' said Simon coldly, appearing from the office to discover the cause of the commotion. 'And while you're at it, change your skirt.' Lizzie fled.

Back in her room in the mess she looked at her skirt and burst into tears again. It looked dreadful. A brand-new uniform skirt that she'd only been wearing for a week, and it was a complete mess. It wasn't the money that it would cost to replace it if it was ruined – all her uniform was insured – it was just the unfairness of the accident happening to her. She sniffed and changed into a clean skirt, then checked her jersey and blouse. They seemed to have missed the deluge, which was something anyway. Lizzie blew her nose and wiped her eyes. She looked at her image in the mirror and carefully removed the smears under her eyes where her mascara had run. She decided that she'd better take her skirt to the dry cleaner's opposite the barracks straight away. Blow the work in her tray, it could wait. If there was going to be any hope for her skirt she felt she shouldn't delay. She had just folded it up and put it in a plastic bag when there was a knock on her door.

'Come in,' she called. Richard Airdrie-Stow appeared looking a bit sheepish.

'I'm sorry about what happened,' he said. 'I was in a hurry and I didn't look where I was going.'

'That's all right,' said Lizzie; his apology was unexpected but welcome.

'No, it's not. Let me pay to have it cleaned.'

'Well . . .'

'It's the least I can do.' He paused and ran his fingers through his blond hair. He looked rather diffident. 'You seemed pretty upset about it.'

'It wasn't the . . .' Lizzie stopped. She wanted to tell him about how impossible her job seemed to be, how rude the colonel and the adjutant appeared, how miserable she was, but she didn't want to be branded as a whingeing female on top of everything else.

'Simon been giving you a hard time?'

'Yes. No,' she hastily corrected.

'Look, I don't know if Jilly told you, but Simon is going through a bad patch at the moment.'

'No, she didn't say anything.'

'That's typical of Jilly.' His normally kindly blue eyes hardened as he spoke. 'She's not one to help others if it means they might do better than her. Oh, friendly and nice to everyone if it puts her in a good light, but forget it if there's any competition involved. You'll probably find that your hand-over left a lot to be desired. She wouldn't want you taking over from her as the CO's golden girl. Likes to be thought of as top dog does our Jilly – perhaps I should say top bitch.' Lizzie didn't respond. 'No, well . . .' Richard stopped. Lizzie felt uncomfortable; she wasn't sure what had provoked this outburst but she didn't like it. 'It would have been a kindness if she'd told you that Simon's wife walked out on him about three weeks ago, *and* that he's also trying to study for his promotion exams *and* that the colonel is being particularly bloody about him having time off for all the courses he should attend. Consequently he's having to work his socks off trying to get his course work done as well as the stuff in the office, and he doesn't even have a decent home to go to any more.'

'I don't imagine it can help having a complete dunce like me to contend with.'

'You'll pick it up. Everyone's at sea to begin with. Try asking the chief clerk for help if you're frightened of Simon. Chiefy's a nice guy and he's been doing that job for ages – there won't be much he can't help with.'

'Thanks.' Lizzie felt this was the first really kind thing anyone had said to her since she'd arrived. She felt very grateful towards Richard, but she shouldn't hang around chatting, no matter how nice he was to her. She would be expected back in the office. 'Look, I'd better get going. Simon'll throw a track if I'm gone too long.' As she walked across the road to the dry cleaner's, she wondered what Jilly had done to upset Richard. He sounded as though he really hated her.

When she returned to her desk some fifteen minutes later, having been assured by the dry cleaner's that her skirt would probably be all right, Simon ignored both her reappearance and the earlier incident. Lizzie, embarrassed by her behaviour, felt she ought to say something.

'I'm sorry, Simon.'

He didn't look up from the signal he was drafting. 'What for?'

'For what happened just now.'

'Not your fault. Richard should have looked where he was going.' The matter was obviously closed. Lizzie felt more of a fool than ever. She sighed and tried to concentrate on her work.

Over the next few days she took Richard's advice and went to the chief clerk, who had endless patience and an inexhaustible supply of good humour. Slowly Lizzie began to feel more confident, and she rapidly realised that the vast majority of the problems which were hers to solve had cropped up before. It was mostly a case of seeing what had been done last time and repeating the procedures. Simon was as silent and moody as ever, but now that she knew the cause, she stopped taking it personally. Slowly she began to feel happier at work and get real pleasure out of being able to efficiently solve most problems that came her way.

Mess life was a different matter. Lizzie had always been used to having other women about her. She had two younger sisters, she'd been to a girls' boarding school and then she'd been surrounded by female cadets at Sandhurst. Suddenly, here she was in an all-male regiment, living in an all-male mess. She knew that for some women – Jilly amongst them, apparently – it was their idea of heaven. But Lizzie felt completely isolated. She found the male subalterns noisy and coarse, displaying their machismo through the use of four-letter words and the telling of offensive jokes. She tried not to look shocked at their outrageous behaviour, knowing it would only goad them to further excesses, but on some occasions it was almost impossible. When Julian, a junior captain, appeared at breakfast one morning, there were cries of 'Well, did you shag her then?' apparently referring to a bet placed the previous night about his chances with a QA nurse. Julian held his fingers under the nose of one of the other officers and said, 'Sniff that. That's Anna.'

Lizzie, red with embarrassment, left the table. As she walked from the dining room a gale of laughter followed her.

Later she tried to phone Edwina but had no joy. According to the barman at the School of Signals mess, Edwina had booked out for dinner, so presumably wouldn't be back until later. He promised to leave a message for her. Lizzie felt a stab of jealousy; Edwina wouldn't be intimidated by young officers, she would give them as good as she got. She wouldn't be embarrassed by their jokes and she wouldn't shut herself up in her room. Sharply, Lizzie told herself to brace up.

While she was getting ready for dinner that evening, she heard the other officers charging about noisily, yelling to each other along the length of the corridor, banging doors and playing their music too loudly. Then suddenly the mess seemed to go quiet. Lizzie, curious, poked her head round her door. Not a soul in sight. She returned to her room and continued putting away her uniform, sorting out some clothes to wash and listening to the news on the radio. At seven fifteen she strolled down the wide, carpeted stairs and across the hall to the bar. Gunner Foulkes, the barman, was alone there, reading the

Sun and listening to rock music on the mess hi-fi. He jumped to his feet and hid the paper when he saw Lizzie.

'Glass of wine please, Foulkes.' Lizzie, not wishing to have to talk to Foulkes, but not wanting to appear rude, walked to the anteroom, collected *The Times* from where it had been abandoned by an earlier reader, and returned to the bar. She folded the paper carefully and studied the crossword before taking a sip of her wine. After a few moments' thought she filled in a clue. She began to enjoy the quiet.

'You didn't fancy going to the party at Larkhill then, ma'am?' queried Foulkes. Lizzie looked up, feeling sad at the sudden realisation that she'd been left out by the other officers. She probably wouldn't have wanted to go to the party with them but she hadn't even been given the option. She couldn't admit to Foulkes that she'd been utterly rejected by her comrades in arms. Huh, some comrades, she thought sourly.

Fixing on a bright smile she said, 'No, I fancied a quiet night in.' Not that she'd had anything else since she'd arrived. The junior officers had hardly wined and dined her. Still, at least she could look forward to a meal where she wasn't going to be the butt of smutty innuendoes, or have to listen to a schoolboy stream of boasts – mostly imagined or exaggerated, Lizzie thought – about who had rogered, shafted, porked, screwed, laid, bonked or knobbed whom. She was just about to order another glass of wine to accompany her solitary meal when the heavy door to the bar opened. It was Simon, carrying a couple of suitcases.

'Which is my room, Foulkes?' he enquired. He was obviously moving into the mess, and planning to stay for some time.

'Top of the stairs, first left, sir.'

Simon nodded, then said, 'Refill Miss Armstrong's glass, please, and put it on my bill,' and abruptly left.

Lizzie didn't know what to say. She accepted the drink, mostly because she hadn't had the option to refuse, and decided it would only be good manners to postpone going in to dinner until Simon returned. If he'd bought her a drink, the least she could do was stay and talk to him – if that was what he wanted. He returned to the bar a few minutes later and ordered a pint of bitter from Foulkes.

'It's quiet for a Friday,' he said conversationally to Lizzie, and took a long pull at his drink.

'The others have all gone to a party somewhere.'

'And you didn't want to go?'

'Not really.' It would sound too self-pitying to tell the truth.

'I don't blame you. Ghastly drunken affairs usually.' He downed the rest of his drink. 'Would you like another to take into dinner with you?'

'Oh, no thanks. I've had enough.'

'Well I haven't. Same again, Foulkes.' They waited until his glass had been refilled and then crossed the imposing entrance hall to the dining room. Looking lost at one end of a huge table designed to sit around thirty people were two places laid side by side. Simon drew back Lizzie's chair for her to sit down and then moved his place so he was sitting opposite her.

'So much easier to talk like this. I don't want to get a crick in my neck.' Lizzie smiled shyly. 'I don't get a proper look at you in the office either.' Their desks were side by side.

'That's probably an advantage,' said Lizzie, not sure how to cope with her boss's apparent friendliness.

The mess steward bringing in their first course of avocado vinaigrette interrupted Simon's answer.

'Thank God it's not beans on toast,' said Simon. 'I'm sick to bloody death of eating stuff I can pour out of a tin.'

'Not much chance of that here.' Lizzie didn't know if she ought to admit to being aware of Simon's domestic problems.

'I'm not cut out for a solitary existence. Being cast away on a desert island would be my idea of hell.'

'There are times when I could quite fancy it.'

Simon looked up. 'Really?'

'I don't mind my own company too much,' Lizzie continued. 'I think it comes of having been to boarding school. Solitude was a luxury there.'

'So having company for dinner when you were expecting to be on your own is a bit of a blow.'

'Oh, no. Not at all.' Oh God, I've said the wrong thing now, thought Lizzie, blushing. They ate in silence for a while, then the steward came and cleared away their plates and brought them their next course: sole, peas, carrots and boiled potatoes. Simon attacked his with gusto.

'My ex-wife would never cook fish. She said it made the house smell. Balls, of course.'

'I don't think it does.'

'That's what I said, but she wouldn't have it. She was nothing if

72

not stubborn. Anyway, she's gone now, as I expect you are aware. You can't keep your personal life secret in the Army.'

'I had heard something.'

'How very discreet you are.'

Lizzie stared at her plate. She didn't want him to tell her about his private life, it was his affair. She was sorry for him, but part of her wondered if he'd been as rude to his wife at home as he was to his subordinate in the office. If that had been the case then she could hardly blame the woman for pushing off. Silence descended again. Lizzie wondered how soon after the meal she would be able to escape back to her room. The dining room door opened and Foulkes put his head round.

'There's a phone call for you, ma'am. Shall I tell the young lady you'll ring her back when you've finished your meal?'

'Did she give her name?'

'Miss Austin.'

'Thank you, Foulkes. Would you get her number and tell her I'll ring in about ten minutes or so.' Foulkes withdrew.

'A friend from Sandhurst?' asked Simon.

'Yes.'

'Well, at least you wait till you're off duty before you take all your personal calls, which is more than can be said for your predecessor. She was never off the bloody phone in the office.'

For the second time in less than a week Lizzie had heard an unpleasant comment about Jilly. Perhaps the paragon hadn't been quite so perfect after all.

Glad of an excuse to hurry her meal and escape, Lizzie returned to the bar to ring Edwina while Simon lingered over cheese and coffee. She wished, however, that the phone were somewhere slightly more private than the bar.

'So what's it like then,' said Edwina, 'being a proper officer?'

'It's OK.'

'You don't sound wild with enthusiasm.'

'Well, I've not really found my feet yet.' Lizzie wanted to sound positive, so she changed the subject and passed on Amanda's news. 'How's the course?'

'It's fine. Loads of work, but not difficult. Well, not yet anyway. And there's lots of hunky chaps here, and we're allowed to fraternise with them, although I don't think shagging on the anteroom carpet is allowed, but I'll check in the mess rules.'

Lizzie laughed. It was good to talk to Edwina; she always found something to joke about and her references to sex were invariably funny, unlike the ones Lizzie had had to endure lately.

'Oh, one piece of good news,' Edwina continued. 'Ulysses passed his SAS selection. He's got a weekend off and he's coming down to see me.'

'Hum,' said Lizzie.

'Yeah, I know you don't approve, but it's only 'cos you don't really know him.'

Lizzie saw Simon come into the bar. He picked up the *Times* she had discarded earlier, ordered a brandy and sat in the corner of the room, seemingly ignoring both Lizzie and her conversation. Even so Lizzie felt inhibited. There were things she wanted to say, questions she wanted to ask, but how could she with the barman and her boss both within earshot?

'Yes, well, I'm sure you're right about Ulysses. Just make sure you're careful.'

When Lizzie had finished her call, Simon joined her at the bar.

'Have a nightcap before you go.'

'No, I don't think I will.'

'Oh, go on. It's early yet. Besides, you haven't finished the crossword.'

'All right then. I'd like a brandy and soda.' Foulkes mixed the drink.

'Were you good friends with Miss Austin?'

'Edwina – yes. She's amazing.'

'Tell me.' So Lizzie recounted the story of Edwina's arrival at RCB, and told Simon about her friend's brilliant running, and the way she'd made them all laugh. As she talked, and Simon laughed, Lizzie realised that perhaps he wasn't so fierce after all, or not off duty anyway. It was past eleven when she went to bed, wondering about the wisdom of the second brandy and soda.

The weekend passed quickly. With Simon living in the mess, the other young officers were much more subdued, and toned down their behaviour to something approaching an acceptable level. Simon also promised to help Lizzie in her quest for a small, reliable second-hand car. What with one thing and another, life suddenly began to look up.

Blandford Forum, May 1988

Edwina returned to the bar after talking to Lizzie on the phone. The mess at the School of Signals was a large modern building; big square rooms with big square windows made it uninspiring architecturally, and rumour had it that it had been built facing the wrong way. Edwina, when she'd heard this, was disinclined to believe the tale, but later, when she'd thought about the poky entrance from the main road and compared it to the magnificent doorway that led into the garden – well, if it wasn't true then it should have been. Besides which, it confirmed what she'd heard about MoD contracts.

The noise in the bar was phenomenal, filled as it was to capacity with thirty or so energetic young officers, who could imagine no better way of celebrating the start of the weekend than throwing pints of beer down their necks as fast as they could.

'Oi, Austin,' shouted a tall, blond man, 'your round.'

'Bollocks,' yelled back Edwina cheerfully. She elbowed through to the bar, collected a large glass of squash and made her way back to the door.

'Aren't you staying?' shouted the blond officer, sounding disappointed. Edwina was a popular member of the course; she had established her credentials right at the start when all the young officers had had to run a basic fitness test, romping in first, a good minute ahead of the next man. After that no one had made any derogatory comments about girls doing men's jobs.

'No, better things to do than stay and drink with this rabble,' she said as she extricated herself from the scrum and headed for her room across the other side of the mess. She wanted to do well on this course. She'd learnt her lesson at Sandhurst about not working hard enough, and she wasn't about to make the same mistake again.

Anyway, the higher up the class she finished, the better were her chances of a plum posting – what she was angling for was a divisional signals regiment in Germany. And if she wanted to be free on Saturday to go away with Ulysses, then she had better get all her homework done tonight. She didn't want anything getting in the way of a couple of days with him.

Edwina felt excited at the prospect of seeing him again. They hadn't become lovers at Sandhurst – there had been too little opportunity and too much at stake for both of them to take such a risk – but Edwina was certain that Ulysses felt as she did. She was pretty sure that he wasn't coming all the way from Hereford just to tell her how many miles he'd walked and run in the Brecon Beacons during the last month. Edwina thought that if he was driving all this way then he was planning for her to massage something more substantial than his ego. Smiling smugly, she sat down at the desk in her room and began to tackle an exercise on frequencies and rebroadcast stations.

By the time she'd finished everything to her satisfaction it was after midnight and the mess had quietened down. She thought about playing some music and reading for a bit, but decided against that in favour of getting her beauty sleep. She was standing naked in front of her washbasin, cleaning her teeth and debating whether to wash her hair now or leave it till morning, when the light in her room went out. She was just wondering if it was a power cut or whether the bulb had blown when both her arms were pinned to her sides and a hand covered her mouth. She struggled frantically and tried to bite the fingers pressed against her teeth but her assailant was too powerful. The shock had subsided now and fear was taking over.

A strangely accented voice, one she didn't recognise, whispered in her ear, 'Stop struggling and you won't get hurt.' Edwina fought harder. She managed to half twist round and jerked her knee upwards. It didn't connect but it elicited a response from her attacker.

'Steady on, Edwina.' The odd accent had gone.

Who was this slimy creep? thought Edwina as anger now superseded fear. Some little pervert of a subaltern? Well, she'd teach him not to go creeping round girls' rooms at night, scaring them half to death. She writhed and twisted in an effort to break his grip. Then suddenly she was aware that he was laughing.

'Please don't shout,' the stranger managed to gurgle between giggles. 'You can go.' As he released her he took the precaution of leaping out of the way of her flailing arms and feet and switching on the light again.

'Ulysses!' said Edwina.

Ulysses was clutching his sides. 'Oh, Edwina,' still chortling, 'oh, you should see your face.' Edwina, relieved that this had been an elaborate joke, smiled thinly.

'You bugger, you. You frightened me half to death. I thought it was some greasy little subaltern planning to rape me.'

'He'd have to be a brave man to take you on.' Ulysses leaned against the wardrobe, weak from laughter and the struggle.

'Well, you thought you could,' Edwina said huffily, having not found the incident quite as hilarious. She reached for her dressing gown, not through modesty but because she was cold. 'Anyway, what the hell are you doing here? You'll get me into a pile of trouble if we're caught.'

'I'm going to whisk you away tonight. I couldn't wait till tomorrow. Now come here and give me a kiss.' He pulled her roughly towards him and kissed her long and hard. Edwina put her arms round his neck, and as she did so her dressing gown fell open again. Ulysses pushed his hand through the opening at the front so he could stroke her smooth back. His hands moved down towards her neat, firm little buttocks. Edwina pressed herself hard against him.

'Fraternising between officers and other ranks is forbidden,' she murmured.

'We're not fraternising, we're fucking,' whispered Ulysses.

'I don't think that distinction was made in Queen's Regulations.'

'Well, there you go then. If it isn't specifically mentioned in the rule book, we must be all right.'

'Just a sec.' Edwina gently disengaged herself from his grip and went to lock the door. 'I don't want any other intruders tonight. Now, Staff Lees, get your kit off.'

'Yes, ma'am.'

'And stand to attention when you talk to me.'

'Some of me is.'

Later, when they were both sated, Edwina, her body tucked comfortably against Ulysses, said sleepily, 'So how did you find my room?'

'I asked the bar steward.'

'You did what?'Edwina was suddenly wide awake. 'How indiscreet can you get?'

'Don't worry. I told them I was from the Army's positive vetting
unit and that I had to deliver some vetting forms to you urgently.'

'You make me sound like a cat – all this talk of vetting. Did he
believe you?'

'Of course he did. Why shouldn't he?'

Edwina couldn't think of an answer to that, but decided that if you
lied with conviction people generally didn't question it. She relaxed
and snuggled down under the duvet again.

They took off for Dartmoor the next day before dawn and long
before breakfast. Ulysses drove his Golf GTi expertly and fast
along the A30 towards the West Country. It was a beautiful spring
morning; the trees, their leaves still the fresh, vibrant green of
May, contrasted with a grape-hyacinth-blue sky. The soil in the
fields became richer and redder the nearer they got to Exeter until
it became the same glorious colour as the Devon red cattle grazing
contentedly in the warm sun. They zipped round Exeter on the by-
pass and carried on for another thirty minutes or so, Dartmoor rising up on their right as they headed west. By ten o'clock Edwina
was complaining that she was suffering from starvation, so at the
next junction Ulysses turned off the main road to find somewhere
to stop and eat. In a minute village consisting of a handful of
white cob-walled cottages clustered round a squat granite church,
they found a teashop offering morning coffee and home-made
cakes.

'Just the thing,' said Edwina as her stomach rumbled loudly in
agreement.

Ulysses parked the car in the tiny sloping square opposite the pub.

'I wonder if they do toasted teacakes,' he said as they walked into
the tiny tearoom. There were only three tables, each with a bright-red
gingham tablecloth and a vase of spring flowers. The smell of fresh
coffee and baking wafted from the kitchen. An elderly couple in
matching husky jackets already occupied the table in the corner.
Edwina and Ulysses sat at the table by the window.

'God, screwing makes me hungry,' said Ulysses as he examined
the menu card propped against the vase.

'Sssh,' said Edwina, giggling and glancing swiftly to see if the other people had heard. They both had such glum faces it was difficult to tell.

'What do you fancy? Apart from hours of sex, that is. There's a dozen different sorts of cakes, scones and cream or teacakes.'

'Scones and cream and jam sound wonderful.'

'Is that with or without sex?'

'Sssh,' said Edwina, still laughing and wondering if anyone had ever been thrown out of a tearoom for improper behaviour.

'Or before sex?'

A dumpy, cheerful woman appeared from the kitchen. 'Morning,' she said in a delicious Devon accent. 'Proper 'ansome day, isn't it?'

'Lovely,' they agreed.

'You'm be ready to order?'

Ulysses asked for three teacakes, two scones and a pot of tea.

'Look,' said Edwina. 'The pub across the road does rooms. What about staying here? We're between the sea and the moor and I could fancy going to the beach. It's years since I've been to the coast.' Ulysses agreed that this village could be a wonderful base. They munched steadily through the plate of food that had appeared in a remarkably short time. The teacakes, thick with raisins and dripping with melting butter, were disposed of quickly, leaving them with greasy chins and fingers. Edwina licked her fingers ostentatiously by way of appreciation. Then she tackled the scones.

'God, that's better,' she said, putting her index finger in her mouth and then using it to mop up the very last crumbs and remaining traces of jam and cream. She saw Ulysses eyeing her with amusement. 'Waste not want not,' she said primly.

'I quite agree. Right, let's get the bill and move off. It's too nice a day to waste.'

They paid a ridiculously small amount for their gargantuan snack, nodded goodbye to the still glum pair in the corner and then wandered across the square to the pub. The landlady confirmed that she had a vacant room and showed them up the creaky stairs to a tiny room dominated by a massive mahogany double bed. A minute latticed window, curtained in a bright-yellow print to match the bedding, looked out on to the square and the church. Behind the church they could see the tors of Dartmoor, craggy grey granite slabs surrounded by golden gorse and lush green spring grass.

'Perfect,' said Edwina happily. The landlady showed them the bathroom, asked if they would be dining in the pub that evening –

which they decided they would – and then left them alone. Edwina fell back on to the bed and sank deeply into the soft eiderdown. 'Now, what were you saying about sex earlier?'

'No,' said Ulysses. 'Randy little minx. We're going to the beach.'

Edwina stuck her tongue out at him. 'You rat. Oh, all right then.'

They drove down deep lanes between hedges frothing with May blossom, catching tantalising glimpses of the Mediterranean-blue sea. Every few miles they passed through villages of snug white cottages under thick thatch, some roofs black with age, some bright yellow, with the telltale remnants of the thatcher's work still strewn about the surrounding hedges and flowerbeds. Suddenly they rounded a corner and the road ended in a near-deserted car park. In front of them was a wide sandy beach and the vast expanse of the sea. Edwina joyously flung open the car door and leapt out.

'Last one to the sea is a sissy,' she yelled over her shoulder as she ran on to the sand. Ulysses watched her go, locked up the car and followed her at a leisurely pace. When he reached her she already had her shoes and socks off and was rolling up the legs of her jeans. 'I'm going paddling.'

'So I see.'

'Coming?'

'No. Too cold.'

'What? You're joining the SAS and you're worried about the cold?' Edwina shook her head in mock disbelief.

They walked along the beach, Edwina swinging her shoes in her hand, her feet splashing in the water, Ulysses beside her, skipping the occasional wave that ventured further up the sand than the norm.

'So are you going to tell me about it then?' said Edwina.

Ulysses looked at her, his eyes squinting against the bright reflection of the sun off the sea, 'Tell you about what?'

'The selection for the SAS, of course. You weren't at Hereford for a holiday, were you?'

So Ulysses told her about the runs, the endless tabbing up and down the Brecon Beacons, the wimps who'd been sacked on the first day, the mountain of kit they'd had to carry, the blisters, the bergen sores and the despondency of those who'd failed. Edwina, so hard to impress when he'd first told her about trying for the regiment, was open-mouthed in amazement.

'Bloody hell,' she said quietly when he'd finished. 'That's some test.'

'Most of it depends on how much you want to pass it. The longer I stayed there the more it mattered to me. The thought of failure was so fucking awful it didn't matter how much my feet hurt or how bad my blisters were, I kept going regardless.'

'I suppose orienteering at Sandhurst helped.'

'Christ, yes! If you can't map-read efficiently you waste time and effort, and you just can't afford to. It's crucial that you get yourself from one checkpoint to another by the most sensible route, as there just isn't any spare time. I mean, apart from the weight that we had to carry, you'd have probably managed it from that point of view; your map-reading is as good as mine and there's no disputing your fitness. But you'd never manage those hills with fifty to sixty pounds on your back.' He grinned at her and shook his head, mocking her. 'So, basically, being a girlie means you'll always be stuck with some fucking crap-hat unit.'

Edwina turned, gave him a huge smile and then drew her foot back and kicked out hard so that a small tidal wave of water soaked Ulysses from the waist down.

'Shit,' he said as he stood there dripping. Edwina, knowing that there would be some sort of retribution, was already racing up the beach to the relative safety of the dunes. Ulysses gave chase and eventually caught her by means of a flying rugby tackle that knocked the wind out of her. Before she had a chance to get her breath back he straddled her and began tickling her until she was begging for mercy.

That evening, over dinner in the pub's minuscule dining room, Edwina resumed her questioning about the SAS – its reputation, mystique and secrecy fascinated her.

'I don't know that much about it all yet. Just because I've passed selection doesn't mean that I'm in. I can still be binned.' Ulysses took a huge mouthful of his steak and chips.

'Yeah, but you'll get to travel lots, won't you?'

'And learn lots of magic new things,' he said indistinctly through his food.

'Sounds better than what I'll end up with when I've finished my signals training.' Edwina pushed some peas around her plate as she felt her jealousy for his new role come to the surface. 'I mean, you'll be doing real soldiering, and all I can hope for is to be allowed out on the occasional exercise.'

'Well, that's what you expected, isn't it? I mean, you knew you'd never be allowed any sort of combat job.'

Edwina sighed disconsolately. 'I know. And to be honest, it didn't matter until today. It's just I'm so bloody envious of the opportunities you're going to have when the best I can look forward to is setting up comms on the training area at Sennelager.'

'Your fault for being a girlie.'

'Heartless bastard,' but she said it with a grin. She didn't resent Ulysses' success, but she did resent that she would never be able to do anything even remotely comparable. Not unless war broke out, and the chances of that seemed unlikely. They munched on for a few minutes, then Edwina resumed her questioning.

'So why were you so determined to get into the SAS?' She realised she still knew surprisingly little about this man.

'Lots of reasons really. Mostly I've always liked being active. I wasn't much good at school and the teachers always gave me a hard time and told me I'd never get anywhere. I looked at most of them and thought that if becoming a teacher was their idea of getting somewhere . . . well, there had to be more to life than that.'

Edwina nodded. She understood. The teachers at her school had also written her off – mainly because she'd been such a rebel. She now felt that getting a commission in the Army had proved them wrong once and for all. She didn't reckon they could have hacked RCB, let alone Sandhurst.

'Your parents must be proud of you,' she said.

'Foster parents.'

'God, I'm sorry. I didn't know.'

'No reason you should. I don't wear a badge saying I'm the product of a broken home.'

'No. Of course not.' Edwina understood exactly what it was like. She told him about her dad, who had buggered off, as her mother always put it, when she had been seven. 'Are your parents . . .?'

'Divorced? I don't think the arrangement was formalised in the first place. My dad might be dead, for all I know. He walked out on my mum about six months after I was born and I haven't a clue who he is, or where he is, come to that. My mum wasn't bad, but she had four other kids and couldn't cope on her own. We all ended up in care.'

'Do you see much of them – your brothers and sisters?'

'Not really. I don't have much in common with any of them. They all live on crap council estates, do crap jobs and have crap families of their own.'

Edwina wondered what it was that had spurred Ulysses to break the family mould.

'So why did you join the Army?'

'It was a way off the dole queue. And when I was in, I discovered I liked it; all that sport, patrolling the streets in Northern Ireland was great, going overseas – I'd never been abroad before. I kept hearing about the SAS, and the more I found out about it the more I wanted part of the action.'

Again Edwina knew exactly what he meant. She wanted some of that action too, but the difference between them was that she knew she could never have it, and it pissed her off mightily.

Ulysses dropped her back at the mess at Blandford after dinner on Sunday. He had to report for further training at Hereford on the Monday morning and wanted to be back there in good time. They kissed farewell in the car park, some distance from the mess. Edwina didn't want too much interest in her boyfriend from the others. It was going to be difficult to carry on a relationship with him, given their difference in rank and the Army's attitude to such matters. The only way was to be very discreet.

Back in her room Edwina thought about what Ulysses had said about the selection – that she would be fit enough to pass it, but not strong enough. It suddenly irked her that she was doomed, as she saw it, to be a crap-hat, as the Paras and the Special Forces referred to ordinary soldiers. As far as she could see the Army was not, and wasn't ever going to be, an equal opportunities employer. Airborne troops and Special Forces would always be men. It just wasn't fair, and she felt a growing resentment because of it. The next day she found that her enthusiasm for the course had waned, and she knew it was going to be difficult to motivate herself to master the intricacies of line-laying, encryption, burst transmissions and the like. Selfishly she wished Ulysses had failed, then she wouldn't feel so bloody envious, as well as hacked off about her own prospects.

She felt more cheerful a couple of days later when a card arrived from Amanda, inviting her to a party at Guildford. 'I don't know how much fun it'll be,' wrote Amanda, 'but Lizzie will be there and a whole load of hairy Paras. Bring a man if you've got one.' Edwina thought that Guildford and an all-female mess wouldn't be Ulysses' scene. Anyway, Amanda and Lizzie would disapprove dreadfully that she was still seeing him. She decided to go on her own.

'Do you want me to meet you at the station?' asked Amanda when Edwina rang her to tell her.

'I don't think so. I've decided to get myself some wheels.'

'Great idea. I can't think how you manage without.'

'Well, there's usually someone I can persuade to give me a lift, but it's not ideal.'

'You'll let me know, though, if Plan A doesn't pan out and you have to come by train?'

'I will. 'Bye.'

Edwina replaced the receiver and wandered into the anteroom. She might have made her mind up about the idea of getting a vehicle, but she didn't have a clue what to buy. She looked at the pile of motoring magazines on the large table by the wall. No one would miss a few copies for an hour or two. If nothing else, it would be a source of ideas. She grabbed a couple of the more recent issues and took them back to her room, where she could read them at her leisure.

Guildford, June 1988

Amanda, waiting to greet Edwina when she arrived in the mess, was taken completely aback by her friend's outfit, which comprised a red leather jumpsuit.

'What's with the kinky gear?' she asked.

'*De rigueur* for motorcyclists,' answered Edwina with a wicked grin.

'You haven't . . . you're not . . .?'

'I have and I am. I've got this beautiful red Ducati sitting in the car park. It didn't half make your guard commander sit up and take notice when she realised I was a female officer.'

Amanda shook her head in disbelief. 'Edwina, you are incorrigible. You'd better come and get changed before any of the crusty old majors see you dressed like that.'

'Dyke's delight, eh?'

'Sssh,' said Amanda. 'You know as well as I do that lesbians are not allowed to join the WRAC. Anyway, it's not a very politically correct phrase.'

'Don't get so sniffy. The boys at Blandford reckon that I'm only here to provide fresh talent for the frustrated old biddies incarcerated at Guildford until they're pensionable.'

'Edwina, really!' Amanda sounded distinctly uptight. 'You have no idea who might be within earshot, and it'll be me that gets hauled up in front of the commandant, not you.'

Edwina just shrugged at Amanda's discomfort. 'Lizzie here yet?'

'No. She's turning up nearer the time. She's not staying the night.'

'Is she bringing a man?'

'Yes. Her boss, apparently.'

'What, the CO?'

'No, stupid, her adjutant.'

'Phew. I thought for a minute Lizzie was doing something outrageous, and we can't have that, can we?'

'Don't be horrid.'

'Sorry, that was mean of me. I shouldn't take the mickey out of Lizzie – she wouldn't do it us, would she?' They'd reached Amanda's room. 'So this is where you hang out.' She looked around. 'Nice. I like your wall hangings.'

'Well, I had to do something to make it different from everyone else's. I got these off a funny little stall up in London that sold all sorts of Oriental stuff. I suppose you've still got those tatty old posters on your walls.'

'Yup. Only they're not tatty. Well, not very, anyway.'

Edwina kicked her holdall into a corner and sat on the bed. She was just on the point of asking Amanda for any juicy bits of gossip when the door opened and in walked a tall, attractive brunette with a wide smile. Despite the welcoming expression, Edwina took an instant dislike to the girl, though she couldn't have said what it was that made her feel such antagonism.

'Hi, you must be Edwina. Amanda said you'd be arriving this afternoon. I'm Bella.' She crossed the room to shake Edwina's hand. 'Gosh,' she said, staring at Edwina's leathers, 'do you have a bike?'

'I certainly do.' There was no reason to be rude.

'Wow! Well, that'll get the old bats talking, won't it, Amanda?'

Amanda shook her head almost imperceptibly at Bella and gave her a warning look.

'Sorry, am I missing some private joke?' said Edwina, catching the glance.

'No, nothing,' replied Bella airily. Edwina looked at Amanda and then back at Bella with narrowed eyes.

Bella changed the subject smoothly. 'So what are you coming as tonight?' The party was fancy dress, with the theme of book titles.

'It's a real cop-out. I'm doing *On the Beach*, you know, by Nevil Shute, and I'm wearing the full NBC kit.'

'Great. God, won't you be hot, though?'

'Well, maybe. But that's the price you pay for no imagination. What about you?'

'Amanda is going as *Gone with the Wind* and I'm doing *Room at the Top*.' Edwina looked askance. 'No, I'm not revealing our costumes, but it'll be a riot, you'll see. Now, I'm going to grab a bathroom and have a long, hot soak.' With that, Bella left the room.

'So how is life here?' asked Edwina when she'd gone.

'Much better than I thought. The majors are a pain but the other subbies are brilliant. It's a bit like being at Sandhurst, only with less work.'

'I don't think I could stand being surrounded by all these women.'

'It's not so bad. Besides, think of poor old Lizzie; she's the only female living in her mess. She says it's terribly lonely.'

'I'd still rather have her posting than yours.' Amanda shrugged. She wouldn't.

As Bella had promised, the party was a riot. Amanda, as *Gone with the Wind*, turned up with a string of empty baked-bean cans around her neck, and slimline Bella, as *Room at the Top*, sported a 48E bra over a figure-hugging black rollneck. Simon and Lizzie had dressed up as Postman Pat and Jess, which, they admitted, was all they could think of.

'Boring,' said Amanda heartlessly, jingling her cans. Lizzie looked miffed. Simon had taken a lot of persuading to come at all, let alone dressed up. But he seemed to be enjoying himself, and as usual with an Army party, where everyone seemed to know everyone else, he was happy to chat and circulate on his own or with Lizzie. Edwina was delighted to see Lizzie again and to hear about her posting. She sympathised about the ghastly subalterns and Lizzie's initial difficulties with getting to grips with the job.

'I've learnt one valuable lesson already,' said Lizzie. 'Never assume anything, always check all the details yourself.'

'Sounds reasonable,' Edwina agreed.

'I've nipped all sorts of potential cock-ups in the bud since the chief clerk taught me that.'

'He sounds like a good bloke.'

'He's great. But like some of the others, he doesn't seem to have had much time for my predecessor. The strange thing is, the CO couldn't sing her praises loudly enough when I first arrived, but all the time I keep hearing the odd comment which makes me wonder about her.'

'You'll probably find it's something really simple, like the CO was shagging her in the stationery store.'

Predictably, Lizzie was horrified by such a suggestion. 'Edwina, how could you? He's a married man.'

'So? I really can't believe that you are so naïve as to think that a wedding ring has ever stopped a man from having sex with someone other than his wife. Why don't you ask Simon? He's bound to know.'

'I couldn't.'

'Well, it's up to you. And I wouldn't worry about it. You're the one doing the job now and you seem to have got to grips with it. Jilly's history.' Lizzie saw the sense in this advice. She changed the subject to ask Edwina about her course – not wishing to sound completely self-absorbed. As usual Edwina related all the funny anecdotes rather than the serious stuff, and Simon came over to see why Lizzie was laughing so much.

'So you're the runner,' he said when Lizzie had introduced them.

'I do a bit,' admitted Edwina.

'Don't believe that, Simon, she runs like the wind for miles on end.'

Edwina grinned sheepishly at the praise.

'Would you like a dance?' Simon asked Edwina gallantly.

'Please don't think me rude if I refuse, but if I bop around in this dreadful suit I'll expire. It's like being in a sauna as it is.' She did look uncomfortably hot. 'Take Lizzie for a dance though, please.'

Lizzie and Simon disappeared into the throng of jigging bodies on the dance floor and Edwina went to get herself a long glass of wine and soda. She felt faintly out of things. Apart from Lizzie and Amanda she didn't know anyone else there. Also, she missed Ulysses. Amanda, as entertainment member, was busy organising the disco, circulating with drinks, introducing people and generally making sure everyone was having a good time. And Lizzie was completely wrapped up in Simon.

Edwina took her drink and went to sit at the top of the steps which led to the subalterns' corridor. She wondered why on earth she'd agreed to come, and why she'd thought it would be a good wheeze to wear this stupid suit. She sipped her drink morosely. She wished Ulysses was with her, but she really couldn't risk going public about their relationship. Damn it, why did she long for his company so much? She felt as though part of her was missing when he wasn't around. She looked enviously at the other couples in the room. Lizzie was gazing adoringly at Simon, although Edwina wasn't entirely sure that Simon was as besotted as Lizzie seemed to be. She watched Lizzie laugh at his jokes and follow him when he moved off to chat to another group of friends. There was no denying the look of utter infatuation that crossed her face when Simon casually put his arm around her shoulder. Lizzie was in love. Edwina only hoped that she wasn't going to get hurt, trusting little soul that she was. Simon struck her as a bit of a Romeo. Still, that was Lizzie's problem, thought Edwina.

She looked around the room to see where Amanda was; she wanted to share the news that Lizzie was smitten. She saw Bella and Amanda talking in another corner, standing very close, too close. Edwina glanced back to Simon and Lizzie and then looked at Amanda and Bella again. It was unmistakable; Amanda, as she talked to Bella, mirrored exactly the way Lizzie leaned towards Simon, the way she looked at him. The body language was identical. Edwina couldn't believe it. Surely not Bella and Amanda. She remembered how chilly Amanda had been when she'd joked about lesbians, and how she'd had the impression, when she'd first met Bella, that there was some sort of secret between her and Amanda. And that would explain Bella's false smile – she probably regarded Edwina as competition.

Edwina tried to convince herself that she was wrong, but the more she watched Amanda and Bella together the more certain she became that she was right. Then she remembered that Amanda had never, not once, produced a boyfriend or even an escort for any of the parties at Sandhurst; even at the Commissioning Ball she said she'd been let down at the last minute. Edwina tried to recall the conversations they'd had over those months, and how the excuse for the lack of male friends had been a steady relationship back home. She and Lizzie had assumed that this had been a man, but now, as Edwina thought about it, she realised that Amanda had never actually said so.

Edwina was convinced she was right, but she wasn't sure what her feelings were about this. She tried to analyse them, which was difficult given the distractions of the noise and lights. Did she care if Amanda was gay? Did it matter to anyone but Amanda herself? She certainly had never made even the vaguest hint of an approach to either Edwina or Lizzie, and she was hardly likely to try to jump on the recruits. And being gay hardly made her a danger to society. But Edwina knew what the Army's official policy was towards homosexuals: a really nasty investigation by the Special Investigation Branch into all his or her friends' sexual proclivities, followed by an examination by a psychiatrist, and finally dismissal for the culprit and anyone else they weren't sure about. Edwina decided she ought to talk to Lizzie about this and get her opinion, but she'd have to prise her away from lover-boy first. She certainly didn't want Simon to get wind of this; Lizzie she could trust, Simon was definitely an unknown quantity. In fact, he looked more like the sort who was likely to go straight to the authorities. She walked slowly down the stairs and went to refill her glass before finding Lizzie.

No, she had to be wrong, Edwina thought. Surely Amanda was as straight as she was. After all, no homosexual in their right mind would join an organisation that held regular witch-hunts to root them out. She must have got hold of all the wrong signals and jumped to a conclusion that was way off-beam.

Still feeling guilty about having doubted Amanda's sexuality, Edwina decided to go to the loo. The room was so crowded that she had to edge round the side of the anteroom to get to the Ladies'. She was just about to sidle past a large pot plant which was blocking her path when she realised that standing on the other side of it were Bella and Amanda. They had their backs to her and were leaning towards each other and laughing. From where Edwina was, she could also see that Bella had her hand on Amanda's bottom and was fondling it.

Edwina felt as if she'd been kicked in the stomach. Quietly she backed away and returned to her vantage point at the top of the stairs, all thoughts of her trip to the loo forgotten. She sat gazing sightlessly at her empty glass, confused and hurt. More than anything she felt betrayed. She didn't understand why she felt like this; after all, it wasn't as if Amanda had lied to her. Nor was it the sort of thing that would affect Amanda's performance as an officer. It was part of her private life so it shouldn't matter to anyone but Amanda. And what should Edwina do about it? Anything, nothing? Should she tell someone? What would happen if the Army found out and then discovered that she knew? Would that implicate her? Oh God, what should she do? These thoughts and more were tumbling around in Edwina's mind and she wasn't aware of anyone approaching her.

'Penny for them,' said Amanda. Edwina jumped. 'Sorry, I didn't mean to startle you. You must have been miles away.'

'Yes, sorry.' She looked at Amanda and couldn't believe what she'd just discovered about her.

'Wishing Ulysses was here?'

'No. Not really.' It was difficult to sound normal.

'Are you all right?'

'Yes, fine.' Edwina tried to sound bright but just ended up coming across as false. 'Well, just a bit hot. That's why I'm sitting out for the moment.' Bella came across the crowded floor to join them.

'I've brought your drink, Amanda, and there's a complaint that the beer's getting low,' she said. Then, 'Hi, Edwina. Enjoying yourself?'

'Yeah, it's great.'

'I haven't seen you on the dance floor. Don't any of our imported hunks take your fancy?'

That's rich, coming from her, thought Edwina. Out loud she said, 'My man couldn't come tonight.'

'Pity.' She didn't sound the least sorry for Edwina, though.

Edwina wished they would both go away and leave her alone. Even if she hadn't found out about their relationship, there was something about Bella that made her uneasy. She knew it was irrational, but she couldn't help herself.

Bella's eyes narrowed as if she sensed Edwina's mistrust. 'I must circulate,' she said, moving away, 'spread a little happiness, that sort of thing. Catch you later.' Edwina didn't trust herself to reply.

'Sorry,' said Edwina after she was out of earshot. 'I don't seem to be very good company tonight.'

'Forget it,' said Amanda. 'It must be hard if you're missing Ulysses. It can't be easy having a boyfriend that you've got to keep secret.'

Edwina couldn't help looking at her incredulously. Of all the people to talk about keeping relationships secret.

Amanda mistook her look. 'I'm sorry. It's none of my business. Your private life is entirely your affair. Look, I've got to go and organise some more beer from the stockroom. I'll talk to you again later. Why don't you get yourself another drink?'

'Yes, perhaps I will. See you later.'

Amanda disappeared into the crowd in the anteroom and Edwina decided that perhaps she would get herself a drink. Something long and cold. Her head was beginning to ache but she didn't know if the cause was the heat or her worries about Amanda and what she should do. Perhaps she should just forget the whole incident.

But as she was standing by the bar waiting to be served, she remembered that to be assured a halfway decent career in the Royal Signals she would have to have a very high level of security clearance. If Amanda was indiscreet and got caught, the fact that they had been so friendly could really balls things up for her. She ordered a pint of water and a large brandy – the former for her thirst, the latter because she felt like getting drunk. She knocked the brandy back in one gulp and then drank the water, ignoring the surprised looks this elicited from the bar staff. Then, possibly fuelled by the brandy, her selfish streak took over and she made up her mind. She would tell Lizzie and together they would confront Amanda.

She found Lizzie on her own a few minutes later; apparently Simon had bumped into some old friend and was talking shop.

'Lizzie, I need to talk to you.'

'Of course.'

'It's really tricky . . .'

'Well, I can't help unless you tell me.'

'It's about Amanda.'

'Oh?'

'It's . . . I think . . . Lizzie, she's gay.'

Despite the ridiculous cat costume and make-up, Lizzie managed to look horrified. Then anger took over. She stepped forward half a pace and hissed, 'What a horrible thing to say about her. How could you? Of course she isn't. Just because she's found another friend you think . . .' Lizzie paused for breath. 'It's jealousy, isn't it? You're jealous that she should like someone more than you.'

Edwina shook her head miserably. 'It's not, honest.'

'Well, I'm sorry, but I just don't believe you. And don't you dare tell anyone else about your sordid little suspicions.'

Edwina realised she'd made a dreadful mistake in telling Lizzie. Lizzie would never be able to contemplate the possibility that anyone whom she knew might deviate from the norm. 'I'm sorry. Forget it.' Lizzie still looked angry.

'It's not me that needs to forget about it. It's you.' She turned on her heel and stormed off back to Simon.

Edwina went back to her place on the stairs. God, what a mess she'd made of that. Well, fuck it. So what if Amanda was gay? It was entirely her own business, nothing whatsoever to do with Edwina. If the Army did find out, there might not be any repercussions for Edwina. And she owed Amanda her loyalty. Being loyal to her friend, even if she was gay, didn't make her a potential traitor or enemy of the state. The best thing she could do would be to try and forget the entire incident. Even so, Edwina didn't really feel in the party mood any more and took herself off to bed – a sleeping bag on Amanda's bedroom floor. In the morning, when she awoke, she wasn't surprised to find that, apparently, Amanda's bed hadn't been slept in.

Lizzie had returned to Aldershot the previous night so Edwina hadn't seen her to say goodbye – which, all things considered, probably wasn't such a bad thing. It would be as well to let things cool between them, thought Edwina, who hadn't ever seen Lizzie so cross before. She met Amanda at breakfast.

'Didn't you come to bed last night?' she said. It was an obvious question to ask.

'It was so late by the time we'd finished clearing up I was beyond sleep, so I went for a walk.' Edwina didn't believe her for a minute, but what the hell – it was plausible.

Edwina chomped her way steadily through a mound of eggs and bacon. When she'd finished and had pushed her empty plate away from her, she said, 'I know I said I'd stay until tomorrow, but I've got a mountain of work to do and I should really get back to tackle it.'

'That's a shame. I was hoping we could go shopping in Guildford together and have lunch at a nice pub I know of.'

'Probably just as well that I've got to go, then. If I go shopping my bank manager will have apoplexy. My overdraft is getting ridiculous.'

Her excuses were all lies, but there was no way she could tell Amanda that her real reason for wanting to go back to Blandford was because she didn't know how to handle her knowledge of Amanda's secret. She simply didn't have the confidence that she could act as though she knew nothing about it.

On the long drive back, Edwina concluded that her decision of the night before, to ignore whatever there was between Amanda and Bella, was not only the most sensible course of action but also the only possible one, and that with time she would come to terms with the issue. She put the whole incident to the back of her mind.

'Didn't you think it was a bit off that Edwina left so suddenly?' said Bella. She was lying on Amanda's bed as Amanda, sitting beside her, painted her nails.

'Edwina's always been impulsive like that. You never know what she'll do next.' Amanda examined her nails and then waved her hands gently to help them dry.

'She didn't like me. I got the vibes as soon as she saw me.'

'Don't be silly. How could anyone not like you?'

Bella smiled. 'You're biased.' Then she added as an afterthought, 'You don't think she guessed about us, do you?'

Amanda stopped moving her hands. 'No, I don't think so,' she said slowly. 'She's got no reason to suspect anything. No.' She shook her head and dismissed the idea.

'You're sure you gave nothing away when you were at Sandhurst?'

'No. In fact, she and Lizzie seemed to think I had a man stashed away at home.'

'You didn't disillusion them?'

'No, my darling, I didn't. I did have someone stashed, but it wasn't a man. The trouble was that after a few months at the RMA we had so little in common the whole thing fell apart.'

'I'm sorry.' Bella wasn't surprised to hear this. Very few of the female cadets' existing relationships with civvies – though more usually they were with men – lasted through training. 'So if you were so sure about your sexuality before you joined up, why did you do it?'

'Oh, lots of reasons: the travel, the lifestyle and the pay, amongst other things. And because, I suppose, I could see that I'd spend a lot of my time working with other women and it's expected that we'll all stick by each other. You know, bags of feminine solidarity. When I was a teacher, if any two of the women staff became friendly the men all commented on it and made smutty innuendoes. It's not like that in the Army because, apart from this posting, hot-blooded men tend to surround us . . .'

'And we're not supposed to shag them,' interrupted Bella.

'Exactly. And if we do, we have to be so discreet about it that no one finds out.' Amanda began to apply a second coat of varnish to her elegant nails. 'But surely your reasons for joining must have been the same.'

'*Au contraire*,' said Bella with a shrug. 'I think I was looking for a way of proving to myself that I was straight. I thought that if I joined an outfit like this I'd find the macho man who would succeed in turning me on. I had a series of appalling relationships which all ended in disaster; I simply couldn't go through with sex when push came to shove. The bloke always ended up storming off, calling me a prick-tease, and I always ended up in tears. About a year ago I finally faced up to the fact that men aren't my thing at all and I had a fling with the PTI here.'

'What, Staff Sergeant Allen?'

'No, the one before her. She's in Germany now.'

'Was it serious?'

'No, so there's no need to be jealous.'

'What was this PTI like – the archetypal predatory dyke that the WRAC hierarchy are paranoid about?'

'Hardly. She was about five foot two, eight stone, blonde and blue-eyed.'

Amanda giggled. 'Not what most people think of as a lesbian, then.'

'Are any of us?'

'So have you told your folks?'

'Not yet. In fact I don't think I ever will, as they're elderly and old-fashioned and live in a village that's in a time warp. Frankly it wouldn't do any good.' Bella paused. 'I mean, look at the reaction you had from yours.'

'I can see I made a mistake there, but what's done is done.' Amanda sighed, shrugged and carried on with her nails.

Blandford Forum, June 1988

Back at the School of Signals, Edwina was so busy with the course that she didn't have time to think much about either Lizzie or Amanda. On a couple of occasions she had tried to phone them, but either their lines had been engaged or there had been no reply. At other times she thought about ringing them, but either it was too late at night or someone else was using the phone in the mess. She dropped a note to Amanda thanking her for the party, but making her peace with Lizzie was too complicated for a letter. She'd get round to it one day soon, she promised herself. But then, somehow, it slipped her mind. The work had begun to pile up and she found her evenings largely taken up with the course work and the urge to keep herself as fit as possible, so her only free time was at weekends, but then her thoughts were filled with getting together with Ulysses.

It wasn't just her friends from Sandhurst whom she found she was ignoring. Although she was still popular with everyone on the course, she was beginning to get the reputation of being a loner: not around after work because she was running, not in the bar later in the evening because she was working, and not around at weekends because of Ulysses. He had absolute priority in her crowded life at this time because he'd told her that soon he'd be going off to the Far East. To make the most of this short period when they could get together, Edwina leapt on her bike early each Saturday and drove north up the A350 to meet Ulysses at one village or another in the Cotswolds. It was a good halfway point for both of them and an area richly endowed with hotels and guesthouses. It was ironic that her route took her past the front gate of the RCB in Westbury. It still gave her the heebie-jeebies to think how close she must have come to failing. And if she'd failed, she'd have never met Ulysses.

As she sped along the road on her smart red bike she counted off the miles. Each one brought her closer to seeing Ulysses again, and she longed for him, his touch, his smell and his humour with a quite frightening intensity. She found herself thinking of him at moments when she should have been concentrating on something completely different – like driving. She'd had flings, relationships, one-night stands and casual sex with more men than she cared to think about, but never before had anyone made her feel like this. Each time she thought about him, seeing him, hearing his voice again, she felt as though her insides were being squeezed in a vice as a surge of desire rushed through her. It seemed to her that when she wasn't working these days, and sometimes even when she was, she spent most of her waking hours fantasising about him. But at their meetings Edwina began to find that the more Ulysses was drawn into the Regiment – as he now invariably referred to the SAS – and the more time he spent with them, the more she felt as though his life and hers were being forced apart. He was completely immersed in his training and his new role in the Army. And worse, he was now doing something separate and different from the rest of the Army – he was part of an élite, and it was a secretive élite to boot. He became less inclined to talk about his training and experiences, which Edwina found hurtful – as though he didn't trust her. She also found it frustrating because, more than anything, she wanted to do a similar job, but knew that realistically her only experiences would be vicarious. Now it seemed she was being denied that too.

Edwina became frightened that if she pried too closely into his military life she would alienate him, so when they met she deliberately tried to keep all conversations general and light-hearted. On long walks in the summer sunshine around the Cotswolds, and during delicious lunches relaxing in warm pub gardens, they talked about their backgrounds and their hopes for the future, about friends and films, about the weather and wildlife. They swapped notes on surviving their childhoods; Ulysses had done it by learning judo to combat the school bullies, and Edwina had learnt to run faster than them. Edwina's unconventional mother intrigued Ulysses, and in her turn she wanted to know about how he'd coped with never enjoying real family life. In common they neither of them had a father who was still around, and they were both wary of committing themselves to creating families of their own. Ulysses said that his family had always been such a crap one, he wasn't sure he would know how to behave with a wife and kids. 'I'd rather not try than screw up and wreck another bunch of lives,' he admitted to Edwina. She could see his point of view. The one thing they didn't talk about was what they were currently doing during the week back with their units, Ulysses because he couldn't and Edwina because she was becoming increasingly frustrated at the lack of opportunities offered to her for some real action. At night, in bed, they were too busy making love to talk.

On their eighth weekend together, Ulysses told Edwina that he was flying to Brunei later that week to start his jungle training. Edwina had known this was coming but the news still came as a physical blow.

'How long for?' she asked, trying to sound as casual as possible. Ulysses, she knew now, would run a mile at the thought of someone getting really serious about a relationship. Edwina had the nous to keep from him how deeply attached she was becoming.

'A month.'

'Oh.' There didn't seem to be much else to say.

'You'll be able to write to me if you want.'

'OK, but I'm not much of a correspondent.'

'Well, neither am I, but I'd like to keep in touch.' This was the closest Ulysses had come to saying that he felt anything more for her than friendship – even though Edwina suspected that he did.

After that the weekend seemed to go flat. Edwina was devastated by the idea of not seeing Ulysses for so long, and Ulysses was preoccupied with his own thoughts about the next phase in his training. When they parted on Sunday evening Edwina, trying to keep her tears at bay, seemed cold and distant. Ulysses, not understanding the reason, wondered if she would wait for him to get back.

Aldershot, July 1988

Lizzie had been angry with Edwina for days after the party. She couldn't imagine what had motivated her to make such a spiteful remark about Amanda, except possibly something to do with jealousy. She had hoped that Edwina might ring her to apologise and had been disappointed when the phone call hadn't materialised. She began to wonder if perhaps she ought to make the first move towards making up. Perhaps she had overreacted? She half thought of telling Amanda about the incident but decided that it would do absolutely no good to anyone to repeat such a malicious rumour. It would be bound to upset Amanda that Edwina had even thought such a thing, and it wouldn't be fair to make Amanda cross with Edwina too. And she certainly couldn't tell Simon about it, even though he seemed much more approachable these days. It was one thing to discuss problems regarding the regiment or duty rosters or the weather, but to broach the question of a friend's sexuality? Gosh, Lizzie didn't think she could even talk to her mother about that.

Since Simon had moved into the mess the young captains and subalterns had had to moderate their behaviour by quite a degree. Several, who had tried to call Simon's bluff, had found themselves doing so many extra duties that they now confined their high jinks to their own rooms upstairs, or other less restricted messes in the area; either way Simon and Lizzie were spared witnessing their bad behaviour. Now that the junior officers spent increasingly less time in the public rooms of the mess, only making sulky and subdued appearances at mealtimes, Lizzie was much more relaxed. No longer was she faced with the excruciating embarrassment of their filthy, tasteless jokes or their sexual taunts and innuendoes. The ground floor of the mess seemed less terrifying and she began to spend an increasing amount of time in the bar and anteroom. Simon, disliking his own company and shunned by the male officers in the mess as a martinet, often joined her, knowing she was a good listener and would provide a sympathetic shoulder. Sometimes, particularly at the weekends, they were joined by some of the married officers who lived on the nearby patch. Their wives quickly noticed that Lizzie and Simon seemed to spend a large proportion of their free time in each other's company. The wives, always glad to have a subject for coffee-morning gossip, began to speculate, and on a couple of occasions the two of them were invited out to supper so they could be observed at closer quarters.

On the Saturday evening that Ulysses told Edwina about going to Brunei, Simon was with Lizzie in the bar, all the other officers having booked out for the weekend, to go home to their families or off with their girlfriends. None of the married officers and their wives had come in for a drink, so Simon knocked the bar steward off early, as there was no point in him staying just to serve them.

'You know we're becoming the subject of regimental gossip?' said Simon. He looked almost smug about the matter.

Lizzie reddened. She hated the thought that she might figure in other peoples' conversations. 'I didn't know. Why?'

'Oh, come off it, Lizzie,' he said, not unkindly. 'We work together, we live in the same building, we're seen together. Work it out.'

'Yes, but it doesn't mean that there's anything else.' Simon looked at her – she was so young, so naïve. He didn't say anything. Lizzie continued, 'Besides which, you're a married man.'

Simon laughed. 'So, my dear, was Cecil Parkinson but it didn't stop him knocking off his secretary. Anyway, I'm only married in law. She's filed for divorce and she won't be coming back.'

'But we're not, I mean, there's nothing . . .' Lizzie stopped. She wished there were. She'd begun by feeling sorry for him, wanting to help smooth his path at work by being efficient. His few words of thanks and kindness she'd treasured because it meant that she'd been succeeding. When he'd moved into the mess she'd spent time with him in the evenings because she hated the thought of him drinking too much on his own, but as she'd got to know him better her feelings of compassion had deepened into something else. At night, in bed, she kept thinking of the moment at Amanda's party when he'd put his arm round her shoulder and given her a cuddle. She would fall asleep and dream of him making love to her. She'd never felt this way about a man before. She looked at the floor, embarrassed that Simon might guess her feelings. He reached for her hand; she leapt, startled by the unexpectedness of his touch. Simon recoiled, worried that he'd made his move too fast and frightened her. She was such a shy creature, so easily alarmed.

'No, please don't. I don't mind,' said Lizzie, aching for his touch again. She reached out. 'I'm sorry.' She smiled at him. She looked more like a child than ever.

'Come here, kiddo,' he said quietly. Lizzie stood up and moved nearer, her lips parted a fraction of an inch. Simon took her in his arms and kissed her. God, how he needed a woman. Lizzie felt herself melting as a delicious feeling of love and security swept over her. Simon's hand moved up her back and his fingers caressed her neck, her hair and her ears. Lizzie, standing on tiptoe, clung to Simon, not sure that her legs were entirely capable of supporting her any longer. The kiss finished. Lizzie didn't know if it had lasted one minute or ten. She put her head against his chest and listened to the steady thump of his heart, so slow compared to hers, which she knew was pounding like she'd just run her BFT.

'Who's the duty officer?' asked Simon, suddenly businesslike.

'Mike Bain. Why?' Lizzie was puzzled. What on earth had that got to do with anything?

'Great.' Simon knew he was married. 'He'll be doing his duty from home. There'll be no one in the mess but us tonight.' Lizzie felt faint with the strength of her emotions. Was Simon suggesting that they made love? Was her dream going to come true? 'Come on,' he said, not wishing to waste any time, 'let's go to my room.'

In a trance, holding Simon's hand, she followed him to his room. He opened the door and turned on the light, and stood to one side to let Lizzie enter first. After the subdued lighting of the bar and the darkness of the corridor, it seemed very bright. Lizzie blinked and looked nervously around. All she noticed was how austere the room appeared – no ornaments, no pictures, nothing to make it personal, not even his own bedding. The only objects seemed to be Army issue. It was like a room in a transit camp – as if the occupant only intended to stay for the shortest possible time. Then she heard Simon shut the door behind her and she turned to face him. He took her in his arms again. Lizzie was trembling and her breath came out in little shudders. Simon kissed her again, hungrily, and then he started to unbutton her blouse. Lizzie went rigid with embarrassment; even at boarding school she'd been shy about undressing in front of the other girls, and the thought of a man seeing her naked was mortifying. Simon felt her stiffen.

'What's the matter?' he questioned, trying to keep the urgency from his voice. Lizzie hung her head; she didn't know how to respond. Simon was a sophisticated man who had probably made love to countless women, and Lizzie was terrified her ineptitude would make him despise her.

'Nothing,' she said unconvincingly.

'Would you like me to switch the light out?'

'Yes please.' It was barely a whisper. Simon had to bend his head to catch the words. Suddenly he realised that Lizzie was a virgin. Dear God, he thought, should I be doing this? His *savoir faire* deserted him. He'd never knowingly bedded a virgin – his girlfriends had always been as experienced as himself, or even more so. He suddenly felt awkward and clumsy and unexpectedly nervous. He hadn't had a women since his wife had walked out on him, and all he'd wanted tonight was a tumble with a willing partner. He'd have had to have been a blind fool not to realise that Lizzie had the hots for him, and he had decided to pull her tonight because, *faute de mieux*, there she was. But suddenly, instead of an athletic romp, he was faced with this responsibility. Jesus, did he want it? Was this what *she* really wanted? He sat down on his bed and pulled her on to his knee.

'Would you rather we . . . Would you rather go back to your own room?'

Lizzie shook her head, and whispered, 'No,' still looking at the floor.

Suddenly he found the prospect of seducing a willing virgin extraordinarily exciting, but despite this arousal he knew he must take his time. He put his hand under her chin and lifted it up until she looked into his eyes. He searched her face. 'Do you really mean that, or are you just saying it because you think it's what I want to hear?'

'Please, Simon, I do want you.' Her voice shook slightly. Simon lifted her off his knee and set her down on the bed. Well, that was good enough for him. He moved across the room and switched off the light.

'Would you rather I didn't look while you undress?' he said.

'Thank you.' He remained with his back to her, looking out of the window, but he could hear the rustle of her clothes and then a faint creak as she got into bed. 'I'm ready.' Simon undressed slowly – he

102

didn't want to frighten her by appearing too eager – then slipped between the cool sheets next to Lizzie's slim, warm figure. 'Simon?' She sounded petrified.

'Yes.'

'I haven't . . . I'm not.'

'I know, I'll be gentle, I promise.' He could feel her shake her head.

'No, it's not that. I'm not on the pill.' She sounded desolate.

Shit! Instead he said, 'Don't worry.' He climbed out of bed and went to the cabinet over the washbasin in his room. The room seemed chilly after the warmth of the bed. He quickly returned and snuggled in beside Lizzie. 'I've got something here.'

Lizzie heard a rustle of paper and felt Simon turn away from her and fumble for a moment or two under the bedclothes.

'All set now.' Then he said, 'If you want me to stop at any time you must say. Promise?'

'Promise.' Lizzie lay next to him and turned her face on the pillow to smile. He could just see her neat little teeth gleam in the soft light of a distant streetlamp. He took her in his arms, felt her silky warm body press hard against his and decided he would start by kissing her all over.

He began with her mouth and face, and as he kissed her he felt her relax in his arms. He was careful just to caress her back, running his hands from her waist to her neck and stroking her shoulders. She was so shy and nervous he didn't want to alarm her with too much intimacy too soon. Having got her this far the last thing he wanted was for her to bolt before he'd got his leg over. He felt Lizzie tentatively move her hands from his chest to his shoulders and then round his neck. Simon gently disengaged one and, taking her hand, kissed each fingertip in turn, then her palm, her wrist, her elbow and her shoulder. Finally, with exquisite tenderness, he moved his mouth down to her breast. He was rewarded with the sound of a sigh of unmistakable pleasure. More daring now, he moved his kisses down to her stomach, her legs, her flanks, and finally the insides of her thighs. Sensing that she was almost ready, he returned this attention to her mouth and very gently felt between her legs with his index finger. Lizzie shuddered with pleasure and excitement.

'Are you ready?' whispered Simon into her ear, knowing that she was because he had felt how wet she was.

'Oh, please.' Her voice sounded treacle-thick with desire. He could feel her heart pounding and knew that this was the moment. He straddled her and parted her legs. He briefly put his hand between her thighs to guide his penis to the right place, and then suddenly plunged forward; there was a split second of resistance, a wince from Lizzie, and he was inside her.

For a few seconds he didn't move, letting her get used to the sensation, but with his next thrust, he felt Lizzie stiffen and then shudder. Christ, she'd come already.

'Oh, God,' said Simon, almost in annoyance, 'you were too quick for me. You don't want me to stop, do you?'

'No, no. Please,' murmured Lizzie, sounding excited and confused.

Her orgasm excited him even more, and an animal driving now took over his body as he began to move back and forth on top of her, all thoughts of gentleness gone. He was unaware of anything beyond his own desire for satisfaction, and his thrusting became fast and more powerful until panting and groaning and with a last tremendous surge he collapsed, exhausted, on top of her. It was only then that he noticed that Lizzie had tears streaming down her face.

'Oh God, Lizzie, what is it?'

'Nothing,' she snuffled.

'Something's the matter, tell me.'

'Honestly, it's nothing,' she lied. She turned and smiled at him. How could she tell him how much it had hurt? She'd had her pleasure – it had been wonderful. What right had she to deny him his? But the agony as he'd got carried away – she felt as though she'd been ripped to shreds. Surely something wasn't right?

Simon, thinking he'd never really understand women – fancy crying just because she'd had an orgasm – and shattered by his physical exertion, rolled half off Lizzie, and with one leg and one arm across her went to sleep.

When he woke at first light he was surprised to discover that Lizzie had gone. But then he realised that she wouldn't want to be found in his bed by the mess steward when he brought round the early-morning tea. He rolled over and went back to sleep for another few hours.

In her own bed Lizzie lay sleepless and worried. As always, problems considered at night assumed ridiculous proportions, and Lizzie's case was no exception. What had she done? What had she been thinking of, sleeping with her boss? How was she going to be able to carry on as normal in the office? What if the others got wind of this? What about the pads on the married patch? How could she stop everyone guessing and talking about her? Oh, the embarrassment if they did. She wondered how cool she could play it. Could she pretend in public that nothing had happened?

It was with trepidation that she went down to breakfast the next morning; she didn't feel ready to put up an act just yet. He wasn't at the breakfast table, which came as a relief, and neither was anyone else. She grabbed a cup of coffee and the *Sunday Times*, and retreated back to her room planning to do the crossword, wash and mend some clothes, write letters and sort herself out. She switched on her radio and was instantly lulled by the perennial familiarity of Alistair Cooke's slow and faintly transatlantic drawl reading his letter from America. She didn't listen to the words but sat quietly in a chair while his steady delivery soothed her and allowed her mind to release its panicky grip on the events of the night before. Perhaps she hadn't done anything wrong; she loved Simon, she'd wanted him to love her, his wife obviously didn't or she wouldn't have left him. And was it so wrong that the two of them had been to bed together? It had seemed to her in the past weeks that all the other young officers in the mess had been getting more than enough sex, if their conversations were anything to go by. As she thought about it while she sewed on a few buttons and restitched a hem, she concluded that she hadn't done anything wrong, really. And as long as she and Simon were discreet, as long as she played it cool – no sheep's eyes or kissing in public – then it shouldn't matter to anyone else.

She was faintly disappointed that she didn't see anything of Simon that day in the mess. She longed for another kiss or some sign of affection. Before lunch she slipped along to his room, first checking that there was no one to see her, and knocked on his door. Not hearing a reply, she tried the door and found it unlocked. She put her head round it and could see that his bed was made and the room was empty. He had obviously gone out. Again, Lizzie was struck by the austerity of his room, but she assumed that his wife had probably taken everything with her when she had moved out of their quarter. That would explain why the poor man only seemed to be in possession of his clothes and a handful of personal items. Not wishing to be caught in Simon's room, Lizzie left again quickly, feeling deeply disappointed that he wasn't around. She wondered if she'd see him again before work on Monday morning.

Guildford, July 1988

Bella came crashing into Amanda's office just after their lunch break and slammed the door behind her. She flopped into the chair by Amanda's desk, her shoulders slumped dejectedly and her expression one of complete misery.

'I've been warned for a posting,' she said. Amanda's eyes widened at this sudden news.

'Overseas?' Amanda could barely keep her voice steady at the thought of losing Bella.

'No, only as far as Bicester.'

'Well, that's not too bad.' Amanda tried to smile. 'It could be worse. At least we will still be able to get together at weekends.'

'If being duty officer, or some mess function, doesn't get in the way.'

Amanda shrugged. Their weekends were supposed to be free but the reality was that they rarely were. Often either Saturday or Sunday was taken up with something: church parade, a duty, a dinner night, a sports fixture – the list was almost endless.

Bella sighed. 'We'll just have to manage as best we can.'

'Yes. But I'll miss you so much during the week. Just knowing that you're in the same building is all I need to make me feel happy.' Amanda stretched her hand across her desk so she could touch Bella's. She wanted to do more than that, she wanted to get up and give her a hug, to hold her and stroke her hair, but they both knew that it was possible for one of the company clerks, or worse, the company sergeant major, to barge in without knocking. The only way for their relationship to survive was absolute discretion and secrecy at all times. 'When are you going?'

'Not until September at the earliest – a couple of months yet anyway.'

'That's something to be grateful for. We'll still be able to get away this summer like we've planned. Two weeks in the sun, just you and me and no prying eyes. God, I can't wait.'

Bella looked marginally more cheerful at this prospect. Resignedly she said, 'I suppose we both knew I'd be due to go soon. It's just I was hoping that the postings branch had sort of forgotten about me.'

Amanda laughed. 'You must be the only person in this entire establishment who wouldn't rather get moved on early.'

'Well, they haven't got what I've got.' Bella blew her a kiss of gratitude and Amanda smiled.

'You'd better get back to your own office. I've got all my reports to do on my platoon, to say nothing of a rehearsal for Passing Out Parade.' She was only partly concerned about her workload. She was more worried about someone noticing how much they liked each other's company and how much time they spend in it, and that, yet again, Miss de Fresne was in Miss Hardwick's office. 'See you at tea?'

'Yes, although I may be late. My in-tray is bulging too.'

It took a while for Amanda to settle back to writing the interminable reports – they all had to be different, but how many ways were there to say that W/Private Bloggs or W/Private Snooks had successfully completed her basic training and had proved to be a reliable, smart, honest and likeable member of the platoon? Amanda had hoped to escape from the tedium of reports when she gave up teaching, but now she found herself doing thirty of the buggers every six weeks instead of once a year.

She sighed and looked glumly at the pile of buff booklets which would have to be completed before tomorrow. Bella's news had thrown her and she didn't feel like tackling this mundane task. She leant back in her hard office chair and looked out of the window beside her, across the parade square where another platoon was drilling. The shouts of the platoon sergeant yelling in annoyance, 'Pick up your dressing. Yes, you!' to some poor recruit who was way out of line drifted clearly into Amanda's office, but she neither saw nor heard; she was wondering how she was going to manage at Guildford without Bella.

She loved the business of turning schoolgirls into soldiers. It was immensely satisfying seeing her platoon pass out, and she got a tremendous kick out of the whole thing. Of course, the job had its down side, but then what job didn't? The reports facing her constituted one of them, as did some of the petty rules and the occasional bitching that went on in the mess. But on the up side there was the tremendous support all the subalterns gave each other, a comfortable lifestyle and, best of all from her own particular point of view, a paucity of men. Having originally envied Lizzie her posting to the Gunners in Aldershot, she now realised that being the only female in an otherwise all-male mess had a lot of drawbacks. Yes, there was plenty of female company to be had in Aldershot, but it wasn't the same as having a friend close by in whom to confide. Hardly a week went by when Lizzie didn't ring her just for the pleasure of some female chit-chat. Amanda had long since decided that she'd had the best deal out of the postings lottery, but it was going to be a different kettle of fish once Bella moved on. She knew the things that niggled now would assume a greater significance once she was bereft of Bella's company and Guildford would lose its appeal. She let a wave of self-pity wash over her.

Although they tried hard to make the most of the few remaining weeks together, their busy and crowded days and the repetitive routine conspired to make the time race by in a blur. Each week, largely indistinguishable from the one before, passed in a rush of parades, inspections, lectures and sport. In their minimal free time they conspired to meet in out-of-the-way pubs and restaurants, leaving and returning to the WRAC Centre in separate cars. The strain of conducting a completely secret love affair was phenomenal, and in a perverse way they almost began to look forward to the moment when Bella was posted. At least then they would not have to pretend to ignore each other at mealtimes, to find spurious excuses to go to each other's offices or rooms, and to maintain a façade of indifference to each other's presence whenever a third party was around. Amanda complained that it was like constantly acting out a part, never able to be herself and always conscious that there was an audience, and she worried she might let the mask slip. Bella admitted she had similar nightmares.

They contemplated the possibility of resigning their commissions – at least out of the Army no one would carp or criticise – but after endless discussion they decided that they didn't want to be forced to make that choice, to sacrifice one way of life in order to pursue another, and that providing they remained absolutely discreet they would probably get away with it. However, maintaining the subterfuge became more and more tricky. As their concern deepened that they might let something slip about their relationship, they began to ignore each other increasingly when in public. A rumour began to circulate that they were at daggers drawn. Wickedly Bella confided to Gina Danby, her least favourite person, that it was all about a man. Amanda and Bella had problems keeping their faces straight as the story gained momentum, thanks to Gina's embellishments: that Bella had been dumped because of interference by Amanda; that Bella's boyfriend had all but popped the question when Amanda got between them; that she'd been practically halfway up the aisle when ... But it least it served to distract their fellow mess members from the real story.

At last their summer leave materialised; a fortnight in northern Greece. It had been Amanda's idea that they should go there. She'd been a Graecophile since her first trip there as a student, when she'd worked as a chambermaid in a resort hotel in order to supplement her grant for the rest of the year – a necessity as her parents had refused to fund her studies further when she'd told them she was gay. In some ways it had been a blessing, as otherwise she would never have discovered the beauties of the area. She'd outlined these to Bella, together with lyrical descriptions of the weather and the scenery, and suggested that an isolated villa in a small village would be a perfect place to unwind and relax. Eventually she'd managed to sway Bella to agreeing to this instead of nightclubs and discos in Spain. Bella had taken some convincing, but Amanda's photographs had eventually persuaded her.

Bella's reward for her compliance was long, sun-baked days spend reading books on the beach, Amanda resting her head on a rock and Bella propped against her. They ate lazy lunches at village tavernas and snoozed through the afternoons, dozing under olive trees, with the cicadas rasping soporifically in the branches above. They explored the delights of Greece by day and the delights of each other at night. They drove into the mountains that towered above the unspoilt coastline and shopped, using sign language, at the wayside stalls for olives, tomatoes, pomegranates and watermelons. Their villa, a grand name for two rooms, minute shower room and tiny but enclosed and flower-filled courtyard, looking across a bay of lapis-lazuli-blue sea towards Corfu, was where they spent their evenings and nights, sipping retsina and making love. Each day was like floating through a succession of sensory delights, with nothing to disturb their idyllic, relaxed contentment. Amanda felt she had never experienced such fulfilment in her life.

When they weren't enjoying the scenery and discovering secluded bays, they were discovering each other and probing mentally for shared experiences, desires and ambitions. They had both been to university, although they had studied different subjects. Bella had a degree in English and delighted in introducing Amanda to a whole host of her favourite modern authors. Amanda had done languages and tried to instil – unsuccessfully – in Bella a basic vocabulary of modern Greek. They had the same humour, the same goals, the same fears, phobias, pleasures and dreams. And this reinforced the sense of mutual security they gave each other. Instinctively each knew what the other would like or dislike, and they revelled in their hedonism. They were so relaxed that they lost all sense of time and had to enquire at the taverna in the village what the date was, for fear of missing their flight home.

After the delights of their holiday the wet and dreary weather which greeted them at Gatwick instantly lowered their spirits. To compound this, on arrival at Guildford Bella was informed that her posting was being brought forward and she was to depart at the end of that week. They spend their last few days together morosely packing Bella's belongings into wooden MFO boxes supplied by the QM.

'You're not even being dined out,' complained Amanda, finding fault with everything.

'I expect they'll invite me back. They usually do.'

'Huh.' Amanda was sceptical. She was in a black mood and didn't want to see the bright side of anything. She knew postings were an inevitable part of Army life, and that she was being childish and immature in her resentment of Bella's departure, but she was dreading the resultant loneliness. It meant nothing that they would be able to see each other at weekends, duties permitting. It was irrelevant that they would be able to telephone each other with ease. All Amanda knew was that she was going to be miserable for five days out of every seven for the foreseeable future.

After Bella had finally left, Amanda sat in the now empty room and fought to control her tears. More than anything she wanted a shoulder to cry on, but how could she confide her problems to any of her other friends? She knew she was too old to be acting like a lovesick adolescent; she was a mature, sensible woman, capable of meting out all sorts of down-to-earth advice to the young recruits in her charge. Yet here she was, deep in despair, unable to come to terms with the posting of her lover. She stood up and returned to her own room, across the corridor. She shut the door and wearily leant against it. Grow up! she silently shouted at herself. Then she sank down on the floor and gave way to her tears.

Aldershot, September 1988

Lizzie sat at her desk and wished for the umpteenth time that day that something would happen to relieve the boredom. Apart from a handful of soldiers, mostly the sick, lame and lazy, she was on her own in the barracks. The regiment had gone on manoeuvres down to Salisbury Plain and she had been left behind as OC Rear Party. She'd balked at this overt sexism but had been told that far from being left behind because she was female, it was because she was the only junior officer who could be trusted to look after the shop properly while both the colonel and the adjutant were away. She'd been mollified by the compliment, although lurking at the back of her mind was the idea that that had been the intention.

For the first couple of days there had been a few admin problems left over to deal with, but once they'd been cleared up there seemed to be nothing else to do. She'd checked that every page of every classified document was still in the safe, she'd brought the regimental history up to date, she'd written the regiment's news for inclusion in the next issue of *The Gunner* and, together with an equally bored clerk, had made sure all the military manuals had their amendments updated. She'd even finished that morning's *Times* and *Telegraph* crosswords. But now there was *nothing* left to do and she didn't dare leave the office early because the instant she did some brass hat was bound to phone up.

She had to look on the bright side of the situation, though. Despite her disappointment at being left behind and missing seeing the guns doing some live-firing, she had to admit that things in the office had been difficult since her night with Simon. And perhaps *difficult* was an understatement. Lizzie still inwardly cringed with embarrassment at memories of the Monday morning afterwards. She hadn't seen

Simon at all on the Sunday so she'd been unable to talk to him. On the Monday she'd woken up early, longing to get to the office and Simon. Too excited to eat, she skipped breakfast and went straight to work. She was stunned to see Simon calmly sitting behind his desk as though he was always to be found there at such an early hour. She had noticed that the clerks' office was empty, not surprising considering the time, and it would certainly be at least an hour before the CO made an appearance. RHQ was deserted but for them.

Lizzie smiled shyly at Simon, not sure of the protocol of greeting one's boss with whom one had recently had sex. She felt a warm glow of love just looking at him.

'You're early,' he said, hardly looking up. Lizzie was thrown. She'd expected him to say something rather more kindly.

'Yes. I . . . I've work to do.' She remained standing by his desk.

'It won't get done from there.'

'No.' She hesitated, longing for some word of endearment, even an acknowledgement of what had happened. 'Um, Simon?'

'Yes.'

'Thanks for Saturday night. It was . . .' She didn't know how to go on. He looked up at her. Lizzie's infatuation was written clearly across her face. His irritation, obvious to anyone, played across his features like a cat's-paw breeze across the surface of a pond. Lizzie realised her mistake with sickening and embarrassing clarity; she wasn't anything more to him than just another lay. With a shock she realised that she had fallen in love, but that for him Saturday night had no deeper significance than just a jolly romp in the sack. There was a stunned pause in her sentence for a moment or two, then, with a commendable recovery, she completed it with '. . . it was a good laugh.' She prayed that it sounded suitably blasé, because she certainly didn't feel it. She was afraid she was going to cry.

Simon looked faintly nonplussed when her words didn't quite match her gooey expression. 'Yes. Well, glad you enjoyed it.'

'It was OK.' Her voice shook, giving her away.

'Look,' he said 'I thought you just wanted a bonk, like me. I didn't think you were going to read more into it than that.'

'No. How stupid of me.' Lizzie felt perilously close to tears.

'I've just escaped from a messy marriage. You didn't seriously think I was looking for any sort of relationship?'

'No, of course not.' Her voice was falsely bright. She didn't dare let her true feelings show, certainly not in front of him. Keeping

113

control of her voice well, she said, 'I've just remembered, I've left my diary in my room.' She turned and left as casually as she could, praying that she wouldn't meet anyone on the short journey back to the officers' mess.

Back in her room, Lizzie sat on her bed, but the expected tears of mortification didn't come. Instead she felt angry. How dare he? How dare he use her like that? Despite her rage she was forced to acknowledge that she'd been a more than willing partner, but that still didn't excuse him for just wanting a cheap conquest. And as for his casual assumption that it would mean as little to her as it patently had done to him – well, that was just adding insult to injury. Did he really expect her to forget that he'd had her virginity? Did she seriously think that she would choose to lose it to just anyone – the first man who didn't completely repel her and who happened to stumble along at the right moment? She was so livid she was shaking. If anything unbreakable had been near at hand she'd have thrown it. Then her anger gave way to shame and worries that he'd tell the other officers that he'd scored with her. She flopped back on her bed, covered her face with her hands and groaned. Oh God, what had she done? And how could she face him every day in the office knowing that all she'd been to him was a free shag? Oh, the humiliation of it.

It took a while for Lizzie to calm down and come to terms with her mistake. She knew that life wouldn't stop just because she'd made a complete fool of herself. She'd have to get on with meeting him every day at work. She slowly came to the conclusion that the only way to play this was to completely ignore the fact that it had ever happened. She walked over to her washbasin and dashed cold water on to her face. As she dried her cheeks she studied her reflection in the mirror, and the face that looked back at her was considerably less naïve than the one she'd seen less than an hour previously. Coolly she made up her mind that in future she wouldn't let herself get close to a man unless she was certain about his feelings for her. And as for Simon, well, he could sort out his own bloody problems from here on – she for one couldn't give a damn about them any more.

Hounslow, September 1988

Edwina thumped the pile of paperwork on to her desk and looked at it miserably. This sort of routine day-to-day admin wasn't at all what she'd had in mind when she'd applied to join the Army. What she'd wanted was to go on exercise in Germany, or to take soldiers on adventurous training expeditions to exciting places overseas. And what had she got now? A troop of female communication centre operators who couldn't be persuaded to leave the warmth of the commcen except in an emergency, and who seemed more interested in knitting patterns than soldiering. What really galled her was that her exam results had placed her in the top three of the troop commander's course, and yet her posting was the most mundane and boring of all. She'd gone straight to her OC and complained bitterly, but had been told that her postings branch felt this posting was the 'right one for her' and they weren't prepared to reconsider.

'Balls, sir,' Edwina had said with her usual directness. She really couldn't believe that she was less well suited to command a signals troop in Germany than any of the men. However, she was also well aware that despite dozens of protestations by the Army that they treated men and women similarly, there were a number of COs who were chary of putting women in charge of men.

Not for the first time in recent weeks Edwina wondered what Ulysses was doing and longed to be allowed to do something similar. She eyed the papers on her desk distastefully, sighed heavily and pulled them towards her. On the top were the day's Part One Orders – the list of duties and notices to ensure the smooth running of the squadron for that day. All she had to do was check it for spelling mistakes and then sign it, ready for duplication and distribution. Really, she thought, anyone could do this. I've spent seven months at

115

Sandhurst, endured three months of special-to-arm training and now I'm doing something a child of twelve could cope with. Desultorily she read the two-page document and was just about to add her signature when one of the notices caught her eye. It was a request for volunteers, male *or female*, for special duties in Northern Ireland. Edwina reread it; she had always thought that the only people carrying out special duties in the Province were RUC Special Branch and the SAS. The RUC wouldn't be advertising for recruits from the British Army and the SAS didn't take women, so what was this setup? Edwina was flummoxed, but she was also intrigued. She wondered whom she could ask for more details. She decided that her best bet would be the adjutant, but he proved to be a dead loss. All he knew was that volunteers' names had to be forwarded to a particular department of the MoD without delay and the signal had to be classified secret.

'But take my advice, Edwina,' he said, not unkindly, 'getting sidetracked by something like this won't do your career any good at all.'

'Why?' Edwina was at a loss to understand his reasoning.

'Because you'll be out of the main stream of things.' This argument cut absolutely no ice at all with Edwina, since she felt that with this current dead-end job she'd already been sidelined from a proper career with the Royal Signals. Running a static commcen was hardly the same as providing comms for an armoured division out in Germany, and all her contemporaries who'd gone to do that would be way ahead of her in experience and skills at the end of their two-year tours.

'Promise me you'll think about this carefully for a couple of days. I don't want you rushing into something recklessly.'

'OK.' Although Edwina felt she had so little information to go on that she didn't actually have anything to think about – except whether she wanted to do something more exciting.

She had a contact number for Stirling Lines at Hereford, which Ulysses had said she could phone in an emergency and they would pass on a message if possible. She hoped that he might know something about what these volunteers were required for. But when she rang she was told that Andrew Lees was away from the unit and wouldn't be able to contact her for several weeks. She didn't ask what he was doing or where – she knew she wouldn't be told.

Since Ulysses had finished his basic training with the SAS he'd been away almost constantly, so Edwina had returned to her old friendships, had made up with Lizzie and had phoned both her and Amanda on a regular basis. Now that she had the luxury of an office to herself and, more importantly, her own telephone, this was a pleasure she was able to indulge in even more easily than before. More in hope than expectation she dialled Lizzie now to see if she knew anything.

'One of our subalterns tried for it,' said Lizzie, glad of Edwina's interruption of her monotonous day.

'And what did he say about it?' said Edwina excitedly.

'Nothing really. He was sworn to secrecy apparently. The only thing I did gather was that you have to be incredibly fit and able to survive on virtually no sleep at all.'

'Did he pass?'

'No. But he was there for quite a while; a couple of weeks or more.'

'Do you know why he failed?'

'No idea. He can't or won't say.'

'So it's unlikely he'll give any gen to me?'

''Fraid so.'

'OK, but if you could ask him to give me a ring if there are any tips he give me – without the pair of us being thrown into the Tower for high treason.'

'I'll mention it to him when he gets back off exercise.'

'Thanks. Anyway, how's life with Simon?'

'I'll be glad when he's gone.' Lizzie had confided all the details of her embarrassing affair with her immediate boss.

'Is it still ghastly?'

'Dreadful. And I'm convinced he's told one or two of the other officers that he's screwed me.'

'Surely not!' Edwina tried to sound horrified but thought that it was only too likely. Most men she knew couldn't resist boasting about their conquests. 'You poor thing. And you still have to share an office with him. God, how gruesome!'

'Not for much longer. He's being posted to Germany, something he's been after for ages. Apparently he needs the experience before he does his promotion exams.'

'Well, that must be a relief for you.'

'You're telling me. The atmosphere in this office is not exactly friendly.'

'I can imagine.' Edwina couldn't think of anything worse, but then she wouldn't have been fool enough to have a relationship with her boss in the first place. It was bound to end in tears. However, now was not the time to lecture Lizzie, who was obviously going through a hard enough time already. Instead she said, 'Do you know who's taking over from Simon?'

'A nice bloke called Richard Airdrie-Stow. He lives out although he's not married. He seems a very private person.'

'So you've met him then?'

'Oh, yes. He's already a member of the regiment.'

'I wish you luck with him.' She nearly added some advice about not shagging her next boss but decided that Lizzie wouldn't find it funny. Instead she steered away from the subject. 'Have you heard from Amanda recently?'

'I phoned to thank her for her card from Greece and she sounded pretty low. She didn't say what it was, although I imagine that once you've trained a couple of batches of recruits it must get a bit tedious.'

Edwina thanked her lucky stars that she wasn't in Amanda's shoes. She promised Lizzie she'd ring Amanda and try to cheer her up, and then she rang off and got back to work. However, she didn't get much done, because she kept trying to remember all the little bits of information that she'd gleaned from Ulysses about SAS selection. If they were looking for really fit people to do something hairy out in Ireland, probably involving anti-terrorist operations, then she reckoned that they – whoever *they* were – must be after people with qualities similar to those needed for the SAS. The one thing she did remember vividly, and which she thought might prove to be her downfall, was that Ulysses had said that the SAS binned candidates who drew attention to themselves. She knew that keeping a low profile and not standing out in any way had never been her style, but could she change her image for this and keep herself under control for long enough to pass? She didn't think that having red hair was going to help and thought about dyeing it, but quickly changed her mind when she remembered what a mess she'd made of it the last time.

The next day she formed up in front of the adjutant and formally volunteered for special duties. He was annoyed but was duty-bound to process her application.

'Now what happens?' asked Edwina.

'Don't ask me,' he said crossly. 'I do know that if you get accepted we're going to be short an officer until the next troop commander's course finishes.'

'You'll manage,' replied Edwina easily. The adjutant gave her a long, hard stare. He didn't appreciate Edwina or her sense of humour.

She was called for an assessment of her fitness and IQ and then she heard nothing more for several weeks, by which time she'd almost given up hope. She'd begun to assume that there was something wrong with her background or her intelligence which made her unacceptable. Perhaps her application wasn't even being considered, she thought bleakly. But then came news that she was to report to a disused barracks in the Midlands. There were instructions on how to get there and what to take, but still no other information on what was going to be expected of her.

Since Lizzie's friend hadn't been in contact with any tips, Edwina thought she'd ring her to see if he could be persuaded to part with any.

'Forget it,' said Lizzie. 'He really doesn't want to talk about it.'

'Why?'

'If I knew that I'd tell you. The only thing he did say was "Tell your friend not to say anything about what she's doing before, during or after selection." '

'Oh.' It all sounded rather mysterious, to say nothing of being faintly intimidating. Edwina was still keen to try for selection but she wished she knew more about what she was getting in to. Most important of all, if she got into it and didn't like it, would she be able to get out again? She knew she wasn't going to be able to find anything else out from Lizzie. If she wanted to know what it was all about, the only way was going to be to report there as directed in her joining instructions.

Aldershot, December 1988

Lizzie replaced the receiver and knuckled down to her work again. Unlike Edwina, she revelled in her role of ensuring the smooth daily running of the regiment, and she was aware that Richard Airdrie-Stow, the new adjutant, was able to delegate an increasing amount of work to her. When he'd first taken over from Simon and had wanted guidance on how the office ran, Lizzie had amazed herself with how detailed her knowledge now was, regarding both the office and the regiment. Until then she'd really had no idea how much she'd learned since her arrival back in May. On a number of occasions he had asked her what the form was for dealing with certain problems, and Lizzie had discovered that if she didn't know exactly how to deal with it, then she at least knew where to find the answer. She now prided herself on her efficiency, the attention she paid to details, and her contacts in other units and formations in the area.

Lizzie had learned early in her career that more often than not, regardless of the nature of a problem, it mattered more who you knew than what you knew. When the wives' club had needed funds to set up a crèche, the colonel's wife's pet project, she had known whom to approach and had got them a grant of two thousand pounds. When the colonel had suddenly decided that he wanted a band to play at the regiment's Remembrance Day service, she had managed to rustle one up, despite being told that bookings for military bands had to be made months in advance. When the regimental boxing team was denied official transport for a match in Germany, she had got them aboard an RAF Hercules, flying out empty to Gutersloh to collect men returning from an exercise. Her stock had improved no end with everyone in RHQ – in fact it had got to the stage when even the CO, having been told by a battery commander that a task was impossible, had suggested that Lizzie should be given a shot at solving it. The battery commander had not been amused.

The junior officers in the mess had got bored with annoying her, and even though Simon had moved out they left her alone. But she wasn't reclusive; having made her ghastly mistake with Simon she'd resolved that she wasn't going to date an officer from her own regiment again, but there were half a dozen officers' messes in Aldershot and Lizzie was a welcome guest in most of them. Her social life thrived. She was often out in the evening, a fact which didn't go unnoticed in her own mess, and which began to make her more attractive to the other officers. If Lizzie spent so much time in the other messes in the area, what could those mess members offer that they couldn't? The junior officers began to try and draw her into their activities more and more, but she was having none of it. She was quite determined not to make the same mistake ever again. The junior officers quizzed her about boyfriends and weren't entirely sure they believed Lizzie's glib answer, 'All my relationships are purely platonic – play for me, tonic for them.'

Lizzie was taken unawares when Richard approached her one morning in the office and asked for her help with a personal problem.

'I owe dinner or supper to most of the married officers on the patch,' he explained. 'The wives take pity on me because I live out and keep inviting me round for meals to make sure I don't fade away.' Lizzie suppressed a grin – Richard was six foot and solidly built. 'The trouble is, I can't keep taking this hospitality and not repaying it. I want to have a dinner party but there are two problems. Firstly I haven't a clue what to cook, and secondly I'll need a hand, someone to pour drinks while I open the door, that sort of thing.'

'I'm sure there are some very good caterers in the area. Or what about asking someone from the Catering Corps to help you when they're off duty?'

'Oh, I hadn't thought of that.' Richard looked glum. 'Truth is, I was hoping you might be able to help.' Lizzie wasn't sure about this at all. The last thing she wanted was for anyone to think that she was setting her cap at Richard after the last débâcle. 'Oh, please, Lizzie. You'll know everyone there, which will make it a much more fun evening. And I'm not asking you to cook. I just thought you might be able to give me some ideas for food – I thought I could probably buy everything from Marks.'

'When had you planned this for?' Lizzie was still wary.

'A week on Friday, the last one before Christmas. People will have started going off on leave if I do it any later, and by the time we get back to work in the New Year everyone will be sick of parties.'

'I'd rather not, if I'm absolutely honest. If you and I do anything together you know what the gossip will be like.'

'You mustn't pay any attention to that.'

'Easier said than done,' retorted Lizzie tightly. She hadn't discussed her mistake with anyone in the regiment but she knew that the rumours – fuelled, she suspected, by Simon – had been rife. Richard must have heard some of them and must surely understand her reasons for refusing his invitation. Certainly the atmosphere in the office hadn't thawed until Richard and Simon had finished the hand-over and Simon had finally departed.

'Oh, come on, Lizzie,' he wheedled. 'Please. Your organisational skills are legendary, and I shall need every bit of them if I'm going to avoid a social disaster.'

'You must know some other woman you could ask.'

'Not really.' Lizzie snorted disbelievingly. 'I broke up with my girlfriend a couple of months ago. I haven't been in the mood to . . . well, you know.' Lizzie did, only too well.

'I'm sorry.' She paused and weighed up the pros and cons. 'Look, I'm free that evening, I'll do it for you, but you're to make it plain to everyone that I'm there as the hired help, OK?'

'It's a deal. Now, have you any idea what we could eat?' Lizzie, who'd helped at innumerable dinner parties that her mother had thrown to help her father up the rungs of the ladder of promotion, said she'd think about it.

She was in the bar that evening, wondering whether smoked mackerel pâté would be a better starter than vichyssoise, when the phone rang. The bar steward answered it and then handed it to Lizzie.

'It's me, Amanda.'

'Hi, how's Guildford? Any better?'

'Don't ask. Horrible. I'm ringing because I can't get hold of Edwina. Her unit says she's adventurous training, but when I asked them where, they got all cagey. What the hell is going on?'

'She's on some sort of selection course, I think.'

'Doing what?'

'I really don't know. I just know that it's something secret.' There was a burst of laughter down the line.

122

'God, Lizzie, you sound like someone from a World War Two film. You'll be telling me careless talk costs lives next.'

'I'm serious, Amanda. I really don't know what's involved. I don't even know what she'll be doing if she qualifies. All I do know is that everything to do with this course is very highly classified.'

'Oh.' Amanda sounded nonplussed. 'Right then. So we just have to wait for Edwina to get hold of us.'

'I think so.'

Amanda sighed desultorily. 'I was hoping to see her again before Christmas, see if she had any plans for the holidays. I suppose you're going home to your folks?'

'Yes – big family get-together. Are you going to be on your own then?'

'Not entirely. I've got a chum in Oxfordshire who's free for the Christmas week, but I've taken the week after as leave as well. I just thought it would be a good chance to catch up with some friends.'

'I wish I could help but I'm duty officer over New Year and I don't get the impression there's going to be any sort of party here. The regiment is on block leave so everyone else is pushing off.'

'Poor you. Well, how about if I come over and see you? That is, if you don't mind. We both look like we're going to be abandoned at New Year.'

'That'd be great. Let me know what day you're arriving so I can book you into the mess. I expect we'll have to fend for ourselves, but at least I can make sure that a bed is made up for you.'

After Lizzie had put the phone down she wondered why she felt sorry for Amanda. Was she really as bored and lonely as she sounded? Obviously there was a dire shortage of men round Guildford way, and if Amanda didn't get herself into some sort of steady relationship soon, she was going the right way to get left on the shelf. Lizzie put Amanda out of her mind and got back to planning her menu.

Partly due to the food, partly due to the company and partly due to the copious amounts of drink that flowed, Richard's dinner party was a huge success. His house, a surprisingly large Victorian terraced villa, had a massive basement area knocked through from two rather poky, ill-lit rooms. This new room, below street level at the front but leading out to the garden at the back, and now beautifully

123

proportioned, had space for a large pine table at which twelve people could sit in comfort. Lizzie played her part as kitchen maid, wine waitress and general dogsbody, joined in the conversations and helped dish up the food, but she left no one in any doubt that she was doing this as a favour to Richard because of his single state. There was something about her brisk efficiency and her attitude towards her boss that emphasised that this was in fact the case.

When the last of the guests had gone. Lizzie stood by the front door and prepared to put on her coat.

'Stay and have a coffee,' offered Richard.

'No thanks. It's late and I need my sleep.'

'I would like you to,' he insisted.

'No,' said Lizzie firmly.

'May I know why?'

'I don't think we know each other well enough for those sorts of confidences.' Richard looked hurt. 'I'm sorry, Richard, I've had a nice evening with your friends but I want to get home to bed now.'

'OK. Well, thanks anyway,' he said sadly.

Lizzie left. As she got into her little 2CV she felt annoyed that he hadn't made more of an effort to persuade her. Then she abruptly started the engine and told herself not to be such a goose. She didn't want to get involved with him – did she?

The West Midlands,
December 1988

Edwina didn't know if she was coming or going, she was so tired. She'd been lying out in a forest, camouflaged under her poncho and a carefully constructed hide, for two days. It was pitch dark, and she was not only tired but wet through, freezing cold and starving hungry. Her feet were completely numb and she knew she had nasty weeping sores behind her knees, in her groin and under her armpits caused by the chafing of her sodden clothes. She and a male partner, whom she knew only by the number 88, were keeping watch on a path. Every now and again either a person or a vehicle would move along it and they were expected to keep a log of all the activity which they saw happening. They had been supplied with cold, meagre rations twice since their arrival in the wood over thirty-six hours earlier, but the tiny snacks had done nothing to alleviate their hunger. Edwina's stomach rumbled again, loudly.

'Christ, that's not very ladylike,' whispered number 88.

'I don't feel very ladylike. I just feel famished. What I wouldn't give for a bacon butty and a cup of tea.'

'Shut up, will you,' murmued 88. 'If anything is going to make me jack this in, it's this mental torture of you talking about food when I'm starving.' He looked at her hard in the gloom under their hide. 'Are you sure you're not on the staff – here to see how far you can push me before I crack up?'

'No, honest. I'm sorry. I'm really only thinking out loud, trying to keep myself awake.'

They had been taking it in turns to keep watch, four hours on and four hours off, but they were now both so tired that neither of them dared sleep in case the other dozed off too. They knew that if they were caught napping, literally, they would both be on the next train home. After getting this far in the selection process neither was prepared to blow it now. Edwina shifted slightly to reduce the dreadful pins and needles in her legs, but it only seemed to make it worse, and she winced as the seam of her shirt dragged across one of her sores. She tried to keep awake by thinking back to her days at Sandhurst and remembering the names of all the Directing Staff. When she'd exhausted that tack she did the same with the names of her classmates at school – Brown, Carson, Curtis, Daniels ... Suddenly 88 nudged her.

'Get the scope, there's someone out there.' With great care Edwina brought the starlight scope up to her eye. Through it she could see a ghostly green image of the countryside in front of her, almost as clear as if it was broad daylight. She panned slowly through one hundred and eighty degrees, watching carefully for any signs of movement.

'Can't see anything,' she whispered.

'I'm sure I heard rustling.'

Edwina panned back the other way. 'Nothing.' It was about the sixth time in as many hours that they'd had a false alarm, though they didn't mind, as it passed a minute or two. As a surveillance exercise this one was easy; it was their stamina and concentration that were being tested.

Then suddenly there was an ear-splitting crash and a lightning-bright blaze of white as a thunder flash went off about a hundred yards away. Edwina was about to jump up when 88 grabbed her arm and held her down.

'Don't show yourself,' he said. 'They're trying to flush us out.' Edwina cursed herself for being so stupid. Thank God her partner was on the ball. They lay quite still, Edwina with her eye pressed against the night sight. In its green light she saw that another pair had emerged from the bushes about fifty yards from the site of the explosion. They stood about, looking bemused, then a figure appeared from behind a tree and motioned for them to walk in the direction of the main track, about half a kilometre away. Edwina didn't think they'd see those candidates again. She felt sorry for them. They'd all been put through hell over the last four weeks or so, and to fail when they must be nearing the end of the selection process – God, that would be depressing.

About fifty of the volunteers hadn't got past the end of the first week, for that week had weeded out everyone who wasn't supremely fit. Each night they'd all been deprived of their promised quota of sleep, woken up in the small hours to do extra PT, or answer dozens of mindless questions so some psychoanalyst could weed out those with the wrong motivations. And yet they'd still been expected to be ready each morning at six thirty to carry out a gruelling variety of tests of observation, concentration, stamina and intelligence. Some had gone because of injury and others had simply thrown in the towel because they weren't fit enough or couldn't hack the constant pressure and exhaustion. One girl, who shared a barrack room with Edwina, had been sacked because she'd asked too many questions of the other candidates. They had been specifically told at the start of the course that all they were to know about each other was the number pinned to their chests. They were not to exchange any personal details, and certainly not their names, with anyone else, neither the other candidates nor the staff. But this girl had asked them all about their parent units, their real names, which school they had been to and so on. To begin with, Edwina had assumed she was a plant, put there to see if any of them would give away more than they should, but judging by the lecture everyone had been given after her departure, it seemed as though she'd just been too curious for her own good. Edwina had prided herself on not giving away anything about herself. She'd kept her trap shut, only speaking when spoken to, and sat in the middle of all the lectures, neither at the front nor at the back, where people got noticed. Not once had she done anything to draw attention to herself, not complaining, not laughing, nothing.

On a couple of occasions Edwina herself had come perilously close to binning the whole thing. Once was after the log race, which had exhausted her to a point she had never imagined possible. It had made running marathons seem pleasant in comparison. Another time it was when she'd been woken up after only a few hours' sleep for the third night in a row. This time all the volunteers had been made to tackle the assault course and had then had to strip down to their underwear, men and women alike and swim across a small lake. Even for December it was bitterly cold, and six of their number had wimped out there and then. The DS didn't care – as far as they were concerned it was no skin off their noses if candidates wanted to leave. It had been made clear to everyone right from the start that no one would be forced to carry on with the selection if they decided to stop, for whatever reason, at any time. Standing by the edge of the lake, shivering in her bra and knickers, covered with goose-pimples, exhausted and bruised from the assault course, Edwina seriously considered taking the easy option and putting her clothes back on and getting on the Bedford truck. But if she did she'd be back to that bloody commcen, so with that thought in her mind she steeled herself to plunge into the icy water. This was her one chance to do something entirely on a par with the men, and which didn't involve running an office. Whatever she was being selected for was going to be infinitely preferable to her outlook if she remained a crap-hat. She'd looked at the icy water lapping at her feet, then, sucking in a lungful of air, had hurled herself into the lake.

But the cold of the lake was nothing to the creeping, aching, paralysing chill of lying out in one set of damp clothes for this length of time. The discomfort was unbelievable, but she wasn't going to jack it in now. Surely they must be getting near to the end of the selection process? She jumped suddenly as the shrill blast of a whistle split the silent night air.

'Now what?' she whispered to 88. He just shrugged. Then they both heard a voice blaring through a megaphone informing them that the exercise was over and they were all to make their way back to the transport.

'Another trick?' said Edwina. Another shrug. They waited for a good minute, but there was no sign of any of the other candidates making an appearance. The megaphone blared again, repeating the message, and this time a few groups could be seen emerging from the undergrowth.

'Come on,' said 88. 'This is for real.' Thankfully Edwina realised that he was right and tried to get to her feet, but she was so numb she couldn't stand up. Even so, the relief of being able to sit upright and massage her calves and ankles was wonderful. After a couple of minutes she was able to hobble about. While Edwina got her circulation going, her partner obligingly collected up the few bits of kit they'd been equipped with, then the pair of them wearily made their way to the four-ton trucks which would transport them back to their barracks. Never in her life had Edwina felt so glad to see a couple of Army lorries.

The drive back to base took only twenty minutes, but all those on board – the three or four dozen remaining candidates from an initial field of over one hundred – were sound asleep as they drew to a halt.

There were a few muted groans of protest as the tailgate crashed down, waking them all up with a start, but they quickly descended from the vehicle and formed up in two ranks alongside it. One of the instructors called out a list of numbers. Edwina's and 88's weren't amongst them, and they were left standing by the truck with about twenty others.

'What's this about?' Edwina whispered.

'I think they're the lot who've passed,' said 88 tonelessly. Edwina, exhausted, cold and miserable, felt completely dejected. All this for nothing. Back to the commcen. Oh, bugger. She sagged slightly and her head dropped. She wasn't going to let anyone see that she had to blink back a tear.

'Squad!' yelled a voice. Instinctively the group braced their shoulders ready for the next word of command. 'Squad, 'shun!' Despite their tiredness their feet crashed to attention as one. 'Move to the left in twos, left turn. By the left, quick march.' And off they moved to the light and warmth of the main lecture hall. They filed in and sat down on the plush-covered seats, Edwina and 88 staying together for mutual support, both fearing the worst. Within a minute the chief instructor appeared and stood, relaxed, next to the lectern.

'Well done,' he said. 'You've passed.' For the first time in a fort-night everyone was smiling and laughing. Edwina and 88 hugged each other, both as delighted with the other's success as with their own. They were told that they could not go on leave until after Christmas, that they were not to return to their old units – their kit would be packed up for them and forwarded to them, if and when they passed the next phase.

'Next phase?' whispered Edwina in horror to 88.

As if her comment had been heard, the chief instructor explained further.

'You will now carry out another month of training. How you fare on that will determine whether or not you progress any further. It isn't so much selection from here on as checking that you really have the right aptitude for the job.'

Edwina felt gloomy again, still not knowing if she'd escaped the tedium of her job forever, or whether she'd be back in the commcen again in only a few weeks.

The chief instructor continued. 'You will be given joining instruc-tions on how to reach our training camp. Please don't divulge your whereabouts to anyone. If you have friends or relations who may need to contact you in an emergency you can give them this phone number. If anyone asks where you are going to be, tell them you're adventurous training.' They were dismissed to grab a few hours' sleep before breakfast and then they were away on their well-deserved leave.

Edwina longed to tell Amanda and Lizzie, but most of all she wanted to share her success with Ulysses and tell him of the direction in which her Army career was now going. However, they'd all been given strict instructions about not revealing that they were being trained to be part of 14 Company, a team of surveillance experts in Northern Ireland. This was for their own safety, they were told. Their lives, and the lives of others, could be endangered if a member of a terrorist organisation got hold of any of their personal details. It might have sounded rather cloak and dagger had they not all been aware of the sort of things that had happened to members of the security forces who had fallen into the wrong hands. Since they were about to be trained, literally, to rub shoulders with these dangerous men and infiltrate their territory, no one doubted the seriousness of the warning. Edwina decided that for the time being she'd just have to lose contact with her friends. It wasn't a decision she enjoyed taking, but from the little she knew about the organisation she was now joining, losing track of a couple of friends was going to be the least of her worries. Frankly, if the training was only half as tough as the selection, she was going to be too tired to worry about writing letters or having some sort of social life. She had a goal now and she was going to focus all her attention on it.

Edwina spent Christmas with her mother. It wasn't her idea of a great time, but if she was honest with herself, she was too tired for the first few days of her leave to care where she was. She was also able to relax in other ways, as neither her mother nor any of her mother's friends and relations understood the first thing about the Army, neither were they especially interested. So when Edwina explained her exhaustion with a tale of too much work and too much socialising, no one batted an eyelid. Well, since when had Edwina been known to be sensible on that score? Nor did anyone want to know why she couldn't be contacted directly until further notice. So Edwina spent ten days contentedly eating, sleeping and going out for the occasional run – just so she didn't let her fitness slip – utterly relaxed and blissfully happy that she was about to do something that was bound to prove demanding, challenging and, above all, exciting. She could hardly wait to continue her training.

Once, on New Year's Eve, she had tried to phone Ulysses to wish him well for the coming year, only to be told yet again that he was away but she could leave a message. She wrote him a long letter instead, which was difficult because she couldn't mention any of her recent exploits. She wondered how they could possibly sustain their relationship when, for the foreseeable future, either one or both of them would be incommunicado.

Edwina arrived at the training camp on the specified train and climbed on the waiting minibus. It seemed a long journey to the barracks, and although it was getting late and she was tired, she was so keyed up she didn't think of dozing. She was shown to her accommodation, a comfortable block with a series of four-man rooms. Edwina noticed that she was, so far, the only occupant in hers. She hoped she wasn't the only woman on the course; she didn't fancy that at all. Apart from making it extremely difficult for her to keep a low profile, it would be miserable to have no one with whom to talk about the course in privacy, away from the staff and the others. But by nine o'clock that night it became apparent that no other women were going to be on the phase, so Edwina resigned herself to being the odd one out for the next four weeks. It made her sympathise with Lizzie's lot in Aldershot.

To her surprise, she discovered that the fact that she was a woman played no part in how the other members of the course – or the staff, for that matter – treated her. To begin with, the men knew that she'd survived exactly the same selection process as they had, and it meant that no one thought for a moment that she was there as the obligatory woman – just to make it all politically correct. It was also explained to them that the skills they would now be taught to equip them for their future role – and still none of them was sure exactly what that was – had nothing to do with brute strength and stamina but everything to do with a propensity to learn, courage and a quick brain.

First off they covered everything to do with high-speed driving techniques. They learned how to drive like rally competitors, to read the road ahead, to handle a car on a skid-pan and to keep control at high speeds on ordinary country roads with other road users around. After a fortnight their driving skills were tested; those who failed disappeared from the course. Edwina and 88, whom she had learned was called Nat, both passed.

Then they had to learn about photography. They were taught about apertures, film speeds and shutter speeds. They learned about developing and enlarging, about lenses and motor drives, about infra-red photography and aerial photography. And just as with the driving phase they were tested at the end.

After each day's training they had to turn out for an arduous session of PT, followed by supper and then more lectures. These would be on vehicle recognition, first aid, signals procedure or Soviet small arms. Time to revise for the photography test was short, but after the selection process Edwina knew she could survive, and function efficiently, on only a few hours' sleep each night, so she swotted instead of sleeping for the few days before the final test.

'Well done, Edwina,' said the chief instructor. 'I'm pleased with both your results so far. How are you finding the course?'

'It's fascinating, sir.'

'Well, keep up the good work. Be sure not to let your standards slip. We make no concessions on this course. If at any stage you don't make the grade we will have to let you go, but we need women desperately and it would be a bonus to the unit if you do pass.'

Edwina left the interview on a cloud. Never had she felt so valued in her life, although she didn't know why women were so important to 14 Company.

She discovered why on the next phase of the course, when they were taught surveillance skills.

'It's quite simple,' said their instructor. 'A man and a woman, mooching along a road hand in hand, whispering sweet nothings in each other's ears, look completely innocent. How could they have anything more on their minds than each other? Even in a rough area of Belfast, no one is going to give them a second glance. But two men walking along the same road are far more likely to be challenged – the IRA is paranoid about the SAS and MI5.'

After two weeks of learning surveillance techniques Edwina's head was swimming. There was just so much information that they had had to learn by rote: the code word for every main street they used, the number given to every junction, and a mound of other codes to cover the variety of targets, vehicles and locations they would be watching. The remaining members of the course were expected to know all of these perfectly, by heart. No wonder so

132

many people fail, she thought, as she struggled to assimilate everything.

At least at the end of this phase she was getting some leave. The trouble was, apart from her mum's, she didn't really have anywhere to go. As a long shot she tried ringing Stirling Lines again, but it didn't come as any surprise to hear that Ulysses was still away.

Aldershot, May 1989

It was becoming increasingly clear to Lizzie that Richard wanted her to be more than just an assistant in the office. Twice he'd asked her to accompany him to some function or other on the pretext that he hadn't had time to find anyone else. Twice Lizzie had refused his offer and then spent a dull evening alone in her room, wondering if she'd made the right decision. They seemed to have so much in common: both of them had a father serving in the Army; both of them were the product of well-known boarding schools; both of them were used to a nomadic lifestyle. And she had to admit that he was an extremely, good-looking man. Unlike most very pale blonds he had dark eyelashes and eyebrows, and his eyes, she had noticed, were a devastating shade of blue – not that it mattered a jot what he looked like, she told herself, as she didn't fancy him. Her experience with Simon had taught her a lesson about office romances, and her head was adamant that she wasn't going to make the same mistake again, although her heart sometimes wished she wasn't being quite so sensible.

But it worried her that, yet again, she was spending more time than she should thinking about her boss. She longed to talk to someone and get some advice, even if it was only 'You'll regret it.' But Edwina was away, goodness only knew where, and it wouldn't be fair to burden Amanda with her problems. Amanda still sounded unhappy, although she wouldn't say why, and it wasn't right to expect her to help with something as trivial as whether or not Lizzie ought to go out with Richard.

Lizzie sometimes felt very lonely in the officers' mess. Many young women would have regarded her situation as heaven on earth; to be surrounded by a dozen or so eligible and well-heeled young men with no competition in sight. But the reality wasn't like that.

Lizzie longed for some female company. It was ironic, she thought. There was Amanda with nothing but women for company and not a man to be had for love or money, while all Lizzie wanted was one girlfriend. As far as postings were concerned, the availability of female company seemed to vary from feast to famine. How she longed to have another female living in the mess with her – someone to gossip with, or to give an opinion about a new hairdo, or to borrow a pair of tights off, or to sympathise with her over period pains. She wasn't used to this complete dearth of women in her life and she wasn't sure she liked it particularly. It was one thing spending one's days at boarding school gossiping about boyfriends and love, but it was another thing entirely to actually experience it. Her brief fling with Simon had taught her that much at least. Some girls, she supposed, would talk to their mothers, but she'd spent too long at boarding school to be particularly close to hers. And her mother had never been much good at talking to her about intimate stuff. Lizzie remembered that her idea of teaching her daughter about adolescence, periods and sex had been to hand her a booklet and tell her to go away and read it. Hardly the best introduction to puberty and its concomitant problems.

Lizzie dragged a comb through her short, neat hair, blotted her lipstick and made sure that she had everything she needed before setting out for the office, ready to start another week. She had made herself up carefully and put a dab of Dioressence behind each ear. She was pleased with her appearance but she didn't stop to think why it should matter how she looked. As always, she was first into the office, neither the CO nor Richard putting in an appearance until nearer nine o'clock. Lizzie liked the thirty minutes she had to herself. It gave her a chance to sort out the morning post, opened by the duty clerk and left on her desk, and to read through the reports from the previous day's duty personnel. If anything dramatic had happened during the night, a road accident or a fight in the NAAFI being the most common, she had a chance to find out as many facts as possible and to be certain exactly what action had been taken to solve the problem before the CO started asking difficult questions. He wasn't the sort of man to accept 'I don't know' as an excuse.

Lizzie flicked through the post and was quite glad to see that there was nothing out of the ordinary, then she scanned the duty reports. A couple of gunners had been locked up for drunkenness on Saturday night – it would have been a bigger surprise if a couple hadn't – but beyond that the weekend had been uneventful. Having established that she didn't have to field any fast balls, Lizzie wandered into the little pantry to make herself a cup of coffee. As she spooned the granules of instant into her mug she realised that she'd been with the regiment for exactly a year. She'd certainly grown up in that time, she thought, as she remembered the day when Richard had made her spill coffee down her skirt and she'd fled in tears to the mess. She'd just poured some milk into her drink when she heard the phone in her office ring. Picking up her coffee she went to answer it.

'Assistant adjutant, good morning.'

'Hi, Lizzie. It's Amanda here.'

'Hi! I was thinking about you only this morning,' said Lizzie. 'How's life treating you?'

'Curate's egg. You know, good in parts.'

'So you're feeling more cheerful?'

'It's difficult to stay down in the dumps for long with the bunch living here. It's a very lively crowd so there is always something fun going on.'

'I'm glad for you.'

'Anyway, hot news, I'm being posted.'

'Great, somewhere nice?'

'I think so. I'm going to an armoured workshop in Germany – just a stopgap. The bloke who's supposed to be going out there broke his leg very badly in a climbing accident and won't be able to join them for about six months.'

'Well, it'll certainly be different from Guildford. But forgive me for asking, what the hell do you know about the REME?'

'I know it stands for "Reck Everything Mechanical Everytime".'

'Only if you want to personally accommodate the CO's set of socket spanners.'

Amanda laughed in agreement. 'Well, perhaps I'll keep that piece of intelligence to myself. As for the technical stuff, I don't suppose I'll have to deal with much of that in the RHQ. How much do you know about gunnery?'

'Point taken. So when do you go?'

'End of the month.'

'Not long then.'

'I think I'm ready to move on, although I would have preferred to stay in the country.'

'Well, all I can say is lucky you. I'd give my back teeth for somewhere more exotic than Aldershot. But I must dash now. The boss will arrive shortly and I haven't read the signals traffic for the weekend. I'll give you a ring this evening and we can chat then.' Lizzie put down the phone, made a note in her diary to send Amanda a good-luck card just before she left, and wondered where she herself would be going next. She knew it would be a while before she heard anything, but what with Edwina and now Amanda off to do a new job, she couldn't help thinking about her own future.

When Richard came into the office Lizzie was still distracted by thoughts of her next posting.

'How much attention will my postings branch pay to where I'd like to go?' she asked him later that morning.

'Probably not a great deal. Why do you ask?'

'Oh, itchy feet, I suppose. I'm halfway through my tour here, two of my friends have been posted early, and I can't help wondering what's in store for me. I really want to go overseas.'

Richard was silent for a moment. 'Oh, I hadn't thought that you might be off in the near future. I though you were here for a two-year tour.'

'Officially, yes. But being short-toured isn't that uncommon.'

'Do you want to go?' He sounded rather sad as he posed the question.

'I don't know. A new job seems quite an exciting prospect, but I've got no special wish to get away from here. Why, do you want me to stay?'

Richard looked surprised. 'Yes, no, I mean, it'll be a pain to train up a new assistant, and she's bound not to be as efficient as you are. Besides, we might get another Jilly.'

'Are you ever going to tell me why you thought she was so dreadful?'

'If you really want to know, I didn't think much of her morals. If even only half the rumours are to be believed, she screwed everyone in the officers' mess from the CO to the cook.'

'You're joking!'

'About the cook – possibly.'

'Heavens.' Lizzie was genuinely shocked.

'I could go on.' Lizzie waited, agog, for further revelations, and Richard obliged. 'She was everything I least admire about a woman. For a start, she always had to be one of the boys: propping up the bar drinking until the early hours, wanting to be part of the regimental hockey team, always loud, always brash. She thought it was OK to tell bawdy jokes and shock the wives, and she regularly got drunk. In short, she was a frightful woman,' he finished.

'Oh,' was all Lizzie could say after the outburst.

'But you're different. Where Jilly was a bitch of Olympic standard, noisy and vulgar, you are quiet, kind and self-effacing.' Lizzie went brick red with embarrassment at this unexpected praise. 'Oh, goodness, now I've upset you,' said Richard, seeing her discomfort.

Lizzie shook her head and shrugged. She didn't know what to say. She'd always thought of herself as rather a wimp and much too shy to boot. She certainly had never thought of those character traits as particularly laudable.

'But it's true, for heaven's sake,' continued Richard. 'You've never even said anything nasty about Simon, and I know he could be a bastard sometimes.'

Lizzie looked up quickly, wondering if Richard was fishing for information. From the kindly and understanding smile on his face, she didn't think he was. 'Well . . . There's not much to say, really. He wasn't a bad boss to work for and he taught me how to do this job properly.'

'There you are, my point exactly – loyal to the end. I know for a fact that it was mainly the chief clerk who taught you.' He grinned at Lizzie. 'See, my spies are everywhere,' he said jokingly. 'Anyway, back to the gritty subject of your future posting. Against my own personal interests, would you like either the CO or myself to have a word with your postings branch? We won't mention that it's you who's curious; we'll make it sound as though the inquiry is coming from us. They're usually more honest with a parent unit than an individual.'

Lizzie's eyes lit up. 'Would you? Would you be able to feed in that I'd like to go to Germany or –' she laughed at the enormity of the idea '– Cyprus?'

'You don't want much, do you? Well, I'll see what we can do. But one thing . . .'

'Yes.'

'It'll cost you dinner with me.'

'That's hardly fair,' said Lizzie. She was so buoyed up by the idea that her preferences for a posting might get proper representation that she barely gave a thought to the invitation. Then she suddenly realised how ungrateful she must have sounded and added, to make it less rude, 'It should be me standing you dinner under the circumstances.'

'We can quibble over the bill at the restaurant.'

'OK. Done.' She wasn't really thinking about the implications of the deal she'd just struck. She was far too preoccupied with thoughts of her future career and travel prospects to notice how elated Richard looked at her agreement to the date.

'Anywhere you fancy going in particular?' he said casually.

Lizzie suggested a pub she'd heard about in a little village between Aldershot and Farnham. 'I don't know how good it is – the recommendation is hearsay.'

Which was how it all began. Once Lizzie had allowed herself to go out with Richard, she discovered that he wasn't the least bit like Simon. Up until then she'd been so busy not getting too friendly she hadn't seen anything more than the officer; she certainly hadn't tried to discover the real person underneath the uniform.

By the time Richard had got a sensible answer from PB16, Lizzie's postings branch, only a week later, their relationship had moved from friendship to lovers. Their first date had finished back at Richard's house. She had made him coffee and he had made her laugh. Nothing had happened that night; they had kissed a chaste goodbye on the doorstep and both had gone to their respective beds wishing that it had been more. Nothing had been said in the office the next day beyond a discussion of the merits of the restaurant, but they had met again that evening for a drink in another country pub in the area. Very quickly their relationship progressed to the stage when Richard hesitantly asked Lizzie if she'd like to stay the weekend at his house.

'It's absurd you toing and froing between here and the mess. No one will be any the wiser; no one from the regiment lives anywhere near me.'

'I don't know. I'm worried about gossip round the regiment.'

'No one will know, honest.' They were sitting in a corner of a tiny country pub near Fleet, one frequented by local villagers and only rarely by any of the large and nomadic Army population.

'I don't know,' said Lizzie. She laughed self-consciously. 'I'm not really that sort of girl.' She knew how prudish she sounded in this day and age, and was embarrassed by it.

'I never thought for a moment you were,' replied Richard. 'I just thought we'd both be able to have a drink and relax. Besides which, my house is a sight cosier than the mess. I'm offering you *a* bed for the night. I have three and I really don't mind which one you choose to sleep in.'

Lizzie looked uncertain. She wasn't sure if he was being serious or not. To give herself time to think she fiddled with the stem of her wine glass. Richard reached across the battered little table and stroked her hand. Lizzie looked at their fingers and then at his face.

'It's not that I . . .' she stopped. Whatever she said about Simon would make her sound spiteful and mean, but if she didn't explain, Richard might not hang around to find out where their relationship was going. Richard smiled encouragingly. Lizzie decided he had a right to know what her problem was.

'I made a fool of myself over Simon. I got the wrong idea about him. I was terrified that everyone in the regiment would get to hear about it.' She spoke jerkily, pausing for a second or two between each sentence. 'I thought I meant more to him than just a night's entertainment.' Her voice was hard and she looked down at her glass again. 'With hindsight, I can see I was stupid, and I can't face being in that particular situation a second time – of working with a man who thinks I'm a little fool. How do I know if I'm being sensible this time?' She lifted her troubled eyes to look at him.

He smiled at her gently. 'It could be that we're both being stupid,' he said slowly. 'Or perhaps we're both being sensible. I'm not sure which it is either, but I honestly think that there's only one way to find out.' Lizzie lowered her eyes and looked at their intertwined fingers. Richard continued. 'I think you had a bad time with Simon because his wife had just put him through the mill. You got him on the rebound when he wasn't really thinking about anyone but himself.' Lizzie nodded. She knew that he certainly hadn't been thinking about her.

'And you?' she asked.

'What about me?'

Lizzie reminded him of what he had said at Christmas about not having a girlfriend to help with his dinner party.

'Oh, that.' Richard shrugged. 'Well, for a start that was all over ages ago, and secondly there wasn't much to it beyond physical attraction.'

'And there's more than that now?'

'Of course there is, you goose. I'm sorry, I didn't mean to sound cross like that.' He continued more gently. 'I think so, yes. Don't you?'

'Yes.' It was barely a whisper.

They announced their engagement in June.

Northern Germany, September 1989

The talk in the mess was of the happenings behind the Iron Curtain, and opinions were divided as to the implications. How many eastern-bloc countries ousting their communist governments would it take before Soviet troops jackbooted their way into crowds of disillusioned demonstrators and fired on them in a repeat of events in Tiananmen Square just a couple of months previously? If that happened, how would the West respond? Could they stand by and watch democracy and freedom being trampled underfoot, or would NATO troops be mobilised to wade in and help the revolutionaries? Europe was holding its breath, uncertain whether to be cheering or praying.

For some members of NATO forces in Germany the build-up for the annual autumn exercises seemed to have a subtext. Were they really just going on exercise, or were they deploying in case events in eastern Europe took a sinister turn? The younger officers, all of whom had missed out on the Falklands War, were itching for some action and were reluctant to see the possibility that, if this was more than just another series of war games, Europe might be a nuclear desert before Christmas. Going on exercise was good fun, but it was still like taking part in a dress rehearsal; what they were waiting for was the real performance.

In the REME officers' mess half a dozen junior officers were gathered in the bar waiting for dinner to be announced. A couple of them sprawled in the deeply comfortable leather armchairs while Amanda and the others sat on stools by the bar. The mess steward polished glasses and emptied ashtrays and tried not to look too interested in the conversation.

'Of course nothing is going to happen,' said Amanda pragmatically, leaning against the bar and sipping her gin.

'You don't know that,' said a young REME captain called Graham Long, from the depths of one of the armchairs. He was a likeable young man who reminded Amanda of a Labrador – blond, amiable and willing to please, but large and solid and probably able to put up a good fight if cornered. 'The destabilisation of the Warsaw Pact,' he continued, 'is more likely than anything else to make them look for some sort of focus, something which will bring all good communists together in a feeling of unity – a war. There are a lot of hard-liners who won't stand by and admit that the great communist experiment is over. A war against the evil capitalists might be just what they want. For heaven's sake, look what the Falklands War did for Maggie and her party.'

Amanda snorted disbelievingly. 'But that was different. And anyway, we were operating from a position of considerable moral strength, to say nothing of the fact that she might have been unpopular at home but at least she'd been voted into power. It would be suicide for the Red Army to go against the will of the people now, and they know that.'

Graham shrugged. 'Not necessarily. Kill enough of the ringleaders, overthrow Gorbachev and train guns on the protesters and things will soon quieten down. NATO couldn't protect all the states which seem to want their independence, and would we really risk nuclear war for a dispute which has nothing to do with the freedom of the West?'

The mess waiter announced that dinner was served. Graham took a swig of beer, which emptied his glass. 'The other half?' he offered, 'Or are you going into dinner?'

'I'm going in to eat. I've got to go back into the office after dinner. I've got a mountain of paperwork to deal with.' Amanda tried not to look too glum at the possibility of a late night working alone in RHQ. She downed the rest of her drink in a swift gulp and slid off the high stool.

'You certainly seem to have a lot on your plate,' said Graham. It was common knowledge how hard the CO worked Amanda. Not that this was unusual. The job of adjutant was always one of the toughest in any unit, but in this case the commanding officer was a sailing freak who spent as much time as possible pursuing his hobby and delegating everything to his second-in-command and Amanda.

The others took their cue from Amanda and finished their drinks and accompanied her into the dining room. Two women, civilian teachers at the local Forces primary school and never ones to indulge in a pre-dinner drink, were already sitting there, tucking into soup and rolls. Amanda greeted them, picked up the menu and contemplated the choice on offer that evening. The soup smelled good but she was aware that her uniform had been getting increasingly tight recently, so she decided against helping herself to some and chose just a salad for a main course instead. She gave her order to the mess waiter and sat opposite the two teachers.

'I'm going back to the UK next weekend. Can I give either of you two a lift?' Neither of the two women, Debby and Gemma, had a car and they were often glad of a lift to the ferry.

'When are you leaving?' asked Debby.

'Straight after work on Friday and back on Sunday afternoon.'

'Not long then,' said Gemma.

'I've got to go to a wedding.'

'That's nice.'

'I hope so. It seems a bit of a rush job to me, but . . .' She didn't continue. It wasn't her business, and if Lizzie was happy to jump into the marriage bed it wasn't up to her to pass comment or judgement. Amanda had seen other dedicated career women marry and then lose the impetus of their prospects as they juggled husband, home and job, to say nothing of having to accept postings that fitted in with their husband's, because invariably the Army saw his career as more important than hers. She was glad that this would never be a factor she would have to take into consideration. She wished Lizzie well but she had little doubt that before long children would come along, and that would be the end of that as far as Lizzie's military ambitions were concerned; she was far too unselfish to even consider handing over the care of her kids to a nanny in order to pursue her own ambitions.

But despite her misgivings about Lizzie's impending, and possibly impetuous, wedding, Amanda was looking forward to it; it was bound to be a jolly occasion, and the chances were she'd get to see a whole host of people she knew. And if she was completely honest, it was good to have a proper excuse for the long drive to the coast and then England and Bella – she didn't like to go too often because the other officers had started noticing it. Speculation was rife as to why she wanted to go back so often, although so far all the theories involved her having a red-hot affair with a married man, thus explaining why she never mentioned him and he never visited her.

She didn't do anything to counter this rumour – it was safer than the truth. However, she missed Bella so much that it was worth the continued speculation, and it was easier for her to travel to England than the other way about; Bella was terrified of driving on the Continent.

'I may take you up on the offer,' said Gemma. 'What about you, Debs?'

'I'll let you know, if that's OK.'

'Sure, no problem.' Amanda was ambivalent. It would be nice to have the company on the long, tedious drive through the flat, dreary industrial heartland of Germany to the coast, but if they didn't come it certainly made for less hassle on the journey back. Neither woman had any idea about timekeeping, and she didn't want to be hanging round the ferry terminal waiting for them to turn up. On balance it was difficult to choose between the pros and the cons.

But Amanda wasn't really thinking about either the journey or Lizzie's wedding, which was planned for three o'clock in Aldershot Garrison Church. What was occupying the majority of her thoughts was her rendezvous with Bella at a small hotel in Windsor on the Saturday. They would have that evening and most of Sunday together, and Amanda could hardly wait.

After dinner she walked from the mess, across the barracks, to the RHQ, a single-storey brick building, featureless and dreary like the rest of the buildings which made up the armoured workshop. The barracks looked more like a minor industrial estate than an Army base, she thought, looking around at the huge hangars where tanks and all manner of other military vehicles were repaired. She let herself into the office block using her key and walked down the brightly lit corridor to the duty clerk's bunk.

'It's only me,' she called, knowing that her voice would be instantly recognisable. The clerk, Corporal Green, put his head out of the box room that contained a narrow bed, a TV and a phone, and acknowledged her. She knew that it appealed to the soldiers' sense of justice that if they had to spend all night on duty in the RHQ then at least one of the officers was in the same boat and wasn't up in the mess swigging gin. One of the duty staff had once even said as much to her face.

'OK, ma'am,' he said. 'I've a couple of signals here, they're not urgent. I was going to leave them until the morning but seeing as you're here now, you might as well take a look.' He handed over the flimsy sheets of paper and Amanda glanced at them, recognising instantly that they were nothing to do with her. One was for stores section about vehicle spares, and the other, surprise, surprise, was about sailing courses during the autumn. She took a pencil, wrote on each the name of the person who should deal with their contents and handed them back without a word. Damn, still nothing about the arrival of the real adjutant. She'd asked to be posted to a headquarters somewhere, preferably in the UK, and was getting more and more impatient as the days passed and her promised replacement didn't materialise. It wasn't that she was so anxious to get away from this unit; after the predictability of the training routine at Guildford, this was quite the reverse. She never knew what was going to be thrown at her from one day to the next, and although some of the things she had to deal with were undeniably dreary, it was fascinating being privy to all the goings on in the workshop. Nothing happened that she didn't know about, from a soldier's wife having a baby to the latest update of the unit's deployment plans in the event of war.

She went back to her office and gazed undaunted at the mound of papers and files on her desk. She knew most of this was routine stuff and wouldn't tax her too much, but this had been a busy week, compounded by the CO's absence yet again, and if she wanted to get away to Lizzie's wedding she had to clear as much as possible ahead of time. There was a bonus, of course; if she was over here in RHQ she was safe from advances from those of the more amorous single officers who believed that with enough persuasion she might transfer her affections to them.

Amanda settled behind her desk and took the top file, entitled 'War Establishment', off the pile. She sometimes wondered if it was right that, with her limited experience – she'd only been commissioned for a little over a year and wasn't even a specialist REME officer – she was expected to take quite so much responsibility, but the feeling of power that she sometimes felt was quite heady. And she knew that if she didn't make a complete mess of things it would look good for her future career. She was so engrossed she didn't hear the front door to RHQ open. It was only when a shadow fell on her desk that she looked up, half expecting to see the duty clerk bringing her a welcome mug of coffee, which some of the more obliging clerks did when she worked late. She was startled to see the commanding officer. She stood up behind her desk, trying to look pleased, but inside she was wondering if he had come to give her another task to be completed in an impossibly short time, something which he occasionally did.

'Ah, good. Glad you're here. I was hoping to catch you,' breezed Lieutenant Colonel Grieve. He looked tanned and weatherbeaten, noted Amanda. Not surprising considering the amount of time he spent out of the office, she thought. No chance he'd comment on how late she was working – he'd told her when she'd arrived that she would find she'd have to work outside office hours, although he never seemed to. The privilege of rank, thought Amanda.

'Did you enjoy your sailing trip, sir?' she asked, trying to sound interested. She wasn't particularly, and was more concerned about getting to the bottom of her in-tray than about hearing his seafaring tales.

'It was very satisfactory, thank you. That's partly the reason I've called in this evening. They said at the mess you were here. I met someone up at the sailing centre at Kiel who I thought you would want to know about.'

'Oh yes, sir. Who would that be?'

'Major Hanrahan.' Amanda didn't have to be told the significance of that name. Major Hanrahan was in charge of posting junior REME officers, and it was he who was to send them a signal as soon as the real adjutant for the workshop was fit to take up the post. Amanda felt her heart leap. Yes! The posting, at long last.

'I wrote to your postings officer a while back and told her what an excellent job you've been doing. You'll be pleased to know she passed the praise on.'

'Thank you, sir,' murmured Amanda, although inwardly she was wishing that he would just get to the point.

'And while we were talking about you I told him that you seem to be very popular in the mess and how well you've fitted in here despite not having a proper REME background.' Amanda didn't say anything, pleased at having such a glowing report. It could only help her in her ambition for a proper staff job. She didn't want to delay the news, for even a second, by interrupting him. 'So we've decided that in light of that, and in all our best interests, you should stay in the job.'

'What?' Amanda couldn't help herself. Her voice was shrill with shock.

'I knew you'd be pleased,' said Colonel Grieve, mistaking her tone of voice. 'I'm sure everyone else here will be as delighted with the news as you are.'

Amanda, feeling completely unsure of the situation for the first time in a number of years, sat down slowly behind her desk. She didn't know how it had come about that she found herself in this predicament, and she certainly didn't know whom she should approach to try and rectify this ghastly situation. As a cadet they'd been taught to go to the adjutant or the commanding officer in the first instance. Well . . . big deal. That was both of her options out of the window. Now what? she thought.

'Right, well, I can see you're busy, so I'll let you get on.' And he was out of the door before Amanda had a chance to say anything else.

Amanda put her elbows on her desk and rested her chin on her clenched hands. Another eighteen months away from Bella, another eighteen months of finding excuses to get to England. Damn. She stared blankly at her desktop, feeling utterly bereft and alone. She longed to tell Bella, but with no solution to offer, what good would it do for them both to be miserable? She sighed deeply and looked at the phone. Should she ring Bella's mess and leave a message for her? No, it would be better to tell her to her face at the weekend. Besides, there was just the slimmest of chances that if she phoned her own postings branch it might be possible to get the decision reversed. Best to see what she could do first before she confronted Bella with the bad news.

Aldershot, September 1989

The Wedding March swelled to an impressive climax and despite herself Amanda could feel her eyes pricking with tears as she watched Richard and Lizzie walk down the aisle of the Garrison Church together. She knew it was a Pavlovian reaction; she was the same when she sang 'Silent Night' at a carol service, or heard the Last Post on Remembrance Sunday or went to any event where the atmosphere became soggy with emotion. She watched her friend progress towards her and there was no doubting that Lizzie looked as radiant and beautiful as any bride had ever done. And Richard, resplendent in his blues and gold cross-belt, was the epitome of a glamorous Army officer. Even Amanda could see why Lizzie must have been attracted to him in the first place; he really was an incredibly good-looking young man. Despite her opinion that Lizzie was making a mistake by getting married so young – good God above, she was only just twenty! – Amanda had to admit that this looked like a perfect match. From where she sat she could see Richard's parents; judging by his black beret and his insignia he was a colonel in the Royal Tank Regiment, and his wife could be a clone of Lizzie's own mother. Amanda felt that it was a dead cert that the two sets of parents would hit it off, which could only be a bonus for any couple embarking on married life.

She felt a little twinge of envy that Lizzie was able to make such a public and beautiful declaration of her love for Richard, whereas she was destined to a life of clandestine meetings and subterfuge with her own lover. She chided herself about this. It wasn't Lizzie's fault that her friend's life would always have a large portion that would have to be kept secret from even her closest friends, whereas Lizzie's happiness was being publicly celebrated and her choice of partner had everyone's blessing. Behind Lizzie trailed a gaggle of small girls, dressed in pretty yellow gingham frocks, all concentrating hard on not treading on the bride's train. Amanda turned to watch the little procession move towards the front door of the rather bleak red-brick Victorian church, and then out to the waiting honour guard with their raised swords.

Trust Lizzie to want the full nine yards when it came to her wedding, thought Amanda, not unkindly. Then it crossed her mind that this sort of military pomp and circumstance was far more likely to be the brainchild of Lizzie's mother. Whatever, it was a splendid wedding, supported by a tremendous turn-out of friends and relations; the Garrison Church was packed. It was a shame Edwina hadn't been able to make it. She'd sent a message from wherever she was these days saying that she'd get away if humanly possible but she didn't hold out much hope. Amanda had been angry when Lizzie had told her; she felt that Edwina wasn't planning on trying. Edwina could be a little cavalier about this sort of thing – she probably didn't realise how much it would have meant to Lizzie that she should be there. However, Lizzie hinted, not for the first time, that Edwina was doing something pretty extraordinary and it was best not to ask questions, and that she knew that if Edwina was able to make it she would. Amanda had to accept that if Lizzie understood – and whose wedding was it when all was said and done? – then it wasn't for her to cast aspersions on their mutual friend's actions. Lizzie always understood, always accepted other people's excuses at face value, always believed the best about her friends. Amanda, who was rather more cynical, was inclined to wonder if Edwina wasn't taking advantage of Lizzie's lovely nature because it was a long way to come for the day. Amanda wasn't best pleased anyway with Edwina these days – she hadn't had a letter from her for ages. OK, she might be busy, but who wasn't? I find the time to put pen to paper, she thought crossly, and sniffed in mild irritation.

Amanda was brought back from her rather uncharitable thoughts by a movement of people at the front of the church as Lizzie and Richard's parents prepared to follow their offspring out into the warm autumn sunshine. Amanda picked up her bag, gloves and service sheet and waited for her turn to edge into the human stream and move down the aisle too. As she emerged from the church, a sea of women in bright dresses and hats and men in uniforms or dapper morning dress surrounded her. It was a superb spectacle and the photographer was certainly earning his money as he organised the guests into some semblance of order and took reel after reel of pictures. It was a shame that the backdrop of Aldershot Garrison Church, though no doubt quite suitable for an Army wedding, really wasn't an architectural gem. In fact it was quite hideous, truth be told, having been built when red brick was the height of fashion and architecture was plumbing the depths of ugliness.

The reception was back in the regimental mess, with the wedding breakfast provided by the Army Catering Corps. This sort of spread was what the Army chefs excelled at. It made a gratifying change for them to supply food to people who were genuinely appreciative, squaddies being notoriously difficult to please. And as for being allowed to show off the full gamut of their abilities with a three-tier wedding cake – well, they thought they'd died and gone to heaven, Lizzie had confided to Amanda in a telephone conversation a week or so earlier.

The reception was a huge success. The mess staff felt quite proprietorial over both Captain Airdrie-Stow and Miss Armstrong – although they'd have to remember to call her Mrs Airdrie-Stow now – and went out of their way to ensure that everything ran smoothly. At first Lizzie's mother had not been pleased that Lizzie was getting married from her own mess, not her father's at Osnabruck, but eventually she'd agreed that it would be much easier for all the guests to travel to Aldershot rather than out to Germany. Lizzie had known that her mother had looked forward to showing off her son-in-law to her own circle of friends, but there were plenty of relations present now to congratulate her on her daughter's match. Besides which, there was the pay-off that she was now getting the kudos of being the bride's mother without having the responsibility of rushing around making sure everything was running properly. It soon became obvious to all that she was actually able to enjoy herself and was doing so in no small measure. Amanda watched Mrs Airdrie-Stow and Mrs Armstrong begin a tentative conversation and then noticed, not five minutes later, that the pair of them were carrying on as if they had been bosom pals for years. Amanda had heard about the sisterhood of long-standing Army wives – how they could form friendships with each other in milliseconds – and was fascinated to see that the rumour was not without foundation. Obviously the shared experiences of frequent moves and life overseas produced a common bond that was as strong between Forces wives as it was between fellow soldiers.

Amanda saw only a little of Lizzie during the reception, although there were a number of other people there that she knew. But despite the enjoyment of catching up on news of mutual friends and the supply of delicious food and wine, Amanda found it difficult not to wish that Lizzie would hurry up and push off on her honeymoon so that she could get away herself. Around her there were happy couples holding hands, embracing, flirting and courting, and it all succeeded in making Amanda feel lonely and miserable and at the same time impatient and excited in her longing to be with Bella.

At last the speeches were made, the cake was cut with a sword, Lizzie slipped upstairs to her room in the mess to change, the junior officers careered out to sabotage Richard's car and Amanda knew that it would be only about an hour till she would be seeing Bella again. She looked at her watch – six o'clock – and decided that as soon as Lizzie had gone she'd ring the hotel where they were meeting to leave a message for Bella that she was going to be later than expected.

Lizzie appeared at the foot of the stairs in a commendably short time and, followed by an excited crowd, ran to the car, where Richard was laughing at some of the bawdier comments written in lipstick across the paintwork.

'Richard!' she shrieked in horror, seeing 'Gunners do it with bigger BANGS' in large letters across the boot. Then she spotted some other comments about negligent discharges and firing blanks that left even less to the imagination. 'We can't possibly drive around with that written on the car. We'll get arrested!'

'You don't mean to say you understand what it all means?' said Richard, still doubled up with laughter.

'Well, I am a married woman now, aren't I supposed to?'

'No time to rub it off. We'll miss our flight. Come on.'

And Lizzie, still muttering things about police and obscenities, walked towards the passenger door. Resigning herself to travelling in a car which was going to raise eyebrows, she turned just before she got in and, with a flourish, threw her bouquet into the air, aiming more or less at Amanda. Amanda made a half-hearted attempt to catch it but was relieved when an athletic QA captain leapt to intercept it to cheers of admiration from her friends. Lizzie mouthed, 'Sorry' to Amanda; Amanda shrugged and mouthed back, 'Good luck' to her friend. As she did so she hoped that luck wouldn't be required in Lizzie's married life. She couldn't see what on earth could go wrong, but she had an awful, shiver-making premonition that something was going to.

As soon as was decent after Lizzie's departure, Amanda left, driving as quickly as the speed limit and the gathering dusk allowed. She felt increasingly excited as she neared her destination. It had been over a month since she'd last seen Bella and each day had been interminable, despite the hectic pace in the office, and each night lonely and miserable. She thought about Lizzie's wedding as she drove along. It brought to mind one of her mother's comments when she had told her parents that she was gay. 'I only ever had one dream for you,' she'd said to Amanda. 'I only ever wanted to see you happily married. I wasn't fussed about jobs or careers but I did want you to have a family of your own. Well, no grandchildren for me then.' Amanda hadn't noticed until later that her mother only seemed able to associate happiness with looking after a husband and the bearing of children. Perhaps that had made her happy, although Amanda sometimes doubted it. Her mother rarely smiled and was always moaning about mess or mud on the carpet. But it hurt Amanda that her mother wasn't prepared to even entertain the idea that she was different; that she had different ambitions and wasn't a clone of her parents. She shrugged her shoulders. Tough, she thought, although she felt a nagging sadness that neither her mother nor her father had had anything to do with her for ten years.

She zipped down the road through Windsor Great Park, the castle ahead towering against the darkening sky, and swung off towards the centre of the town. It was only when she had parked her car and was removing her holdall from the back seat that she remembered with a lurch that she had yet to break the news about her job. Her elation deflated in an instant. She went into the hotel feeling apprehensive as to how she was going to tell Bella, and what her reaction would be once she knew.

Careful and discreet as always, the girls had booked two rooms, though only one would be used. Amanda asked for and received the key to hers and carefully noted Bella's room number as she signed the register. They sometimes wondered if perhaps they were ridiculously paranoid, but then they reasoned that they only had to make one mistake and their careers would be in tatters. If they weren't as equally in love with each other as they were with the Army, then life would have been so much easier. Heterosexual couples didn't have to choose between personal relationships and their jobs – well, not unless they were knocking off a spy from some undesirable country, Amanda joked. It's all so unfair, Bella complained almost every time they met. But unfair or not that was the way things were, and they both knew that unless they respected the rules they could kiss their commissions goodbye.

Amanda climbed the stairs to the second floor of the family-run hotel. It was more like a guesthouse, she thought, but obviously *guesthouse* didn't have the same cachet for the American visitors who provided the main source of income in this tourist-oriented town. A small plastic plate, screwed to the wall opposite the top of the stairs, directed Amanda towards her room. However, she turned in the other direction and knocked quietly on Bella's door. It opened immediately and Amanda, with a surge of delight at seeing her lover, almost ran through it, slamming it behind her so not a second might be wasted before she was hugging and kissing Bella. After a few minutes they moved slightly apart, their hands still resting on each other's shoulders, and studied each other's face.

'You look tired,' said Bella.

'I feel it. Absolutely shattered, to be honest. I had to make sure I had everything squared away properly before I went off this weekend. It meant burning the midnight oil rather a lot.'

'And the CO has been away sailing too?'

Amanda sighed, and nodded her head disconsolately. 'It's not just his fault. If I had more experience I think I would be able to get through a lot more work. I seem to spend an awful lot of my time looking up rules and regulations. And on the bright side, the 2iC says it gets a lot easier in the winter because the weather is too shitty for the CO to want to go out in it.'

'Well, here's hoping it's a really foul winter.'

'No, you mustn't wish for that. I won't be able to drive over if the roads are too bad.'

'Oh, my poor darling, you're right, of course. Well, let's just hope his boat sinks.'

'At least that would keep him at his desk.' They both laughed.

'Now then, EF or FF?' Bella used their private code to discover whether Amanda's appetite was for food or something more carnal.

'Would you mind awfully if we eat first? I'm famished. Lizzie's wedding reception was wonderful and elegant, but the food was pretty rather than filling.'

'Of course, we can fuck later. There's a Chinese down the road looks pretty good, how do you fancy that?'

'Chinese – wonderful.' Amanda debated whether or not to tell Bella the news before they went out, but she quickly decided that it would be easier over a meal. She knew that she was procrastinating, but she was dreading the moment so much that any excuse was welcome.

They left the hotel and walked the hundred yards or so to the restaurant. Because of the relatively early hour it was almost empty and they were able to select a corner table in the ornate red and gold room. A plaster dragon, coiled up a pillar, leered down at them, and behind Bella's chair a shoal of monstrous koi carp swam lazily around their huge tank. They had barely sat down when a waiter appeared, offering menus, drinks and a bowl of prawn crackers to stave off any possibility of starvation setting in before his customers made their choice. Bella and Amanda tucked into the frothy white crackers while they pondered over the delicious selection on offer.

'I really fancy the crispy duck and hoi-sin sauce,' said Amanda, already salivating at the very thought of it.

'Oh yes, my favourite. How about a quarter of a duck between us? And what about some rice and the sizzling beef?' They chose a couple of other items on the menu, selected a bottle of wine and then settled back in their chairs to nibble the crackers and wait for their order to be taken. Amanda knew that she couldn't put off imparting the news for a moment longer.

'I had some bad news last week,' she began, hesitantly. Instantly Bella looked concerned for her.

'Oh, I'm sorry. What was it?' From the tone of Amanda's voice she was expecting to hear that a relation had died or a friend had been killed, at the very least.

'The CO has arranged for me to stay on with the workshop as adjutant.' Her voice rose in indignation. 'He didn't even consult me, he just went ahead and did it, thinking I'd be over the moon.' She looked desolate. 'I wouldn't mind so much if it wasn't for you, but I was really counting on getting back to the UK.'

But Bella was concerned more about the strain the job and its heavy responsibilities were putting on her friend than about the effect on their relationship. 'What about the hours you have to work

155

and the responsibilities he expects you to take? It's ridiculous for him to expect you to be able to carry on for a full tour when you've only been commissioned for eighteen months.'

'I know, but I think that because I'm so much older than the average subaltern he forgets that and thinks I've been in the Army for years.'

'Well, don't you tell him?'

'When I see him, which is once in a blue moon.'

'Didn't you ring our postings branch?'

'Yes.'

'And what did they say? Surely they're on your side?'

'Not really.' Amanda took another cracker and ate it whole. After she'd finished it she said, 'Basically they told me it's a huge compliment and it'll be very good for my career in the long run. I could hardly say that I was less interested in my career than being posted near you.' She smiled ruefully at Bella.

'Couldn't you use the argument that your lack of experience is making an already difficult job too tough?'

'But the CO is telling everyone that I am coping and doing really well. It makes that argument a bit tricky.'

'You could kick up a stink. Go to your brigade commander, for example.'

'But on what grounds – that I don't like the hard work? And as the CO is saying that I'm doing such a great job I don't really think they'll take much notice.'

The waiter appeared to take their order. When he'd gone Amanda said, 'I suppose I could always say I want a posting to UK to be near my future partner.'

'I somehow think,' said Bella with a chuckle, 'that when they start examining your vetting forms you'll be posted to civvy street, not Oxfordshire.'

Lisburn, September 1989

Edwina had remembered that it was Lizzie's wedding day when she'd been woken up by her alarm that morning and had wished that she could be there. But there was no way. They had a big operation planned for that day – providing everything worked out – and the leave she had asked for had been cancelled. Since that first moment she hadn't had another chance to think about Lizzie, for despite it being a Saturday, from the instant her feet had hit the floor at six o'clock that morning she hadn't stopped. Now, even though it was after five, she was making her way across the barracks to the ops room for a briefing on what was going to happen that night.

The 'hot int' was that some guns were going to be moved from a house in Twinbrook to another one in Portadown in the next few weeks, possibly within the next few days. According to the RUC Special Branch, the tout who'd supplied the information was pretty reliable, and had also hinted that amongst the consignment was the large-calibre high-velocity rifle which a sniper had been using to systematically pick off British soldiers. About a dozen in as many years had already fallen foul of this deadly weapon and everyone was desperately keen to get hold of it and prevent any more victims. This was not the first time that the Special Forces had had a tip-off about it, but it was the best one they'd had for some time. To this end, Edwina and half a dozen other members of 14 Company were staking out the area around the estate. However, hanging around in parked vehicles or on street corners was not an option in this neck of the woods – they'd have been spotted at once. It might have been acceptable practice for the police catching petty criminals in London, where no one paid any attention to what was going on around their neighbourhood, but the people Edwina and her colleagues were monitoring were professional terrorists operating in their own territory. Every man, woman and child who lived on these streets knew to keep watch for anyone who looked out of place, anyone who didn't belong. No one had any doubts as to what would happen to members of the security forces who got caught in the wrong place at the wrong time.

Already that day Edwina had made a couple of trawls past the house they were monitoring. On the first pass, early that morning, she'd walked slowly down the street, a small, reluctant dog trailing along behind her, her hair crammed into a woolly hat and her slim figure bulkily disguised by a massive shapeless coat. Un-made-up and with a slightly shambling gait, she might have passed for forty-something given a cursory inspection. She'd allowed the dog, the property of their armourer back in the barracks, to stop and sniff at a nearby lamppost while she'd had a long look at the front of the target house, logged that there was only a Yale lock on the front door and noted that there was absolutely no cover from prying eyes anywhere along the street. Gaining access from the front was going to be difficult, but they'd checked the back the night before and that looked like even more of a non-starter. There was almost no cover to be had as the garden was no more than just a tatty lawn surrounded by a fence of low chain link, but more importantly the garden could only be accessed from neighbouring ones – all of which seemed to contain dogs. The risks of getting caught that way were far too great.

The second time Edwina had checked out the house, and the neighbourhood, she'd jogged past wearing a tracksuit. She was confident about her disguises because she knew that people tended to assume that joggers and dog-walkers were doing just that and had no other agenda. Once she was well clear of the estate and the target house, she'd rendezvoused with a car and driver.

'It's no good,' she'd reported. 'Every house in that street is occupied. Certainly those either side of the target are, so there's no chance of getting through the roof somehow. I tell you, the only way in is going to be through the front door.'

The rest of the team considered this.

'And there's no cover,' said Nat.

'None at all.'

'Right, well, we'd better come up with some sort of workable plan,' said their ops officer.

Obviously someone was going to have to walk down the street and go in through the front door, but even under the cover of darkness, there was no way they could ensure that none of the neighbours would see. The problems this created seemed almost insurmountable.

'What about some sort of disturbance, or a fight, outside the house? Couldn't we get the lock picked and someone in while everyone is distracted?' said Nat.

'It might work in some situations,' said the ops officer, 'but this is a quiet street. You're more likely to end up with everyone hanging out of their windows to see what's going on. And if people are looking out of upstairs windows, we'll never be able to smuggle someone in undetected.'

Nat looked downcast as his idea was rejected.

'What about blocking the street with a big vehicle? Then no one opposite would be able to see – even from upstairs,' suggested Edwina.

'That's not bad. But it's not the sort of street big lorries would ever turn down.' Everyone nodded in agreement with the ops officer.

'A removal van might, especially if the driver looks lost and needs directions.'

'I think we're cooking,' said the ops officer. 'Right, Bill,' he said to one of the old hands in the team, 'you've got some good contacts. Do you think you can come up with something suitable?'

Bill sniffed thoughtfully and scratched his head. 'I'll see what I can do. No promises, mind.'

'OK. Everyone else is to work out an exact plan that we can put into action as soon as the target house is vacated by chummy. I want you to report back here at seventeen hundred hours for a briefing. Any questions?'

Edwina was one of the last to arrive in the ops room, even though she was five minutes early.

The ops officer cleared his throat to get everyone's attention. 'OK, sorry about this, folks, but Bill tells me there's nothing doing on the van front for a couple of days. We can get hold of one but we've got to paint the right logos on the side. That can't be done before tomorrow and the paint must be given time to dry. Everyone can stand down for today. We'll just have to hope that the gun stays put for a while.'

A rumbling of discontented muttering filled the room. Everyone felt deflated at the operation getting called off.

'Bugger,' said Edwina with feeling. She could have gone to Lizzie's wedding after all.

'We'll go on Monday, assuming nothing else goes wrong,' Nat said in an effort to cheer both Edwina and himself up.

'We'll get the green army to keep an eye on the place, make sure there's not too much activity while our backs are turned,' said the ops officer.

'Christ, now we've almost got that gun where we want it, the last thing we want to do is lose the fucker again,' said Nat.

Everyone agreed, but they also knew that they couldn't just go into the house and pick the cache up, much as they longed to, because such an action would compromise the informant. And the informant had warned his handler once already that if anything happened to endanger him, in any way whatsoever, then they'd never get another word out of him. As a valuable source of reliable information, this tout's wishes were sacrosanct. As they couldn't lift the guns, they were going to attach minute transmitters to them – 'jarking' in Army slang – so that they could be monitored on their journey. It would then be the runner's tough luck if he just happened to run into a snap RUC checkpoint before he got to Portadown and the weapons were found during a routine search of his vehicle.

Edwina left the briefing room feeling more than a little frustrated and at a loss as to how to spend her evening. She had nothing planned, she wasn't especially hungry – she'd been snacking all day, which was her way of dealing with tension – and it was too early to turn in for the night. She decided that, in spite of the lowering clouds threatening rain and the chill breeze which cut across the barracks, situated as they were on top of a hill overlooking Lisburn, she would go for a run. She returned to her Portakabin from the ops room, threw off her jeans and sweater and dragged on her tatty and none-too-clean tracksuit. If she was honest, jogging round the barracks was beginning to drive her mental, but there was no way she could run anywhere else. It was strictly against regulations for her to be seen openly entering or leaving any Army property. The only time they got out was on operations, but they nearly always travelled in specially adapted vehicles on those occasions.

She walked between the closely packed Portakabins until she reached the car park behind the NAAFI shop, noted the time on her watch and set off at a steady lope along the road past the soldiers' quarters towards the top end of the barracks. She was just about to turn into the QM's compound when she heard the guard dogs kennelled there setting up a tremendous din, which meant that someone was passing them, coming the other way. A second later she'd stopped dead in her tracks.

'Ulysses!' she shrieked.

'What the fuck . . .? Edwina, what the hell are you doing here?'

'I've got a posting here.'

'With the HQ?'

'No.' She wriggled with excitement, longing to see his reaction to her news. 'I'm with 14 Company.' Ulysses' reaction was all that Edwina had expected. His jaw literally dropped and his eyes goggled. 'And now you know my secret, I'll have to kill you,' she said with a huge smile.

'Christ, Edwina . . . I mean, well done. God, I don't know what I mean. I should have known you'd do something off the wall like this.'

'It's only because of you, you know. You were the one who said I'd be stuck with a crap-hat unit for the rest of my career because of being a girlie.'

'I know, but I didn't expect you to see the comment as a challenge. It was only a throwaway line.' Edwina thought that Ulysses sounded more than a little put out. It crossed her mind that he had enjoyed his lofty position of being one of the élite, of being admired and envied by a Rupert – as he invariably called all officers, male or female – and that she had now stolen his thunder. Still, she thought, he was big enough and ugly enough to get over it.

'Let's go back to my room,' she said. She felt ridiculously excited at seeing him again, but she tried to sound casual. 'It's too cold and wet to stand here gassing and I didn't really want to run anyway.'

'I thought I wasn't allowed to fraternise with officers,' said Ulysses, linking his arm through Edwina's and giving her a peck on the cheek. Yup, she thought, he's getting over it already.

'Christ, we don't bother with any of that shit in 14 Company. As far as they're concerned, I'm just Edwina.'

'Great. Lead on.' As they walked Edwina told Ulysses a little about her selection process and they compared notes about the degree of toughness each of them had had to attain. It was beyond question that Ulysses had had to produce feats of much greater physical strength and stamina, but all the same, he couldn't hide his admiration for Edwina's survival and success on her course. Hers had required an amazing level of fitness together with intelligence – more like winning *Mastermind* after taking part in a triathlon and then playing chess with Gary Kasparov. His had been more to do with having the endurance to run marathons day after day.

Back at Edwina's Portakabin they were greeted by a blast of warm, welcoming air as they opened the door. Edwina switched on the light and quickly kicked her dirty clothes under the bed, out of sight. It did little to improve the overall appearance of the room. Chaos reigned: papers and books were strewn across the floor, used tissues overflowed the waste bin, odd shoes and socks were scattered by the wardrobe and dirty mugs seemed to be on every available flat surface in the spacious but featureless room – by the bed, on the dressing table and even a couple on the bookshelves, which were crammed with dog-eared paperbacks. Ulysses ignored the mess, walked across to the books and began examining the titles.

'We spend a lot of time hanging around waiting for something to happen,' she explained.

'So I see.' The sarcasm was obvious.

'Hey, hang on a minute. I've been out on a hillside for four days at a time, in bandit country, lying around in a muddy field and getting fuck-all sleep. I don't read books all that often, I just like a good selection to choose from when I do.'

Ulysses was surprised at how defensive she sounded. Then he realised that she was used to most of the Army having the wrong idea about what these people did. Because of the absolute secrecy which surrounded their operations, none of the members of 14 Company were ever able to justify or explain their role to outsiders. He knew she was only telling him because the SAS were often involved with their operations and knew exactly what they got up to.

'I must admit that when I first heard about 14 Company,' Ulysses said, 'I thought you were all a strange bunch of nerds living in a fantasy world. Some of the lads call you Walts . . .'

'I know,' interrupted Edwina, somewhat wearily, 'after Walter Mitty and his imaginary world. It's rather an old joke.'

'Yeah, well.' Ulysses grinned sheepishly. 'They drop the phrase once they work with your mob and see what you really get up to.' He left the bookcase, went over to the bed and lounged across it.

'I suppose I should be grateful.' Edwina changed the subject. 'Coffee?'

'Got anything stronger?'

'Sure. I've got some great Irish whiskey, will that do?' Ulysses nodded and smiled, making a smacking noise of appreciation with his lips. Edwina found two glasses on the shelf above the washbasin, gave them a perfunctory rinse under the cold tap and poured two generous measures of Bushmills.

'What do you like in it?'

'More whiskey?' asked Ulysses hopefully. Edwina put another slug in the glass and passed it to him.

'So how come I haven't seen you around here before?' she asked. She sat beside him, but on the very edge of the bed.

'Haven't been in the Province long.' Edwina noticed his tan for the first time. Bronzed skin in Ireland had to mean a trip somewhere else to get it. Summer in the six counties was supposed to be a fortnight in May – if it was a good year. God, with his blond hair and blue eyes it made him even more hunky – if that were possible.

'Somewhere hot?' She tried to sound bored because she was almost squirming with the pleasure of seeing him again, but she didn't want to frighten him off by showing it.

'Maybe.'

Edwina knew better than to press further. She sipped her drink and fiddled with a thread pulled out of the bed cover.

'You never wrote,' she accused suddenly.

'Neither have you since January.'

'I was busy.'

'And I was in the middle of fucking nowhere.' They dropped the subject – they were both at fault – and silence descended once more. They sat beside each other on Edwina's unmade bed, not touching or even making eye contact. They both had a lot to say but neither really knew where to begin. It had been a long time since they'd last met, more than a year, and although they both knew that the reason for the separation was involuntary it still made them feel awkward in each other's presence. So much could have happened in that time. Christ, thought Edwina, if Lizzie can meet and marry someone in the space of a year, so might Ulysses. But how could she ask if she still meant as much to him as she had before when she didn't know how much she'd meant in the first place? She took a large gulp of her drink. Ulysses raised an eyebrow.

'Dutch courage?' he asked.

'Why do you think that?'

'Because I could do with some.' He turned towards her and the anger he was feeling showed clearly on his face. A muscle twitched and pulsed with tension in his strong clean-shaven jaw. 'When you buggered off without a word I wondered where the hell you'd gone, or if I'd done something to upset you. I mean, even girlies can cope with the advanced technology of the phone system and leave a message. So I rang your unit and all I got was some bollocks about you being on an adventurous training course. For six months?' His ice-blue eyes stared at her angrily. 'I knew I was being fed crap but I didn't know why. So I assumed it was because you'd found someone else and were too chicken to tell me, and you'd persuaded some sad scaly to give me the bum's rush.' Edwina didn't rise to the phrase 'scaly' to describe someone in the Royal Signals; now was not the moment to nit-pick over the use of this pejorative term. But Ulysses did deserve to know what she'd been up to and she was also touched by his concern over her whereabouts and activities. It proved he cared for her.

'I'm sorry.' Her contrition was genuine. 'I phoned on a couple of occasions, but you were always away, and I could hardly tell a complete stranger what I was doing. For heaven's sake, I wasn't even supposed to tell my family what I was getting up to, let alone some telephone operator, even if he did work in Stirling Lines. And,' before Ulysses could continue, 'you'll be pleased to hear that there's not been anyone else. Not even a one-night stand.' She didn't add that this was mostly due to lack of opportunity, lack of sleep and lack of privacy rather than feelings of fidelity. Her room in the Portakabin was the first one she'd had where she knew no one would walk in without knocking, but she'd been far too busy since she'd arrived in the Province to even think about bonking.

Her apology and her explanation mollified Ulysses. He knew she was right, of course; she couldn't have told one of the clerks at the SAS base in Hereford details of what she was up to. He took a slurp of his drink and shrugged. It was the nearest he'd get to an apology for his outburst, but Edwina didn't mind.

'I don't know why it never crossed my mind that you'd get yourself tied up with this gang, but it didn't. I'd have slept a lot better if I'd worked it out.' The tension eased and he smiled.

'I'm sorry.'

'What for? Getting involved with this outfit or for me losing sleep.'

'The sleep.' She grinned back at him. 'And talking of sleep, how about a bed for the night here?'

164

'I can't.' He sounded genuinely disappointed but soon perked up a little. 'Well, not the night anyway.' He smiled wolfishly. 'Our transport's going back to our own base in a couple of hours. We came up here to support some operation your lot was supposed to be setting up, but then it got postponed – I suppose you know more about it than I do.' Edwina nodded. Ulysses continued, 'We decided to stay up here in Slipper City and have a few drinks in the Greenfly Club.'

'Forgive me asking, but where the hell is Slipper City?'

'Here, you donkey. Everyone calls it that because you've got it so cushy up here: riding stables, NAAFI, indoor tennis courts, library. Christ, even the fucking families live in style here.'

Edwina couldn't argue with that; the officers' quarters within the barracks looked as though they'd be more suited to the wealthy stockbrokers of Sunningdale than the less than generously paid members of HM Forces. She knew that accommodation for unaccompanied soldiers in some places in the Province was little better than slum standard. She'd had to visit the infantry battalion in North Howard Street Mill and had decided that Dartmoor Prison looked more homely than the huge, run-down flax mill with its bricked-up windows and hot and cold running cockroaches. She knew where the SAS were billeted, and it wasn't as bad as some places; even so, she found it annoying that it was automatically assumed by everyone that all the personnel in Thiepval Barracks had it soft.

'So why aren't you down the Greenfly Club with the others?'

'I was, and then I remembered that I needed more razor blades and I was rushing down to the NAAFI before it shut.'

Edwina checked her watch. 'Well, you're too late now.'

'Never mind. I'll swipe some from one of the others. Now, back to serious matters, you were talking about bed a few minutes ago.'

'Was I? Well . . .' But she didn't have a chance to say anything else because Ulysses kissed her hard on the lips. With a rush and a lurch she remembered his smell and his taste. Christ, she wanted him.

'If you were a gentleman,' she tried to mumble, despite his exploring tongue, 'you wouldn't do this without asking permission first.'

'If you were a lady you wouldn't talk with your mouth full,' Ulysses retorted equally indistinctly.

'Bastard.'

Aldershot, December 1989

'Our first Christmas,' said Lizzie with a huge grin as she sat up in bed on Christmas morning, surrounded by the detritus of her stocking and unwrapped presents. Richard paused in the investigation of the contents of a large parcel, leaned towards her and kissed her.

'The first of dozens.'

'How many dozens?'

'I don't know, about five, I should hope. I can't do sums at this hour.'

'And you don't mind that we won't be on our own for this one?'

'Of course not, you goose. Amanda's your best friend, and judging by the time that the two of you spend on the phone to each other you'll get withdrawal symptoms if you don't get to natter to her over the holiday. I reckon having her to stay for twenty-four hours will save a fortune on the phone bill!' As he said that Lizzie glanced at the clock and let out a shriek.

'The turkey!'

'What about it?'

'It's got to be in the oven in about ten minutes or we won't be eating it till Boxing Day.' Lizzie scrambled into her slippers and dressing gown and sped out of the room.

'You're coming back to bed again, aren't you?' shouted Richard, hopefully, as her footsteps faded down the stairs. A distant 'yes' floated back. Richard switched on the radio and listened contentedly to the sound of a solo treble voice singing 'Once in Royal David's City'. In the distance he could hear faint noises emanating from the kitchen. If Lizzie got a move on with the bird there might be time for some quick lovemaking before he nipped into the barracks to take gunfire to the duty staff. He checked the clock again – perhaps not, after all. If he were going to serve the soldiers remaining in barracks their Christmas treat of early-morning tea laced with rum he'd have to get a move on. Reluctantly he pulled back the duvet and clambered out of bed. When he appeared in the kitchen twenty minutes later in his number-two dress uniform, Lizzie was still struggling with the turkey.

'Oh, is it that time already? Time for a cuppa before you go?' she asked.

'No, I'll get one in the guardroom. What time is Amanda arriving?'

'About twelve, I think. You are sure you don't mind?' she asked yet again.

'Honestly. She's your best friend, she's a lovely lady, she's on her own; what possible objection could I have?'

Lizzie stood on tiptoe and kissed him.

'Don't bother getting dressed,' said Richard, ruffling her hair. 'I'll only be gone about forty minutes or so. I'll just wish all the duty staff a happy Christmas and then I'll be back here again. We can resume our lie-in then.'

Lizzie giggled. 'OK stud.' Richard kissed her goodbye and bounded up the stairs to the front door. She heard it slam and then resumed her battle to get the turkey wrapped in foil and into the oven. She had just succeeded when the phone rang.

'Hello,' she said, expecting to hear her mother's voice, or even Amanda's. It was neither.

'Lizzie, it's me,' said Edwina.

'Edwina! Happy Christmas. Where are you?'

'Ireland. I've got New Year off so I'm on duty today. I thought I'd ring and see how you are.'

'I'm really well. Busy, of course, and our social life has been unbelievable. Married life is great. You should try it.'

'One day, perhaps.' Edwina was laughing too. Lizzie's good humour and happiness were infectious. 'Have you seen or heard anything of Amanda recently?'

'We're having her for lunch today.'

'That'll make a change from turkey.' Lizzie doubled up with laughter. 'I haven't seen her for ages,' continued Edwina. 'What with operations here and her being out in Germany, it's just not been possible.'

'Thank goodness for the phone.' There was an awkward silence.

167

'You haven't phoned her for ages either, have you?' Lizzie didn't have to remind Edwina that she'd only rung Lizzie once since her wedding.

'Uuhh,' groaned Edwina in embarrassment. 'I have tried, honestly, but her office phone is always engaged and at weekends she's often away, and I work odd hours . . .' Her voice trailed off as her excuses ran out and she remembered she'd used them with Lizzie six weeks earlier.

'You're hopeless,' remonstrated Lizzie.

'And you're so good at keeping in touch with us all. I love getting your news and Amanda's from your letters.'

'Yes, but that's not the point.'

'I promise I'll try harder next year, but always remember that if you don't hear from me it generally means I'm well and happy.'

'I'll bear it in mind.' Lizzie was mollified, but even so Edwina decided to get off the dodgy subject of her communications skills.

'So why aren't you off seeing relatives, or have you got thousands staying with you?'

'No, it's just Amanda and us. Richard volunteered to do duty officer today so we can't go anywhere. Amanda is going to some friends on Boxing Day but needed someone to take her in today.'

'Still not talking to her parents?'

'No. I can't imagine that. My mum's on the phone to me every week.'

'Thankfully mine isn't, but it doesn't mean we don't get on. Anyway, I'm glad she'll be with you this year. It would be miserable for her if she had to spend Christmas on her own.'

'But what about you? Aren't you on your own?'

'Good God, no. There are dozens of us here. Work doesn't stop just because it's Christmas. The cookhouse has got a huge meal planned and we'll all have a few drinks and a great time.'

'You're sure you won't be lonely?'

'Of course I won't. Hey, shall I tell you a funny story?'

'Go on then.'

'The soldiers on the gate here got presented with a huge tin of chocolates by a couple of the local slappers. They were dead chuffed to read the note on the tin that said how much the local girls fancied them. Anyway, they opened up the tin and instead of two pounds of Quality Street it had two pounds of Semtex in it.'

'How awful.' Lizzie was aghast.

'Not really. It was a crap bomb and it didn't go off, but the local bomb-disposal man was cross because he'd hoped that there would be at least *some* chocolates in it to make up for getting called out on Christmas Eve. Now tell me what you gave Richard for Christmas, apart from a good seeing-to . . .'

After fifteen minutes they had run out of news, and Edwina pleaded that she had some other calls to make and rang off. For the umpteenth time Lizzie wondered about the strange job she did which allowed her to find humour in stories like the one she'd regaled Lizzie with. She checked that the turkey appeared to be cooking properly and returned to the warmth of her bed. She had barely tucked herself in to await Richard's arrival when the phone went again. Lizzie raced downstairs to answer it before the caller rang off. This time it was her mother calling from Germany and complaining that she was missing her daughter. Lizzie was still talking to her when Richard returned, stamping his feet against the cold. He cocked his head questioningly.

Mother, mouthed Lizzie. He went to put the kettle on to make tea. This could be a long session.

By the time Lizzie got off the phone the turkey needed basting.

'Aren't you ever coming back to bed?' groaned Richard.

Lizzie checked her watch. 'Well, if we don't get any more interruptions . . .'

Decisively, Richard took the phone off the hook and led her upstairs.

When Amanda arrived a couple of hours later, Lizzie was immersed in cooking the feast and Richard was busy fielding complaints from his own mother that the phone had been engaged all morning. He was finding it difficult to keep a straight face. The smell of turkey filled the house, Christmas music played softly and Amanda suddenly felt a pang of sadness that she was an interloper into Richard and Lizzie's happy intimacy. Richard, seeing Amanda, made his excuses to his mother, hung up and greeted her warmly, giving her a big hug and handing her a glass of champagne and the present he and Lizzie had bought for her. Instantly Amanda felt welcome, but as she sipped her drink and unwrapped a thick sweater she wondered if she would ever find the deep contentment that Lizzie so obviously had. Her thoughts about her future were banished a minute or two later as Lizzie insisted on hearing all about life in Germany.

'And there is one really good perk,' finished Amanda.

'What's that?' asked Lizzie as she sliced carrots into batons.

'I'm going skiing with the Army next month for a fortnight, all expenses paid. Your lovely jersey will come in really handy.'

'You jammy thing! How come?'

'Can you believe that it's considered to be part of winter warfare training? Of course, everyone knows it's really a two-week jolly in the Bavarian Alps. The REME have got themselves so well organised that they run a sort of hotel down there. I can't wait. I've always longed to learn how to ski.'

'Absolutely,' said Lizzie with undisguised envy. 'My mother has got a photo of me on skis when I was about five, but I don't remember it. After that my dad was either posted in the UK or I was at boarding school. Richard asked me how I'd feel about a posting to Germany if one came up, and I wasn't too keen because it would mean leaving here, but I'd forgotten about the possibility of skiing.' She tipped the carrots into a pan of cold water and turned her attention to the sprouts. 'Promise me you'll send me a postcard and ring to tell me all about it when you get back.'

'Promise.'

Later, as the two women sat drowsily in the little upstairs sitting room, picking desultorily at a bowl of nuts and waiting for the Queen's Speech, while Richard finished off the washing-up downstairs, Amanda admitted to Lizzie that she envied her having her own home.

'But you'll have one of your own one day.'

'I don't know. I sometimes think of investing in a little place, but where? There's no point in buying somewhere near my parents –'

'It's so sad you can't make up,' interrupted Lizzie.

Amanda didn't want to talk about them, so she didn't allow herself to be drawn on the subject. 'Yes, well . . . Anyway, I don't feel as though I belong anywhere much. I can't buy a house while I'm stuck out in Germany. And then if I do get a place one day, I can't count on living in it for too long.'

'We don't know how much longer we'll be able to live here. I'm still waiting to hear where I'm posted next, and goodness knows where they'll send Richard.'

'Haven't they made up their minds what to do with you yet?'

'They thought they had me sorted out a couple of times, but then things fell through. The CO is getting quite ratty because he doesn't really like having a husband-and-wife team in the office. He keeps muttering about discipline and things. Richard and I don't mind, but it's not really up to us – it's his regiment after all.'

'Are there any ideas about what might be available?'

'I gather there's possibly something in Aldershot but they won't tell me what. Apparently they've got to convince someone I'm up to it.'

'Sounds intriguing.'

'Richard thinks it might be a staff job. I'm awfully junior to be run for one, not to say rather young.'

'You'd be brilliant at it, though,' said Amanda, gamely hiding the twinge of jealousy she felt. After all, a staff job in the UK was what she had been requesting for months.

Aldershot, May 1990

'How's the new posting then?' Richard asked Lizzie when she walked through the door of their house.

'It seems pretty good,' she said. 'It's terribly busy of course, because I seem to have loads of briefs and minutes which I have to write, but the brigadier seems charming, although Bob, he's the SO2 –'

'Yes, I know who he is,' said Richard. He sounded slightly exasperated. 'I deal with him about disciplinary matters, remember? Lizzie knew that Richard was a little jealous of her posting as a grade-three staff officer at the Command Headquarters in Aldershot. Not only had she received promotion, but on certain administrative matters Richard would now have to answer to her and her office. She was very conscious of this fact and had made a promise to herself that she would try her hardest not to refer to this at home if at all possible. But he had asked her about it first.

'Well, I expect I'll cope,' finished Lizzie, not wanting to say anything that might rub Richard's nose in her rather desirable posting. It was a compliment to have been given it, quite a feather in her cap, although she knew she'd only got the job and the promotion which went with it because it was all that was available in the area just then; she also knew, however, that she wouldn't have been offered it if there was the least suspicion that she wouldn't be up to it. Her posting hadn't just caused a twinge of jealousy to surface in Richard; it had also made him extra work, because he now had to break in a new assistant, which didn't help matters as it increased his workload hugely. Lizzie felt that she should have been issued with a pair of kid gloves at the same time she'd been awarded her third pip.

'I'll go and see what there is for supper, shall I?'

'Mmm. I'm famished.' She went into the kitchen and peered into the fridge. There was the remains of the Sunday joint, which needed eating up, some broccoli and a handful of new potatoes. That would do, she thought. She gave the spuds a quick rinse and a scrub and put them on to boil before going upstairs to change.

Richard's uniform was carelessly strewn on their bed as usual, so Lizzie went to the wardrobe, collected a hanger and carefully hung his barrack-dress trousers on it. While she was at it she checked that he had a clean and ironed shirt ready for the morning. It didn't occur to her that Richard, who had probably finished work a good half-hour ahead of her, might have not only done this but made a start on supper too; her mother had always done these things for her father, and it seemed to Lizzie that it was what wives, especially Forces wives, were expected to do. Male officers were used to the perks of living in the mess and expected the lifestyle to continue in their own home. Despite having fended for himself for a year or so before Lizzie had arrived on the scene, Richard had soon got used to the pleasures of being waited on hand and foot by a loving and caring wife. She quickly changed into jeans and a sweatshirt, ran a comb through her hair and returned to the sitting room to ask Richard if he wanted a drink before supper.

'Gin and tonic, please,' he said from behind a copy of *The Times*. Poor man, he looks shattered, thought Lizzie. Perhaps his day had been particularly lousy. She went to the sideboard to make his drink and remembered guiltily that they'd run out of tonic the day before and she had forgotten to buy any more. She owned up. Richard sighed deeply. Obviously this was the final straw at the end of a rotten day.

'Can I get you a beer instead?'

'I suppose that'll have to do.'

'I could nip out and buy some tonic now, if you'd rather.'

'No, beer's fine.' Lizzie brought a can of bitter and a tankard to where he was sitting. 'I think there's something boiling over in the kitchen,' he said, taking them from her and returning to his paper.

'Blast.' Lizzie charged down to the kitchen, turned down the gas and mopped up the pool of water from the top of the stove. God, she was bushed, she thought, as she wrung out the cloth in the sink. And it was only Monday. What she really needed was an early night. She sighed tiredly and got the joint out of the fridge to carve the last of the meat off the bone. A few of the pieces were rather scraggy and somewhat fatty; these she put on her own plate, selecting the best and leanest meat for Richard. Then she trimmed the broccoli and popped it in the microwave so it would be ready at the same time as the potatoes. Finally she laid two places at the table before pouring herself a sherry.

Housework was certainly no joke, Lizzie thought as she took her drink up to the sitting room to watch the news while the potatoes cooked. Perhaps it would get easier as she became more efficient at it. Efficiency had certainly been the key to her last job, and she hoped that it would prove to be the same in her new one, but housework was another matter entirely. After a childhood spent at boarding school and a subsequent existence being looked after by mess staff, Lizzie knew that domestically she was a disaster. Yes, she could iron shirts with razor-sharp creases; yes, she could bull shoes and boots; yes, she could quote chunks of the Manual of Military Law, but cooking and shopping, just working out what they were going to eat each evening, was a nightmare. She never seemed to have everything she needed for a meal, and try as she might to do just one big shop each week, she invariably found that a couple of days later she was out of cooking oil or flour or some other essential, so back she would have to go to the supermarket.

She drained her sherry and returned to the kitchen to check on the spuds. She picked a knife out of the drawer and prodded them. They seemed to be done, so she drained them and shared them out between the two plates, dished up the broccoli and put the meal on the table. She called to Richard that it was ready.

As she sat down at the table, Lizzie reflected back over the six months of her marriage. She didn't like to admit it, even to herself, but she was beginning to wonder if she was up to coping with this new role of being a working wife. And just lately, since she'd begun to hand over her old job and take on the new one, she'd started to feel so tired all the time that she spent half her day just longing to crawl back into bed again. She was sure it was just the extra work and hoped against hope that it wouldn't be long before she felt better. But it didn't help matters that, being newly-weds, Richard assumed her desire for early nights had precious little to do with sleep. Lizzie wondered if, despite her assurances to all and sundry that she had no intention of sacking her career, she was going to have to admit defeat. Admit that she just wasn't up to the challenge of holding down a job and running a home.

Richard joined her and Lizzie put these thoughts from her mind and tried to look cheerful while he told her about the latest scrape a particularly accident-prone young subaltern had got into. Apparently he'd ridden his motorbike through the mess for a dare, lost control on the polished hall floor, crashed into the hall table and demolished a flower arrangement completed by the CO's wife only an hour previously. Worse than that, he had also broken her favourite vase. Lizzie laughed dutifully.

'So how many extras did he get for that?' she asked.

'I let him off with just fourteen.'

'You're all heart,' said Lizzie with a wry grin. 'When will he have worked that lot off?'

'The RSM reckons that when we've added these to his previous ones, and if he doesn't get any more, and if he is orderly officer every alternate day, he should complete all his extras by Christmas – but this does assume, as I said, that he doesn't get any more.'

'Well, there is some compensation for him.' Richard looked askance. 'He must be top of the popularity stakes. Duties for all the other subbies must come round only once in a blue moon. To say nothing of the fact that as he hardly ever gets out of barracks to be able to spend his pay, his bank account must be loaded.'

'I'll remind him of that next time I see him. I've no doubt the thought that, instead of a busy social life and a girlfriend, he has a tidy sum in the bank must cheer him up hugely.'

'What about having him to supper one evening?'

'He may be Mr Popularity with the subbies but I don't think I am with him. Don't forget, it's me handing out the extras.'

'OK. Well, perhaps we could have a few of the others over one day; have a little dinner party?' Lizzie didn't know why she was saying this, as if she didn't have enough on her plate without entertaining as well – some sense of duty, perhaps. It was, after all, what other wives did, but then most of the other regimental wives didn't work. They'd long since sacrificed their jobs and careers to follow their husbands round Europe, moving every couple of years. Organising coffee mornings and dinner parties gave them a justification for their existence. They were expanding their circle of friends, and everyone in the Army was aware that things happened in the Forces – from promotions, postings and recommendations for medals to the painting of quarters and the allocation of new carpets – because of who you knew. Lizzie knew that to be a real help to

Richard's career – or at any rate to be seen by the other wives to be a help, which was almost as important – a bit of networking and socialising on her part wouldn't come amiss. She'd been married for over six months now and she hadn't done anything in that line. She really ought to pull her finger out and throw a couple of drinks parties at the very least. But the very thought of the organisation that it would entail made her feel more exhausted than ever.

After supper Lizzie cleared away the plates, stacked the dish-washer and then took herself up to have a long, hot soak in the bath, praying as she went that Richard wouldn't want sex and she could go straight to sleep. A good ten hours would surely sort her out. As she lay in the bath, her eyes shut, letting the warm, scented water relax her, she wondered why she'd been feeling so tired recently. Other officers seemed to be able to cope with changing jobs without going into a decline. Perhaps there was some other reason why she felt knackered morning, noon and night. Maybe she ought to see the MO about it, but there was nothing obviously wrong with her and she was terrified of being thought a malingerer or a time-waster. She decided against it. Surely it was a case of too much bed and not enough sleep, coupled with having a lot on her plate at work. She allowed her mind to drift and wander as her limbs half floated in the hot water . . .

With a start she realised she'd dropped off to sleep in the bath, and the water was now stone cold. Shivering, she got out and towelled herself down vigorously, then she slipped her nightie over her head and began to clean her teeth. She looked at her reflection in the bath-room mirror and noticed the dark circles under her eyes. She decided that if a good long sleep tonight didn't help erase them she'd better start disguising them, because they made her look dreadful; as if she'd gone a couple of rounds with a prizefighter.

Her plans for a long, refreshing sleep were destroyed by the arrival of Richard who, discovering his wife already in bed, washed and sweet-smelling, decided not to waste the opportunity. Lizzie, although flattered that he found her so irresistible, suppressed a groan as her early night vanished. Perhaps she'd get one tomorrow, she thought. She tried to look and sound enthusiastic as Richard indulged in seemingly endless foreplay – why couldn't he get on with it more quickly? – and she prayed he wouldn't notice that twice she swallowed a yawn. She felt enormously guilty that she really didn't want his attentions. She loved him to distraction, she adored everything about him, but she was desperate for some sleep. Oh, why wouldn't he get on with it? Eventually, sated with kissing, sucking, fondling and feeling, Richard began to make love to her properly. Lizzie resisted the temptation to look at her watch to see how late it was, but she did fake an orgasm in the hope that thinking she'd come, he'd hurry up just a little. No such luck! It was at least twenty minutes before he allowed himself to climax.

'That's the best bit,' he'd told her the first time they'd made love. 'Once I've come it's all over. I like to tease myself and make it last as long as possible.' Which had been fine then, when lovemaking could only take place at weekends and Lizzie had the rest of the week in which to recover. But now? Why couldn't he be like other men; the ones about whom various girlfriends had complained that their idea of foreplay was removing their socks before they got into bed, and whose idea of stamina was to have lovemaking last for four strokes, not four hours.

When he had finally finished, he thanked Lizzie courteously, gave her a kiss goodnight and was asleep within a few seconds. Lizzie leaned across and gave him a peck on the cheek.

'Goodnight, darling,' she whispered. Richard snored by way of an answer. Lizzie, dog-tired herself, slipped instantly into a deep sleep.

It seemed to Lizzie that the alarm went off almost immediately. Quickly she shut it off before it woke Richard and slipped out of bed, making as little noise as possible. She took her uniform from where it hung on the wardrobe door and went into the bathroom to dress. Gazing into the mirror, she saw that the circles under her eyes were no better, and even a heavy layer of foundation did little to improve their appearance. Giving up on it as a bad job, she deftly applied some mascara and a touch of lipstick before going downstairs to make Richard's early-morning tea and unload the dishwasher while the kettle boiled. Her early-morning routine was a masterful application of advanced ergonomics, with Lizzie achieving as much as possible of her housework for the day before Richard was even out of bed – she liked him to come down to a tidy house. She returned upstairs with his tea and grabbed the pile of dirty shirts from the washing basket in the bathroom, which she took back to the kitchen to bundle into the machine. She would be able to take them out and hang them up in her lunch hour; too bad that she'd have to skip lunch.

Neither of the other two staff officers with whom she shared an office commented on her tired appearance when she arrived at her desk just before eight thirty, but they both noticed it. Later, at lunchtime, when Lizzie had raced off to sort our her laundry, the SO2 – her immediate boss – couldn't resist a remark.

'She looks shagged out,' said Bobby Yates.

'Lucky Richard!' William Davies, an SO3 like Lizzie and the third member of the office, said lasciviously. They both laughed, although they were both wondering privately what Lizzie was like in bed. They couldn't help it. They knew they'd probably never find out, but at least they could fantasise. She must go like a train and want it all night, every night to look as exhausted as that. They had both reached the stage in their marriages when sex, although still fun, was less frequent and more predictable than in the early years and were envious of Richard's position of having a young wife, eager to please and not yet jaded by ten or so years of monogamy.

'Even so, she doesn't look well,' said William.

'Perhaps she's going down with something?' offered Bob. But they didn't wonder any further. After all, Lizzie was an adult, an Army officer and a married woman; whatever her problem was, it was up to her to sort it out, not her colleagues.

After a few days, Lizzie found that her new job in Headquarters was becoming marginally easier as she gained in experience. She was lucky that she had a quick brain and was naturally efficient. She was also helped by an ability to write clear, concise English, so she rarely had to spend time redrafting documents, letters or briefs that had been rejected by the brigadier for being woolly or rambling. This did mean that both Bob and William all too frequently interrupted her train of thought to pick her brains for a neat turn of phrase or the *mot juste*, but she appreciated the compliment that it implied. In return they never complained if she was a few minutes late back from lunch because she'd been getting some shopping, picking up uniforms from the dry cleaner's or queuing at the bank, although they both wondered why Richard couldn't take a turn at doing some of these errands occasionally. And if doing these chores made her late back, then they both knew that she'd not leave in the evening until her in-tray was empty. How she managed her day was up to her, as long as the work was done. Lizzie just wished she didn't still feel perennially tired.

May drifted into June, bringing with it a round of cocktail parties to celebrate the Queen's birthday. In Aldershot there was to be a

Beating of the Retreat followed by drinks. Lizzie, still feeling below par, was up to her ears in preparing guest lists, issuing invitations, co-ordinating the replies and liaising with the Catering Corps and the mess manager about the food and drinks.

'We've one hundred and eighty-seven definite replies,' she told them two days before the event, 'and another thirty-four who haven't replied despite being chased.'

'It probably means they aren't coming,' said Sergeant Wallis, who'd run more mess functions than Lizzie had had hot dinners.

'All of them?'

'Probably, but we'll cater for around two hundred.' The catering officer nodded in agreement.

'Right, then,' continued the mess manager, 'the form is that the guests arrive at the Command Headquarters and the soldiers detailed from the Gunner regiment and the Paras will show the VIPs to their seats. There's no problem with their units, is there? They know to have the duty personnel here for eighteen hundred hours, don't they?' Lizzie nodded in affirmation to both questions. 'Right. The other guests will be invited to fill up the stands on a first come, first served basis.'

'Will we need rugs?'

'Only for the VIPs, and I've ordered them from the QM. I'm afraid, ma'am, everyone else will have to shiver if it's cold.' He returned to his check list. 'OK, after the Last Post the band will play the National Anthem and the general will invite everyone back to the marquee on the lawn for drinks. That should be at about seven o'clock.'

'What are we going to do if it pours with rain?'

'The Beating of the Retreat will be cancelled if we get a down-pour and everyone will go straight to the marquee. If it's just a shower or a spot of drizzle it'll go ahead and we'd better hope people bring brollies. The decision on the weather will be taken at six o'clock.'

Lizzie checked the list of canapés proffered by the catering officer.

'They all sound mouth-watering,' she said appreciatively.

'We didn't have any complaints last year.'

'Sorry,' said Lizzie. 'You've both done this before.'

'Don't worry, ma'am,' said the mess manager. 'We know that it's you that'll have to face the music if things go wrong. We don't mind you double-checking.' Lizzie smiled wanly.

In the event, in the best tradition of military parades, everything went off like clockwork and the weather obliged by being dry, albeit a touch chilly. The band marched past in quick time and slow time, the music was stirring, the audience appreciative and the Last Post moving. As soon as the National Anthem had been played the assembled guests began to gather their belongings together and move towards the yellow and white marquee, pitched on the grass in front of the Headquarters.

'Where do we get a drink?' asked Richard, looking expectantly through the entrance of the huge tent.

'The waiters should be round in a second,' said Lizzie, glancing anxiously about her. Where were the staff? They should have been by the entrance to greet the guests, but everyone had been very quick off the mark in heading for the relative warmth of the marquee. Just then a battalion of waiters appeared from the far end of the tent bearing trays laden with a variety of drinks. Lizzie began to relax as she realised that all the arrangements were perfect.

She and Richard both took a drink and began to cast round for a group they could join. Behind them other guests poured into the big tent. The temperature began to rise rapidly.

'Aren't you going to introduce me to your high-powered colleagues?' said Richard.

'Yes. Bob's over there. Let's go and talk to him.'

They made their way through the noisy press of people to where Bob Yates and his wife stood. He was with a group of about half a dozen other officers from the Headquarters, most of whom Lizzie recognised, even if she wasn't entirely sure of all the names. She hoped Bob would bail her out over the introductions.

'Hi, Bob,' she said cheerily as she and Richard got close enough. 'May I introduce Richard?'

'At last we all get to meet Lizzie's husband in the flesh,' said Bob. He'd spoken to Richard on the phone on a number of occasions about work matters. 'Nice to meet you, Richard. You are a lucky man to have such an efficient wife.'

Lizzie felt Richard stiffen beside her. Oh God, she thought, she should have warned Bob to lay off the 'Lizzie's husband' bit. Richard was very good about this matter most of the time, but she knew it rankled none the less. Why didn't her work colleagues realise how insulting they were being to Richard by implying that Lizzie was socially more important?

180

'I'm glad she's not letting the side down in the office,' said Richard.

'Richard taught me everything I know,' said Lizzie, wanting to boost his moral. Everyone laughed politely.

'Lizzie,' said Bob, 'I'd like you to meet my wife Ginny. Ginny, this is Lizzie the paragon I've been telling you about.'

'Delighted to meet you, Lizzie,' said Ginny, a large, pleasant-faced woman who gave the impression she'd be more at home baking scones in a farm kitchen than here. They shook hands. 'Can you tell me where I can ditch my coat? I'm going to expire in a minute. It's completely airless in here.' Certainly her round face was very red. She wasn't a bit the sort of woman Lizzie would have imagined as Bob's wife. She'd expected Ginny to be svelte and fashionable.

'I tell you what,' said Bob. 'While you two go off and find the cloaks, I'll take Richard off to meet the brigadier.'

'OK,' said Lizzie. 'We'll catch up with you in a minute or so.' She forged through the press of chattering, laughing officers and their wives, towing Ginny behind her to the corner where there were some rails for coats. She found a spare hanger and watched while Ginny carefully arranged hers on it and brushed out some imagined creases. These meticulous actions seemed incongruous in a woman who gave the outward impression of being such a frump.

'Let's go and join our men again,' Lizzie said. 'Though God knows how we'll find them in this crush.'

'OK.' Ginny looked redder than ever as they both squeezed and eased their way between the guests, trying not to jog drinks or tread on toes, 'Excuse me, can we get through, thank you, sorry' being repeated like some sort of mantra by both of them as they made their way back across the marquee. Lizzie was uncomfortably hot, and she began to feel a little panicky and claustrophobic. She was aware that she'd begun to perspire heavily. Suddenly she came to a place where the crowd wasn't quite so thick, and she stopped and leaned against one of the huge poles holding up the roof of the tent, waiting for Ginny to catch up.

'Phew,' said Ginny, now an interesting shade of puce. 'I vote we find our husbands and then get out of this tent and into some fresh air.'

'Absolutely,' agreed Lizzie, feeling increasingly more uncomfortable.

'I must just catch my breath for a moment, though.' Ginny fanned a hand ineffectually in front of her face before diving into her huge handbag to extract a man's hankie, with which she mopped her forehead. Lizzie wished she'd get herself sorted out so they could escape. Every second she seemed to feel hotter and iller.

'That's a bit better. How do you like working for Bob?'

'He's a nice boss. Honestly.'

'Not that you can really say anything else.'

'No, but he is all the same.'

'Bob said you had some problem with your last posting, which was why you were only sent a mile or so down the road.' She was obviously fishing to find out the cause. Lizzie didn't mind her obvious curiosity but she would rather they left the conversation until they got into the fresh air. She moved off tentatively, talking to Ginny over her shoulder.

'It was nothing, really. Richard was my boss and we went and got married. For some reason the Army thinks it's bad for discipline to have a husband and wife serving in the same unit, so one of us had to go. It was easier to move me than Richard, that was all.' Lizzie was beginning to feel most odd. There was a strange ringing in her ears and she longed to get some fresh air. 'Come on, let's find Bob and Richard and get out of here.' With relief she saw a group of men which included their husbands. 'They're over there,' she gasped to Ginny, and pushed her way towards them.

'Lizzie, are you all right?' said Richard, his face creased by a worried frown. His voice sounded odd, distant. Perhaps it was because the ringing in her ears was even louder.

'I think I need some fresh air,' Lizzie tried to say, but a wave of nausea swept over her and she felt her head spin. She was vaguely aware of a crash of glass, of some hands grabbing her and a voice calling her name, but the next thing she was really conscious of was lying on the grass outside the marquee with Richard bending over her, patting her hand.

'Don't get up,' he said, seeing her open her eyes.

'I don't think I could even if I wanted to.' She still felt very dizzy and rather sick.

'What brought that on?'

'The heat, I think, and all those people.'

'You'll be all right now. Ah, here's Ginny with some water, and the fresh air will help too.'

Ginny crouched beside them and held the water out. Richard supported Lizzie's head so she could drink.

'Better?' Ginny asked.

'A bit.' Lizzie smiled thinly. 'I expect everyone thinks I was pissed.'

'Not at all. Frankly, I think a few other people were feeling pretty ropy too. It was completely airless in there.' And indeed there was quite an exodus from the tent as more and more people decided that conditions were nicer outside.

'Ah, Lizzie,' said the brigadier. 'Feeling better, I trust?'

Lizzie nodded weakly. It seemed odd to be lying down looking up at her boss rather than standing to attention in front of him. She felt very self-conscious about the scene she'd just made, and rather stupid.

'I was thinking of taking her home, Brigadier,' said Richard. 'If that's all right with you.' Everyone knew that under normal circumstances no junior officer would dare to commit such a breach of protocol by leaving before the principle guest.

'Certainly, dear boy. Have you got transport?'

'Oh yes, thank you, sir.'

Lizzie, the fresh air at last reviving her and making her feel considerably better, struggled to sit up.

'Can you make it to the car?' asked Richard.

Lizzie nodded. Richard helped her to her feet and slipped his arm around her waist to support her.

'I don't expect you in on Monday unless you feel completely better,' the brigadier called after her as she left.

'I'm sure I'll be fine by then,' she replied.

But she wasn't. On Monday she was in a side ward of the Louise Margaret Maternity Hospital in Aldershot, recovering from a miscarriage.

'Do you feel up to visitors?' asked Ginny, putting her head round the door.

Lizzie smiled sadly. 'I'm not much company. I keep getting weepy,' she said. Ginny pulled out a few magazines from her shopping bag and put them on the bed, before perching on a hard plastic chair.

'You poor dear, you must be feeling wretched. No wonder you were so unwell at the cocktail party. I'm so sorry about the baby. How very sad for you.'

'Yes. But the silly thing was I didn't even know I was pregnant.' Ginny looked more than a little surprised. 'I know, I know. I'm a

183

grown woman and I know the facts of life, but my periods have always been completely irregular, and what with this new job, I've been so busy recently that I just didn't notice they'd stopped altogether.'

'But what about feeling sick?'

'No. I'd been feeling shattered for ages but I put it down to the new job. I never felt the least bit sick.'

'Bob said to me once that he thought you weren't looking well, that you looked very tired.'

'Yes, well . . . I thought I just needed a few early nights. I didn't think . . .' Her voice tailed off and she gulped back a sob.

'How's Richard?' asked Ginny gently.

'He's being sweet. I think he's as upset as I am but he's being ever so brave about it. He says I must have been doing too much, what with the house and working full time. He says I must get a proper cleaner so I don't have to do so much at home.'

'Typical man's reaction,' said Ginny with a snort. 'Get another woman in to do it rather than help out himself.' Lizzie felt she was being a bit harsh, although the thought had crossed her mind briefly too. 'Well, you take it easy for a few days. Bob says that the office will cope without you, and when you get home you make sure you put your feet up. Get Richard to run around after you for a change.'

'I'm sure he will. I'm being allowed home tomorrow and already he's asked me about what I want to eat.'

'Well, you just make sure he doesn't expect you to cook it.'

Belfast, July 1990

Edwina eased herself on to the wall and ran along it. In black clothes and with no lights around, she was almost invisible. Silently she jumped off, carefully avoiding a muddy flowerbed, and tiptoed to the window. Crouching down beneath it she listened assiduously for any noise, either inside or outside the house. The occupant, a known IRA player code-named Bravo One, had taken his large Alsatian and gone out. Bravo One was high on everyone's list of priorities because, despite their previous efforts, they'd lost the big sniper's gun they'd been after, and they had been told that this man had been instrumental in moving and hiding it. There was supposedly some 'hot int' to corroborate this. They'd been watching him for several weeks and knew that on a Friday night he went to his local and rarely returned till close on midnight. Others in the team were keeping tabs on him while Nat and Edwina went for a snoop around his house. The only problem was that tonight he'd left later than normal and they'd already missed half an hour of darkness. Assuming he was still returning at his usual time, they didn't have long, but they were going ahead regardless because Special Branch were desperate for the information that should result from this operation. Anyway, they had reassured themselves, an hour should be ample time.

Edwina turned her mouth to the tiny microphone, hidden in her coat collar and whispered, 'OK, Tango. All clear.' That told Nat to join her. In a couple of seconds she could hear Nat following her route along the wall and into the garden. With a soft thud he landed beside her. She reported this back to the other call signs, again using a minimum of words.

'Tango and Whisky in position.'

'Roger,' she heard through her earpiece.

185

Quickly Nat picked the lock of the back door. Both he and Edwina had their fingers crossed that it wouldn't be bolted from the inside. They would be able to overcome this problem but it would take time. He carefully twisted the handle and felt the door give slightly.

'Great,' he murmured. Swiftly he pushed the door open far enough for both him and Edwina to slip through and shut it again, noiselessly, behind them.

'Whisky and Tango complete.' Their back-up team needed to know they'd got inside safely. They both stood for a moment in the darkness before they reached into Edwina's backpack and pulled out their passive night goggles. This weird apparatus, which looked like a cross between an SLR camera and a pair of binoculars, allowed them to see clearly in the dark and was strapped to their heads, leaving their hands free. They switched their goggles on simultaneously and instantly a muted high-pitched whine could be heard.

'I hate that bloody noise,' complained Edwina in a low voice.

'We all do, so shut up about it.' Edwina knew that Nat was only snapping at her because he was as nervous as she was, but she had to bite her tongue to stop herself answering back.

They looked around their surroundings using the goggles and an infra-red torch, which gave everything a funny greenish-grey tinge. They were standing in the squalid kitchen. The sink was piled with plates and pans, soaking in greasy washing-up water, cold by the look of it. On the table in the middle of the room were a half-eaten loaf of bread and a couple of dirty plates. They quickly checked the surfaces for letters, papers or diaries – anything that might contain useful information. There was nothing. Edwina's earpiece hissed for a second, which warned her someone was about to come on the net.

'Bravo One in place.'

Edwina gave her transmitter switch a double click that meant she understood that their target was now in the pub. All being well, they had at least an hour. She began to relax.

Nat patted her arm to get her attention and pointed towards the door to the rest of the house. She nodded. They knew that the walls of some of these houses were thin and noise had to be kept to an absolute minimum. They certainly didn't want nosy neighbours coming to investigate what was going on in a supposedly empty house. They went through into a small sitting room. It contained a television, a couple of chairs and a low table, and it reeked of cigarette smoke. The grate in front of the fire was littered with butts.

Edwina automatically went to check the piles of paper on the table for something interesting while Nat quickly unscrewed the mouthpiece of the telephone and inserted a tiny bug. Then he extracted a screwdriver from a pocket, swiftly unscrewed a wall socket and placed another bug in that. He had the whole thing back in place in under a minute. Edwina, meanwhile, was sifting through the stuff on the table. Delightedly she extracted an address book. It might be useless – just his relations and girlfriends – but on the other hand . . .

'Hold this open for me,' she said in an almost imperceptible murmur. Nat replaced his screwdriver in his pocket and held the book open as Edwina clipped an infra-red flashlight to her camera and clicked. The light popped, seemingly flooding the room although they both knew it was only visible courtesy of their goggles. Even so the sudden flash still made them both jump involuntarily. Without being asked, Nat turned the pages so Edwina could photograph each one. Their earpieces hissed again just as Edwina was dismantling her camera and putting it back into the poacher's pockets in her jacket.

'Bravo One is foxtrot on Green.'

'Roger,' replied Edwina. Shit! They looked at each other in horror. Their target had apparently left the pub and was walking along the road code-named Green. What on earth was going on? It was just possible that he wasn't coming home, but it was equally possible that he was. If it was the latter option they had ten minutes before he arrived back.

'Upstairs, quick.'

'OK,' said Edwina. Her soft voice was calm but she could feel her heart thudding as if she'd just done the log race again.

They both sped up the stairs, the soft, supple soles of their black plimsolls making virtually no sound. Taking a bedroom each, they repeated the procedures of downstairs, removing a socket cover and inserting a tiny bug inside. Edwina was aware her hand was shaking. She tried to tell herself that in a dentist's chair, having a tooth drilled, ten minutes would seem an eternity, but it didn't help.

'Fuck,' she swore under her breath as she dropped a screw. She fumbled for it on the floor and found it. Her earpiece hissed again.

'Bravo One turning left on to Brown.' He *was* returning home. What the hell had happened to make him change his plans? It crossed Edwina's mind that perhaps there was some sort of passive alarm in the house, something that had warned him his house had been broken into. Hell, if that was the case, he might have others converging from another direction to help him. Bravo One was hardly small fry in the IRA hierarchy and this estate was thick with IRA members, supporters and sympathisers.

She spoke softly into her concealed mike again; she wanted to know what was happening at the back of the house.

'Whisky. What activity to rear of Alpha One?'

'Nothing on Blue.' That was the alley clear.

Another voice chipped in, 'Red quiet.' Edwina smiled to herself as she recognised Ulysses' voice. It gave her comfort to think he was out there and on her side. If things got rough he'd be her knight in shining armour – well, SAS trooper in combat kit really, but what the heck.

She got the screw into the socket cover and began to turn the screwdriver. Blast, she'd crossed the threads. More haste, less speed, she thought. She extracted it and tried again. This time it went home smoothly.

'Bravo One, three minutes.'

Time to go. She ran quietly into the bedroom Nat was working in. He'd heard the message too. She checked he'd left nothing behind and he did the same for her, then they scampered silently down the stairs, keeping close to the wall to minimise the risk of the treads creaking, and out of the kitchen door. They both crouched down as Nat tried to relock the door using his lock picks.

'Bravo One, one minute,' they heard.

'Hurry up,' said Edwina.

Nat just grunted in exasperation and fiddled again with his instruments.

'Bravo One, thirty.' Edwina could feel the adrenaline pumping.

'The fucking thing won't turn,' snarled Nat, more to himself than to Edwina.

'Shit.'

'Bravo One at Alpha One.' He was home.

The click as the lock turned was audible to both Edwina and Nat. There was not time for any congratulations. They wheeled around and headed for the wall. They knew from experience that it would be easier for Edwina to give Nat a leg up and then for him to reach down and pull her up. In the deep shadow by the coal shed she crouched and cupped her hands. Nat put his foot into it and with an almighty heave she thrust him to the top of the eight-foot wall. Suddenly part of the garden was bathed in light flooding through the kitchen window. Nat, sprawled on top of the wall, swivelled on his stomach so that he could reach down for her. Edwina glanced over her shoulder to see what was happening in the house. To her horror she saw Bravo One in the kitchen.

'Go,' she said to Nat. Without a moment's hesitation she opened the door of the coal shed and slipped inside. She didn't wait to see what Nat did. If he had any sense he'd be away on his toes.

'Whisky, are you OK?' came Nat's voice through her earpiece. Even with the static she could hear the concern.

Click, click, she transmitted by using her pressel switch.

'Are you trapped?'

Click, click.

'Do you have cover?'

Click, click.

Edwina pressed her face to the crack between the door and the jamb and peered through. To her horror, she saw the back door open. The Alsatian came flying though it, propelled by a hefty kick.

'And you can stay out all night, you filt'y cur.' The back door slammed.

Oh, God, she thought, not the fucking dog. Now I'm bound to be found. Her heart rate racked itself up another notch. She felt physically sick with terror. She knew exactly what to expect if she was discovered. And unless she could get the first shot in, being shot herself would probably be the least of her worries. The terrifying images of the two fated corporals who'd strayed into an IRA funeral cortège were still vivid in many minds. Involuntarily she checked her pistol in the waistband of her trousers as she watched the dog paw at the back door and whine loudly. The light in the kitchen went out, although Edwina could see from a remaining glimmer that the light in the front room was still on. Bravo One was obviously settling down to watch the TV. The dog continued to whine.

Edwina knew from experience that you couldn't stay frightened indefinitely, and slowly, as it became apparent that the dog was only interested in getting back into the house, her heart rate and her breathing began to slow down.

The dog was whining incessantly. No one in the neighbourhood was going to pick up Edwina's voice over the noise, if she kept it low. She whispered into her mike, 'Whisky. I'm safe. I'll need assistance to exit Alpha One.'

'Roger.'

'Whisky. Not immediately. Bravo One is still awake.'

'Roger. All stations, did you copy?' Edwina heard all the other call signs acknowledge. She sat down on the sacks of coal, hungry, dispirited and frightened, and waited. Despite the fact that it was July and not cold, she shivered. The whining of the dog began to wind her up. Surely it was going to attract attention, the last thing she wanted. She felt her situation was bleak indeed. Her only comfort was that at least it was summer and no one was going to be coming out to the coal shed for fuel.

After what seemed an age, the whining stopped. Edwina was instantly alert again. Why? She pressed her eye to the crack in the door and saw that the dog had given up and was lying across the doorstep, its nose resting on its paws, looking utterly miserable. You and me both, thought Edwina. As she moved to lean back again, she dislodged a few lumps of coal, which skittered on to the floor. Instantly the dog was alert. Shit! Edwina's heart rate accelerated again as she saw the dog cock its ears up and sniff the air. Obviously it had now found something to take its mind off its misery. It got to its feet and began to prowl round the tiny back yard, sniffing around the base of the wall. Edwina held her breath as the dog approached the coal shed. Suddenly there was a flurry of barking and snarling; it had obviously caught her scent. It paced backwards from the shed and standing in the middle of the yard barked frantically. Edwina debated whether she could get herself out of the shed and over the wall before the dog caught her. She knew she didn't stand an earthly. She saw a light come on. From the angle of the shadows on the ground it was upstairs and next door. Her ears strained to hear any noises over the barking of the Alsatian. She caught the unmistakable sound of a sash window being thrown up.

'Shut up, you fucker,' shrieked a shrill Irish voice. 'John McGuinness, if you'se don't shut your dog up . . .' The dog barked even louder. The window slammed down again.

'Tango. Whisky, what's happening?' The whole of Belfast must be able to hear this bloody dog, let alone the remainder of the team hanging around in the vicinity.

'Whisky. The dog has found me.'

'What's your situation?'

'OK, over.'

Edwina could see that the neighbour's light was still on. She didn't need this either. It meant yet more light in the garden, thus hampering even further her chances of escape.

The dog was still going ballistic in the middle of the yard. Bravo One was bound to come out in a minute, even if only to shut the mutt up. And even as Edwina thought that, the kitchen light went on again. Edwina willed herself to stay calm. She fingered her pistol again. At least she would have the element of surprise on her side, but would she be able to shoot Bravo One *and* the dog before one of them got her? She knew her training should have prepared her for exactly this, but there was one hell of a difference between training and reality. She drew her pistol and cocked it, then pressed her eye to the crack again. She saw the back door open and yet more light flood into the yard. Bravo One stood in the doorway, a silhouette against the brightness behind him. Another figure joined him. Oh, God. Two and a dog. The odds were shortening frighteningly.

Suddenly Edwina had an almost overwhelming desire to laugh as she heard, '. . . and I tell you, John McGuinness, you tell that dog to shut the fuck up or I'll have it taken to the pound. That I will.' His neighbour was yelling at the top of her lungs to be heard over the barking, her voice shrill with anger and indignation.

'You mind your own fuckin' business and get out of my house.'

'I'll not go until you've shut this dog up.'

'Oh, shut up yourself, you old bag. You had no right to barge in. Who the fuck do you think you are?' He turned his attention to the dog. 'Come here, you'se.' The dog continued to bark frantically. Edwina watched as Bravo One strode forward a couple of paces and yanked viciously on the dog's collar. 'Shut up,' he yelled at it, and hit it hard across its muzzle. Despite the anguish the dog had caused her, Edwina felt sorry for it as it yelped in pain. It was still straining towards the coal shed but Bravo One was deep in his slanging match.

'You piss off, you.' Bravo One, still grasping his dog by its collar, pushed his neighbour towards the house.

'Not till that dog's inside.'

'Don't you tell me what to do.' The pair of them made their way towards the door.

'If that fucking animal wakes us up again, I'll call out the law.' They disappeared inside, taking the dog with them, and their voices faded as the door slammed shut.

Edwina sagged with relief and uncocked her weapon. She noticed her hands were shaking. Softly into her mike she said, 'Whisky. I'm preparing to exit Alpha One.'

'Roger. Tango proceeding.' There was a pause of a few seconds, then, 'Tango. In position.'

Edwina opened the door to the coal shed, took two paces to the wall and looked up to see Nat grinning down at her like a Cheshire cat. She reached up and in a fluid movement Nat had grasped her hand and hauled her up so that she was able to sprawl on the top of the wall. Without stopping to thank him, she swung her legs over it and dropped down into the relative safety of the alley. A second later there was a soft thump as Nat joined her. They both ran to the unmarked car waiting to collect them at the end of it.

'Whisky and Tango complete,' Nat said into his mike as the car drew away.

'Roger.'

Edwina leant back against the seat of the car and grinned sideways at Nat.

'That was hairy,' she said, trying to sound nonchalant and cheerful.

'I've known smoother operations.'

'What the hell happened? Why did he come back?'

'According to Bill, some dope fed the bloody dog a packet of crisps while McGuinness wasn't looking. The dog choked on them and threw up all over the floor of the bar. The landlord chucked them both out.'

'You mean the whole operation nearly went tits up because some mangy mutt honked in the pub.' The ridiculous story, compounded with the relief of getting away in one piece, was too much for Edwina. She began to laugh. Tears ran down her face as she threw her head back and roared and roared with laughter. She was still chuckling when she got back to her Portakabin.

'What's so funny?' said a voice in the darkness.

Edwina leapt as if she'd been stung. 'Ulysses! You bastard! Christ, I don't need any more frights.' But she felt a warm glow of desire start to spread through her.

'But I didn't think sneaks like you got frightened.'

'Sneaks who think they're about to be torn to bits by some rabid Alsatian do.' As she spoke she began to undress.

'Don't exaggerate.'

'I'm not – well, not much.' She pulled off her undies and leapt into bed. Ulysses drew her close to him and wrapped his arms round her. The feeling of instant security was the perfect antidote to the strain of the last few hours. 'Ooh, that's better,' she said, trying to sound casual. 'I wondered what I was going to warm my feet on.'

'It's not your feet I was planning on warming up.'

'Special Branch have put a barrel of beer behind the bar at the Greenfly, to thank us for last night,' Edwina told Ulysses when she returned from a briefing the next day. 'Can you stay until this evening? We're going to have a bit of a party to celebrate yesterday's operation.'

'Yeah, sure.'

'Well, don't sound too enthusiastic,' she snapped. She was feeling touchy. The elation of her escape the day before had worn off, and lack of sleep had taken its toll. She went off for a run to work her bad temper out of her system. When she got back she found a note from Ulysses telling her that he'd gone to practise on the range. Edwina eyed her bed longingly. Shit, she was tired. She flopped down on it for just five minutes . . .

She woke with a start. Blearily she looked at her alarm clock. Hell's bells, six o'clock. She leapt out of bed. Ulysses, sitting in the armchair by the window, glanced up from the book he was reading.

'Welcome back to the land of the living.'

'Why didn't you wake me?' she demanded angrily.

'What for? So you could bite my head off again?'

'I'm sorry. I was a bear, wasn't I?' She went over to him and gave him a long, lingering kiss. 'Am I forgiven?'

'All right,' said Ulysses, grudgingly. 'On one condition.'

'Name it.'

'Get your kit off and get back into bed.'

It was after eight o'clock when they strolled, arm in arm, across the car park towards the corner of the barracks where the Greenfly was to be found. Edwina was feeling fully recovered. A decent sleep had helped her to get over the trauma of the night before, and now she was on a high again. After all, the operation had been a success – albeit through luck rather than judgement – and everyone could now see the funny side of things. On top of that Ulysses was around and didn't seem to be under any pressure to return to his own unit – well, not before morning anyway. She felt so good about life that she was even able to overlook the stink of the glue factory, which pumped its noxious fumes over Lisburn whenever the wind was in the right, or, rather, the wrong direction.

The Greenfly Club was a single-storey hut near the stables. From the outside it didn't look particularly inviting and inside the décor was basic, but the beer was good, the glasses were clean and the seats comfortable, and for most members of the unit that was more than enough. Edwina and Ulysses were no exception.

They walked through the door and Ulysses went to the bar to get the drinks while Edwina walked to the one table that was free and sat down. After a minute she heard a movement beside her. Someone was standing next to the table.

'Well, well. If it isn't Miss Austin.' Edwina recognised the voice instantly – Cathy Roberts, her platoon commander from Sandhurst. She closed her eyes, quickly counted to ten and took a deep breath. Remembering not to call her ma' am, she turned and smiled.

'Cathy. How nice.' She tried to sound sincere – but not very hard.

'I haven't seen you around before,' said Cathy. 'Have you just arrived in the Province?'

'No, I've been here six months.' Edwina tried to keep the antipathy she felt out of her voice.

'Where're you based?' Edwina quite fancied telling Cathy what she really did, just to score a point, but it was strictly against the rules. Shame, though.

'Here, in Lisburn.' She wished Ulysses would hurry up and come back with their drinks, but the bar was crowded and the single bar-man was only just coping.

'Well, I haven't seen you,' said Cathy flatly.

'I don't work in the Headquarters.' Perhaps even Cathy would be able to deduce Edwina's role in the Province from those few words. 14 Company's *raison d'être* and its personnel were a huge secret, but most people in the HQ knew the unit existed, and knew its personnel didn't socialise much outside their own kind.

'I see,' said Cathy, although Edwina was pretty sure she didn't. 'And how are your friends, Amanda and Lizzie?' Superficially the words were friendly, but Edwina could hear that the tone wasn't.

'They're fine. Lizzie got married last year.'

'What about Amanda?'

'She's out in Germany.'

Cathy sat down uninvited at Edwina's table.

'So, you've been split up?'

'Yes, so what?'

'Oh, nothing. Are you waiting for someone?' said Cathy, noticing that Edwina was on her own and without a drink.

'Yes. My boyfriend is at the bar.'

Cathy looked at the crush waiting to be served. She recognised a face she knew from Sandhurst days amongst them. 'Staff Lees?' she asked, stunned.

'So?' Edwina almost asked her if she wanted to make something of it, but decided that would be going too far. After all, Cathy was still her superior officer, although the gap between subaltern and captain was a far lesser chasm than that between cadet and captain.

'You are aware of the Army's views about officers fraternising with other ranks?' asked Cathy pompously.

'I work with him.'

'I work with my chief clerk but I don't go out with him.'

'Only because he's got more taste.' Edwina regretted what she'd said the instant it was out, but it was too late.

Cathy flared up in anger. 'If I'd had my way you never would have been commissioned, Edwina. You were a poor cadet and you're obviously a worse officer.'

'Just as well you can't touch me then, isn't it, Cathy? I don't work for the WRAC, so as far as you're concerned I'm fireproof,' said Edwina coolly.

'Don't you believe it. You know what they say in the Army?'

'No, do tell me.'

'It's not what you know, it's who you know, and I've got lots of friends in all sorts of places.'

'You surprise me. I wouldn't have thought you'd got any friends at all.'

Cathy completely lost her temper. 'I'll wipe the smile off your face, so help me I will.'

'You wish!'

Ulysses appeared with the drinks. 'Sorry to be so long, Edwina. Glad to see you've got company.' He stared at Cathy; her face was familiar but for a split second he couldn't place it. Then, as she spoke, he remembered her from Sandhurst. He also remembered a rumour he'd heard about this officer since she'd arrived in the Province. He looked at her with curiosity, trying to work out if it could be true.

'Staff Lees,' said Cathy. 'How nice to see you again. Don't worry,

I'm just going.' And she swept off to a table where she joined a man Edwina recognised as the SO3 (Intelligence) at the Headquarters. So that was how she'd got herself invited to this exclusive club. Edwina had been wondering about that, as no one but the Intelligence Corps and Special Forces was welcome.

'Christ, you could have cut the atmosphere between you two with a blunt palette knife it was so thick. What the hell was going on? I nearly told her to fuck off.'

'Back of the queue!'

'She doesn't like you?'

'It's mutual. She reported me for having a man in my room at Sandhurst.'

'So out of character.' His voice was larded with irony.

'Piss off. I was a model cadet in that respect.' Ulysses just raised one eyebrow by way of reply, and Edwina punched his arm hard.

'Ow! What did you do that for?'

'Because I was telling the truth.' Up went his eyebrow again. 'Anyway, I didn't. She was mistaken and I think she got a rocket from the company commander. I don't think she liked me much before that incident, but afterwards . . .'

'Off her Christmas card list?'

'Something like that.'

'Well, she can't touch you now you're working for 14 Company.'

'That's what I told her too. She didn't like it.'

'Do you want to hear something about her?'

'What?' Edwina was delighted at the thought that Ulysses had some gossip on her.

'Rumour has it she's bonked her way round most of the officers in the Province.'

'The local bike?'

'She's had more rides than Disneyworld.'

Aldershot, September 1990

'Hi, Lizzie! How's tricks? Life treating you well?' Edwina sounded cheerful, as she always did when she took the all-too-infrequent trouble to phone. Lizzie, cradling the telephone, stared miserably around the sitting room of her home and wondered how to answer Edwina's question. Should she tell a bare-faced lie? 'Hello, Lizzie? Are you still there?'

'Yes, sorry. Um . . . never mind. Sorry. What did you say?'

'I asked how you are?'

'Oh, fine, thanks. And you?' It wasn't really the truth, but she didn't want to talk about how she was. It only made her worse. She could put on an act at work, she could manage some semblance of pretence when Richard was around, but when she was on her own, like now, she slipped into this awful morass of misery, lethargy and despair. But she couldn't admit how awful she felt, not to anyone, not even Edwina and Amanda.

'Great,' said Edwina, taking her answer at face value. 'I've got some leave coming up. I was wondering if I could come and crash out for a few days at your place. I really can't face my mum's again.'

'When were you thinking of?' A tiny part of Lizzie perked up slightly at the thought of seeing Edwina again, but another, bigger part couldn't face it. She didn't think she could cope with Edwina's constant cheerfulness and relentless optimism, to say nothing of the effort of looking after a visitor. And would she be able to conceal her miscarriage from her? There were still only a very few people who knew about it and Lizzie wanted it to stay that way. She'd had enough sympathy, and she didn't think she could cope with any more.

'A week on Friday?' asked Edwina. 'Would that be OK? It'll just be me. Ulysses can't get leave at the same time.'

'I think that'll be OK.' Lizzie was relieved Edwina hadn't asked her to accommodate Ulysses too. That she couldn't have coped with. 'I'll have to check it's all right with Richard, though; that he hasn't anything planned.'

'And to make sure he doesn't mind having such a bad influence in the house.'

Lizzie didn't answer. She knew Edwina meant it as a joke, but she wasn't sure, things being the way they were, that Edwina would be entirely welcome. She knew that Richard was still worried that anything extra might hinder her slow, fragile recovery. He tried to protect her from anything that he thought might upset her or tire her. The reality, and they both knew it, was that Lizzie was perfectly recovered physically – it was just the emotional side that had to heal now.

'Right,' said Edwina. 'Ring me if there's a problem. If I don't hear from you I'll assume everything is OK and I'll see you a week on Friday.'

'Great. I'll look forward to it.'

''Bye.'

Lizzie put the phone down. She wished she'd had the courage to put Edwina off. She really didn't feel up to this. Everything these days was such an effort: work, shopping, sex. Richard was being wonderful, patient, understanding, and she knew that she should be able to snap out of this awful, miserable sluggishness which had overtaken her. But since she'd lost the baby things had seemed so pointless. There were only a few people in Aldershot who were privy to what had happened just after she left the cocktail party – the awful, stabbing pain and her second collapse in the car park beside the Headquarters, the ambulance, the blood and the mess. Those few were all so kind and sympathetic, but Lizzie knew that even they were beginning to think it was about time she pulled herself together and got on with her life. And she knew they were right. She wasn't the only person in the world who had lost a baby. She was young, she was fit, and she could have another. So there was no excuse, she told herself, for her to be moping around feeling sorry for herself. But it didn't help.

Neither did it help that Saddam Hussein seemed to be doing everything he could to goad the West to declare war on his troops in Kuwait. The Americans had already flown thousands of troops out to the Gulf, and units from the British 7th Armoured Brigade were about to follow. Lizzie was horrified that some of her friends from Sandhurst days were facing the prospect of going to war. She consoled herself with the thought that Richard was probably safe in his new posting at the Ministry of Defence, although she knew that given the opportunity to go to the Gulf he'd take it like a shot. But, she told herself, like everyone else in that huge building he was working flat out organising a massive deployment of British troops, and it was unlikely that they would be able to spare him to go, despite the fact that he was a fluent Arabic speaker. Underneath, though, she had a nasty, sneaking feeling that this situation might change.

The down side of his relatively safe job at the MoD was that, with this emergency brewing in the Middle East, he rarely seemed to get home before ten o'clock at night, which meant Lizzie had even more time to brood and feel miserable on her own. This evening was obviously going to be no exception, Lizzie though dully. She went into the kitchen and checked the shepherd's pie in the oven. Despite its protective cover of foil it was beginning to look unappetising. Lizzie switched the oven off and took it out. Perhaps if she scraped some of the potato off the top when Richard came in he might not notice that it had got a bit burnt. She looked at the clock on the kitchen wall: ten thirty. Lizzie sighed. She was tired and famished, and she wanted to shower and wash her hair. She considered having her supper and going to bed and to hell with Richard, but she couldn't. He was working his socks off and he deserved to come home to a bit of sympathy and support. It would be unfair of her to leave him to eat his supper on his own.

She heard his key in the latch. She switched on a smile and went into the hall to greet him.

'Hello, darling. You must be shattered after such a long day. Let me get you a drink while you have a sit-down. Supper'll be ready in a moment.' She stood on tiptoe to kiss his cheek.

'Get me a gin, would you, sweetie. Make it a large one.'

As she went into the dinning room to make it, she heard him collapse into his favourite chair.

'Supper will only be a few minutes,' she said to him as she handed him his drink.

'Great. I'm famished.' He took a noisy slurp of his drink. 'And shattered.' He looked up at her and smiled. 'How was your day?'

'Oh, so-so. You know, busy.' Everyone was these days. Just

because she worked in a headquarters in Aldershot didn't mean the increased workload didn't percolate down to their level. 'I think I prefer being busy.' She didn't say that it stopped her brooding. She didn't have to.

Lizzie went into the kitchen to dish up and returned a couple of minutes later with Richard's meal on a tray.

'Don't wait for me,' she said as she returned to the kitchen to fetch her own meal. They ate in silence; both of them too tired to be interested in conversation. Lizzie completely forgot to mention Edwina's telephone call, only remembering it the next day after Richard had already left to catch the train to London.

That evening Richard amazed Lizzie be being home just after seven. Something good had obviously happened at work, because he had a broad grin on his face as he walked through the door.

'I'm going out to the Gulf,' he announced without preamble. 'One of the Gunner regiments needs to be brought up to its war establishment and I've been offered the chance to fill one of the slots.'

Lizzie's heart sank. Her worst fear, that she'd hoped wouldn't come true. Already the press and TV reports had been full of descriptions of Hussein's chemical and biological arsenal. The defence correspondents on every channel had been harping on for days now about the casualties in the Iran–Iraq war. They didn't think things would be any better for American and European forces, and it could possibly be worse. Lizzie, despite outwardly sympathising with Richard's frustration at not being involved directly with Operation Granby, had inwardly been praising heaven that his post at the MoD would surely prevent him from going out there.

She fixed a smile to her face to mask her feelings. 'When are you . . .?' but despite her expression the tears began to pour down her face. She rushed downstairs to the kitchen. Richard followed her.

'I'm sorry, I'm sorry,' she sobbed. 'I should be so pleased for you, I know you want to go really. I'm just being silly.' Richard put his arms round her and gave her a hug. Lizzie buried her face against his chest and sobbed even more.

'Oh, don't worry, Lizzie.' He sounded embarrassed at her concern. 'We'll get over there, rattle our sabres and Saddam will back down. You'll see.' But the excitement in his voice belied his soothing words. He patted her shoulder. 'I've got four days' leave and then I have to report to my new unit. You'll have to help me sort my kit out, although most of what I'm going to need won't be issued till I get to

Hohne. I'll be doing some training with my new regiment before going to Saudi.'

Lizzie sniffed miserably. She knew how important this was to him. But was she going to be able to cope with it on top of everything else?

Over the next few days Lizzie didn't have time to worry about the future. This was a busy time for everyone in the Army, not just for the troops who were heading for the Middle East. The units going to war all had to be virtually doubled in number, which meant poaching soldiers and officers from anywhere that could spare them, and even from units and formations that couldn't. Bob Yates, Lizzie's boss, was being sent out to join 7th Armoured Brigade, which left Lizzie and William Davies to do his work as well as their own. They didn't complain – no one did. It was the same throughout the Army. The excitement of the unfolding scenario in Kuwait gave them all the energy to keep going despite their increased workloads. Lizzie – feeling exhausted again but knowing that this time it definitely *was* work that was the cause – kept telling herself that she could catch up on her sleep once Richard had departed. What with the amount she had to do at work, to say nothing of the extra burden Richard's departure was creating at home, sleep was a luxury that was in preciously short supply.

'There's one good thing about all this,' she told William in a rare lull in the office.

'What's that?'

'I haven't had a chance to brood about what's going on. I'm either working, helping Richard get ready or asleep.'

'Don't overdo it, will you?'

'No, I promise.' And she realised that with all this activity, she'd had so little time during the last few days to think about her own problems that they – at last – seemed to be receding. Perhaps, she thought, it takes a new crisis to get rid of the old one.

'I'm glad to hear it. I don't want you off ill again. I couldn't run all three desks on my own.' Although he made it sound like a joke, they both knew he was being serious.

'Don't worry. I won't leave you in the lurch.'

'When Richard has gone, would you like to come round for supper with Sophie and me? It might help to take your mind off things. We thought we'd get Ginny round too. You'll both be in the same boat and perhaps you'll be able to cheer each other up.'

Lizzie gladly accepted the invitation. She liked William and she'd heard his wife Sophie was a real character. They had a large circle of friends and, so the rumour went, a chaotic house. Supper there was bound to be fun. For the first time in months, Lizzie realised that she actually relished the prospect of going out and enjoying herself. She even found she was looking forward to Edwina's imminent visit.

With her depression finally lifting, Lizzie was able to get a grip and tell herself sharply that she had no right to feel sorry for herself about Richard going to the Gulf. She felt she was getting more than her fair share of sympathy from her colleagues at work because of the baby, but she knew that really there were others who were far more deserving of such kindness and support; Ginny, for example, who had two small children. At least Lizzie didn't have to worry about children as well as everything else; perhaps the miscarriage had been a blessing after all.

When Lizzie drove Richard to RAF Lyneham to catch his flight to Germany, he barely kissed her goodbye before rushing off. Lizzie thought he was more like a small boy going to a party than a grown man going off to war.

'I'll write every day,' she said as they parted.

'I don't know I'll be able to, but I'll write when I can, I promise. Look after yourself.' And he pecked her on the cheek and disappeared into the passenger terminal.

As Lizzie watched him go she wondered if she'd ever see him again. Tears streamed down her face as she drove from the base. She couldn't bear to wait to watch his plane take off, as some of the other families planned. She felt that if she didn't see the plane go, she could tell herself that he hadn't gone either. She could hold on to the delusion as some sort of comfort.

'Have you heard from him yet?' asked Edwina, when she arrived to stay with Lizzie a few days later.

'Not yet. I don't suppose he's had a chance to do anything much. He was told that he was being met at the airport and being taken straight out to join the regiment on exercise out on the ranges. I think it'll be a while before he can find a phone or a postbox.' Lizzie was arranging the rather battered bunch of flowers that Edwina had bought at a garage on her way rather than arrive empty-handed. She'd hoped that Lizzie wouldn't notice that they were beyond their sell-by date, but once the cellophane wrapping had been removed it was rather obvious. Better than nothing, though, Edwina thought breezily. Lizzie finished doing the best she could with the sorry selection of blooms and carried them into the sitting room to put them on the windowsill. Edwina followed her.

'Why don't we go for a drink? There must be a decent pub near here. Or what about the mess?'

'It's not a very lively place. There's a nice pub in a little village down the road. I'll drive if you like.' Lizzie was well aware that Edwina claimed to be allergic to soft drinks.

'Great.' Edwina wasn't going to argue.

It was still light when they got there and the evening was warm, so once they'd bought their drinks, they opted to sit in the garden. There was a bench free in the spacious, sunny garden. Edwina plumped herself down on it and turned her face, cat-like, towards the last rays of the evening sun.

'This is great,' said Edwina appreciatively as she took a large gulp of her Guinness.

Lizzie wrinkled her nose in distaste. 'I don't know how you can drink that stuff.'

'It's easy. I open my mouth, tip the glass and swallow.'

Lizzie laughed. 'I didn't mean that, stupid.'

Edwina was pleased that she'd made her friend laugh. She'd been shocked at Lizzie's appearance when she'd arrived at the house. Lizzie had never been anything but slim, but now she looked positively emaciated – her face in particular was all eyes and cheekbones. And she look strained too. There were lines around her mouth and her eyes had lost their sparkle. There was something about Lizzie which made Edwina think she'd been doing a deal too much crying recently. She had a suspicion that, whatever the problem was, it was more complicated than just Richard going away.

'How's married life?' Edwina asked.

'It's fine.'

'Only fine?'

Lizzie stared at her tomato juice and didn't answer. Her eyes began to fill with tears.

'Lizzie, what's wrong?' Edwina moved closer to Lizzie and put her arm around her. 'Come on, poppet, tell me.'

Lizzie suddenly knew she had to tell her. Edwina had obviously worked out that something awful had happened and she would be so dreadfully hurt if Lizzie couldn't bring herself to confide in her. The tears spilled on to her cheeks as she began to talk.

'I wasn't going to tell you or Amanda. I didn't think I could face any more sympathy, but actually, just recently I've been a lot better.' She took a deep breath and paused, oblivious of Edwina's impatience to hear what dreadful event had befallen her. 'I had a miscarriage back in the summer,' she said finally.

'Oh, you poor thing. How ghastly.' But because Edwina had never been the least interested in babies, either her own or anyone else's, she was really thinking, *Is that all?*

'It was awful. And it's taken me ages to get over it, which was ridiculous because I didn't even know I was pregnant until it happened.'

'But I'm sure there's nothing unusual in that, not being well afterwards, I mean.'

'No. But it wasn't physical. It was all in my head. I got completely down and couldn't get out of it. And it was Richard's baby as well and he had to help me when he must have been disappointed too. So then I began to feel guilty about that and I just got worse and . . . Oh, it was awful.'

'But you seem much better now.' Edwina could sympathise with her friend's depression, even if she couldn't over the baby.

'I think I am better. Yes, mostly I am. But the crazy thing is that it seemed to take Richard going off to the Gulf to get me to snap out of it. So now I feel guilty about that.'

'Don't be silly. You've had a rotten time. I expect it's having so much else to do, so much else to think about, which has helped. And perhaps it was just a question of time. Perhaps whatever it was that got you feeling so low has just run its course. Aren't these things supposed to have a lot to do with hormone balances?'

'Like women getting baby blues? You could be right, I don't know.'

'Didn't your doctor tell you?'

'I didn't see one. When I got out of hospital there was nothing wrong with me physically. I wasn't ill; I could go to work each day. I could mostly function after a fashion. I couldn't bear the thought of being on these ghastly pills that turn you into some sort of zombie.'

'So you put on a brave face and got on with it?'

'Yes.'

How typical of Lizzie, thought Edwina. Never one to make a fuss about her own trials and tribulations.

'There'll be heaps of time for breeding once Richard gets back home, randy as anything!' Lizzie nodded and smiled at Edwina's characteristic coarseness. Yes, there would be. She realised that she could move on now and put the sad episode behind her.

Edwina patted her friend's hand and took her glass. 'Right then, another drink, and I shall tell you all about my most recent encounter with the ghastly Cathy.'

Lizzie basked in the sunshine as Edwina fetched two more drinks.

'So,' Lizzie said after a sip. 'What's the low-down on Captain Roberts?'

Edwina gave her a blow-by-blow account of their conversation.

'She really hates me, you know,' she said cheerfully.

'I can't think why you are so unconcerned. She could be dangerous.'

'How?' said Edwina.

'I don't know, but if she has made her mind up to get her own back I wouldn't put it past her to do her damnedest to achieve it.'

'I'll be all right. You know me, I'm indestructible.'

Northern Germany, September 1990

Amanda slumped across her desk, exhausted. It was almost midnight and she'd been in the office since daybreak. For a change the CO was next door in his office, working equally as hard, all thoughts of sailing being put to one side as the workshop desperately organised itself to deploy to the Gulf. Their vehicles had to be ready to move by sea in the first week of October, and all personnel, less the rear party who were staying behind to look after the families, would be departing two weeks later. But unlike other units in the area, once in Saudi the workshop would have the task of helping every other unit get their tanks, Land Rovers, armoured personnel carriers, radios, gun sights and every other piece of mechanical equipment serviced and ready for war. Consequently they had to have all their own kit sorted prior to departure, and on top of that they were to be one of the first units out to the Gulf. To get ready in time was proving a nightmare of hard work and ingenuity. The workshop fitters were operating round the clock, and consequently so were most of the other departments.

Amanda's training at Sandhurst had done little to prepare her for the problems she now encountered, but she was constantly amazed at how helpful and co-operative all the agencies that she now had to deal with were towards her. Now that there was a real emergency on which to focus, the attitude had changed to one of 'if the unit wants it they can have it' – not in the least like the response she'd been used to in the past. In particular the MoD and the soldiers' records office seemed to be able to solve almost every problem she threw at them regarding bringing the unit up to its war establishment. But these higher authorities, whether in Germany or back in UK, weren't just dealing with Amanda's problems, and the knock-on effect was that just about everyone working with or in the British Armed Forces was having to work all hours to cope. Answers to units' problems arrived at any time of the day or night, and someone had to be around to take the calls or answer the signals.

'Go home, Amanda.' She looked up. It was the second-in-command.

'I can't, sir. I'm waiting for a call from the MoD.'

'Can't the duty clerk take it?'

'I don't think so. I just thought I'd crack in forty winks while I was waiting.'

'You ought to get a camp bed put in this office.'

'I know. I've asked the QM for one but I think he's forgotten about it. I don't like to pester him; he's got enough on without me wanting something I can make do without. Anyway, I'll be all right once you lot have pushed off and left me and the rear party to get on with things in peace and quiet.'

'Oh God,' said the 2iC almost under his breath.

'What's the matter? What have I forgotten?'

'You haven't forgotten anything. It's nothing like that. It's just that you're not going to be rear party; you're coming with us.'

This came as a bolt from the blue to Amanda, who'd resigned herself to the fact that, being the only woman in the workshop, naturally she'd be OiC rear party. It had never crossed her mind that, in her capacity as adjutant, she would be required to deploy. After all, women didn't go to war, did they? She shook her head, baffled, trying to come to terms with the news.

'But I don't know anything about a workshop operating in wartime. I'm only a stopgap here, remember? I haven't done any of the right courses, I haven't got an engineering degree and in case you haven't noticed, I'm a woman.'

'So you don't want to do it?' The 2iC didn't sound surprised.

'I'm not saying that.' Amanda didn't know what she did want to say. She'd been caught completely off guard by this sudden turn of events. She'd always assumed that she wouldn't be going and had accepted it as her lot, although if she were honest with herself she'd felt annoyed at the idea that it would be her who would miss out on the adventure. She knew that looking after the families, keeping up their morale and organising Wives' Club events, though vitally important to them and their husbands, would be as dull as ditchwater compared to what the rest of the unit might get up to out in the Gulf.

But she didn't feel it would be fair for her to go too, especially given her lack of training and experience. The last thing she wanted to be was a lightweight or a liability, especially when things might get a lot more serious for them if providing a show of force didn't work. She drew a long breath and said, 'It's just that . . .'

But she got no further. The 2iC seemed to sense her concerns. 'Don't worry, you won't be up with the fighting troops. We'll be a long way behind any of the action, especially as I don't think that it'll even come to that. It's one thing Saddam waltzing into Kuwait, but trying to invade Saudi too would be completely illogical.'

'I know that.' She'd been following the news on BFBS, the Forces radio station, as avidly as anyone else since this whole matter had blown up. And she'd learnt enough about tactics and army organisation at Sandhurst and on subsequent exercises to know the place of a workshop RHQ in the massive scheme of a battlefield. 'It's just that it's come as a bit of a surprise.' That was an understatement. The phone rang. She picked it up. 'Hello, Adjutant.' *It's the MoD*, she mouthed silently at the 2iC.

'Don't worry about it, you'll be all right.' He left the office, closing the door behind him, leaving her in peace.

After her call Amanda walked tiredly back to the mess. She passed the main buildings where the fitters and artificers were frantically modifying armoured vehicles ready for the coming desert war. It looked like a scene of complete confusion but she knew that in fact the speed and efficiency of the work was already earning the workshop considerable praise. She felt a swell of pride that she was part of this. Yes, she thought, I ought to go with them, even though she felt a frisson of fear at what she might be letting herself in for.

She was so tired that she undressed and got into bed on auto-pilot. She was asleep in an instant. When, after several attempts, the mess steward woke her the next morning, Amanda found that she couldn't remember getting there. She groped for the cup of tea left by him on her bedside table and drank it quickly, hoping that it would have some magical reviving power. As soon as she'd finished it she swung her feet out of bed, not daring to lie there for even a minute because she knew she'd fall straight back to sleep again. She flicked the switch on her radio and heard the DJ on BFBS read out a stream of requests from wives to 'my darling husband and tell him not to get too sunburned', or other such attempts at jokes from women who were using humour to hide their fear that if the coalition's show of strength didn't work they might soon be widows. Their husbands might be treating this like a *Boys' Own* adventure but many of their wives were scared stiff about the future. Not being kept busy like their partners, they had time to brood, read the papers and watch the endless television reports about the crisis in the Middle East. Amanda pulled on her tracksuit and headed out of her room, thinking that it was going to be as tough on those left behind as it would be on those going.

On the stairs she met Graham Long. His normally tidy blond hair was tousled and he looked as if he hadn't been to bed, which in all probability he hadn't, considering he was in uniform despite the fact that it was only six thirty.

'God, you look awful,' said Amanda.

'Thanks.'

'When did you last get a decent night's kip?'

Graham rubbed his face and yawned. 'A couple of nights back.'

'Then go to bed now.'

'I can't. PT parade.'

'Sack it. I'll square it with the CO. This must be about the only perk of being adjutant.' Graham smiled, grateful, and tottered up the stairs towards his room.

Amanda jogged from the mess to the sports pitch where almost the whole unit was gathered. Everyone was ordered to attend daily, even those unfit for active service or detailed for rear-party duties. If those who were going to endure the rigours of the desert climate, living and working in the appallingly high temperatures, had to do early-morning PT as part of their preparations, then it wouldn't do the others any harm to join them in their fitness training. Amanda, never a natural athlete, dreaded these early-morning sessions, but she knew that, as an officer, she was expected to set an example. Furthermore, as the only woman, she knew that her performance each day was all the more visible. And anyway, now that she knew she was expected to go to the Gulf too, she had an extra incentive to improve her personal fitness.

At the front of the assembled mass of soldiers the PTI bellowed instructions for star jumps, squat thrusts, press-ups and running on the spot. After ten minutes of warm-up exercises he led everyone on a two-mile run around the camp.

'Come on, ma'am. Keep up,' he yelled at Amanda as he sprinted past her to egg on the tail-enders. Amanda was reminded of Edwina and Sandhurst and wished she hadn't let her standard of fitness slip quite so markedly. As she ran she could hear Edwina's voice in her head, 'Breathe in, two, three, four, out, two, three, four,' the counting keeping time with her feet slapping on the pavement, and she repeated this to herself like a mantra as she pounded along.

The rhythm of the words and the drumming of her feet lulled her mind into a waking dream about her time as a cadet. Old memories slid in and out of her head as she ran mechanically, parallel to the chain-link and razor-wire perimeter of the barracks. She was unaware of the distance her unwilling feet were covering because of her day-dreaming, and it seemed almost no time before she was passing the guardroom, where the PTI was jogging on the spot and haranguing them all to sprint in to the finish. Suddenly Amanda was aware of how puffed she was, but with a supreme effort she drove herself to race the two hundred yards to the door of the gym – the finishing line. There, she doubled over, quivering with exhaustion, spitting and coughing and wishing, not for the first time, that she was back training recruits at Guildford. At least there she'd been competing against women, not men.

After five minutes she felt fit enough to walk back to the mess for a shower and breakfast. She looked at her watch; it was still only seven o'clock, too early to ring Bella, as England was an hour behind. Amanda didn't fancy making the call from the office, which was more like Clapham Junction these days, with a constant stream of people coming to see her with information or problems. But she had to speak to Bella soon. If nothing else, she wanted to talk to someone to whom she could voice her fears and worries. Her fellow officers in the mess were no good. They were all thrilled at the prospect of going to war, winning medals and putting into practice the constant training. They'd voiced considerable disappointment when Eastern Europe had solved its political problems without the intervention of NATO, and they now saw the defence of Saudi and the possibility of liberating Kuwait as a consolation prize. Amanda didn't think they'd understand the sort of worries she had about the awfulness of what they might have to face. It probably wouldn't cross their minds that they might crack up under shell fire – that wasn't the sort of thing that men even thought about – but the possibility was at the forefront of Amanda's mind. What would it be like to be fighting for one's life? How would she react? She liked to think that she'd acquit herself well, but supposing she didn't? And what about the tricky matter of personal hygiene? Amanda knew from experience of exercises in the field that this was never an easy matter for women. But out in the desert? God, it didn't bear thinking about.

When she got through to her later in the day, Bella was horrified.

'But surely you don't really want to go?'

'I don't know. I've been with the unit for well over a year now and I feel part of it. I think that if I don't go I'll really regret it later. You know, copping out. And it wouldn't be right, would it? There are lads with young families who aren't complaining that they have to go. Besides, no one else gets given a say about it, so why should I?'

'I know, but that's not the point.'

'I think it is. I'm dreading it. I'm absolutely terrified about what might be thrown at us. I did the NBC course when I was at Guildford, remember? I know the effects of some of these weapons that Saddam has got stockpiled. And I'm most frightened of going to pieces if it gets really hairy.'

'Oh, Amanda. What I would give to be able to go there with you – or instead of you.'

'I know, my darling, but that's the way it is. Promise me you'll write.'

'Daily. Twice a day,' Bella promised. 'I'll get a stack of blueys from the post office this morning and there'll be a letter waiting for you when you get there.'

Amanda found it a comfort to know that whatever happened to her in the Middle East, someone would be thinking about her, and possibly even praying for her.

In the days that followed, Amanda found sleep becoming more and more of a luxury. She still had her job to do: posting out those soldiers who were unfit or who had family problems, organising the unit's NBC training, arranging the first phase of their injections and inoculations, conferring with the chief clerk about what stores the RHQ would require for an indefinite stay in the war zone . . . The list of what needed doing seemed endless, and it didn't leave any time for social calls to her friends in the UK. She'd write to Lizzie and Edwina when she got the chance. Although goodness only knew when that would be.

Around the barracks the armoured recovery vehicles were being transformed from British Army green to Desert Rat beige; plans for

211

the convoys from the barracks to Bremerhaven were finalised; route maps produced and convoy procedures and drills issued. Activity became ever more frantic as the day for the equipment to move to the port of embarkation approached. Once they'd got rid of their vehicles there would be much less to do. There might even be a chance for a few days' embarkation leave before they all flew out to Saudi a fortnight later, the idea being that the personnel would arrive by air at the same time as their kit arrived by sea.

'I'll believe it when I see it,' the CO had said dourly.

'I'm sure it'll all work out fine,' Amanda has said. 'We've planned for almost every contingency.'

'And you believe the rule of the six Ps will hold true? That prior planning prevents piss-poor performance?'

'We can only hope,' replied Amanda, thinking that perhaps the CO wasn't such a bad sort after all.

'Well, it'll be a triumph of hope over experience.'

Al Jubayl, October 1990

It was just after dusk when their VC-10 touched down on the airstrip. They had been informed that it would be appreciably cooler than earlier in the day, but as they stepped out of the aircraft and on to the top of the steps the heat hit them. That, compounded with the exhaust fumes from the engines and the smell of the distant petro-chemical refinery belching a variety of pollutant gases into the atmosphere, was enough to make their eyes smart.

'Christ,' said Graham Long, shouting over the whine of the engines, 'what the hell will it be like when it isn't cool?'

'I dread to think,' answered Amanda, her mouth close to his ear. 'I'm not looking forward to rushing about in this with NBC kit on. We'll frazzle.' They walked across the concrete, which was hot under their feet, and Amanda found she was sweating quite profusely before she'd gone more than fifty yards. The warnings the medical officer had given them prior to departure about the necessity to drink large quantities of water each day suddenly didn't sound as alarmist as they had done in cool, cloudy Germany.

'I wonder if all that guff about snakes and scorpions is true too?' said Amanda to Graham as they neared the hangar which served as a passenger terminal.

'I expect so. It's the camel spiders I'm not looking forward to meeting.'

'Do you really think it's true that they can jump three feet?' Amanda shuddered at the thought of it. She wasn't very good with any sort of spider, let alone ones with gold medals for athletics.

'True or not, I'm not hanging around with a measuring tape and a rep from the *Guinness Book of Records*.'

They entered the hangar, and were hit by an even hotter waft of air

– the building had a metal roof and had been heated up during the day to blast-furnace temperatures. There the first fifty or so off the plane had occupied a few benches and chairs arranged haphazardly around the building. Amanda and Graham moved towards the edge of the huge hangar and flopped down on the floor, leaning wearily against the corrugated-metal wall.

'I feel knackered and we've only walked a few hundred yards.' Amanda shut her eyes and tried to get comfortable.

'It's the heat.'

'Oh, well done, Einstein.'

'They say we'll get used to it.'

'Great.' The conversation, such as it was, tailed off. They were waiting for their kit to be unloaded from the plane. No one was going anywhere until that had been sorted out. Outside, a convoy of buses and four-ton trucks was waiting to take the unit to its lines at Al Jubayl. It seemed an eternity before the bergens, backpacks and rucksacks which comprised the passengers' personal possessions were dumped in a heap on the floor of the hangar. The RSM stepped into the middle of the hangar.

'Listen in,' he yelled over the hubbub of voices. Silence fell. 'The four-tonners are for the kit, the buses are for personnel. I want all this,' he pointed at the mound of dark-green canvas luggage, 'loaded on to the trucks. Once that is done, you are to embus.' The RSM had flown out the week before with the advance party in order to get things organised ahead of the main body of troops arriving.

Amanda made to move but Graham restrained her. 'Leave it. Let that lot get it sorted out.'

'Good thinking.' Amanda sank back against the wall again, thankful that for the moment she didn't have to exert herself, and watched the soldiers organise themselves into chain gangs to shift the pile. Outside, the VC-10 that had brought them wound its engines up to full power and hurtled down the runway, heading back to Cyprus and the next load of troops waiting to be ferried out.

After twenty minutes or so, when most of the kit had been thrown unceremoniously on to the trucks, Graham and Amanda wandered over to the buses and took their places in the queue to board. Amanda claimed a front seat as hers by virtue of being a lady and the adjutant. No one minded. By now darkness had fallen completely and with it the temperature, although it was still extremely warm. As they left the lights of the airstrip, the lorry was engulfed in complete darkness. The headlights pierced it, illuminating the road and the truck in front, but beyond the two pencil lines of light cutting through the blackness ahead, nothing could be seen. Amanda knew that even in daylight the scenery wasn't going to be up to much. When they'd been descending into Al Jubayl, there had still been a glimmer of sunlight illuminating the ground, and she didn't think she'd ever seen anything which so closely resembled a moonscape outside of sci-fi films. She'd pointed at the ground.

'Christ, I wouldn't like to get lost in that. Not a lot in the way of landmarks.'

'It's like looking at a kid's sandpit,' Graham had agreed.

The bus rumbled on down the road. After a few minutes lights appeared as they drew into the outskirts of the port of Al Jubayl itself. They drove towards the sea, across an empty, flat expanse of land lit by giant floodlights like those in marshalling yards. The lights illuminated the occasional pile of containers waiting to be shipped outwards or onwards, and a few massive metal sheds. At one stage they passed what was going to be a vast tented village. Some of the tents were up but the majority were lying flat on the ground, the poles to complete the task in bundles besides them like garden canes. The bus drove along a large mole, with the sea on one side and a row of hangars on the other. About halfway along, it pulled off the road and drove directly through the open doors of one of the sheds. It stopped inside the bleak interior and the doors hissed open.

'Look welcoming, doesn't it?' said Amanda.

'I think this is where we get off,' said Graham.

They climbed off the bus and stood on the bare concrete floor, wondering where to proceed. The RSM had got there in advance. He approached them and saluted.

'Sir, ma'am. Please go to that table over there, where you'll be processed.' Amanda and Graham looked at the queue of personnel already waiting patiently, and groaned.

'At least it's getting cooler now it's dark,' commented Amanda, trying to find something cheerful to say. But by the time they'd reached the clerks putting details of number, rank, name and next of kin on to computer records, her good humour had long since evaporated.

Along both sides of the hangar were stacks of wooden pallets dividing it up into a series of giant rooms. The workshop had been allocated a couple of these where everyone would be billeted until their vehicles arrived by sea. Before they'd finished erecting their camp beds the soldiers had already christened their rooms the 'cattle pens'.

'So much for home sweet home,' said Amanda as she assembled her camp bed and arranged her bedspace. She gazed forlornly around at the lack of privacy, the lack of creature comforts and the lack of air-conditioning.

'It's only for a couple of days,' said Graham consolingly. Amanda sincerely hoped so.

It was four days before their vehicles arrived at the port. Daily more and more troops poured into Al Jubayl, filling the cattle pens to capacity. Outside, the tented camp was finished and the amount of equipment that became stockpiled around the port assumed mind-boggling proportions. The idea was that as soon as the heavy kit arrived by sea the soldiers would transfer to the tented area. There they would complete the last-minute preparations prior to moving out in their vehicles to training areas in the desert. The cattle pens were so dreadful that any option seemed a better one.

In the time they spent at the port they settled into a routine that revolved around the few daily high spots of meals, showers and the arrival of the post. Amanda, her office now the back of a box-body truck, had work to do organising endless rotas for the soldiers to attend further inoculation sessions, physical training periods, spells of sentry-go and NBC training. She found she worked at half the speed that she was used to and put it down to the appalling midday temperatures, which climbed to a blistering one hundred and forty degrees. At that temperature her brain just seemed to cease to function. They'd all been told that they would slowly acclimatise, but Amanda found it hard to believe. The heat was infernal.

'Would you like a drink of water, ma'am?' asked the chief clerk when Amanda took him that day's orders. Amanda nodded gratefully. They'd been told to make sure they drank pints of the stuff during the day – 'That'll make a change from gin for you,' Graham had said to her, somewhat unfairly, since she only ever had one gin before dinner each evening – and Amanda found that despite copious quantities of liquid she felt almost permanently thirsty. Chief handed her a plastic mug of water and Amanda sipped it.

'How I long for really cold water. This stuff is always lukewarm.'

'I know, disgusting, isn't it? By the way, the post is here and there's a letter for you.' He handed Amanda a blue airmail letter-gram. She recognised the writing immediately and couldn't help a small smile of pleasure. 'Your boyfriend, ma'am?'

Amanda was thankful that the heat and exposure to the sun had given her face a permanently crimson complexion. There was no way she could glow any redder. She lied, 'Yes, Chief,' and shoved the letter into the pocket of her desert combats. She'd read it at lunchtime.

'We've had a signal to warn us that our vehicles will be arriving tomorrow, ma'am.'

'Hallelujah!'

'So once we've got everything off the ship we can move over to Baldrick Lines, prior to moving out for training.'

'The tents have got to be better than the cattle pens.'

'I think so. I don't think they get quite as hot. And it'll be better for you, ma'am.'

'It certainly will.' There were a few tents that had been allocated specifically to the handful of women out there. Amanda couldn't wait to get away from sharing with two hundred sweating, swearing soldiers.

'Attention, attention. This is an air-raid warning. Incoming Scud missiles . . .' blared the tannoy system rigged throughout the port area. Amanda dumped her mug of water and reached into her webbing for her gas mask. She pushed her hair off her face and pulled the mask on, making sure that the seal between the rubber and her skin was airtight. Having done that, she scrambled into her charcoal-lined NBC suit.

'Is this a practice or the real thing?' she asked the chief clerk, her voice muffled and distorted through the mask.

He shrugged. There was no way of knowing. Amanda peered out of the door of the box-body. Everywhere personnel were dressed in the same weird kit, looking like mutant humanoids off *Doctor Who*, with black rubber faces, hugh fly-like eyeholes and an odd protuber-ance where there should have been a mouth. It was a surreal scene but Amanda felt strangely calm. So this is an air raid, she thought. There was nowhere to go for shelter, there was no point in being any-where else, or running around like a headless chicken. Everywhere was equally at risk. If her number was up, well, so be it.

After fifteen minutes she was aware that worse than fear was the discomfort. There didn't appear to be any enemy activity, but as the all-clear hadn't been given, no one was going to risk taking off their suit. Inside the dark, thick protective garment the heat was stifling. Her face had begun to itch as sweat trickled down from her forehead to her chin. She longed to be able to rub her face, but she knew that if the air was contaminated with chemicals or bacteria, the last thing she should do was remove any bit of her protective clothing, least of all her mask. Because she could do nothing about it, the irritation of the dripping sweat became almost unbearable. She tried shaking her head and scratching her skin through the soft rubber of the mask, but nothing seemed to help. She wondered how long this torture was going to continue.

Eventually the all-clear sounded. With a sigh of relief Amanda ripped off her mask and mopped her face on the sleeve of her protective suit.

'God, that was unpleasant!'

'It will be if it's for real,' said the chief clerk. He looked at her closely.

'It's all right, Chief.' It was obvious that he was wondering if she would crack up under fire. 'I don't mean the Scuds, I mean these ruddy suits in this heat.'

'Oh.' He sounded relieved.

The next day, their vehicles having arrived at the docks, the workshop moved into the tented city prior to their eventual deployment into the desert. Amanda, like everyone else, moved out of the cattle pens and into her new quarters with alacrity and pleasure. She might have to share with four or five other women in the near future, but for the moment she had a tent to herself. She could hardly believe the luxury of having some privacy after the horrors of the cattle pens. It didn't matter that the tents were utterly basic and smelt fusty and airless. Neither did it matter that they were obviously going to be unbearable in the heat of the day.

Amanda threw her kit down on the floor, assembled her camp bed and lay on it revelling in the peace and quiet. She was too hot, but now she could unbutton her combat jacket and let the air get to her naked skin. Oh, the bliss of it. She looked around at the empty space and wondered how long it would be before other women joined her. It didn't really matter. Compared to what she'd just endured, the company of four or five others would be nothing. Besides which, it would be nice not to be the token woman. She'd heard somewhere

218

that 4 Brigade was coming out to the Gulf too and that there would be forty-five thousand British troops in Saudi Arabia by Christmas – they couldn't all be men, surely? Amanda found it hard to visualise the sort of logistic problems this number of soldiers and their kit would create, but judging by the size of this camp, the problems were going to be massive.

Having got her bedspace sorted out, Amanda went to find some lunch. The Americans, who'd been in Al Jubayl longer than the British and were therefore more organised, were running the central cookhouse. The food generally was excellent, and delicacies like hash browns and muffins made a pleasant change from bangers and mash. Amanda grabbed her water bottle and walked over to the canteen. Her stomach had been rumbling for a while in anticipation of the meal and her internal complainings got louder as the smell of food wafted towards her. As always there was a queue of soldiers waiting to be served, and Amanda tagged herself on at the end. In her pocket was yet another letter from Bella, and she had been looking forward to reading it since its arrival.

Amanda was quickly deeply immersed in Bella's letter, which included news of her posting to Headquarters United Kingdom Land Forces in deepest Wiltshire, and amusing descriptions of how she was going to miss life in darkest Oxfordshire and the odd assortment of officers who'd shared her mess. She was so engrossed she didn't hear a voice tentatively saying hello. When she was tapped on her shoulder she jumped, startled.

'I'm sorry. I didn't mean to scare you,' said Richard.

'Richard! What a wonderful surprise.' Amanda stuffed her letter in her pocket. She'd read it later.

'So what the hell are you doing out here? I mean, surely you didn't volunteer; you could have asked to stay behind and look after the families.'

'I assumed I would be doing exactly that, but when I found that it was expected of me I was actually quite pleased.'

'I get it,' Richard said. 'It was the thought of all these sex-starved men stuck out in the middle of nowhere which appealed to you.'

'Don't be ridiculous.' The temperature plummeted several degrees, and instantly Amanda regretted her rebuke. She moved away from this particular minefield. 'What about you? I thought you had some cushy desk job up at the MoD.'

'I did, but when I was told I was needed to make up numbers, I didn't like to refuse. Anyway, I'm an Arabic speaker – did a course before going out to the Oman some years ago. I expect the brass thought it might be useful.'

Poor Lizzie, Amanda thought. It must be miserable to be stuck at home worrying. 'How is Lizzie? I've been meaning to write for ages but I simply haven't had the time.'

'Oh, fine. Well, she was when her last letter came through.' They shuffled forward, a few paces nearer to the serving point.

'I expect she writes loads of letters to you.'

'Yes.' They reached the makeshift counter where the food was laid out. Amanda picked up a plastic plate and thought for a couple of seconds before she chose pizza and salad. The cook helped her to a large slab of pizza. American portions seemed to be in proportion to the size of their country – huge. It lapped over the edges of her plate. Amanda shuffled on a few paces further in the queue and filled up her water bottle. She waited for Richard.

'I'm going to sit outside in the shade. Would you like to join me?'

'Great.' They walked around the side of the mess tent, found a patch of deep shadow and squatted down on the ground. Around them were dozens of soldiers, in sunglasses, stretched out on the sand, using their lunch hour to soak up a few rays.

'I go like a lobster if I get too much sun,' said Amanda. 'Or perhaps I should say *more* like a lobster.'

'I have that problem too. That's the trouble for us fair types.'

'I'm told that it can be quite miserable out here in the winter.'

'But haven't you heard?'

Amanda stared at him quizzically, not knowing which piece of intelligence she'd missed.

'It'll all be over by Christmas.'

She laughed. 'Oh, yes. Like it always is.'

'I gather the skiing was a great success.'

'It was fantastic. It seems an absolute age away, though. I can't believe it was only about nine months ago. I was hoping to go again after Christmas, but . . .'

'Maybe you'll be able to after all.'

'Yeah, and maybe pigs fly.'

Over the next few days Amanda found herself running into Richard with increasing frequency. She didn't mind it – it was nice to have a friend who wasn't also a colleague – but she hoped that no one was going to construe their friendship as anything else but that. It would be dreadful if a rumour got back to Lizzie about them seeing each other, especially as it would be so completely wrong. Amanda didn't know if she ought to say something to Richard, warn him off about meeting her as often as he did, or whether he'd be offended that she thought he might be sniffing round. It was a delicate matter. She decided to trust to luck, not to say anything and rely on the fact that shortly they'd all be off into the desert and it'd be extremely unlikely that they'd run into each other again.

One evening she was returning from her shower when she saw him heading towards her yet again.

'Oh, hi, Amanda,' he said. 'Fancy running into you again.'

'Yes, fancy.' She began to wonder about his intentions. Surely this time it couldn't be coincidence.

'How are you?'

'Fine, thank you.'

'Look,' he said, 'I must come clean. I didn't just run into you this time. I wanted to tell you that I managed to smuggle some vodka out here, disguised as tonic water.'

'You and the rest of the troops. I know what the directives all said before we came out here, but everyone and their dog has got a little stash waiting for End-ex.'

'Well, I thought that when this is all over, assuming we both come through unscathed, we ought to get together for a little celebration. What do you think?'

'Oh, Richard, I'm not sure. I mean, it sounds a great idea, but we've seen quite a bit of each other recently. My chief clerk asked me whether I knew you before we came out here, so even he's noticed. We both know that it's as innocent as the day, but supposing Lizzie heard something?'

Richard roared with laughter. 'But Lizzie has been encouraging me. I wrote to her the first time we met and she wrote straight back and told me to be nice to you. She said that you must be awfully lonely out here, as there are so few women. You didn't think . . .?'

Amanda felt foolish and relieved in equal measure. She tried to cover up her embarrassment that she had thought there was a hidden agenda. 'Thank God for that then,' she said. 'In which case we *must* get together when it's all over, although goodness knows when or where that'll be.'

'Let's hope it's not too far in the future. I'm getting fed up hanging around here. The sooner we get out there,' he waved at the distant desert, 'the sooner we can all go home.'

Amanda agreed wholeheartedly.

Amanda was delighted when the next day the CO announced that the workshop would be moving into the desert just as soon as all the personnel had been given the last of their jabs. She and the chief clerk ran themselves ragged, organising all the inoculations to take place within the shortest possible timeframe. She didn't have a chance to see Richard to tell him that they were off, but she knew that his unit would be pulling out of the port within a couple of days too. Then it was her turn to have her final cocktail of jabs.

After that she wasn't much use for the best part of a week, as she was hospitalised with flu – or it might have been a reaction to the jabs, no one would say. Whatever, Amanda felt too lousy to give a stuff one way or the other. It certainly felt like flu; every joint ached and she had the most appalling shivers despite the heat. God, she thought, what a time to let the side down. And despite the assurances of the CO and everyone else, she was sure that they all thought she was being a wimp. She thought it was grossly unfair that none of the others had caught what she had, because if a man had he would be moaning just as much, if not more, about how bloody awful this illness was, and then the others might realise how rotten it had been. As it was, everyone else in the workshop assumed she was just being a pathetic girlie.

Aldershot, January 1991

Lizzie's alarm rang and she rolled sleepily over in bed and turned it off, then with her index finger flicked the switch on her bedside radio. She listened transfixed as she heard the reporter announce that the air war in the Gulf had started. Instantly she was wide awake.

'The sanctions have failed,' said the voice sombrely, 'the deadline has passed, the time for talking is over. Now there is no going back.' He went on to describe the Tornadoes and the F-16s going into combat. 'Strategic targets in Baghdad have been bombed with what we have been told was surgical precision . . .'

Lizzie stopped listening and sat in bed, tears streaming down her face as she thought of her husband, Amanda, her friends, all the young men, the lads she'd known as cadets, now facing the massive might of the Iraqi troops. What would become of them? Pundits were talking of twenty to thirty per cent casualties, while defence correspondents spoke about Saddam's use of chemical weapons in his country's last major conflict and how America might respond with tactical nuclear strikes if he tried it again. The public was being prepared for the news of thousands and thousands of casualties. All the 'what if . . .' scenarios were just a softening-up process so the worst news would be more acceptable. Armageddon and Dante's inferno were going to look like the teddy bears' picnic if all these forecasts came true.

Lizzie wondered how long it would be before the ground troops engaged, now that the air strikes had started. Perhaps they were about to; perhaps Iraqi troops were already advancing towards their defences and the ground war had started too. It was almost too awful to contemplate.

Suddenly, with a rush of guilt, she thought about Ginny. How on earth would she be coping, having to keep a brave face on for her two little girls? At least Lizzie didn't have to pretend to anyone. She told herself to pull herself together. There were those who were much worse off than she was. She got out of bed and washed her face. Whatever was going on, staying in bed wasn't going to change things. With great practicality Lizzie decided that she'd be better off at work, where at least she'd have something to do to occupy her mind.

William stood up and gave her a comforting cuddle when she got into the office some forty minutes later. As he did he remembered guiltily that he'd promised Lizzie an invitation to supper, but their social life had been so hectic up till Christmas that it had gone clean out of his mind. He must organise something with Sophie soon.

'How do you feel?' he asked her.

'Sort of numb. Inside I'm terrified of what Richard and everyone else must be going through, but I can't do anything except worry, which seems pretty futile.' Her forehead creased with the effort of holding back tears.

William rubbed her shoulders and gave her a peck on the cheek. 'You're probably better off here. I think if I was in your shoes I'd be glued to the TV at home, and that would be worse.'

'It's terrible. I switch it on whenever I get home, and I know I shouldn't as it upsets me so. They keep on going on about the casualties we can expect.'

'Don't. I'm sure it won't be as bad as they say. They're only doing it because they've got nothing better to occupy the endless TV coverage. Have you had a letter from Richard recently?'

'Yes, about a week ago.' Letters came through much more slowly now the mail had to be collected from all around the desert. 'Things have been pretty busy, he says, lots of exercises and live firing. And the weather has been awful, cold and wet. I thought the desert was supposed to be hot and dry, but Richard says it's been like the Somme out there.' Lizzie stopped and put her hand over her mouth. 'Oh my God.'

'What? What's the matter?'

'The Somme. Why did he have to say it was like that?'

'He only means the mud.'

But Lizzie had got the image of the carnage of that dreadful battle in her head. She looked stricken.

'Would you rather go home?' asked William. 'No one would mind.'

'No. As you said, I'll only sit and worry. Honestly, I'm better off here. That is, if you can stand sharing an office with me behaving like a wet weekend.' She sat down at her desk and pulled her in-tray towards her, but the first file she took from the top she just sat and stared at. After a few minutes William buzzed the clerks' office and asked them to bring in some coffee. When it arrived he sat on the edge of Lizzie's desk with his mug and handed one to Lizzie.

'Do you want to talk?'

'There isn't really anything to talk about. I'm being pathetic, aren't I?'

'Hardly. You wouldn't think it unreasonable if Sophie was in some sort of danger, say ill in hospital, and I was pacing up and down.'

'No, but that's different.'

'Oh, hardly.'

'I'm being so selfish, just worrying about Richard when there's thousands of men out there.'

'And don't you think that the other wives and mothers are only worrying about their husbands and sons?'

Lizzie tried to smile. 'You're probably right. Anyway, he's not the only person we know out there, is he? What about Bob? And every time the news comes on the television I seem to recognise a couple of faces. One of my best friends from when I was a cadet is out there, and I've hardly given her a thought.'

'Her?'

'Yes. She got sent to a REME unit as a temporary measure and then all this blew up.' Lizzie explained that Amanda hadn't got an engineering background; she was just there because she was a good administrator.

'It could easily have been you that went, then,' said William. 'She just happened to be the right person for the right job at the right time.'

'Or the wrong time.'

Though William had been in the Army just long enough to have been around for the Falklands War, his regiment hadn't gone and he had missed out on an active role.

'I think you'll find,' he said, 'that when this is all over there will be plenty of people who will be jealous of missing the action, regardless of how awful it turns out to be. Afterwards there will always be the "them and us" situation. Speaking from experience, I'd say that whatever happens – providing Richard comes out of this in one piece – he'll be glad he went.'

Lizzie took his word for it.

William's wife Sophie was a big woman in every respect. She was tall, with bubbly blonde curls, an ample bosom and a loud voice. She also possessed a huge sense of humour, a big heart and a penchant for white wine, which she drank in large quantities. When William suggested that they should have Ginny and Lizzie over for supper she wasn't the least put out.

'The poor dears must be so miserable sitting on their own every evening, watching the news and fearing the worst. Of course I'll have them round. You should have organised this ages ago, William.'

William accepted the blame. It wasn't in his nature to argue with his wife. He liked a quiet, uncomplicated life, and in his experience he'd found that confrontation always made things more difficult than they need be. Besides which, they had an unspoken agreement about the division of labour regarding every aspect of their lives, and while Sophie organised their social life when it involved either her friends or their relations, anything to do with the Army or William's friends was strictly William's business.

'Get them round on Saturday, but for God's sake warn Lizzie about what to expect. At least Ginny is used to us.'

Lizzie stood on the doorstep of the Davies' quarter, clutching a rather good bottle of white wine and a bunch of flowers. As she rang the doorbell she wondered what the interior would be like.

'We're not very house-proud,' William had said when he issued the invitation. 'Sophie likes people to know so that it doesn't come as a shock.'

How bad can it be, thought Lizzie, that they have to warn their visitors? After all, they didn't have any kids, so there couldn't be that much chaos. Lizzie herself was naturally tidy. She came from a tidy family – her mother had always insisted on her toys being put away at the end of every day – and boarding school and three years in the Army had completed her aversion to mess.

The door was opened by William, who greeted her with a smacking kiss on the cheek and a glass of wine, which he would have thrust into her hand she not already been somewhat laden.

'Come on in,' he said, throwing the door open wide. 'Ginny's only just arrived.' But Lizzie barely took in his words as she stared past him at the mounds of half-unpacked tea chests in the hall. William followed her gaze. 'Don't mind the mess, please. We both hate unpacking so we don't bother. When we need something we ferret in the boxes till we find it.'

'Fine,' said Lizzie, not knowing quite what to say and scarcely believing what she saw. 'Um, would you like to take the wine? The flowers are for Sophie.'

William put down the glass he was carrying and took the presents, which he dumped on the stairs. 'I'll look after them both properly in a minute,' he promised. Now Lizzie had her hands free he gave her the glass of wine. As she took it she reflected that it looked as if they were in the throes of moving in that day, not as if they'd been living in the house for nearly a year. She edged past the crates and into the sitting room, which proved to be not much better. Here, instead of boxes, there were piles of newspapers. William made a space for her to sit down on the sofa by dint of picking up one of the piles and dumping it on the floor.

'Packing material?' asked Lizzie tentatively. As she said it she smiled a greeting to Ginny, who waved back at her.

William roared with laughter. 'Lord, no. These are the Sunday papers that we keep promising we'll read in entirety one day. The trouble is, we never catch up with the backlog. Anyway, drink up and I'll give you a refill.' Lizzie had barely had a chance to touch her wine but she obligingly took a swig. Instantly William topped her glass up to the brim. 'You and Ginny know each other, don't you? Great, well, you two have a chat while I go and help Sophie in the kitchen for a minute.' He disappeared, and Lizzie moved another pile of newspapers from the coffee table on to the floor so she could put her drink down.

'How are you getting on?' she asked Ginny.

'So-so, thank you. You must know what it's like.'

'Yes. I don't know about you but I spend my life listening to or watching the news.'

'The early-evening news, the six o'clock, Channel 4, the nine o'clock . . .'

'Hang on, don't you start the day with Radio 4?'

Ginny laughed, 'I do,' and then, more seriously, 'but God knows why, because it always upsets me.'

William returned. 'Sophie says supper will be about thirty minutes. It's curry. OK?'

'Delicious,' said Lizzie.

'I don't want to sound ungrateful,' said Ginny, 'but Sophie could produce anything and I'd lap it up. I'm so sick of eating nursery food that it's a real treat to have something grown-up.'

'I don't see what's wrong with nursery food,' said William. 'I love boiled eggs and toast soldiers.'

'But you know what she means,' said Lizzie. 'I've been living on sandwiches for supper. I go to the mess for lunch so I don't have to bother cooking for myself in the evening. It's wonderful to have someone cooking for me.'

'Great, I'm sure you'll enjoy it. Soph's a wonderful cook,' said William. He splashed another drop of wine into Ginny and Lizzie's glasses.

'Steady on, William,' said Lizzie. 'I've got the car outside.'

'You can always leave it here and get a taxi home. And Ginny, you've no excuse, because you've only had to come a hundred yards.' He disappeared to the kitchen again.

'Are they always this generous with the booze?' asked Lizzie, her face a picture of horror.

'Invariably. They have a reputation a mile wide for their parties. I'm surprised you haven't heard about it.'

'We didn't socialise very much after the miscarriage.'

'No, of course you wouldn't have.' Ginny smiled kindly. 'And then this.' She was referring to the Gulf crisis.

'Well, there's more to life than dinner parties,' said Lizzie, a little sadly.

'So one way and another you've escaped the Davies' brand of eating, drinking and being merry?'

'Being very merry if I have much more wine,' said Lizzie. She thought of Richard, out in the Gulf with not a drop of drink anywhere to be had, and only camels and Scud missiles for company. But they'd been invited to Sophie's to enjoy themselves, to get away from the dreaded TV with its constant newscasts. She raised her glass to Ginny. 'Let's forget everything for an hour or two,' she said determinedly, and downed her drink.

'Why not?' replied Ginny.

The curry was delicious. As William had promised, Sophie was a stupendous cook. They sat and ate and drank, and then picked at the leftovers and drank some more. At every opportunity, William filled their glasses, and, by the time the plates had been cleared the Davies' wine cellar had taken a battering and Lizzie was obviously rather the worse for wear.

'I know what a nanac . . . an acanon . . . a python must feel like after eating a goat,' she said to William, and smiled fuzzily. 'That was wonderful.'

'Have some more wine,' offered Sophie, returning from the kitchen.

'No. I mushn't,'

'How about some coffee?'

'Wunnerful. Hic.'

'Let's go into the sitting room,' said William. 'We can be more comfortable there. I need to loosen my belt.' He patted his stomach and kissed his wife on the cheek. 'One of your best curries, darling,' he said appreciatively.

'Thank you. Now, you take the girls through while I make the coffee.'

William helped Lizzie to her feet. She was extremely unsteady.

'I think I mush 'ave 'ad, hic, too mush wine,' she said with a giggle. 'Wouldn't Rishar' be jealoush if he knew.' She giggled again as William took her arm and guided her to the sofa in the sitting room. 'I don't usually drink mush, hic. I've always thought that women who get drunk look schtupid.' She sat down and beamed up at William. 'But I think I mush have been wrong. What do you think?'

'I think you could do with some coffee, sweetie.' He met Ginny in the doorway. She'd been helping Sophie stack the dishwasher in the kitchen. 'Keep an eye on Lizzie. I don't think she's used to drinking, she's smashed.'

'She didn't have that much, did she?'

'A few glasses. Well, perhaps four or five.'

'So virtually nothing by your standards.'

'Bitch,' said William with a smile.

Ginny went into the sitting room to find that Lizzie had already passed out on the sofa. She tucked Lizzie's legs up and put a cushion under her head, made sure that she couldn't roll on to her back again, just in case she was sick, and went to join her hosts.

'Out cold,' she reported.

'Oh, Lord,' said Sophie. 'Did you make sure she's all right?'

'Yes. She's on her side and I've wedged her with cushions.'

'Thanks. Well, she'd better stay the night. I'll tuck her up in a rug in a minute.' She finished making the coffee. 'She's going to feel bloody awful in the morning.'

'I'll lay you a pound to a penny that this is the first time she's got absolutely blotto,' said William.

'I think it's because she's just miserable at Richard being away. And I think it took her an age to get over that dreadful business of the miscarriage. What with one thing and another I think she let herself go tonight to get it out of her system.'

'You're probably right,' said William. 'You know, for weeks after she lost the baby she'd come into the office looking terrible. Bob and I both tried to get her to take time off but she wouldn't hear of it. Kept insisting she wasn't ill; that she was fine.'

'Which she patently wasn't,' said Ginny. 'I saw her and she looked like a panda, with huge dark rings round her eyes. Even worse than she did when she was pregnant.'

'And that's saying something,' said William.

'And she's just getting herself sorted out and her husband gets sent off to war,' added Ginny.

'Some people get all the tough breaks.'

'And I can't think of anyone who deserves them less.'

Lizzie couldn't think where she was when she awoke the next day. She came to slowly, aware that her head throbbed, her eyes felt gritty and her mouth was dry and tasted foul. Then, with a dreadful feeling, rising horribly from the pit of her stomach, she knew she was going to be sick. She sat up and cast about wildly for a receptacle but all she could see was a wicker waste basket. Hopeless. She felt her gorge rise, and knowing it was too late she grabbed a newspaper from a nearby pile and held it open on her lap as she retched over it. After a few minutes the heaving stopped and with shaking hands she carefully made the soggy mess into a tidy parcel, using a second paper off the pile. She felt mortified with embarrassment both about what had just happened, and regarding her vague memories of the previous evening. Try as she might she couldn't remember anything after the meal; she couldn't even remember leaving the table. With horror she realised she must have been drunk. Well, that explained how she felt, she thought wretchedly.

She looked at the newspaper parcel on her lap and knew she must dispose of it quickly, before its contents began to seep out. She stood up slowly, frightened that she might be sick again, and tottered into the kitchen. She prayed that she wouldn't run into either of her hosts until she'd disposed of her revolting package in a dustbin and had had a chance to wash her face and rinse out her mouth. She peered round the kitchen door. Thank God! Not a soul about. Lizzie scuttled across the floor to the back door, hoping against hope that the bins were kept in the conventional place – although in this house nothing would surprise her. Quietly she unlocked the door and stepped out into the freezing early-morning air. Despite the fact that it was still almost dark, Lizzie found the bins easily enough and got rid of the evidence of her previous night's excess. Guilty, but relieved, she crept back into the house and came face to face with Sophie. Her face reddened as a surge of embarrassment engulfed her. Sophie pretended not to notice.

'How are you feeling, my dear? I heard you get up and I thought you might like a cuppa.'

Lizzie smiled weakly. 'I'd love one. But could I have a glass of water first?'

'Aren't you feeling too good? It's all William's fault. He's got a heavy hand with the drink and he never takes into account that not everyone has a head as hard as his.'

'No.' Lizzie didn't feel strong enough for a conversation. Gratefully she accepted the water and sipped it. Even that made her stomach lurch ominously again.

'I'll get you an Alka-Seltzer,' said Sophie, practically. 'You must be feeling dreadful.' She rummaged in a kitchen cupboard and found the packet. She took Lizzie's glass from her, dropped in a couple of the big tablets and swirled the water round to help them dissolve. As the fizzing subsided she handed the glass back. Lizzie drank it down and then burped loudly.

'I'm sorry.' She suppressed a second belch. 'I can't think what came over me last night. I've never drunk too much in my life before.'

231

'We thought so,' Sophie said bluntly. 'And you didn't have that much. Anyway, we're a bad influence. It's me who should be apologising. I should have stopped William before you got to that stage.' She handed Lizzie her tea. 'Drink this slowly. It's hot and sweet and should make you feel a lot better. If you think you're going to be sick again, the loo's at the end of the corridor.'

Lizzie found Sophie's practical manner a bit daunting, but she appreciated the lack of fuss. Obviously Sophie was fazed by very little. She perched herself on a stool and clasped the cup in both hands. She felt dreadful; cold and shivery, to say nothing of nauseous. God, if this was what a hangover was like she never wanted another one again in her life.

Sophie looked at her. 'You'll live, despite what you may think right now.'

'I'm so ashamed.'

'Why on earth should you feel like that? I've already said it was William's fault.'

'But I should have know when to stop.'

'Don't worry about it. Honestly, it really doesn't matter.'

'You won't tell anyone, will you?'

'Of course not. Why on earth do you think I might?'

'I'm sorry, of course you wouldn't.'

'And don't worry. You were completely ladylike. You went into the sitting room and fell asleep on the sofa. You didn't charge around the house trying to grab my husband's nuts with the salad tongs, you didn't strip your clothes off, you didn't even tell any dirty stories. If you knew some of the behaviour we've witnessed in our house, you'd realise just how restrained you've been.'

Lizzie smiled in relief. 'Thanks for the reassurance.'

'But one thing, Lizzie –'

'Yes.'

'I think you tied one on last night as a reaction to some of the rotten things that have happened to you recently. Am I right?'

'Possibly. I don't really know.'

'Well, promise me you won't ever get drunk to solve a problem. I'm sure you wouldn't – though God knows you've had reason enough recently. Believe me, it doesn't help. It might get you through the evening, but the morning you have to face afterwards has all the same horrors. Added to which, you feel physically awful.'

Lizzie didn't resent this advice. She had a feeling that Sophie's

232

little homily might even have been based on personal experience, although she was too shy to ask if this was so. She smiled and nodded to show she had understood, then she said, 'Now I know what a hangover is like, I don't think I'll *ever* consider it.'

'And if you need a shoulder to cry on, there's always mine.'

Lizzie was very grateful for this offer. There was something about Sophie's capable, forthright, generous nature that would be immensely comforting in a crisis.

Saudi Arabia, February 1991

A Tornado jet screamed overhead, heading for the border with Iraq.

'The poor buggers are about to get another pasting,' Amanda said to no one in particular. Sometimes, depending on the whereabouts of the target and the wind direction, they could hear the crump of the laser-guided bombs exploding. It was an unpleasant sound.

'Don't waste your breath with any sympathy,' said the chief clerk dourly. 'If they had the technology it'd be us on the receiving end.' Amanda knew this to be true. But she'd seen the live-firing exercises and knew the power of the heavy artillery and the devastation of the aerial bombardments, and the idea of being underneath such terrible and indiscriminate destruction was dreadful. It didn't matter to her that the Iraqis were the enemy; they were also human beings, and she couldn't help herself from feeling compassion towards them. She wondered if she would be able to kill any of them if it came to hand-to-hand fighting. She supposed that then it would be a question of her or them. If she ended up fighting for her life she might be capable of anything.

She stepped out of the back of the box-body vehicle that was her office and took a deep breath. The stink in the vehicles was appalling. It would be bad enough if it was just sweat and imperfectly washed socks, but permeating everything was something evoking drains and sewage. Not that it was anyone's fault, but one of the side-effects of the pills they had to take to help them against a possible nerve-gas attack was dreadful wind. Amanda had long since given up apologising each time she let rip; it was the same for everyone. Had anyone told her three months previously that she'd be able to fart with impunity in front of a group of men, she knew she'd never have believed them – she got embarrassed enough when it

234

happened with Bella – but life in this grim scenario had coarsened everyone, and Amanda was no exception.

She gazed around the flat, bleak, desolate scenery and thought for the umpteenth time that the desert wasn't a bit like she'd imaged it to be. She'd had this romantic picture of *Beau Geste*-type sand dunes, crescent-shaped and yellow, with craggy foreign legionnaires trudging across them in smart navy tail coats and kepis. The reality was a featureless, trackless and barren moonscape of grey pebbles and grey sand, or grey mud after one of the many winter storms. She hadn't even seen a bloody camel, she thought.

An ominous grumble emanated from behind her navel, followed by a sharp pain. Oh, God! Not another trip to the loo already, surely? It had only been a couple of hours since she'd had the last bout of squits. And the latrines had to be the absolute worst aspect of a desert campaign, consisting as they did of a line of euphemistically named thunder boxes placed back to back and side by side, a hundred yards away from the main camp area. No tentage, no cubicles, no anything around them – so no privacy either. Amanda had found that she could cope with most things: the variety of unpleasant creepy-crawlies which seemed to want to share her sleeping bag, the sand storms which drove grit and dust into her every nook and crevice, the constant Scud alerts, the cold and the rain, not to mention the fact that they were on the brink of a full-scale land war. But the latrines were the limit. Communal farting was one thing, but having to shit in public was something else entirely. Someone had suggested that the soldiers of the Pioneer Corps ought to be detailed to dig a separate latrine for Amanda, but they were stretched to the limit already without having to worry about her arrangements. The suggestion had been dismissed, primarily by Amanda herself.

She gave the latrines a quick glance and was relieved to see that no one else was using them. Swiftly she walked over to them, chose the furthest one, undid her belt and trousers and slithered them down to her knees, using her shirt-tail as best she could to provide a modicum of decency. The flies and the stench were sickening, but if she wanted any sort of privacy then she couldn't have the luxury of going for a crap when the contents of the drums under the latrines had just been burnt off. There was always a queue of men waiting to take advantage of the only period of the day when they were vaguely tolerable. She tried not to breathe more than was absolutely necessary as she let nature and gravity ream her out. Her mind drifted to thoughts of hot baths, soft loo paper, clean clothes, washed hair and a comfortable bed. Then she became aware that two squaddies were approaching. Quickly she tidied herself up and departed. After all these weeks she felt she ought to be used to this, but all that had happened was that she had just become more adept at being discreet. She dabbled her hands in the bowl of disinfectant, dried them on her combat shirt and returned to work.

The smell as she re-entered the vehicle was even more apparent, but it had to be said that it was almost fragrant when compared to the latrines.

'Post's here,' said the chief clerk, handing her three blueys. 'Your boyfriend must love you to bits, ma'am. He writes ever such a lot.'

'Well, it's nice to get letters, isn't it?' she replied ambivalently.

'I don't know. My missus just sends me lists of things I'm going to have to sort out when I get back: the car's not running too smoothly, the washing machine won't spin properly . . . It's just one bleeding complaint after another.'

Amanda laughed. 'But I bet you can't wait to get back to all that domestic drudgery, Chiefy.' Before he could reply a sound like a bugle call rent the air from the region of his trousers. 'Oh, come on, Chief. Couldn't you have gone outside?' said Amanda.

'I'm sorry, that one caught me unawares.'

'Well, that's it.' And Amanda extracted her gas mask from its holder and put it on. 'I'm sorry, Chief, it's nothing personal, but enough is enough.'

Graham Long, watchkeeping at the other desk in the vehicle, shook his head. 'Phah, that's disgusting. It smells like a rotting rat.'

'I wouldn't know. I've never smelt one,' said the chief clerk.

'I'm sorry, Chief. I'm with Amanda.' And Graham put his mask on too.

The chief clerk looked morosely around the cramped confines of the vehicle, feeling ostracised, albeit justifiably. Then a light breeze off the desert sands blew through the open door of the vehicle and stirred the air, wafting afresh the foul odour. The smell rose up to his nostrils and it made even him blench. It was truly gag-making.

'You're right,' said the chief clerk. 'It's beyond a joke. I can't think what on earth is making them so bad.' And with a resigned shrug of his shoulders he reached for his own gas mask.

Five minutes later a signaller came in with the transcript of a message from the Divisional Headquarters. Seeing his superiors sitting around in their gas masks, he assumed that he'd missed notification of an imminent Scud attack and that in the next instant he might be dead from some unspeakable biological or chemical weapon. Perhaps there had already been an airburst and deadly droplets of some lethal nerve agent were drifting, unseen, towards their position. In his haste to get his own gas mask fixed in place he stepped backwards, fell head over heels out of the open door and knocked himself half unconscious as he hit the ground. His cry as he lost his footing caused Graham, Amanda and the chief clerk to look round and catch a glimpse of the poor lad disappearing, arms flailing. It was some minutes before the reason for his panic became clear, and even longer before they stopped laughing.

Later that morning the order came to move closer to the Iraqi border. Neither Amanda nor Graham read any particular significance into the event; changing position was not an unusual occurrence. Sometimes it was done as an exercise to see how quickly they could bug out, and at other times because their position had become threatened by the repositioning of Iraqi troops or artillery. Certainly, at their level in the massive chain of command, they were not privy to the whys and wherefores of the tactical decisions made at the top.

'Talk about pawns in a bloody chess game,' Amanda had complained to Graham on one occasion, after they'd been ordered to move to a new location at night and in the middle of a sandstorm. 'I wish, just for once, they'd let us know what the big picture is, so we understand what the hell is happening.'

'I think you're wrong there. I think that ignorance is bliss,' said Graham. 'If we don't know what's planned, we can't worry about it.'

'That's what you say. I wasn't the least bit worried about the jabs we got just before we deployed out of Al Jubayl. "You'll feel a bit shivery," the nurse told me as soon as she'd done it. A bit shivery, my arse! I was laid up for a week, terrified that I might die and scared shitless that my reaction was unusual – you know, like kids that are allergic to the whooping cough vaccine. The fear of what *might* be happening to me was almost worse than what actually *was*.'

'Yeah, but if you'd been told beforehand how bad your reaction was going to be, you'd have been worried sick before you had the jabs.'

'Well, I still think I'd have preferred that scenario.' They'd agreed to differ on that occasion.

Once the move had been completed and they'd set up comms again with the Brigade Headquarters, they settled down into what they assumed would be their normal routine. Amanda was busy compiling statistics about breakdown frequencies of certain types of vehicle and checking the number of fully serviceable power packs – REME-speak for an engine and gearbox combined – while Graham was monitoring the radio traffic on the brigade net. The chief clerk was pottering about somewhere dealing with the day-to-day admin that had to be done despite the war. It was a scene of peaceful diligence.

Suddenly Graham said, 'Christ, this is it.'

'What's *it*?' said Amanda, looking up from the stack of statistics and paperwork she was preparing to send to the Force Maintenance Area.

'The war. The bombardment has started, the Sappers are breaching the berms and once they're got through the defences, the division is going to cross the start line. We've just been placed on two hours' notice to move.'

'Christ.' Amanda didn't know what else to say. The news hardly came as a shock – after all, this latest order from their higher formation was one they'd all been expecting for some time now – it was just that Amanda had expected to feel more when it came. She was nonplussed that she felt so calm. She thought she ought to be afraid, but curiously she wasn't. Perhaps the build-up had been going on for so long, and there had been so many times when she'd been frightened, that she had run out of fear. Or perhaps she'd just grown fatalistic. If something dreadful was going to happen to her, there wasn't much she could do about it.

'It had to happen,' she said.

'Is that all you've got to say?'

'I don't know. There isn't much else *to* say – is there?'

Graham thought for a minute and then replied that he didn't think there was.

Amanda went outside for a moment to see if she could hear the bombardment, but they were too far away and the wind was blowing in the wrong direction. She didn't linger outside; it was cold, wet and miserable. So much for the parched desert, she thought as she went back to her statistics so she could send off her return before the due deadline. Then she pulled an air-letter form from under her mill board and wrote a quick note to Bella. As she wrote she imagined Bella receiving it in the future. Perhaps when she got it Amanda might already be dead. The thought saddened her but her feeling of calm remained. She stopped writing to flex her aching fingers and to think of the right words to tell Bella how she felt about the war, their love and her hopes and fears for the future. As she thought, she twisted the signet ring that Bella had given her round and round on her little finger, then tried to take it off to reread the inscription inside it, but her knuckles had swollen and it wouldn't budge. Amanda decided that the cold and wet was enough to make anyone's knuckles swell – it could explain why they'd been aching so much recently. In fact, all of her joints had been giving her gyp. It's my age, she thought.

Time was ticking on and there were things to be done. Amanda finished off her letter and dropped it in the mail sack before being swamped by the frantic activity as they prepared to move up to the front line, ready to follow the fighting troops through Iraq and towards Kuwait.

The bustle and industry around her as everything was squared away and sorted out ready for the battle was in sharp contrast to the quiescence of her mind. The soldiers shouted and swore as they prepared everything for the move, everyone grabbed a hasty meal – no telling when there might be a chance for another one – jerrycans of fuel and water were checked and topped up where necessary. And then the order came for them to move to the start line. More shouting, engines revved, a towline organised for the truck bogged into soft, wet sand, a last check that nothing and no one was forgotten, and then they were off to the war.

The road to the front, which they joined shortly after dark, was surfaced by little more than oil sprayed on to sand and then rolled and compacted till it was hard. Hardly a motorway, which was a shame, because when they joined it it resembled the M25 on a Friday evening at the start of the summer holiday rush – three lanes of traffic at a complete standstill, except that in this instance, despite the darkness, there were no headlights blazing. They were driving in their box-bodied truck on convoy lights, playing follow-my-leader and hoping that the guy at the front stuck to the main route. They didn't dare use proper lights in case of a counterattack. The traffic jam ground to a total standstill, and after ten minutes of going nowhere Graham switched off the engine.

'I wonder why the hold-up and how far we are from the border.'

'Pass on both,' replied Amanda. She opened the door of the cab and got out to stretch her legs. There was no moon and the darkness was absolute. The wind was getting up and the sky looked threatening. It was obviously going to pour with rain again, which wouldn't make things any easier. She checked her torch, walked a few hundred yards away from the road and gazed back at the traffic jam. The dim lights, glimmering in the darkness like a stream of tracer bullets, stretched for miles in both directions. Incredible.

'We might as well try to get some shut-eye. I don't think this is going anywhere for a few hours. I've never seen so many vehicles. I'm not joking, but there can't be *anything* left in Germany.'

Graham got out to have a look and returned equally impressed.

'Now I know what migrating wildebeest must feel like when they're on the move. I can understand why they think the idea of safety in numbers is such a good wheeze.'

There was silence in the cab for a few minutes as they both thought about survival and mortality and their odds of achieving either.

Then Amanda said, 'Are you afraid?'

The question took Graham by surprise. 'I don't think so. More excited, I think, but I don't really know. What about you?'

'I'm all right, I think, like you. But I suppose it's just that I've no idea what to expect. No one has ever shot at me before.'

'Me neither. When I was at Sandhurst, a chap who came to talk to us about the Falklands War said that when he came under fire he was so busy fighting back and thinking about his next manoeuvre that he didn't have time to be frightened.'

'I suppose that's true. I don't fancy being captured, though. I don't think I could stand being tortured or interrogated. I've got a nasty feeling that they'd only have to wave a pair of red-hot pincers at me and I'd tell them everything they could possibly want to know, from the strength of the unit to the CO's shoe size.'

'Quite, torture doesn't appeal at all.' They both thought about the unpleasant prospect. Graham tried to lighten the mood. 'I've heard they shag their POWs. Hands up anyone wanting a gang-bang,' he said with a laugh. Amanda was repelled by the thought.

'Christ, that would be awful.'

'Probably worse for me than you,' said Graham with a wry smile.

Don't you believe it, thought Amanda. Then she realised exactly what Graham was saying. 'You mean they . . .?'

'I don't think many women are allowed in the army in this neck of the woods, so female POWs would be an unheard-of luxury. Anyway, I don't think they're as fussy about gender-benders in the Iraqi Army as we are in Britain. It probably stems from their choice in barracks being limited to wanking, shit-stabbing or shagging camels, due to the lack of women.' Amanda forced herself to chuckle at Graham's attempt at humour. He was obviously appalled by the idea of homosexuality. She wondered what his reaction would be if she revealed her secret. Total horror, she suspected.

'I think I'd rather top myself than get raped by a load of hairy soldiers,' said Amanda with feeling.

'Death before dishonour, you mean?' asked Graham.

Amanda nodded and shuddered.

'Nah,' continued Graham. 'I've too much to live for. Just promise you won't tell the boys in the mess that I was buggered senseless.'

'And you promise the same for me – whatever happens, the story is that I came out of this war as pure as I was when it started.'

'Deal.' Beside him Amanda shuddered again at the prospect of being raped by a gang of enemy soldiers. Her earlier doubts about being able to kill another human being wavered considerably as her imagination ran riot with the idea of her fate at the hands of the Iraqi Army. She was fairly certain that if they were ambushed she'd be perfectly capable of slotting as many of the enemy as she could before being taken. And as for the idea of committing suicide rather than being captured – well, she dismissed it. Realistically she knew she'd probably forget to count the rounds in her magazine properly and run out of bullets. She decided she'd be better off praying she didn't get captured.

They dozed fitfully in their cab, the rain beating on the windscreen and the cold wind whipping though the ill-fitting doors and windows. Occasionally they would be able to switch on the engine and chug forward a few hundred yards, before switching off again and trying to grab a few more minutes of shut-eye. Amanda tried to combat the chilly conditions as best she could, but with a strict limitation on the amount of kit they'd been allowed to bring from Germany, she didn't have much for cold weather. They'd been warned about the heat but there'd been no mention about this sort of weather. What with the cold, the lashing rain and the hardness of the seats, Amanda found that the discomfort and her exhaustion were making her joints ache more than ever.

As the sky began to lighten and the stars faded, Amanda gave up the struggle for sleep. The rain had eased, although the wind was still whipping around. She put on her combat jacket and gloves and jumped down from the cab. Her knees jarred painfully as she landed on the hard ground. God, she felt stiff. She eased her aching limbs and joints and stretched like a cat. Suddenly she realised she was bursting for a pee. She hobbled away from the road, her ankles and knees still complaining about the night in the cramped cab, and headed towards a dip in the flat landscape that might afford a bit of privacy. As she walked she was aware of a surreal stillness, as if the massive army, assembled ready to join the battle, was holding its breath. Amazingly, despite the thousands of vehicles, the battalions of troops, and – somewhere, allegedly – a battle raging, she was conscious of the sound of her footsteps crunching across the stony ground.

She'd barely reached her objective and squatted to relieve herself when the air was rent with the sound of shouts and engines revving. A vehicle backfired like a pistol shot and she could see Graham standing by their vehicle, waving at her frantically. Why, thought Amanda in annoyance, can one never have a wee in peace? She hurried as best she could but in her haste she piddled over her desert boots. When she'd finished she ran back to the vehicle, doing her flies up as she went.

'What's the matter?' she panted as she clambered into the cab.

'They've opened up another lane through the minefields. We're going over the top in just a short time.'

Amanda gulped. So this was it. She'd barely got her breath back when the truck in front began to move off. Graham slipped their lorry into gear and then followed it slowly along the track. It was still stop-start, but the progress was much faster than it had been overnight, and within a couple of hours they were driving through the gap ploughed through the berms, the system of defences between Saudi and Iraq, and then over the border and into the Iraqi defensive minefields. Their path was clearly marked with tape but Amanda worried that it would be just their luck to hit a mine that had been missed by both the Sappers and all the other vehicles ahead of them. She voiced her fears to Graham.

'A bit unlikely,' said Graham.

'I don't care. I still don't fancy the prospect. And keep your eyes on the road,' she yelled as he turned his head to smile at her. 'For God's sake, don't leave the marked path.'

'As if I would,' said Graham, all innocence. Then he suddenly swung the wheel from side to side, causing the truck to slew and swerve crazily.

Amanda screamed. 'Don't be stupid, you mad bugger. You'll get us killed.' Graham drove straight again. 'Thanks,' said Amanda coldly. Her sense of humour was struggling with her anxieties and losing the contest.

'No problem.'

'Where are they all?' said Amanda, gazing across the desert. 'I expected to see some signs of fighting, but there's nothing. You don't think this is some sort of trap, do you?'

'It's a bloody clever one if it is. What with aerial reconnaissance, to say nothing of satellite photography, I would imagine that Schwarzkopf has a fair idea of where the enemy is.'

'OK, OK. I'm a girlie, remember?'

'I hadn't forgotten.'

'All the same, I did expect to see some evidence of fighting. I mean, I'd have thought that the border would have been defended, at the very least.'

'There's something over there.' Graham pointed to a smouldering shape about a quarter of a mile away.

'What is it, do you think?'

'A tank?'

'Could be. Ours or theirs?'

'Don't know. Too far away to tell yet.'

They drew closer. They could see the hole in the side of the hull and a couple of bodies lying on the sand by the tracks. A third figure hung out of the turret like a discarded child's toy. All the figures were burned black, with their teeth still screaming through their charred lips.

'It's one of theirs,' said Graham. Amanda was mesmerised by the horror of the scene.

'How ghastly,' she whispered.

'Get real. They're only rag-heads.'

Amanda stared at him, aghast; he wasn't joking. She hoped she would never, ever get that callous. She knew that the war had already changed her, hardened her, made her more self-reliant, to say nothing of honing her military skills. But she didn't ever want to stop feeling compassion for her fellow human beings. Briefly she wondered if this was a part of Graham's character that had always been there but had only recently had the chance to surface, or whether the war had made him like it. Either way it didn't really matter, and either way it was unforgivable.

As they drove deeper into Iraq they came across more and more evidence of the push through the enemy defences by the fighting troops of the 1st Armoured Division. In some places they passed huge groups of demoralised enemy troops, squatting miserably on the ground, waiting for transport to take them to a camp and guarded by a handful of soldiers.

'They seem to have given up without a fight,' said Amanda, puzzled.

'It certainly looks that way,' said Graham.

When they stopped later that day to refuel and get a hot meal, they were able to catch up with the day's monumental events. It transpired that the bombing of the enemy positions before the start of the ground war had been so effective that before the coalition forces got anywhere near the Iraqis, most of them had already thrown in the towel and deserted. A handful had tried to fight but they'd been hopelessly outnumbered. It seemed that the main problem for the advancing army had been dealing with the vast numbers of the enemy who wanted to surrender.

Amanda was thankful that the 'Mother of all Battles', as Saddam had claimed it would be, was turning out to be the 'Mother of all Walkovers'. If nothing else it sounded as though the coalition casualties were negligible. She hoped this trend would continue, even when they got to Kuwait.

Northern Ireland,
February 1991

Edwina listened to the news with increasing frustration. She longed to be out in the Gulf, fighting through the desert, facing the enemy, winning medals. Since their first lectures at Sandhurst on tactics she'd always been envious of the Desert Rats at El Alamein. It had been an classic battle played out in classic circumstances with masses of movement, feats of derring-do and wide-open spaces in which to manoeuvre and outmanoeuvre. And now the Desert Rats were engaged in an action replay and she was in the wrong place. Perhaps if she hadn't volunteered for 14 Company she might have been sent to the Gulf . . .

Bugger, she swore under her breath as she watched the early-evening news, riveted by the pictures being sent back from the battle zone. She knew she was being ungrateful; she had a wonderful job in Ireland and six months ago she wouldn't have swapped it for the world. But she just had this uneasy feeling that now she was missing out on the real action, that she'd made the wrong decision, and if she'd stuck with the Royal Corps of Signals she might have been out there in the thick of it too. Her only consolation was that it was apparent that the land battle in the Gulf was going to be over almost before it started, whereas the fight against terrorism would continue long after the excitement in the Middle East had stopped. All the same, it was difficult not to feel envious as she watched the report of the conflict. The TV showed a multi-launch rocket system in action at night, the rockets streaking across the pitch-black sky like giant fireworks. Wow, thought Edwina, all that power! It didn't cross her mind to wonder about the enemy squaddies on the receiving end; she was just impressed with the firepower it provided. Then the pictures changed to the scene at a briefing, somewhere in the desert. General

245

Sir Peter de la Billière was standing in front of a map, pointer in hand, and as the camera panned around the tent there was Richard Airdrie-Stow, right in the middle of the shot, looking earnest and attentive.

'Good grief,' she said out loud, taken aback by the sight. She'd never met him but there was no doubt. Lizzie's sitting room had been full of photos of their wedding day, and besides which, his green name tape, stitched across his uniform, was clearly in focus.

'What's the matter?' said Ulysses.

'I know that bloke,' and she lunged forward to point him out before the picture changed.

'Oh.' Ulysses sounded uninterested.

'Don't you play "spot the face" then?' asked Edwina. It wasn't the first time she had seen someone she knew out there, although it had usually been the more senior officers that she recognised.

'I don't think any of the people I know will be too keen to get their faces on the box.'

'You mean the Regiment is out there?'

'I didn't say that.'

Edwina stared at him. 'But you implied it.'

'If that's what you want to think.'

'Oh, come on, Ulysses. We're on the same side, we both do the same job.' He just shrugged. 'So what are they doing? Are they going to assassinate Saddam?'

'I honestly don't know,' Ulysses declared with finality.

'Liar, liar, your pants'll catch fire,' chanted Edwina.

'If you say so.'

Edwina felt infuriated, but she knew that nothing she could say would make Ulysses divulge information if he didn't want to. To take her mind off her annoyance she turned her attention to a bit of personal admin that she'd been putting off for far too long. Her earlier thoughts about the continuing war against terrorism had reminded her that if she wanted to be a part of it, then she had to extend her posting beyond the time she'd been allotted. Besides which, the news had shifted from scenes of the Gulf War to the next story. Boring.

'Shift yourself,' she ordered Ulysses, who was lounging in the one easy chair the room possessed. She wanted to get some writing paper out of her desk and Ulysses was sitting in the way. She took a fresh sheet of paper, found her fountain pen, checked it had ink in it and carefully began to draft a formal letter to her postings branch via her commanding officer.

'"Sir, I have the honour to apply . . .",' read Ulysses over her shoulder. 'What sort of arse-licking is this?'

'I want to extend my current posting by a year and this is how I go about it,' she explained.

'So "keep me here for a bit longer, please, darlin'" isn't the proper wording?'

'Not exactly.'

'What about "keep me here or I'll fuckin' slot ya'"?'

Edwina couldn't help laughing at the thought of the reaction of some senior officer receiving such a letter. Still giggling, she took her head. 'No. Now shut up and let me finish this.' She wrote on carefully and slowly, checking her spellings as she went. This sort of letter was utter bullshit and she knew it, but if it wasn't done properly it wouldn't be received favourably and she didn't want to jeopardise her chances. *I have the honour to be, Sir, Your obedient Servant*, she finished, ignoring Ulysses' hoots of laughter and his tugging of his forelock. 'Don't mock, it's only a means to an end.' But Ulysses was laughing too hard to reply.

Neither of them laughed a week later when Edwina was told that her application had been turned down flat and that she was to be posted back to the Royal Signals in April.

'But why?' she protested to her boss.

'I've no idea. If I had anything to do with it you could serve on for the next decade. You're a bloody useful member of the team. To be honest, I was thinking of asking you if you'd be prepared to be DS at the next selection.'

Edwina stared at him morosely. Big deal, she thought, but she was too upset to say anything. She knew that if she spoke, she'd cry. She could feel her eyes pricking, and the colonel saying nice things to her wasn't helping her composure. She mumbled some incoherent thanks and walked swiftly from his office and back to her Portakabin. The rest of the Army was celebrating the successful conclusion of the ground war in the Gulf, and Edwina felt she must be the only miserable person in uniform.

When Ulysses found her half an hour later her sobs had finished and she was lying, inert, staring at the ceiling.

'Your boss told me,' he said without preamble. Edwina didn't reply. 'You can't just leave it at that. There must be some action you can take, some sort of appeal.'

'Oh, yeah. Like what?'

'Don't get at me,' said Ulysses, hurt. 'I'm only trying to help. Surely, as the boss wants you to carry on, he can put in a word for you?'

'Suppose so.'

'And why don't you ask why they turned your application down? If they haven't got a good reason, or if the reason is crap, then surely you've got better grounds for a redress of grievance?' But Edwina still didn't respond. She just sighed and turned her head to the wall. Ulysses gave up, exasperated. 'I had you down for a fucking fighter but I was wrong. If you take this shit without a murmur then you're a loser.' More annoyed with himself at losing his temper than he was with her, he left, banging the door behind him.

After several minutes Edwina sat up. She swung her legs off her bed and thought about Ulysses' words. He was right, of course. She couldn't just accept this kind of rejection. She had to confront whoever had made the decision, and even if she couldn't alter it, at least she would have the satisfaction of having her say.

Three days later Edwina boarded the shuttle from Belfast International to London Heathrow. The flight was surprisingly crowded and Edwina hadn't been able to get a window seat as she'd hoped. As it turned out, it made no difference, as the sky was ten-tenths cloud for the whole journey and no one was able to catch the least glimpse of the ground until they had almost landed. Edwina, her luggage consisting of her handbag, zipped through the terminal and down to the tube – Piccadilly Line to Green Park then change on to the Jubilee Line, all the way to Stanmore. As she climbed on to the train she did a rough sum to calculate the length of her journey – someone had once told her it was about three minutes a station. Oh, God, an hour and a half on the tube. She wished she had a book. What the hell was she going to occupy her thoughts with, other than her fears about her impending interview? Part of her wanted the journey, to say nothing of the whole day, to be over and done with. But part of her wanted time to stop. She had a feeling of dread in the pit of her stomach that, however cogent her argument for her retention in 14 Company, however carefully she stated her case, the outcome had been decided and nothing would alter that. She knew that by the end of the day her fate would be decided one way or the other. She wasn't sure she wanted that moment to come.

As the train rattled and swayed its way along the line, stopping occasionally at the dreary stations along its route, Edwina went over and over all the things she had to say. She read and reread her OC's letter of recommendation, and although his glowing report gave her some comfort, she still felt that this exercise was fruitless. She knew she shouldn't feel so despairing, and she tried to feel positive – but what was the point? She just knew the day was going to be a bust and she might as well accept it.

It was only a short walk from Stanmore station to the MoD department that planned officers' postings and careers. It wasn't signed – part of the campaign to confuse terrorists – but the directions Edwina had been given were impeccable. It didn't take long for her to find the old hutted army camp, grandly named Government Buildings. It was reminiscent of the huts beloved by film directors in movies about the Battle of Britain. She half expected to see a group of young men, dressed in air-force-blue battle-dress, lounging around in deckchairs and all set to scramble at a moment's notice. She dismissed her flight of fantasy and followed the signs that directed her towards her particular PB branch.

The warrant officer who greeted her offered her a cup of tea and told her that her interview would take place shortly. Edwina sat on the edge of her seat, sipping her tea and trying to look calm and ignore the ducks flapping around in her stomach.

A buzzer sounded discreetly.

'You can go in now. The room across the corridor.' The warrant officer smiled reassuringly at Edwina. Edwina smiled back and nodded, and handed back her half-drunk tea.

She paused for a second outside the closed door, and as she did so she heard the sound of high heels clicking along the corridor towards her. For some reason she turned to see who was approaching. It was Cathy Roberts! Suddenly, intuitively, Edwina knew that this completed the picture. Although she had not a shred of proof, she somehow knew that if Cathy was working in postings at Stanmore, she was the one to blame for Edwina's career with the Special Forces getting screwed up. That had to be the explanation. She'd said she would wreck things for Edwina. It wouldn't matter that being mainstream WRAC Cathy would only have responsibility for posting members of her own corps; she could still spread rumours, network, sow seeds of doubt about Edwina's reliability. And those who didn't know Edwina personally – and certainly her own postings officer didn't – would accept the word of a fellow postings officer as gospel – especially as Cathy would have convinced them that she had no personal axe to grind and that she just had the interests of the Army, as a whole, at heart.

Cathy smiled triumphantly at Edwina as she passed, and Edwina resisted the temptation to smack her, then she knocked briskly and entered.

'Sit down, Edwina,' said her postings officer. 'I gather you're not happy that your tour in Ireland is about to end?'

'You could put it like that.'

'But you've been there for nearly two years. It's essential, in the interests of your career profile, that you move on, return to regimental duties or a junior staff job.'

Edwina thought this was bollocks, but she didn't say so. She had a huge amount of specialist training and experience, far too much to be wasted on some dreary desk job. Instead she said, 'My boss would like me to stay on, to help with selection and training.'

'I know. I have his letter in front of me. You've certainly been an effective member of the team. I also hear that you get on with your colleagues *extremely* well.' There was something about the way the major opposite her said this last bit that put Edwina on her guard.

'The team doesn't gel if you don't,' she said warily.

'But you get on with others, outside the team?'

'Not especially. We keep ourselves to ourselves. You know that.' She wished this man would either piss or get off the pot; she couldn't stand people who didn't come directly to the point. He was heading in some direction or other and she couldn't quite determine which.

'What about Staff Sergeant Lees?'

So this was it – her friendship with Ulysses, their meeting witnessed by Cathy, who had no doubt dug around to find out some more about the two of them. Cathy had used that information to blow the whistle on Edwina and had told them she was fraternising with an Other Rank. What a bitch! And as for this drongo sitting across the desk, playing some sort of inane game – why didn't he come right out and ask her if she was screwing an NCO? As if it made her any less useful in the Province? Well, she decided, she wasn't going to admit to anything. They could take a running jump.

'What about Staff Lees?' she asked belligerently.

'You see him a lot?'

'At least once a week.'

'Is this wise?'

'Extremely. He's the best shot I know. I wouldn't have anyone else guarding me when I'm surrounded by bastards who would like to shoot me in the back.'

The major had the decency to look uncomfortable. He knew what she was getting at. 'I see. He's Special Forces too, then?'

'SAS.'

'But you see him off duty too?'

'Yes.'

'Often?'

'If operations permit.'

'Do you think you should?'

'You mean, isn't it bad for discipline? Well, frankly, no, because we don't need the sort of stupid claptrap about dress codes and behaviour and fraternising that we learn about from Queen's Regs to know where we stand with each other. We all respect everyone in our unit because it's a respect that is earned, and not just demanded because of a little gold pip that you can buy from Moss Bros and stick on your shoulder, and which means damn all. And I don't just see Staff Lees, I also see my oppo, Nat, off duty too. For all I know Nat could be a bombardier or a brigadier. We don't know each other's ranks, we don't even care what they are. Nor do we know who's using their real name and who isn't. And it doesn't matter. But we do care about being loyal to each other and backing each other up and not letting the enemy stick knives into us.' Edwina sat back in her chair, breathless and aware that she had said far too much.

'I see.' The voice was cold.

Edwina knew she hadn't done her case any good. She knew she'd been insubordinate to this officer but she didn't care. He obviously didn't have a clue about her work in Ireland. He had been told to post her back to a Signals unit somewhere and to do it pronto, and nothing was going to alter it. Cathy, manipulating the system, had won – for the time being. But Edwina remembered what her boss had told her before she'd left to catch the shuttle: that if her postings branch was intransigent she could volunteer again and her application would have to be forwarded. Well, perhaps she'd better resign herself to that course of action. She didn't think that a real head-to-head battle was going to advance her cause. Maybe patience was the answer.

'OK. So where are you planning to send me?'

The major sagged with relief that the hellcat in front of him wasn't going to fight any more. She'd looked as if she might get violent.

'Admin officer of 3 Squadron. Your posting date should be about mid-May.'

'Aldershot?' Edwina raised her eyebrows.

'That's right. Look, I know you think that this is a personal slight, but honestly, this posting is in your best interests. You simply haven't got the experience, at a regimental level, to move on to the next stage in your career. You can't afford to jeopardise your chances of promotion by staying away from a mainstream signalling job.'

'But I'm not interested in promotion. I like doing what I'm doing.'

'That's as may be, but the Army didn't spend all this time and money on training you to be a signals officer to see it wasted.'

She held her tongue about the cost of her training for 14 Company. Instead she said, 'So what the system wants the system gets, and to hell with the individual?'

'That's not true and you know it.'

Edwina shook her head sadly. She wondered how quickly she could apply to rejoin 14 Company. Christ, Aldershot, home of the British Army. She couldn't think of anywhere she was going to hate more. But on the bright side, at least Lizzie and Richard were there.

She got back to Ireland that evening just in time to join in the unit's darts marathon down at the Greenfly Club. They'd been organising it for weeks, in between operations, with the aim of helping to raise funds for a scanner for the Royal Victoria Hospital in Belfast. A member of the RUC Special Branch had started the campaign after his son had to be flown back to the mainland for some specialist treatment. No one in 14 Company minded helping with this; the kids in Northern Ireland had as much right to this equipment as anyone else, and anyway, it was a cracking excuse for a piss-up.

Edwina rarely needed much of an excuse to knock back the odd drink or two, and after the day's events she felt she had more than enough reason to get slaughtered that night. It was after three in the morning when she left the Greenfly Club and began to head back to her quarters. It was a dark, moonless night and the lighting at that end of the barracks, near the stables, wasn't good.

'Come on, Nat, hurry up,' Edwina said as she swayed past the loose-boxes. The horses were looking out, annoyed by the distur-bance. Beside her the stable cat slunk down in the shadows, wary of this intruder into its nocturnal world.

'Just slow down. I can't see a damn thing.'

'There's nothing to see, stupid. It's pitch . . . Oops. Oh, fuck!'

'Edwina? Are you all right?'

'Yeah. I've just trodden in a pile of horse muck.'

'I told you to slow down. Oh, there you are.' Nat caught up with Edwina, who was trying to scrape the manure off her shoes. He could just discern her standing like a stork on one leg while she poked ineffectually at the sole of her shoe with a stick. He had to admire her sense of balance, even though she'd had what could be called a skinful, in anyone's terminology. 'Why don't you wait until we get to some grass and wipe your shoes on that?'

'OK.' Edwina threw her stick away, narrowly missing the stable cat, which hissed and spat at her and skulked away. She resumed her uncertain progress through the stable yard.

'Ooh, goody! A gate. Watch me leap it, Nat.'

'Stop horsing around, you silly cow. You'll hurt yourself.'

But Nat's exhortation fell on deaf ears. Edwina put both hands on the top bar of the gate, planning to push up hard and swing her legs high over it. But in the dim light and under the influence of far too much Guinness, she misjudged it, caught one foot on the gatepost and fell, crashing hard on the other side.

'Shit!' she bellowed. 'My fucking arm.'

Nat negotiated the gate carefully and bent over her. 'What's the matter?'

'I think I've broken my bloody wrist.' She was kneeling up, nurs-ing her arm against her chest.

'Let me have a look at it.' He moved to touch it, but Edwina snarled at him to leave her alone. She knew that the least touch, how-ever well-meaning, would be unbearable. Just up ahead, where the officers' married quarters were, a couple of bedroom lights came on as the occupants, disturbed by the noise, decided that perhaps they ought to investigate the commotion. A face peered blearily from an upstairs window.

'Now we've woken those people up, do you want to go to them while I get help, or can you make it to the medical centre?'

'It's my arm that's broken, not my leg.' The pain made her temper even shorter than normal. She winced as she got to her feet. 'Shit,' she swore as she jolted her arm. The pain was making her feel sick. 'Come on,' she said through lips tightened against the awful throbbing ache. 'And thanks for not saying I told you so.'

When Edwina finally arrived at the medical centre five minutes later she found she had to wait a further twenty minutes while the medical officer was telephoned and hauled out of his bed to come and examine her. His bedside manner was not at its best and it was with a distinct lack of sympathy that he told her it was only a sprain, not a fracture.

'To be honest, as far as the discomfort goes, there's not much to choose between the two,' he said sourly, angry at having yet another disturbed night.

'That's just great,' she replied, trying not to swear as the nurse strapped up her arm.

The MO refused to give her painkillers because of the amount she'd had to drink – or at least that was what he said. Edwina suspected he wanted her to suffer a bit to get his own back for being called out.

'Bastard,' she swore at him, but he wouldn't be budged.

She spent an uncomfortable night, her arm giving her hell and, because of all the Guinness she'd consumed, having to get up twice for a wee, which didn't help matters. The next morning, with her arm in a sling, it was impossible to conceal the fact that she'd had an accident, and she was the butt of any number of jokes when the cause of it got out. Finally, to add insult to injury, it stopped her taking part in any operations for a least two weeks, possibly more.

'So what am I supposed to do to keep myself busy?' she complained to the ops officer.

'You can help me out for a start.' He didn't feel particularly sympathetic towards her. Her injury could almost be classed as self-inflicted.

Edwina's main disappointment was that she wasn't able to meet the tout she was supposed to be running. There was no way she could go out with a sprained wrist because for one thing, she couldn't drive properly. OK, her shooting wouldn't be affected – she could use either hand with equal effectiveness – but she wouldn't be able to defend herself properly if she got into a situation where she couldn't use her gun.

'Nat will have to meet your tout tomorrow,' said the ops officer. 'So give him a proper briefing. I don't want any more fuck-ups.'

Edwina felt rightly chastised. What she'd done had been stupid. Her penalty had been this injury, but it wasn't just affecting her. It meant extra work for everyone.

'Sorry,' she said.

'It's a bit bloody late for that.'

Edwina told Nat everything she knew about her tout: the agreed signal he would use if something wasn't right, his mannerisms, his habitual turns of phrase, anything which might alter if he was under stress or lying.

'I wish we could postpone the meeting,' she said. 'I'm worried that something might go wrong.'

'What could go wrong? You've told me everything a dozen times. And it isn't as if I haven't run my own informants,' said Nat, annoyed that she didn't appear to trust him.

'I'm sorry. I know you're not a novice. It's just there's ... Oh, I don't know. I'm just not absolutely happy this time. I've got this feeling something isn't quite right.'

'But this tout has always come across. Why don't you trust him all of a sudden?'

'I don't know.' And she didn't. It was nothing more than a vague niggle.

'Sounds like a case of an overactive imagination to me,' said Nat.

'Yeah, you're probably right. Anyway, if he finally leads us to whoever has got that bloody gun, it'll be worth it.'

They were still chasing the sniper's gun. Whenever they got within spitting distance the IRA spirited it back across the border into the Republic for a few months. It was as if they knew when 14 Company was about to move in. Edwina's unit was getting more and more determined to bug it so they knew where it was going next. Then they could set up an operation and, with any luck, capture the gun and slot the sniper. He'd killed enough of their side – it was time to pay him back. Edwina's tout, who'd produced rock-solid, first class information in the past, was now hinting that the gun was back in Belfast and hidden in an old factory. He'd promised to have more information for her at their next meeting. In fact, she'd had an idea that he was on the brink of telling her which disused factory in particular was the hiding-place. Now Nat would be the one to hear the gen and have the cachet of running the subsequent operation.

Edwina wasn't out for gongs or personal glory – she was too much of a team player even to consider such things – but she had a special interest in this. It was her informant, her hard work that had got them to this stage and she wanted to be there at the conclusion. Also, it wouldn't be long now before she left the Province and she suspected that this would have been her last chance at a serious contribution to the team's list of successes.

Oh, what the heck! It was her own stupid fault. But she watched Nat go off to his rendezvous feeling more than a little bit sorry for herself. If only she hadn't got rat-arsed.

'Right, this is the factory here.' Nat pointed to the building marked on the large-scale map, then to a large aerial photograph showing the run-down complex clearly. It had been taken from one of the military helicopters that habitually hovered over Belfast. 'We will need to keep watch from here, here and here.' His pointer tapped the map to show where he meant. 'I don't want there to be any risk of the opposition, or some of the local yobs, stumbling across our team once they're inside. Access is through the car park, here,' he tapped his pointer on the picture, 'but the lighting is almost nonexistent so it shouldn't be a problem. Then we go via this wicket gate,' tap, 'in through the main goods entrance.' Tap. 'We've already done a recce and it's not locked. The gun, according to our man, is in a pipe-hide in the inspection pit in the old vehicle-servicing bay, which, also according to our tame Mick, is here.' Tap. 'The green army has been told this area is out of bounds from eighteen hundred hours today. We don't want some keen squaddy being overenthusiastic and checking out any activity in the area. It could blow the whole operation.'

A murmur went round the crowded briefing room as they all remembered a recent occasion when exactly that had happened. A member of 14 Company had nearly been shot by a uniformed soldier – a member of the green army – who'd thought the agent's actions were so suspicious he must have been a terrorist. The quiet rumble of voices died down to listen to Nat detailing who was to be positioned where, undertaking which tasks, when and how. His audience listened intently. Most of what he was saying was routine stuff, procedures they'd all carried out dozens of times, but even on a routine operation like this one there was always the potential for something to go wrong, and everyone was a little tense as a result.

256

'OK then, I want each pair at their locations by twenty-one fifteen hours at the latest. We've timed it then, while people are still around, because we'll be less conspicuous. Half an hour after the pubs close there's no activity in this area, so from about twenty-three hundred hours we'll stick out like dogs' bollocks. I'll be going in with Mark, now that Edwina is out of action, at twenty-one thirty. We want to be clear before closing time because this site is sometimes used by the local lads to have their wicked way with their girlfriends on their way home. I don't want to trip over a courting couple on my way back to the RV. Right, any questions?'

Everyone seemed happy with what was going on, and even Edwina had to admit that the operation appeared to have been planned to cover every possibility and option. Because it only involved a static piece of kit, with no terrorists to follow, arrest or avoid, it was a straightforward exercise. All they had to do was get two men into the building, find and bug the gun, and then get them out, picked up and away again without being seen by anyone else. Teams of two would be stationed around the area to warn the pair inside of any possible danger – easy-peasy. They'd all done it before. Edwina was sorry she was going to be missing it, but at least she'd be able to make herself useful by manning the radio in the ops room.

As the teams went out into the miserable, wet winter night, Edwina took up position at the radio set, listening in on the net to them calling their status and position. One by one everyone moved into their appointed place, exactly as Nat's plan had ordained. Edwina felt redundant as she heard the quick, terse messages. It was all going smoothly, so it was unlikely she would be required to co-ordinate anything. She glanced at her watch, then at the television droning away quietly in the corner. The ops officer sat in the only armchair, doing the crossword. It looked as though he was going to be redundant too – no need for him to get involved with something going as smoothly as this. Each of the call signs radioed in that they were in position, then confirmed that the surrounding area was deserted. At this rate everyone would be back in base by midnight.

As she sat in the stuffy ops room, listening to the radio set humming and crackling and waiting for the next transmission, surrounded by maps and photographs, empty mugs of coffee and full ashtrays – the clutter of a rarely empty office – Edwina imagined in her mind's eye what was going on. She visualised Nat and Mark, clad in black, sneaking swiftly up to the wicket gate of the factory entrance, watched closely by the others to check that they hadn't been pinged by any dickers. If this was going to be a trap the IRA would have someone watching closely, ready to alert an active service unit to move in for the kill – or worse, capture. But it was obvious from the traffic on the net that there was no one around. If there was, a contact report would be sent and the operation aborted. The word *contact* was the all-important one that watchkeepers, ops officers, everyone was tuned into; it was supposed to indicate that the sender could see the enemy or had an indication of their presence. But in Ireland, where the enemy didn't use conventional warfare tactics, it more usually meant that the soldiers had run into an ambush. This operation, however, was specifically designed to avoid contact, and anyway it was going to be a piece of cake, judging by the traffic so far.

She had just accepted another coffee from the duty clerk when she heard Nat laconically informing everyone on the ground that he and Mark had made it into the factory. Silence followed as they made their way through the building to the vehicle servicing bay and the inspection pit. This was the most frustrating time for all the others involved as they waited for news of their progress. Edwina sipped her coffee.

'Delta complete,' she heard eventually. Great, she thought, Nat and Mark had found the inspection pit. They should soon find the hide, deal with the gun and be back out.

Then, behind her, the radio tuned to the brigade frequency crackled for a second prior to someone coming on that net. Edwina recognised the initial call sign as that of the Girdwood Barracks' watchkeeper.

'Contact. Wait out,' he said. Then a pause.

Edwina sat bolt upright; her coffee slopped over the rim of the mug and on to her trousers but she didn't notice. Swiftly she put the mug down on the table as she pulled the log towards her, grabbed a pen and noted the time of the report. The ops officer put down his paper.

What sort of contact? they were both thinking. The word could mean a number of things.

'Explosion, unknown location. Direction North Belfast,' from the Girdwood watchkeeper.

'Shit,' the ops officer mumbled. 'That's where they are.'

Edwina scowled. She knew that just as well as he did. He crossed the room to stand behind her chair.

Then, on her own net, she heard what she'd been dreading for those few seconds.

'Zero, this is X-ray.' It was one of their call signs. The voice, even over the radio, sounded fraught. 'Explosion this location. Out.'

'Delta.' Edwina looked up from her frantic scribbling of events on to the log sheet. This was Nat and Mark's call sign. 'We've been fucking stitched. It was a booby-trap. Nat's hurt. I need dressings.' Oh, God. Not badly hurt, please. Edwina had no idea of the size of the explosion, though it must have been fairly big to be heard at Girdwood. How much of the force had Nat taken?

'X-ray, roger. Zero, do you copy?'

'Zero, roger,' Edwina acknowledged.

The ops officer had already picked up the red telephone and contacted the local infantry brigade HQ. It was answered before the first ring was complete.

'We need the quick-reaction force and an ambulance to this grid reference.' He read the list of numbers to the brigade watchkeeper. 'There's been an explosion, casualties, one serious and there may be another, I don't know.'

'OK,' the watchkeeper acknowledged. There was a second's pause while he translated the grid to a location on his map. 'You mean the out-of-bounds area?'

'Yes. That's because of our operation.' The out-of-bounds order was irrelevant now; the operation had gone tits up and they needed back-up at the factory from the green army, and fast.

'Roger.'

The line was kept open and Edwina and the ops officer listened with one ear to the radio traffic so they could relay to the watchkeeper what scant details were available.

'X-ray. Has anyone got more dressings? Nat is bleeding heavily.'

Oh, God, thought Edwina, it sounds bad. A wave of guilt surged through her. If she'd not been so stupid she'd have met the tout herself and might have realised that this was a fucking set-up. If only she'd gone to the meet . . . How could Nat have picked up the signs that something might be wrong if he'd never met the man before? If only she hadn't got drunk, if only she hadn't shown off, if only, if only . . .

The radio set on the other side of the room, tuned to the brigade net, crackled into life again as the watchkeeper crashed out the QRF and the ambulance attached to them.

'That tout of yours,' said the ops officer.

'Yes?'

'Do we need to get him out?'

Edwina hadn't thought of that; she'd been taken up with worries about Nat. What the ops officer was inferring was that the IRA might have deliberately fed him information to check out his reliability. That way they would not only score a hit against the Special Forces; they'd also identify an informant. Edwina felt guilty that she hadn't considered that aspect; she'd automatically assumed he'd double-crossed her and her team.

'I don't know,' she said. 'But let's get the RUC to bring him in anyway.' Once in police custody, he was safe from his enemies and handy for them to talk to. Either way, they couldn't lose. Edwina hoped she'd be given a chance to have a chat with him. She'd trusted him, and if he was the bastard she suspected him to be, she looked forward to asking him a few questions. She got on to the RUC and gave them his address.

The net was frantic with radio calls as those on the ground and directly involved got to grips with the situation. The QRF arrived in a matter of minutes, evacuated the casualties and organised a cordon round the area. Felix, call sign of the ammunition technical officer, was tasked – 'a bit fucking late now,' said Edwina when she heard, even though she knew that the first explosion might have been a come-on, designed to entice more troops into the area for an even worse ambush. But she wasn't concerned with the troops now at the scene. All she was worried about was the state of Mark and Nat. Back in the ops room they still had no idea as to the extent of the injuries, and they weren't going to clog up the net with irrelevant questions to allay their worries. They'd find out the details after-wards. In the mean time, all they could do was listen to the radio traffic and glean what they could.

Gradually the situation was brought under control and things started to calm down. The activity slowed and the tension began to ease. Then the RUC phoned them back. The tout wasn't going to be any help to anyone. He was dead in his sitting room, shot through the head.

'Let's hope his is the only death resulting from this cock-up,' said the ops officer grimly, staring at Edwina.

Oh, God, she thought, he was blaming her for all this too.

Kuwait, March 1991

'Do you know what the definition of luxury is, Graham?' asked Amanda, sitting in a deckchair beside their vehicle on the outskirts of downtown Kuwait City. In the last couple of days she'd had the time to attend to her own personal admin and now she was thoroughly washed and shampooed, in clean clothes and feeling quite comfortable for the first time in weeks.

'Not having a slit trench for a bedroom?'

'No.' Amanda didn't much mind sleeping in a trench beside the vehicle. In fact, now she'd got used to it she quite liked the feeling of security the confined space gave her.

'Pass, then.' Graham was lounging in a chair opposite her, reading a copy of *The Times*. It was nearly a week old, but as he hadn't seen a copy for some months he didn't really care.

'A hot shower and a flush loo.' She still hadn't experienced the luxury of either, but at least her shower had been in complete privacy, as had her trip to the latrines. Now that they were stopped in one place for the foreseeable future, Amanda had at last managed to organise her ablutions to her own satisfaction.

Graham laughed. 'I will never, *ever* complain again about the standard of mess accommodation. There is nothing quite so nice, and so taken for granted, as having a shit, shower, shave and shampoo in comfort.'

'Right,' said Amanda, looking at her watch. 'Nearly time to go on duty, I suppose.'

'Yup.' Graham heaved himself out of the low chair. 'Come on, lazy. You can't lie around here all day soaking up the sun.'

Amanda laughed mirthlessly. They hadn't seen the sun for days. The sky above, which should have been deep blue, was an apocalyptic black as the smoke from hundreds of oil-well fires was belched over the Gulf. They both knew that their current feeling of cleanliness wouldn't last, as everything, even the air they breathed, was laden with minute droplets of oil which would make them dirty again in a short space of time. But while the feeling did last, it was wonderful.

Gathered around them were vehicles from any number of units. They no longer had to think tactically, so now the criteria for their base were things like the most convenient water supply, good hardstanding for the trucks, and shade. Despite the unpleasant atmospheric conditions, morale throughout the units was excellent. The war was over, they'd been promised a swift return back to their families, they were alive and they'd seen incredibly few of their own side injured or killed.

Things weren't so cushy for some of the other units. Part of the Divisional Headquarters was parked up on a rubbish dump because it was the most convenient piece of open space available. Graham had been to visit them to sort out an admin problem and had reported back to Amanda that they had to contend not only with the polluted air, but also with the stench of rotting rubbish and the sight of maggot-infested animal corpses. Amanda thanked her stars that their allocated area was a relative beauty spot in comparison.

In the distance they could see Kuwait City itself, but this was strictly out of bounds. Amanda and Graham had discussed the possibility of a spot of sightseeing but had decided that the dangers of falling foul of the authorities were too great.

Amanda hauled herself to her feet and began to head towards the rear of their vehicle, ready to do her next stint of duty. She didn't mind the idea of sitting in its squashed interior, hunched over a desk, for the next eight hours, as at least it meant she would be inside. The vehicle was so cramped that only those people on duty were allowed in it – off-duty personnel had to make their own arrangements outside, which was not particularly pleasant because of the revolting air conditions. As she was about to duck through the door of her inadequate office a Land Rover drew up about ten yards away. A figure jumped out of it and began walking towards them.

'Richard,' yelled Amanda, recognising him instantly.

'Hi! My spies told me your lot was holed up here.' Amanda, delighted to see a familiar face, gave him a hug. 'And what did you do in the war?' asked Richard.

'Oh, this and that. What about you?'

'Had a wonderful time. I've never done so much live-firing in my life.' He saw Graham hovering near Amanda. 'Aren't you going to introduce us?'

'Sorry. Richard, this is Graham Long. Graham, meet Richard Airdrie-Stow.' The two men shook hands.

'Hi! Look, Amanda, I'll go and take over the watch for you,' said Graham. He went into the vehicle to relieve the chief clerk.

'I'm sorry, Amanda,' said Richard. 'Is this a bad time to arrive?'

'Well, not really, except that I'm just about to take over on watch. It'll be as boring as sin with nothing to do, but . . .'

'I know. Duty calls.'

Amanda smiled. 'How about tomorrow morning? Can you come over again then? I'll be free until four.'

'I don't think that'll be a problem, especially as I now know where to find you. See you then.'

Amanda found she was looking forward to the next day. It would be nice to have a conversation with someone other than the people she'd been spending the last months with.

She had just finished her breakfast of eggs and beans and was cleaning out her mess tins when Richard drew up in his Land Rover.

'You're early,' remarked Amanda.

'I have to give the Rover back to my OC at lunchtime, so I thought if we were going to do some sightseeing we'd better get cracking.'

'But Kuwait City is out of bounds.'

'I know that. We're not going there. Ready?"

'Give me a minute or two.' Amanda put her mess tins back in her large pack and grabbed her camera, checking she had a spare film. She hadn't had much chance to take any pictures for a while and she wanted a record of what she'd seen and done – she didn't think it likely that she'd be going to war again.

'I'm ready,' she announced as she joined Richard.

'Great. Let's go.' They both climbed into the vehicle and Richard started the engine and swung the wheel so they were heading north.

'We're not going to the Basra Road, are we?' Amanda had heard stories of the appalling carnage inflicted on the Iraqis fleeing in their looted vehicles, and had no wish to see it.

'No fear,' said Richard. 'I've had to go along it twice now and it's not a pretty sight. Though actually it's not the sights that are so bad, it's the smell. I don't think I'm every going to be able to eat roast meat again.'

Amanda could tell from the look on his face that his last comment wasn't as glib as it sounded.

'That bad?'

'Worse.'

She didn't feel inclined to probe further.

'So where are we going?' she asked.

'There are some Iraqi tanks which appear to have been surrendered without a fight. I thought we could go and have a look at them.'

'OK.' Amanda didn't feel particularly thrilled at the prospect of climbing over some lumps of metal in the middle of a desert, but, what the hell, it was a trip out, the company was congenial and it might just conceivably prove interesting.

Richard drove carefully, with his headlights on, because even though it was broad daylight the oil fires had created a permanent dusky gloom. He headed out across the desert, mostly retracing the route Amanda's unit had taken a week before when they'd followed behind the main force that had liberated Kuwait. The route was pretty well defined and had been heavily used, but they both kept their eyes open for any unexploded bomblets.

'You know what we're looking for?' Richard had asked Amanda as they had set out. She'd nodded. While they'd been camped at Al Jubayl they'd had a lecture about the multiple-launch rocket system which was capable of firing up to twelve rockets. They'd been shown a memorable film of MLRS being fired at night and had been awestruck at the sight of the rockets arching away from the launch vehicle, like some infernal fireworks display. After the film the lecturer had got on with the rather more tedious details about the precise weaponry dispensed by each rocket over the enemy positions. It would either be hundreds of small sub-munitions designed to explode on contact with whatever lay beneath them – armour, vehicles, buildings, et cetera – or mines, both anti-armour and anti-personnel. A highly impressive and effective delivery system, the lecturer had explained, but had then gone on to say that the downside of this weapon was the failure rate of the bomblets, which meant the battlefield could be strewn with a significant quantity of these armed – and now dodgy – bits of ordnance.

'So, if you find anything like these,' and a series of slides had been flashed on a screen, 'don't touch them,' the lecturer had concluded.

Don't you worry, Amanda had thought.

She reassured Richard that she knew exactly what to keep her eyes peeled for, and just hoped that the shifting sand hadn't recently uncovered something unpleasant. The small ones wouldn't be especially dangerous to the occupants of a vehicle unless they were particularly unlucky, but it would be a pain to have a tyre blown off or the sump punctured. However, the bigger variety, designed for attacking tanks, would probably kill them. It certainly ensured that they were both extremely alert.

After about twenty miles Richard crested a small ridge and stopped the Land Rover.

'There,' he said. About a hundred yards away was a T55 tank, abandoned by the Iraqis out in this empty piece of desert. It looked completely unscathed. 'I reckon the crew of this one decided that the game was up and just got themselves to a position where they could pick up a lift from our boys and get taken to the nearest POW camp.'

There was certainly nothing to indicate that the tank had seen any action. It obviously didn't look as if it was straight out of the showroom, but apart from being mud-splattered it seemed perfectly OK.

'Have you ever fired a machine-gun?' asked Richard.

'You mean we're going to use it as a target?'

'No, silly. You see that heavy machine-gun on top?' Amanda nodded. 'Well, that's a twelve-point-seven-millimetre Dsh K.' He pronounced it like *dushca*. 'Impressed?'

'I think I ought to be.'

'It's not just the Iraqis who play with these. The IRA has a couple too.'

'Lucky them.'

'Come on then. Let's go and see if it's loaded.'

'Surely we can't . . .'

Richard swept his hand in a wide arc. From the top of their ridge they could see miles in every direction. Not a building, vehicle, bird or animal could be seen. 'And who is going to know?'

'OK then. Why not?'

They drove across to the tank, lying silently on the desert sand.

'Take a picture of me,' Amanda asked, and handed Richard her camera. She clambered up on to the turret and posed extravagantly.

'Cheese,' called Richard, and Amanda grinned. Richard chucked the camera on to the seat of the Land Rover and climbed on to the tank to join Amanda.

'Great. Look.' He indicated the belt of ammunition still loaded in the gun. He crouched behind it, grabbed the cocking handle with both hands and pulled it. The working parts slid back with a satisfying clunk. 'There you go.' He lined it up on a knocked-out tank three hundred yards away. 'Hit that!'

'Where's the trigger?'

'See those two handles.' He pointed to the rear of the gun. 'The trigger is in between them. Push it down with your thumbs.'

'OK.' He moved back to let her get behind it and she crouched down on the closed hatch on top of the turret. A whiff of something unpleasant made her wrinkle her nose, but she ignored it. She assumed Richard had broken wind but didn't know him well enough yet to comment. She took a firm hold of the handles and tentatively pressed the trigger. The gun thundered and she let go of the trigger after only three rounds, startled by its power. In the sudden silence she heard the empty cartridge cases clatter off the turret and on to the main body of the tank.

'Not like that,' said Richard with a grin. 'Put your fingers in your ears.' He took the handles from her, pressed the trigger and held it down. As she stood behind him she saw chains of green tracer arching off towards the other tank. Even with her fingers in her ears she was shocked by the noise. The other tank erupted as the armour-piercing incendiary rounds struck it, then the gun stopped, not because Richard had taken his finger off the trigger but because it had run out of ammunition.

'Wow!' She grinned. 'Now I'm impressed. Give us another go.'

'Got to find some more ammo first. There's bound to be some inside.' He grabbed a handle and pulled open the commander's hatch.

The nauseating stench that erupted was almost instantaneously followed by a cloud of flies. They both recoiled and threw their arms up to protect their face as the horror and the insects hit them.

'Shit,' exclaimed Amanda involuntarily.

The tank commander sat where he'd died. His head had slumped back, and he was staring directly up at them. His mouth sagged open as if he was still screaming. Such features that were left amongst his rotting flesh were putrid and heaving with the off-spring of the escaped flies. Below his shoulders his torso was a mass of pulped flesh and dried blood. Amanda didn't look at him for more than a few seconds but her brain took in every detail, and when she looked away she could still see him, his image as clear as a photograph.

The tank hadn't been abandoned as they had assumed. Its crew hadn't been cowards, fleeing rather than fighting. Amanda somehow knew that, although they couldn't see the other crew members, they were still present, killed by the fin-stabilised round that had smashed through the armour, showering the inside of the tank with a hail of steel fragments.

'Poor bastards,' said Richard, closing the hatch. 'I had no idea. I'm sorry.' Amanda didn't know if he was apologising to her, or to the dead Iraqis for the desecration of their coffin. 'We'd better go back and tell the burial parties they've missed a few.'

Amanda jumped off the tank. As she did so she saw the entry hole made by the allied round. Small and almost insignificant on the outside, yet the cause of a second of unbelievable carnage and horror for those trapped inside as the splinters of metal whirled through the tank, slicing, cutting, pulping and killing. She suddenly felt guilty. Not a minute ago she'd been completely caught up with the power of the machine-gun on top of the vehicle and hadn't given a thought to its primary purpose of causing death and destruction. And while she'd been getting a cheap kick from some live-firing, aiming at another tank without a thought of what it would be like to be on the receiving end, beneath her feet were the poor sods who'd been shelled a couple of weeks earlier. She felt sickened by the incident. The vision of the dead commander, looking up at her with his staring eyes, was ingrained into their consciousness. Did he have a wife and family? A mother? How old was he? She couldn't tell. The carefree outing had turned sour.

Richard looked across at her as they got into the Land Rover. 'Are you OK?'

'Yes, fine.' But the life and sparkle had gone out of her eyes and her voice was dull.

'Let's go then.' He put the vehicle in gear.

On the journey back Amanda didn't feel like talking and couldn't get the tank commander's staring face out of her mind. She knew in her head they'd done nothing wrong, but in her heart she felt guilty.

They arrived back at her unit and Richard parked up the Land Rover.

'Will there be any chance of seeing you again before you return?'

Amanda replied that they were only waiting for the last of their heavy kit to be low-loaded back to Al Jubayl and then she would be flying out.

'First in, first out,' she said, trying to sound cheerful.

'Soon then,'

'I hope so. What about you?'

'We've got a lot of ammunition to unload and process. Not long though.' He remembered something. 'I promised you a share of my vodka to celebrate our safe arrival in Kuwait.'

Amanda didn't feel like celebrating – not after today. All the pleasure at the victory and their impending return to Germany had gone. 'Do you mind if I pass?'

'Not at all. But why don't you come over to our lines one evening anyway? Tomorrow?'

'I'll be on duty.'

'Can't you swap with someone? Come on, come and meet some of my lot. You must be sick of the sight of everyone here.'

Amanda knew he was trying to cheer her up after the day's unpleasant outcome. And it *would* be nice to meet some other people. 'OK. I'll see what I can do. I'll get a message to you somehow if I find someone to stand in for me.'

'Great.' He jumped into the Land Rover and drove off.

'Nice day out?' asked Graham when Amanda joined him on duty later that day. After his reaction when they'd spotted the burned-out Iraqi tank, Amanda didn't think she could face his comments if she told him what had happened. But she had to say something. After all, she'd been gone most of the morning.

'We found some enemy kit that had been abandoned and I fired a heavy machine-gun.'

'Cool.'

'Yeah.' Then, to change the subject, 'Would you stand in for me tomorrow evening?'

'Why, where are you going?'

'I've been invited over to the Gunner lines.'

'Oh yes?' Graham's scepticism at the innocence of the invitation sent his eyebrows up almost to his hairline.

'Richard is my best friend's husband,' said Amanda, shaking her head in exasperation. Why did men think that a woman could only be interested in a man for sex? Probably, she thought, because most of them were only interested in women for that reason.

The next evening Richard sent the duty driver over to fetch her.

268

Their messing arrangements were as basic as everyone else's and their Catering Corps cook couldn't do much more with the compo rations than any of the others. However, the cook on duty obviously had a great sense of humour, because when Amanda approached the giant camping stove where he was dishing out the food, she was astounded to be offered boeuf Bourguignonne, haricots beans and pommes de terres façon militaire. It transpired that the reality was tinned stewed beef, baked beans and instant mash, but, the chef had explained, if you shut your eyes and dreamed . . .

'He does this every mealtime,' said Richard. 'It cheers us all up no end. The food is always basically the same but you want to have the next meal if only to find out how it's being described. The battery commander had a birthday a while back and the chef produced a birthday cake for him. It was even iced. It looked wonderful.'

'Crikey. How on earth did he do that on compo rations?'

'That's what we all wondered, until he cut it. It was corned beef iced with instant mash.'

'But what an imagination!' said Amanda.

Even Richard's imaginative cook couldn't do much to perk up the dreary rations, but as Richard had observed, it was nice to have a change of company. It seemed as though all the young officers with Richard's regiment had a supply of smuggled booze, and consequently there was quite a choice on offer. They tried to persuade Amanda to have a drink with her meal.

'No, honestly,' said Amanda. 'I'm not a great toper at the best of times – the odd glass of wine sometimes, and an occasional gin – and having gone without for so long I hardly miss it at all now.'

'We've got gin if you'd like it?' pressed Richard, who had obviously had a couple of vodkas before she got there.

Amanda smiled and remained adamant that she'd be happy with plain tonic water.

The jolly conversation of Richard and his friends began to cheer her up and lift the gloom she'd felt since finding the body in the tank.

'Hey, have you heard the latest joke?' asked Richard as their meal drew to a close. He sounded quite drunk.

'I've heard a few, try me.'

'OK. What were the only two things working in Saudi after August last year?'

'I don't know, what were the only two things working in Saudi after August last year?'

'Patriots and ex-patriots. Get it?' Richard roared with laughter and Amanda smiled, not at the joke but at Richard's reaction to his own humour.

'And what about this one – the Sappers were going to build a defensive berm from NAAFI pork pies, because the Iraqis, being Muslim, wouldn't be able to risk touching them to breach it.'

'So?'

'Then the brass realised that the plan was completely hopeless. There's no pork in a NAAFI pork pie!' Richard fell about laughing again, tears rolling down his face. Amanda wondered how much of his private stash of vodka he had left.

'Come on,' he said as he controlled his helpless laughter. 'How about a drink now?'

'I'd love a coffee.'

'Boring,' he said, not unkindly, and went off to organise it for her, staggering slightly as he walked over the uneven sand to the huge urn. He managed to spill quite a bit of Amanda's coffee as he returned to her but she didn't comment. Why shouldn't Richard and his friends tie one on? They were young men, they'd been through a war, they'd been denied all the pleasures and comforts that they'd grown used to in peacetime barracks – surely they deserved to let their hair down now? Even so, Amanda didn't feel like joining in and, deciding that she was verging on being a wet blanket, she asked Richard if he could organise the duty driver to take her back to her own lines.

'No problem.' A young gunner was detailed to bring the Land Rover round. 'Will I see you again before you go back?'

'I don't think there's going to be time. Tomorrow we've got to organise the last of our vehicles to be moved and I think we're flying out the day after. But we must get together when you're back in Aldershot. It'll be a grand excuse for a party!'

Richard took another slug of his drink. 'A party! Yes, we must have a party.' He swayed on his feet.

Amanda wanted to tell him that she didn't think he should drink any more, but that really would be interfering. He was a grown man, after all. And presumably it wasn't going to be the first hangover in his life – or the last.

'Well, see you back in Blighty! Give my love to Lizzie when you get home.'

The driver started the engine and Amanda leant out of the window to wave to Richard. He waved back and then staggered off to join the other junior officers.

The next day they moved up to the Armoured Divisional Administrative Headquarters position at the notorious rubbish dump, where their vehicles were organised into convoys southwards and the last details were made to airlift the remaining personnel back to Al Jubayl.

As Amanda took in the grim position of the Headquarters – the dreadful smell, which was apparent despite the smell of burning oil, to say nothing of the outlook across piles of rotting rubbish – she was aware of a flap going amongst the Divisional staff.

'What's up?' she asked a passing major.

'Some poor bloody Gunner got out of a vehicle in the wrong place, trod on a bomblet and was blown to fuck.'

Amanda's shoulders sagged. What a waste! And what of his family, presumably happily celebrating his imminent and safe return from the front? How horribly unfair. She felt her eyes pricking with tears and sniffed angrily. Crying wasn't going to bring the poor bloke back. Then, more practically, she wondered if Richard had known the man or if the death was going to cause his regiment a load of extra work.

Aldershot, March 1991

'Go on, have another glass,' wheedled William, waving the bottle of champagne in Lizzie's direction.

'Oh, all right then, providing there's enough for Ginny as well.'

'Plenty. I've put another bottle in your fridge.' William carefully poured the foaming golden wine into Lizzie's glass. Lizzie waited for the bubbles to subside before taking a sip.

'Yum! I do love champagne.'

William, Sophie, Ginny and Lizzie were sitting round the big pine table in Lizzie's kitchen. The war was over, Bob and Richard had both come through unscathed and Lizzie had invited William and Sophie to supper to help her and Ginny celebrate. On the stove behind Lizzie, a pan containing rice hissed and bubbled; a huge bowl of salad stood in the middle of the table and the smell of baked spiced chicken wafted deliciously across the room.

'I think we should have a toast,' said Sophie. 'Here's to the conquering heroes.'

'The conquering heroes,' the others replied as they chinked glasses.

Lizzie looked around the room at her friends. It was such a different feeling from when they'd last been together for a meal, the night she'd got disastrously drunk. Then, even though they'd tried to hide it, they'd all been worried sick about their relatives and friends. They'd seen pictures of the battered faces of captured pilots, they'd heard the details of Saddam's stockpile of chemical and biological weapons, and their imaginations had been working flat out as to what might happen. But now they were relaxed and happy, knowing that everyone they knew well had survived intact, that the casualties had been minimal and it was all over. Lizzie felt she didn't really need the champagne to feel tipsy; she'd been as high as a kite ever since she'd heard that a ceasefire had been ordered just one hundred hours after the big allied push had started.

She got up from her seat and went over to check the rice. There wasn't a trace of water left and she could hear it just beginning to sizzle. She spooned out a couple of grains and nibbled them.

'Perfect,' she announced, pulling the pan off the hot plate.

'Let me lay the table,' offered Ginny.

'OK.' Lizzie pulled open the cutlery drawer to show Ginny where everything was kept.

'What can I do?' asked Sophie.

'Nothing.' Lizzie deftly got the plates from the warming drawer, took the earthenware dish of chicken from the oven and tipped the rice into a serving bowl. By the time four places were laid, she was ready to serve up. William busied himself topping up glasses while Sophie passed the filled plates along the table.

'Right. Tuck in,' said Lizzie. The words had barely left her lips when the doorbell went. She began to get out of her chair. 'I wonder who that could be,' she said.

'Stay put. I'll see who it is. It's probably Jehovah's Witnesses or something,' said Sophie. Lizzie, who had been on her feet all day, shopping and cooking, didn't argue.

As Sophie clattered up the stairs out of the basement kitchen the others began eating. It was only when Lizzie was chewing her third forkful that she began to wonder what was keeping Sophie. She went to the foot of the stairs.

'Sophie, is there a problem?' she called. There was no reply. Instead, Lizzie saw Sophie come to the head of the stairs, followed by two men. It was the brigadier and the padre. Both William and Lizzie rose automatically at the sight of their superior officer; then they realised the significance of the visit.

'Lizzie,' said the padre. 'Would you like to come up to the sitting room?'

Lizzie's eyes widened; and expression of sheer terror appeared on her ashen face.

'It's Richard, isn't it? What's happened?'

'Come and sit down, Lizzie,' the brigadier insisted gently.

'Tell me.' Her voice was barely a whisper.

'Please, Lizzie, I'd prefer it if you sat down.'

'For fuck's sake, tell me!' she shouted, using language she'd never used to anyone before, and certainly never to such a senior officer.

'It was a mine, an absolute accident. He died instantly.'

Sophie saw Lizzie sway, and even though she lunged to catch her she didn't manage it and Lizzie crumpled to the floor.

Amanda arrived in Aldershot from Germany in time for the funeral, while Edwina had managed to get leave from Ireland in order to be there. Richard's body had been repatriated and he was to be buried in Aldershot's military cemetery with full military honours. The two women sat beside each other in the ugly Garrison Church where Lizzie and Richard had been married less than two years previously. They were silent, both feeling numb with shock that it was Lizzie's husband who was being buried. And over and above the feelings of sorrow and shared misery for their friend's pain, Amanda had convinced herself it was partly her fault. It was immaterial to her how often others, who knew the facts surrounding his death, had tried to tell her it had been a ghastly accident, just one of those dreadful things; Amanda believed that if she'd stopped him from drinking so heavily the evening she'd had dinner at his lines, he would be alive now. If he hadn't got so drunk and suffered the subsequent hangover he would not have felt sick, and if he hadn't felt sick he would not have had to get out of the Land Rover and so he wouldn't have stepped on the mine.

'But where he stopped his vehicle and not spotting the bomblet were entirely down to him,' Graham had explained patiently.

'That's not the point,' sniffed Amanda miserably. 'I saw him getting drunk and I knew it was a mistake. I should have interfered; I should have made him stop. How will Lizzie ever forgive me?'

At this Graham had lost his temper. 'Don't you dare tell his wife what you've told me. She doesn't need to know the details. She doesn't need to know that he was puking at the side of the road when he was blown to bits. All she needs to know was that he was killed when he stepped on an unexploded bomblet. If you go and sob on her shoulder so she feels sorry for you it will be sheer self-indulgence on your part at her expense. Whatever you may be going through is nothing to what she is suffering. OK?'

Amanda had been quite surprised at Graham's reaction, but she knew he was right. She wanted Lizzie to forgive her to make herself feel better – it had nothing to do with Lizzie's welfare. If she *was* guilty by omission, as she believed, then that feeling of guilt was her punishment.

The funeral service, dignified and sombre, progressed slowly. From where she sat, Amanda could see Lizzie sitting rigidly in her seat, clutching a hankie, although she appeared to be dry-eyed. Next to her were her mother and father, who had flown back from where they were now stationed in Germany. As the organ began the introduction to the next hymn, 'Abide with Me', Amanda was overwhelmed by the emotion of the occasion, and even though she tried to sing, no words came out. She glanced at Edwina and saw that she too had tears streaming down her face.

Six soldiers slowly moved forward, and without a word of command shouldered the coffin. As the congregation began the last verse the soldiers began to slow-march out of the church. Lizzie followed, the black of her mourning contrasting with the stark white of her face. She saw Edwina and Amanda as she passed and tried to smile at them but her expression of utter desolation barely changed.

'Poor, poor Lizzie,' muttered Edwina. 'Of all the bad luck.'

After the committal everyone returned to Lizzie's mess for a reception.

'Lizzie, I am so sorry,' said Edwina, giving her friend a hug. 'How are you?'

'Oh, not too bad.' Lizzie's voice was absolutely dead and devoid of emotion. 'Everyone is being very supportive.' She saw Amanda approaching. 'Amanda. It's kind of you to come. Aren't you on leave?'

'Yes. I've got a fortnight, and then I'm posted to a new job.'

'Somewhere nice?' Lizzie was going through the motions of normal social intercourse, although it was automatic rather than anything else.

'I'll be at Andover, so I don't think *nice* is necessarily the right word.' But it was a staff job, which she'd requested, and it was in the south of England, which she had also asked for, so Amanda was pretty pleased with what she'd been offered. 'When I've got myself settled perhaps you'd like to come and stay?'

'Yes, I'd like that.' Lizzie tried to sound pleased at the offer.

'Did you know that I saw Richard the day before he died?'

Lizzie's face was transformed by a smile. 'Did you? How was he?' Talking about Richard seemed to bring him back to life. The problem was that most people got embarrassed when he was mentioned and treated his name like some sort of taboo. Lizzie had very quickly discovered that no one seemed to know how to treat the recently bereaved, and frightened of saying something crass, they didn't say anything at all. She felt lonely enough without Richard, and now she found she was socially isolated too.

'He was in good form. He told me what a great time he'd had firing all that live ammunition.'

'I know. I had a letter telling me all about it. I think he quite enjoyed it out there one way and another.'

'I think most of us did, once we got used to it.' Amanda suddenly had a vision of the dead Iraqi soldier. She couldn't help adding. 'It was pretty grim for the other side, though.'

'Yes. I keep trying to remember that I'm not the only one who has lost someone.'

'That's typical of you, Lizzie,' said Edwina. 'Trust you to be thinking of others even now.'

Lizzie smiled sadly. 'It beats thinking about some other things. Look, I'm sorry, but I'd better go and talk to some other people. We must get together again before too long.'

Edwina and Amanda watched her move across the room, accepting condolences and thanking those who had travelled miles to be there, doing it all calmly and with such immense dignity that they both found it quite humbling to watch her.

'I think I'd be a wreck if I was burying someone I loved as much as she loved Richard,' said Amanda.

'He must have been a popular bloke,' said Edwina. 'There's a lot of people here.'

'You never met him?'

'No. By the time I managed to get away from Ireland to stay with Lizzie, Richard had already gone off to join the war effort.' Edwina suddenly remembered something. 'I don't know if she told you this, but there's something you ought to know.'

'What's that?'

'Did you realise she'd had a miscarriage last summer?'

'Oh, no! She never mentioned it.' Amanda was so appalled at this further blow Lizzie had suffered that she didn't feel the least bit hurt that she'd been excluded from her best friend's confidence. In fact it didn't even register that Lizzie had told Edwina and not her.

'She kept it to herself because it left her really depressed. It took her quite a while to get over it.'

'It just isn't fair, is it, that she's had all the tough breaks. I mean, when I think of some people I know ... I wouldn't actually wish such bad luck on anyone, but I do feel Lizzie deserves it least of everyone I know.'

'Precisely,' said Edwina with feeling, thinking that Cathy Roberts could have picked up the bad luck on Lizzie's behalf and not many people would have complained. 'Anyway, I'll be able to keep an eye on her soon.' Amanda raised her eyebrows in question. 'I'm posted back to Aldershot in a couple of months.'

'Away from whatever it is that you do at the moment?' Amanda still wasn't exactly sure what Edwina did do, although she could make an educated guess.

'Yes.'

'For good? I mean, away from your trade for good – not posted to Aldershot for good.'

'I think so.'

'Is that what you want?'

'No, but I screwed up recently so I can't really expect much else. I did something really stupid and as a result a friend got hurt. He's going to live, but he's lost a leg and he'll never be able to have kids. I blame myself, because if it wasn't for me, I don't think he would have walked into the trap.'

'Oh, come on, surely not.'

'Some of the others in my lot thought so too. Oh, they didn't say as much, but ...' Nor would they, but Edwina knew it had crossed their minds that her absence at a critical moment in the operation had played a part in Nat's ambushing. 'I think I'm better off in a desk job for a bit.' My penance, she thought grimly.

'I'm sorry, Edwina, I really am.'

Edwina shrugged dejectedly. 'It's how the mop flops, isn't it? We've all been through it recently, haven't we: poor old Lizzie losing first the baby then Richard, you having a hard time out in the Gulf, and me buggering up someone's life in Ireland.'

'I've got to be honest here; the Gulf wasn't too bad, not once I got used to the conditions, and in retrospect I wouldn't have missed being a part of it for the world. So, compared to you and Lizzie, I don't think I've been through that much.'

'But you must have seen some grim things.'

Amanda told her about the Iraqi tank. 'I still see it in my mind's eye, but I'll get over it. Frankly, from what I heard, there were many

277

worse sights that that. The only thing about the whole campaign that I find really hard to take is Richard's death. I suppose it's because I partly blame myself for what happened.'

'Huh?'

Amanda recounted her worries over the amount Richard had drunk the night before he died.

'Believe me,' said Edwina, 'if you had told him to stop he'd only have ignored you. Or he'd have said he'd stop and carried on as soon as your back was turned. I wouldn't feel guilty if I were you.'

'But I do.'

But Edwina didn't have much sympathy. She'd cornered the guilt market over Nat; Amanda's role in Richard's accident was nothing in comparison, and she said so.

'I see,' said Amanda rather stiffly, and went to find someone else to talk to. She would have liked some sympathy, a little understanding, and Edwina's curt reaction had been hurtful.

Edwina looked at Amanda's disappearing back view and wondered what she'd done to upset her. After all, there was nothing for Amanda to feel guilty about – not like she did over Nat, anyway.

Andover, May 1991

The large pine table in the centre of Amanda's cottage kitchen was covered with plates of delicious-looking food, and the work surfaces were stacked with wine bottles, cans of beer and boxes of glasses. Amanda looked around her with satisfaction.

'Right, I think that's everything,' she said to Bella.

'How many did you say were coming?'

'About fifty, I think, I'm not quite sure.'

'Anyone from the workshop?'

'No.' Amanda said it very firmly.

'Oh? I was looking forward to meeting some of the characters you described in your letters. Too far for them to travel, I suppose?' It wasn't unheard-of for officers to travel to or from Germany for a really good party, as the cost of an air fare wasn't that much of a burden for a well-paid single officer with few financial commitments.

'No, it wasn't that. I haven't told you about what happened when we finally all got back to Germany. It rather tainted my whole tour with the unit.'

'Oh?' said Bella. 'Do you want to talk about it now?'

'It seemed great at first. We got flown out of Al Jubayl and spirits were really high – of course I didn't know about Richard then. We were one of the first units to be repatriated and we'd been told a big party had been organised by the Wives' Club to welcome us all back. So, like everyone else, as soon as I arrived back at the mess I went and had a wash and brush-up and then got myself down to the gym where the bash was. To begin with it was really good, and then I suddenly began to notice that whenever I joined a group the atmosphere went sour. It took me a while to convince myself I wasn't being paranoid.'

279

'So what was causing it?'

'I didn't twig until one of the subaltern's wives came up to me. She'd had too much to drink and she didn't pull her punches. Of course, I should have realised for myself.'

'Realised what?'

'Well, it's a well-known fact, isn't it, that all members of the WRAC have a special release mechanism in their pants so that every time a member of the opposite sex walks past they can drop their knickers. This woman thought that while her husband had been knocking himself out fighting the Iraqis, I'd been knocking him off. Obviously, being the only woman with an all-male unit, I wouldn't have had anything better to do with my time. It was so ridiculous it was laughable, but the problem was, they all believed it. Everywhere I went I got snide comments about me knowing their husbands better than they did, that sort of thing. And when I tried to tell them I really didn't fancy their man – well, they just thought I was being deliberately insulting by questioning their taste.'

'And your real defence –'

'Was absolutely useless. Not if I value my career, anyway. Can you imagine the reaction if I'd said in front of all those people that the true reason I didn't touch one of their precious menfolk was that I was actually angling for the QAs working in the field hospital.'

'So after everything, all you went through, you came back to be treated like the enemy?'

'You've got it. The women had it worked out that I'd wheedled my way out of the Gulf in order to get a clear run at the blokes. I tried to tell them that even if I looked like Meryl Streep and had wandered around without a stitch on, no one in their right mind would have fancied me under the conditions we endured out there. But they'd made their minds up that no end of hanky-panky went on, and that was that. I'm afraid that whatever loyalty I felt for the unit rather evaporated after that.'

'What a shame.' There was a pause as both women thought about the unfairness of it all.

Amanda shrugged. 'Worse things happen at sea,' she said pragmatically. She changed the subject. 'I'm going to have a bath.'

'I'll come and scrub your back.'

'Mmmm, yes, please.'

'We've got at least two hours before anyone will arrive, so we could always have our bath afterwards.'

'After what?' said Amanda, although she already knew the answer. Bella just giggled and took her by the hand. Amanda winced at the sudden pressure on her knuckles.

'Are they still sore?' said Bella, putting Amanda's fingertips to her lips and kissing them.

'They come and go,' which wasn't exactly the truth, but Amanda hated to bang on about the subject. She knew that even one's nearest and dearest soon got bored of constantly having to provide sympathy for some nagging but invisible illness. The MO had implied to her that in his opinion she was malingering. Outwardly there appeared to be nothing wrong with her, no symptoms beyond joints which sometimes ached as if she was about to go down with a severe bout of flu. To humour her, more than anything else, the MO had put her on a course of anti-inflammatory drugs, but they'd done absolutely no good at all and she hadn't dared go back to him. All she could hope was that now that summer was fast approaching, the warm weather would ease the twinges.

The imminent party was a house-warming to celebrate having a place of her own at long last. One of the benefits of her time in the Gulf had been her inability to spend her pay for the duration of the campaign. Thus, on her return from Germany, she had more than enough for a deposit on a house that would now give her and Bella the privacy they'd so longed for. As a sop to leaving her with the armoured workshop for two years when it should only have been a couple of months, her postings branch had done everything in its power to find her a posting as requested in southern England as quickly as possible. So she also had a second, private, reason for the party, which was to celebrate the fact that she and Bella could now see each other every weekend – with complete discretion.

By the time nine o'clock was struck by the large clock on the kitchen dresser, its solemn bongs could barely be heard above the din in the cottage. Amanda had invited almost everyone she knew, and they, in turn, had brought other friends whom she didn't. Not that it mattered; there was ample food for everyone, and with the amount of beer and wine donated by the guests, Amanda's kitchen had taken on a close resemblance to a Calais duty-free warehouse. Amanda heard the clock chime and faintly wondered where Edwina had got to. She had been more than keen to accept the invitation when Amanda had phoned her a couple of weeks previously.

'Great, a party. Are you going to invite Lizzie?'

'I don't know. What do you think? I'd hate for her to think I'm being callous by asking her so soon after Richard's death, but if I don't, she may feel terribly hurt.'

'If it were me, I'd ask her. Tell her of your dilemma. After all, she can always say no.'

'Would you ask her for me?'

'I don't think it would look right if I did. The invitation has got to come from you.'

'OK, if you're sure.'

'I am.'

So Amanda had invited Lizzie too and had been slightly surprised that she'd accepted, but pleased that she felt ready to get out and socialise. Did that mean she was beginning to come to terms with her loss?

The front door stood wide open, partly to provide some much-needed fresh air and partly to save Amanda from having to answer it constantly. The evening was balmy and many of the guests had spilled out into the tiny garden.

'Thank God we haven't got neighbours to worry about,' Amanda had said to Bella, as some wag let off a volley of party poppers.

Just then Lizzie squeezed through the front door, a huge smile on her face at the thought of seeing Amanda again. The guests cluttering up the hall pressed against the walls to allow her access into the kitchen. Behind her came Edwina, who had a bottle of wine in each hand.

'Amanda,' yelled Lizzie over the racket. 'You look wonderful. You've lost weight.'

'I'm not the only one,' commented Amanda, giving her friend a huge hug. Lizzie must be down to eight stone at the absolute outside.

'Oh, it's good to see you again.' Lizzie put her arms round Amanda and returned the hug. Amanda winced in pain, but Lizzie didn't notice. 'Here, have this, a house-warming present.' She delved into a carrier bag and handed Amanda a beautiful book on home decorating.

'Oh, Lizzie, that's wonderful.' Amanda was incredibly touched that Lizzie could manage to be so thoughtful when she'd only recently been through such an appalling tragedy. She glanced through the book. 'This will be brilliant. I haven't got a clue about any of that sort of thing. Gosh, wonderful ideas. Look.' She showed Lizzie a page that had caught her eye. 'Now, come and have a drink.'

'And what about a drink for me, you old bag?' said Edwina. Amanda had been so busy welcoming Lizzie she hadn't spotted Edwina.

'Hi! And sorry, but less of the *old*, you cheeky wench. And how are you both?' quizzed Amanda.

'Not so bad,' answered Lizzie. 'I have some good days and then I go through a bad patch. Someone says it takes eighteen months to get over it.'

'And I'm enjoying living near to Lizzie, although I'm bored to snores in the new job. Still, it keeps me in beer money, so I'll put up with it for the time being.'

'Only the time being?'

'I'm toying with the idea of sacking the Army. Ulysses is coming out. He's fed up with getting slagged off by the boys who were out in the Gulf.'

'I didn't know any were,' said Amanda.

'Apparently there were quite a few, although I don't suppose we'll ever find out what they got up to. But Ulysses feels there's a big them-and-us thing about it now, and it cheeses him off.'

The party flowed around them while they chatted. Guests came into the kitchen to demand the whereabouts of the corkscrew – 'surely you must have more than one?' – or a cloth – 'some prat's knocked over a glass of beer' – or more food – 'pass us the trayful and I'll see if anyone else wants some' – and Lizzie, Edwina and Amanda dealt with each interruption and then returned to their conversation.

'How's work?' Amanda asked Lizzie.

'William and Bob are great – very kind to me and very understanding. And in fact, I think having to get up each day, sort myself out and go into the office has been good for me. I expect Edwina told you about the miscarriage?'

'Yes.' Amanda wondered if this was the right thing to say; she didn't want to drop Edwina in it, as it had appeared to be something Lizzie had wanted to keep quiet.

'It knocked me for six and I was worried that Richard's death would send me into a complete decline, but I've been relatively OK.'

'You've been brilliant,' corrected Edwina.

'Not really. I cried solidly for a fortnight.'

'Which probably did you good. Allowed you to grieve properly. What's the word?' Edwina's grasp of the more unusual words in the English language had never been brilliant.

'Catharsis?' supplied Amanda.

'Exactly. You tried to pretend nothing nothing had happened after you lost the baby, and I think you bottled everything up and that's why you got so low. This time you did the opposite.' Edwina looked pleased at her psychoanalytical skills.

'You could be right. Anyway, postings have offered to move me away from Aldershot, if I think that it would help.'

'And will it?' asked Amanda.

'I don't know. I've still got a year to do in this job and I really love it. I think I'm better with paperwork than I am with people; I just love problem-solving, I've decided. And anyway, I wouldn't want to go too far at the moment, because of the house. Because we were so happy there I can sort of still feel him there.' Lizzie looked embarrassed. 'That sounds silly, doesn't it?'

'Not in the least. It must be very hard for you.'

At the moment Bella entered the kitchen. She greeted Lizzie with standard words of condolence and then turned to Edwina.

'Last time we met was at Guildford, wasn't it?'

'That's right,' replied Edwina, but she was thinking, *So Amanda and Bella are still an item*. She wasn't surprised that Amanda hadn't told her of the continuing friendship; it wasn't the sort of thing she would want to make too public, obviously. However, Edwina was surprised to discover that, unlike previously, when her uncovering of their relationship had put her thoughts and loyalties into turmoil, now she didn't care a jot. Amanda's performance in the Gulf had more than proved her abilities as an officer. It seemed unlikely that her private life was going to affect her career now. In fact, Edwina was almost happy that apparently Amanda had found a partner and had formed a long-term relationship. She linked her arm through Bella's. 'Come on then, Bella, introduce me to all these guests. You must know heaps more than I do. Apart from you, Amanda and Lizzie I hardly know a soul.' If Bella was taken aback by Edwina's sudden and somewhat unexpected display of friendship, she didn't show it.

Aldershot, July 1991

The Garrison Mess in Aldershot is a distinctly unimpressive building. It is situated on top of the hill overlooking the town, sandwiched between the Cambridge Military Hospital and the Louise Margaret Maternity Hospital, both of which are built of best-quality Victorian red brick. In contrast, the prefabricated concrete exterior of the sixties Garrison Mess resembles a faintly tacky motel, an impression further strengthened on entering by the positioning of the bar in the main lobby.

Lizzie, who had known the building all her life – she'd been born in the adjacent maternity hospital – didn't notice any of its architectural faults as she parked her car and then rang the bell at the front door. It was sad, she reflected, that the permanent threat to security had long ago stopped messes from providing open house to any passing officer; but if officers could walk in off the streets, so could terrorists, as indeed one had when a bomb had been planted in the para mess in 1972. Through the heavy glass door she could see Edwina approaching. They'd arrange to go and see a film and then have a bite to eat afterwards.

'Hi, Lizzie,' Edwina said as she held the door open for her friend. Lizzie was surprised by the strong smell of spirits on Edwina's breath as she pecked her on the cheek. 'I was having a drink in the bar while I waited. What can I get you?'

'Just an orange juice, please. I've got the car.'

'OK.'

They walked across the thickly carpeted lobby to the bar. Apart from the barman there was no one else there.

'Same again for me, please, Briggs, and an orange juice for the lady.'

Lizzie noticed that the barman poured a double measure of gin into Edwina's glass. Drinking doubles, and alone, this early – it was barely six o'clock. Lizzie wondered if she ought to comment, but decided not to.

'How's the signal squadron?' asked Lizzie.

'Oh, don't ask! Do you know what I did today?' It was obvious that Lizzie was about to find out. 'I spent this morning renegotiating a debt that one of my servicewomen owes to the NAAFI. Two hours I spent with the NAAFI manager, sorting it all out. "Got any other debts I need to know about, Private Snooks?" I asked. "No, ma'am. Three bags full, ma'am." So I get back to the office to find a letter on my desk from Lloyds Bank in Aldershot telling me Private Snooks is overdrawn to the tune of five hundred pounds and what am I going to do about it?' Edwina took a gulp of her drink. 'Fucking debt-collector, that's what I am these days. Sorry, Lizzie,' she said, suddenly realising that she was whingeing about trivia – after all, sorting out her squadron's personal problems was what she was paid to do. It was nothing to the sort of troubles Lizzie had had to cope with recently.

'You wish you were back in Ireland?' asked Lizzie.

'I don't know. It was fun – no, wrong word' – she frowned in concentration as she fumbled in her mind for the right one – 'fulfilling, yes, that's it, fulfilling doing something important –'

'But sorting out that kid's finances is just as important.'

'To her, maybe. Not to me.' Lizzie was shocked at how heartless Edwina seemed to have grown. Personnel management was one of the most important things an officer could do. Happy soldiers equalled a happy unit, and everyone knew that nothing worked properly in the Forces if morale was bad.

'So why don't you volunteer to go back to wherever it was you were based?'

'It's not as simple as that.' Edwina finished her drink. 'Another one, Lizzie?' Lizzie shook her head. Edwina ordered another double gin, waited for the barman to serve her and continued. 'As I was saying, it's not that simple. And I'm not sure I'd be welcome.' She told Lizzie the bare bones of the incident that had left Nat critically injured. 'I went to see him last week. He's at Headley Court, being rehabilitated. That's Army-speak for getting him used to his tin leg before they throw him out; you don't see members of the Special Forces zipping along the streets of Belfast in wheelchairs. He was

286

very sweet to me. He doesn't blame me for what happened, he says it was all his own fault for not checking for a pressure plate. But frankly, it makes things worse. I would almost rather he did have a go at me. Him being all forgiving is the last thing I need.'

Lizzie didn't say that Edwina's needs were probably pretty minimal compared to Nat's now, and she was disappointed that her friend's selfishness didn't allow her to see it for herself. She decided to change the subject.

'Have you seen much of Ulysses recently?'

'He'll be back in a few weeks. He's got a resettlement course he's got to go on before his terminal leave. Until then he's being kept busy. Right.' Edwina finished her drink. 'Let's go.' She stumbled as she got off her bar stool and bent to pick up her handbag. 'Oops.'

Lizzie led the way out of the mess to the car park opposite. 'I'm looking forward to this film.'

'I haven't been to the flicks in ages.'

'Then a chip supper afterwards.'

'And back to the mess for a nightcap.'

Lizzie didn't think that Edwina needed anything else to drink that night, but then she'd always knocked it back. Only whereas before she'd drunk for recreation, now it struck Lizzie that it was desperation which drove her.

Back at home later that night, having dropped Edwina back at the mess, Lizzie wished, for the hundredth time – or was it the thousandth? She didn't know; she'd given up counting – that Richard was around to talk to. He'd always had such sensible advice; he'd always seemed to know instinctively what to do. She tried to imagine what he would say if she told him about Edwina's drinking. Would he advise her to confront Edwina, tell her boss, tell Ulysses? She didn't know.

'Oh, Richard,' she whispered. 'Why did you have to leave me?'

A month later Ulysses moved into the sergeants' mess at the Army School of Physical Training, ready to start his resettlement course. On his first evening there he arranged to meet Edwina at the nearby Queen's Hotel.

'I suppose we'd better obey the Army's rules until you become a proper civilian,' Edwina had said when Ulysses had turned down her suggestion of meeting in her mess.

'I don't think it would be wise to push our luck, even when I do become plain Mr Lees.'

'Coward. Right, see you there at eight.'

Ulysses had found a seat tucked away in a corner so he could see without being seen, and Edwina didn't spot him for a few seconds when she walked into the bar of the smart hotel. He waved to attract her attention.

'You've put on weight,' he said accusingly.

'A bit. You know what it's like, cushy mess life, three meals a day, and then eight hours sitting behind a desk.'

'I wouldn't. Haven't sat behind a desk once since I left school–well, apart from the odd course.'

'Lucky you, that's all I can say.'

Ulysses went to the bar to order Edwina a drink.

'Guinness?'

'I'd rather have a large gin.'

'OK.' He got the drink and returned with it to where Edwina was sitting. She downed half of it appreciatively.

'So how's the resettlement going?'

'I'll tell you when I've done a bit more.'

'And what *exactly* are you going to do?'

'I'm going to be a personal trainer for unfit people with more money than sense.'

'I like it! Fleecing the rich appeals to my sense of justice.' She polished off the last of her gin. 'I'm going to have another. Can I get one for you?'

Ulysses looked at his almost untouched pint and shook his head. 'I'll pass on this round.' Edwina shrugged and went to the bar.

When she returned, Ulysses said, 'Tell you what, instead of drinking together tomorrow, why don't we go for a good long run?'

'Nah. I don't fancy that.'

'Aren't you training every day?'

'Not really. There's not much point now I'm back with the crap-hats.'

'What's the matter with you, Edwina?'

'Nothing, why?' She looked affronted.

'Forget it.'

Edwina shrugged. What did it matter if she let herself get a bit out of condition? She'd be able to sort herself out easily enough when it came nearer the time to pass her next fitness test. Ulysses was just being boring.

Ulysses changed the subject. 'I'm going to go house-hunting at the weekend. Do you want to come with me?'

'Sounds cool. Where are you thinking of living?'

'I don't know. West London, maybe; somewhere where there's a bit of space but getting up to town won't be too much hassle.'

'Kingston would be good.'

'Why?'

'I could move in with you then. Aldershot is straight down the M3.'

Ulysses hadn't thought of that. 'Oh,' he said noncommittally.

'Don't you want me to?'

'I don't think I could afford the gin.' He looked pointedly at Edwina's glass, which was empty again.

'Rearrange this well-known phrase or saying then: off fuck!'

Ulysses picked Edwina up from the mess the following Saturday. He wasn't best pleased at being kept waiting for half an hour, as Edwina had overslept.

'Late night?' he enquired sourly.

'Not really,' said Edwina, although she couldn't actually remember. After going out with Ulysses for a meal in a local restaurant, she had returned to her room to watch the TV and have a glass or two of wine from the three-litre box she'd purchased at the NAAFI a couple of days before. One glass of wine had led to another, and if she was honest she couldn't recall switching off the light and going to bed. She'd woken at about four in the morning with a splitting headache and a mouth like the Gobi Desert. She'd taken an Alka-Seltzer and gone back to sleep but hadn't been roused by the mess staff delivering her early-morning cup of tea. By the time she'd discovered it, it was stone cold. Ulysses refrained from remarking that her face looked puffy and her skin had lost its glow of health. He also noticed a fine tracing of broken veins on her cheeks. How long had she been drinking far too much? he wondered.

They drove up the motorway towards Kingston and Richmond. It didn't take very long to get there but they hadn't reckoned with the problem of parking. In the end Ulysses got completely fed up with queuing for the multi-storey car parks and dumped the car in Richmond Park.

'We can walk from here,' he said, locking the vehicle. 'It can't be more than a mile or so to the town.'

Edwina didn't say anything, just followed him through the park gates and down a smart residential road. They passed a pub.

'We could come back here for lunch,' she suggested hopefully.

'I've got that all planned,' replied Ulysses. He continued at his normal walking pace, which was very fast. Edwina noticed that she was finding it a struggle to keep up.

'Where's the fire?' she complained.

'I'm not going that fast. You're out of condition.'

'I'm not,' replied Edwina resentfully.

'Look at you, you're puffed out. You're turning into a fat, knackered crap-hat, just like the ones you used to take the piss out of in Ireland.'

Edwina stamped past Ulysses, refusing to acknowledge his comment. In her heart she knew he was right; she was out of condition and putting on weight. It had been weeks since she'd gone for a run, she knew she was drinking more than she should, and her diet was none too healthy, but what was the point of being superwoman when all she did all day was things like room inspection and writing apologetic letters to bank managers? And she resented the fact that Ulysses had taken it upon himself to comment about it. She wanted his sympathy and support, not his criticism.

Edwina sulked for the rest of the walk into town and childishly refused to look at the selection of flats and bed-sits offered by the first estate agent they came across. Ulysses patiently listened while the young man explained about the desirability of some addresses compared to others: this one was in the catchment area for a particularly good school; that one had once had a minor royal living next door; another was within walking distance of the station. Eventually Ulysses grabbed the pile of details and headed out of the office.

'God, all I want is somewhere with a front door, a kitchen of sorts and a room big enough to take a bed. I couldn't give a stuff about the sitting room,' and he began to mimic the smooth young salesman, '"having the considerable advantage of getting the evening sunlight". What do I need with evening sunlight, for fuck's sake?' Edwina didn't answer. 'Come on. If you're going to be like this then you might as well piss off. I thought you wanted to help me choose somewhere because you had ideas about moving in too?' Edwina shrugged and continued to remain silent. 'I can't be doing with this. Either you stop acting like a spoilt brat or you make your own way home. Which is it to be?'

'I'll stay,' she mumbled, knowing she had been completely unreasonable.

'Good. Come on then,' he said more gently, knowing that this was the closest he would get to an apology. 'Let's see what they want to sell us in this one.' And he led the way into another estate agency.

After about three hours they had two carrier bags full of pieces of A4 paper, each detailing a flat or rooms that they had been assured, in every case, was just the place they needed.

'I've had enough,' said Ulysses as they left the eighth agency they'd visited that morning. 'Lunch.'

'I've spotted a few nice pubs,' offered Edwina hopefully.

'I told you, it's all organised. Back to the car.' Ulysses carried both bags of bumph, and without making it obvious, he slowed his pace a fraction so Edwina had no problems matching his stride. But despite his consideration she was still hot and sweaty when they returned to the car. Ulysses unlocked it and Edwina flopped down, panting, on to the passenger seat. She put her tiredness down to the sultry heat of the day rather than her lack of condition.

'Phew. Good job you parked in the shade.' As it was, the internal temperature was tropical, despite the deep shadows cast by the huge limes, oaks and chestnuts that surrounded the car park by the gate of Richmond Park.

'I hope the picnic is OK,' said Ulysses.

'Picnic?' The disgust in Edwina's voice was unmistakable. 'Picnic?'

'What's wrong with that? I thought we could find a quiet corner of the park and have a lie-around in the sun. We could also go through this lot,' he waved a hand at the property details, 'heave out all the rubbish and have a quick snoop round some of the more likely ones before we head back this evening.'

Grudgingly Edwina accepted the logic of the plan. 'All right,' she said.

They drove deep into the park before leaving the car and striking out through the tall bracken to find a secluded spot for their picnic.

'Easier said than done,' commented Edwina. 'This place is heaving with people.' She indicated the kids flying kites, the joggers and cyclists on the bridle paths competing for space with the riders and dog-walkers, to say nothing of the motorists and pedestrians.

'Well, what do you expect? Where else is there for half of west London to find some fresh air?'

Edwina shook her head at the thought that for some people this was the nearest they ever got to the country. 'Poor buggers.'

After about ten minutes they crested a small rise and found themselves looking eastwards, across London, towards Canary Wharf.

'Christ,' said Edwina, 'We can see for miles.' She glanced around and saw that they had come sufficiently far from the nearest path to have found relative solitude. They could still see cars moving along one of the main roads that ran through the park, and there was a dogwalker within hailing distance, but beyond that they were alone. 'OK, make with the food then.'

Ulysses began to unload a rucksack he had slung over his shoulder. 'Pork pie, smoked salmon sandwiches, potato salad, tomatoes, fruit, crisps. How about that?'

'Smoked salmon! That's a bit upmarket for you, isn't it?'

'Mess caterer's idea.'

Edwina wasn't the least surprised. She had been certain that given those ingredients Ulysses had had nothing to do with making up their packed lunch. 'Where are the beers?'

'No beer.'

'Very funny, but I'm gagging for a drink.'

'No. No beers. I've brought some water.'

Edwina gave him a hard stare and then lunged for the near-empty rucksack. She danced off with it, rummaging in the bottom. Ulysses made no attempt to retrieve it.

'You bastard. You weren't lying.' Edwina, in disgust, tossed the plastic bottle of mineral water on the ground next to Ulysses.

'And you're drinking too much. It'll do you good to go without a drink.'

Edwina snorted. 'Who says?'

'I do.'

She flounced off a few yards. 'I don't have to take this from you,' she called back to him over her shoulder.

'No, you don't, but you know it's true.'

'You'd go a bit wild every now and again if you had my grotty job to do.'

'That's a pathetic excuse. You're not going a bit wild every now and again; you're drinking too much, too often. Besides which, no one is forcing you to stay in the Army. If you don't like it, get out. I did.'

Edwina looked completely downcast. 'But it's not the Army I hate. It's just my present posting, and I've only got that because of Cathy Roberts and some petty vendetta.'

'That's bollocks and you know it. You got posted to this job because that was what they had earmarked for you next. No one could exert that sort of influence and get you moved from 14 Company.'

'I didn't think you'd believe me. No one does.'

'"Nobody loves me, everybody hates me, I'm going down the garden to eat worms",' chanted Ulysses.

'Oh, piss off,' yelled Edwina in anger and frustration, before turning on her heel and marching back towards the main road through the park. Ulysses watched her disappear, then gathered up the picnic things and loped after her.

When Edwina arrived back at the mess that evening she found an invitation from Lizzie waiting for her in her pigeonhole.

'Amanda has come up to Aldershot for the weekend unexpectedly,' it read. 'Come and have supper. About 7.30.'

Edwina looked at her watch. Seven forty-five. Blast. She ran to the payphone in the lobby and rang Lizzie.

'I've been out for the day,' she explained, 'and I've only just got in. Can I still come?'

'Of course. It's only cold meat and salad, so there's no problem. When do you expect to get here?'

'Well, if I come as I am I'll be about ten minutes.'

'Great. See you then.'

Edwina hung up and went to the bar to get a quick gin to keep her going while she went to fetch her jacket and comb her hair. She remembered what Ulysses had said to her about drinking, but then thought to herself that everyone had a drink before supper, so why shouldn't she? It didn't occur to her that she might wait until she got to Lizzie's. She took a gulp of the gin as she made her way along the corridor to her room, and finished downing it as she tidied herself up a little. She returned the empty glass to the bar and legged it out of the mess. She began to head for her motorbike but then had second thoughts – Lizzie was bound to have a bottle or two of wine, possibly some gin too. Considering the dim view the Army authorities took of its personnel getting done for drink-driving, she'd be better off on foot.

Putting her keys back in her bag, Edwina set off down the hill that led to the commercial part of Aldershot. She crossed the dual carriageway, walked past the civic centre and carried on up the road on the other side for about half a mile till she came to Lizzie's house. Because she had walked, it had taken her nearer twenty minutes than ten, but Lizzie didn't care and greeted her effusively when she arrived.

'I'm so glad you could come. Amanda arrived about an hour ago. She's downstairs in the kitchen.'

'Hi, Amanda,' Edwina called out as she descended the stairs into Lizzie's cheerful basement.

'How are you?' said Amanda. 'You look well.'

'Is that a euphemism for "you've put on weight"?' The best form of defence is attack, thought Edwina.

'I didn't say that,' said Amanda, but she didn't add that she'd thought it.

'Anyway, I can't complain, bar bitching about my grotty job. And you?'

'Oh, so-so. Busy, you know.' Amanda involuntarily rubbed her knuckles.

Lizzie offered Edwina a drink.

'Gin and tonic, please.'

'Coming up. What about you, Amanda?'

'No, I'm fine.' She'd barely touched her glass of wine.

'You're not going to be a party-pooper and be an old sobersides?' said Edwina bluntly.

'I'm just not that keen on drinking these days. I got used to going without any when I was in the Gulf and I haven't really got a taste for it again.' Edwina's eyebrows shot up. 'Honestly.'

Edwina took a sip of the drink that Lizzie handed her. 'Is there any gin in this? All I can taste is tonic.'

'I'm sorry, Edwina, have I made it too weak?'

'Well . . .'

'Let me do you another.'

Edwina downed her drink and handed Lizzie the empty glass. 'Thanks.'

Lizzie virtually half filled the glass with gin before adding a splash of tonic. This time it was Amanda's eyebrows that disappeared skywards. Lizzie handed the glass to Edwina.

'Mmm. Much better,' said Edwina after an appreciative sip.

By the time the food was ready to go on to the table, Edwina had drunk two more such gins while Lizzie was sticking to orange juice and Amanda was still nursing her wine. Edwina didn't notice that her voice had got quite loud and she was slurring some of her words.

'Grub's up,' said Lizzie, placing a basket of baked potatoes on the table next to a big pat of butter.

'Great,' said Edwina, pulling out a chair and helping herself.

Amanda sat down opposite and waited for Edwina to finish with the salad.

'Glass of wine, Edwina?' asked Lizzie.

'Please. This is lovely, Lizzie. Just what I need after a crap day.'

'Why?'

'Oh, just Ulysses and I didn't see eye to eye about something. We had a bit of a disagreement, and I ended up hitching back to Aldershot from Kingston.'

'You did what?' cried Lizzie, horrified.

'Hitched. It's not as dodgy as you think, providing you're careful. Anyway, I can look after myself.'

'I don't doubt it,' said Amanda dryly.

Lizzie placed a glass of white wine by Edwina's plate and helped her to a baked potato.

'Pass the butter, would you?' Edwina asked Amanda. As she reached to take it her elbow caught the rim of the full wine glass and tipped it on to its side. A tide of Chardonnay flooded across the table towards Amanda, who leapt out of her chair, partly to get out of the way and partly to fetch a cloth from the sink.

'Oops!' said Edwina.

'Really, Edwina. You are clumsy,' said Amanda crossly.

'It doesn't matter,' said Lizzie. 'No harm done.'

The mess was cleared up, Lizzie refilled Edwina's glass and the three women settled down to enjoy their meal.

'So how's your job, Lizzie?' asked Amanda.

Before she could answer, Edwina interrupted. 'You know, I don't know why you work. Surely you don't need the money?' She was unaware of how tactless she sounded.

'You're right, I don't need to work – I'm loaded, as they say – but I want to. And I suppose I'm lucky because I love my job and I work for nice people. Bob and William are lovely and their wives are great, so I've had lots of support.'

'Yeah, I know all that,' said Edwina, none too clearly, 'but if you don't have to work, why do you?'

'It gives me a reason to get out of bed in the morning. What would

I do if I didn't work – sit around the house all day in a darkened room and feel sorry for myself? Is that a better alternative?' For Lizzie this was a pretty belligerent little speech, but Edwina didn't notice the tone.

'No, I suppose not. But William and Bob aren't going to be there for ever.'

'No, they won't be. In fact Bob has already been told that he's going to be posted to Salisbury towards the end of the year. But it's four months since Richard was killed and each day gets a little easier. There are some days I get through now without crying.' Lizzie looked defiantly at Edwina as if she expected her to challenge this statement. Edwina finally got the message and dropped her gaze to concentrate on her food.

'Do you find people are more willing to talk to you these days?' asked Amanda. She felt acutely embarrassed about Edwina's behaviour, as if she was somehow responsible for it, and she wanted to get the conversation away from the rights and wrongs of Lizzie wishing to work.

'Yes. I've almost lost my status as a social outcast,' said Lizzie without bitterness. 'How can I tell friends that I'm not hurt if they mention Richard? It's them *not* mentioning him that hurts; it's as if he never existed, and they don't understand that I like to talk about him. He did exist and he was real and he was a big part of my life, and I don't go into a decline if I hear his name.'

'So you're happy to stay here in Aldershot then? You're not looking to go anywhere else?' asked Amanda.

'Not for the moment. I'm happy here in the house, I like my job –'

'Lucky you,' mumbled Edwina morosely. 'Can't stand mine.'

Amanda glared at her. Why, she thought, could Edwina only ever see things that related to her? She hadn't once asked Lizzie how she was or how she was coping, and now she was bringing her problems into a conversation that was about Lizzie and her future. How selfish could you get?

'Do you know what I did last week?' continued Edwina. 'I organised some adventurous training, and none of the girls in my squadron wanted to go on it. I couldn't believe it. So I went to my OC and told her I was going to cancel it and she said –'

'Will you shut up!' exploded Amanda suddenly. There was silence around the table. 'Sorry,' she mumbled. 'It's just that this has nothing to do with Lizzie and her problems. To be honest, what do we care about your squadron and how much you hate it? Everyone in the Army gets a posting they don't much like at one time or another. It can't be a jolly picnic all the time. You've got a duff posting now but it's only for two years. Richard's dead and that isn't going to alter, so I'm sorry, Edwina, but the world does not revolve around you.'

Edwina looked for a second as if she was going to cry. 'God, everyone hates me: Ulysses, you. I expect Lizzie only invited me round tonight out of pity,' she sneered.

'That's unfair,' yelled Amanda. 'Don't you be horrid to Lizzie. She hasn't a nasty bone in her body, and how dare you be rude to her?'

'Stop it!' shouted Lizzie. There was silence. 'What is the matter with the pair of you?'

'Sorry,' said Amanda.

'Sorry from me too.' Edwina sobered up. 'I shouldn't have said what I did. I've had a rotten day and I'm feeling a bit sorry for myself.'

'There you go again,' said Amanda. 'Your rotten day is nothing compared to the sort of problems Lizzie has to overcome all the time.' At the end of the table Lizzie began to sob quietly. 'Now look what you've done.'

'Why is it all my fault? It takes two to have a row.' Edwina glared at Amanda.

'Oh, just shut up.'

'Don't worry, I will.' Edwina picked up her glass, gulped down the last of her wine, and then, grabbing her bag, flounced out, slamming the front door so hard the windows in the basement rattled.

Andover, September 1991

'Won't she answer your messages still?' asked Bella as yet again Amanda left word with the mess at Aldershot that she'd like Miss Austin to contact her.

'It doesn't look like it. It's not like Edwina to sulk. Fly off the handle, yes, but she's not a sulker. I tried ringing her in the office a couple of times but she just slammed the phone down on me.'

Bella began to massage Amanda's shoulders.

'Mmm, that's nice.'

'It must have been a terrible row.'

'That's the stupid thing, it wasn't that bad really, and she knew she was in the wrong. Of course it didn't help matters that she was half pissed.'

'It never does.' Bella felt Amanda wince. 'Sorry. Did that hurt?'

Amanda shook her head. 'Not really.'

'From what you say, she's drunk a good deal too often these days.'

'She always used to drink like a fish. Even when we were cadets, and most of us were terrified of having to perform the next day with a hangover, she would be knocking it back in one of the bars, but she never seemed to be affected by it then. Now, according to Lizzie, who sees a lot of her, she never seems to sober up.'

'Surely that's an exaggeration,' said Bella, playing devil's advocate.

'I don't know. Lizzie's worried sick about her. I feel I ought to be able to do something, but what?'

'What about asking Lizzie to help? She's in Aldershot.'

Amanda shook her head vigorously, which made her neck ache. She rubbed it to ease it. 'No. The last thing Lizzie needs is to take on Edwina and her problems. She's doing so well sorting herself out and Edwina could drag her right back down.'

'What did she say? That it takes eighteen months to get over a bereavement?'

'Six months down and a year to go,' said Amanda grimly. She stood up, her face contorted into a grimace as her weight was transferred to her toes and feet. 'I'm going to have a hot bath. It might help all these aches and pains.'

'I'll come up and help you.' Bella knew that Amanda sometimes found it difficult to undress herself; her fingers just didn't seem to bend in the right way to unhook her bra or pull down the zip of her dress. Bella ran her bath and tenderly helped her lover to get out of her clothes. 'You ought to go to the medics about this again, you know,' she said, when Amanda bit her lip to stop herself from crying out as she had to bend her arms to slip the sleeves of her dress off.

'And what good will that do? They've said I've got arthritis, they're giving me some pills for it and if I bang on about it they'll look at downgrading me medically.'

'But you've got nothing to lose. If you don't pass your BFT that'll happen anyway. You must be due to take it any day now.' Bella tipped a generous helping of Radox into the bath. Neither of them knew if it helped or not, but Amanda's stiffness had got to such a pitch they were happy to try anything.

'I am. I'm supposed to be running it this month, and I don't know that I will pass it.' A year ago Amanda had romped through the test with minutes to spare to prove she was fit enough for further service, but since the Gulf she had had problems walking across a car park, let alone running the required mile and a half.

Amanda leant on Bella's arm as she gingerly lowered herself into the bath. She gave a sigh of relief as the deep warm water supported her aching joints. 'Ooh, that's better,' she sighed.

'I've had a thought,' said Bella, closing the lid on the loo and settling herself on it so she could talk to Amanda in some comfort.

'Tell me about it.' Amanda shut her eyes and let the water wash over her.

'Well, if Edwina won't talk to you, and we're agreed that it would be unfair for Lizzie to get involved . . .'

'Yes,'

'Well, what about asking that boyfriend of hers?'

'Ulysses?'

'Why not? From what I've heard about the two of them they were

299

very close at one point, so I'm pretty certain he would have had, or possibly still has, quite a lot of influence with her.'

'But he's left the Army, and apart from the fact he lives in Kingston, I haven't a clue where to find him. I bet he'll be ex-directory, so there's no point trying to find him that way.'

Bella sighed as this avenue seemed to turn into a blind alley. 'And Edwina's the only one who's likely to know, and we can hardly ask her, can we?'

'Not without making her very suspicious. Anyway, I'm not entirely sure they're still seeing each other.'

Bella began to soap Amanda. 'I know, do you have contacts in the Army pensions office?'

'No. And even if I did, I expect his current address is not the sort of thing they'd let me have.'

'But they'd forward a letter, surely,' Bella stopped soaping Amanda's shoulders while they both considered this option.

'It's worth a try.'

They decided to write to him, or at least that Bella should write at Amanda's dictation – she was finding it increasingly difficult to hold a pen these days, though luckily she mainly used a word processor at work.

A fortnight later Ulysses phoned.

'I got your letter,' he said without preamble.

'Thanks for getting in touch with me. I'm sorry I had to bother you but I'm concerned about Edwina. Are you still seeing her?' asked Amanda.

'Not really. I got fed up with her moaning about the unfairness of life and we had a bit of a row.'

'Was that the day the pair of you went to Kingston?'

'Yes.'

'Did you know she hitch-hiked back?'

'I should do; I had the devil of a job tailing the car she got a lift in to make sure she got back all right.'

Amanda laughed. 'So you still care about her?'

'If I'm honest with myself, I do, but she's just such a pain to be with at the moment.'

'That was why we wanted to get in touch with you. We're really worried about her.'

'She's still drinking then?'

'So you'd noticed too?'

'Fucking difficult to miss, if you'll excuse me for being blunt.'

'She can't go on like it. The Army'll notice soon – that's if she isn't done for drinking and driving first.'

'What do you think I can do? I'm assuming you didn't want me to phone you just to help you guess what her mess bill is each month?'

'Could you have a word with her about it?' asked Amanda. She heard Ulysses sigh down the phone.

'I honestly don't think it'll do any good. It was me having a go at her which sent her storming off in the first place.'

'Oh dear. She won't talk to me, and the only other person who might be able to get through to her is Lizzie, and I'm really loath to ask her.'

'Is she the one who lost her husband?'

'Yes.'

'You can't expect her to take on Edwina. She'd eat her alive.'

'Lizzie's tougher than people think,' said Amanda, despite the fact that she'd already decided to keep her out of this.

'It's still unfair to ask, though. OK, I'll see if I can mend some bridges and invite Edwina up for a weekend. No promises, mind.'

Amanda put the phone down feeling relieved.

She was surprised when Ulysses phoned again the next night.

'We're too late, I'm afraid. Her boss carpeted her this morning. Apparently she returned to work yesterday afternoon reeling drunk, and got sent back to the mess to sober up.'

'You're joking!' Amanda was aghast. She'd thought that Edwina would at least have been professional enough to confine her drinking to when she was off duty.

'I only wish I were. She's in bits, as you can imagine. Not just because her career is in tatters, but also because she imagines we're all going to say I told you so.'

'Which we won't, of course.' Amanda paused fractionally. 'Even though it's tempting.'

'She's been put on warning. She said that her boss had been on the brink of calling her in about the size of her mess bill, and going to work drunk was just the last straw. She's got six months to sort herself out, and if she doesn't she'll be out.'

'Surely they can't do that?'

'They can. She's on a short service commission and at the moment it's due to end next spring. If her behaviour wasn't in doubt it could be extended if she asked to serve on, but as it stands . . .' Ulysses didn't have to say more.

'Poor Edwina. What's she going to do?'

'She's been told to take leave till the end of the week, so she's coming to stay with me. The only trouble is, she'll be on her own most of the day. I've got clients for fitness training and there's no way I can put them off.'

'So there's no one to make sure she doesn't go on a bender?'

'I don't know that's what she's got planned, but if it is, well . . .'

'I see. I imagine you've got rid of the booze at your place.'

'Everything. I nearly poured it down the drain but I just couldn't stand the waste. A neighbour is looking after it for me. But I can't stop her going to the shops or the pubs.'

'Do you think she will, under the circumstances?'

'Look, if she was low enough to be hitting the bottle before her OC had a word with her, then she's going to be taking it intravenously now.'

'Shall I come up at the weekend?'

'I don't think that'll do any good' – Ulysses realised this sounded churlish – 'but you can if you want, of course.'

'I don't know. I'll see.'

Ulysses gave her his address and phone number so that she could visit if she decided to. After Amanda put the phone down, she rang Bella on her mobile – Bella had invested in one to keep her private phone calls away from the public gaze of mess life – and quickly told her of the latest misfortune to befall Edwina.

'Stupid cow,' said Bella with feeling.

'I know, I know, but we've got to help her get back on her feet.'

'How? Can you see her standing up at an AA meeting and saying, "Hello, I'm Edwina and I'm an alcoholic"?'

'No. But there must be some way.'

'Well, I've told you how I gave up smoking by taking up knitting.'

'Because you couldn't smoke and knit,' finished Amanda.

'But can you see Edwina knitting? That's even more unlikely than her going to an AA meeting!'

'If she had something to occupy her she might forget to pick up a glass quite so often, but what on earth would appeal to her as a hobby?'

* * *

302

Amanda found it difficult to concentrate at work the next day. Edwina and her problems seemed to dominate her thoughts to the exclusion of her job, which involved the logistics of supply and demand and which Amanda found pretty dull at the best of times. With something more pressing to occupy her mind, the procurement of clothing for Her Majesty's Forces easily slid on to a back-burner. What could Edwina do that she might find interesting, would occupy her, especially in the evenings, and would get her out and about and away from anywhere she might get a drink? Amanda toyed with the idea of some sort of sports club but she wasn't sure that would appeal. Edwina had always been such a loner in that respect; running marathons as a personal challenge, with her goal being the improvement of her own best time. Competing against other people held no appeal for her. No, thought Amanda, a group activity was probably not the answer, but what the hell was?

She telephoned Ulysses that evening to talk over the problem with him. She was worried that Edwina might answer the phone but Ulysses assured her that she was out cold on the bed, having apparently started drinking at lunchtime and continued until oblivion had overtaken her.

Ulysses accepted that giving Edwina an interest that might keep her occupied and away from pubs, bars and off-licences was a good idea.

'I'll give it some thought,' he said. 'But God knows if we'll be able to think of anything which will give her sufficient motivation. Anyway, I've got a pretty quiet day tomorrow. I've a couple of clients early in the morning and then nothing till late afternoon. I was supposed to be taking a couple of sessions in the gym but I've managed to swap, so I'll be able to keep a closer watch on Edwina and I may be able to talk some sense into her.'

'Good luck,' said Amanda, because Ulysses would certainly need it.

Kingston-upon-Thames, September 1991

In her heart, Edwina knew that what Ulysses had said to her, when she'd finally woken up at nine o'clock the night before, made sense. She was wrecking her life, destroying her health, she was weak-willed and she was annoying the hell out of her friends. The problem was that the morning after, with a hangover to contend with as well, the words still cut and the harsh words on top of nausea did little to improve her low self-esteem. And low self-esteem was a large part of the cause of the problem to start with.

She lay, dry-eyed, on the double bed that filled the bedroom in Ulysses' tiny flat, oblivious to the sound of the nearby trains on the main line to Waterloo, which rumbled regularly up and down the line. Ulysses had gone to work an hour ago and now her mind was filled with the sound of his voice, saying over and over, 'No one can help you but yourself. You've got to want to do this, we can't make you.' Round and round the words went as she wallowed in self-pity. No one understood the guilt she felt over Nat's accident, no one believed that Cathy Roberts had somehow engineered her posting away from 14 Company to this dreadful unit she was with now, no one realised how unhappy she was. And it didn't help having Lizzie on her doorstep coping so wonderfully with her problems, which only made Edwina look even more useless. Life was unfair and her friends despised her, she hated herself and she was about to lose her job. And worst of all, there wasn't anything to fucking drink in the house!

God, she wanted a drink. But there was no chance of getting hold of any because nothing would be open at this early hour and Ulysses had hidden or got rid of every last drop. After yesterday he'd also taken her cards and money so she couldn't buy anything anyway.

Bastard! Wearily Edwina got up. She'd have to have some sort of fix, and it looked as though caffeine was all that was on offer. She wandered across the living room to the cupboard that passed for a kitchen and switched on the kettle. Then she walked across to the other tiny, windowless cupboard which contained the shower and the loo, and which the estate agent had optimistically described as a bathroom, to have a pee while she waited for the water to boil. She flushed the loo and looked at her reflection in the spotted and grubby mirror over the basin. She had to admit that she looked awful. Her hair needed a wash, she had a rash of pimples and her skin had a greasy, unhealthy sheen. She cleaned her teeth to rid herself of the stale, early-morning taste and looked at herself again. Still dreadful.

Edwina padded back to the kettle and poured boiling water over the coffee granules. More in hope than expectation she checked the fridge to see if there was any milk and was surprised to find a carton of semi-skimmed. She poured a splash in and was disgusted to see it curdle as the sour milk, patently well past its sell-by date, mixed with the hot water. 'Bugger,' she swore, and threw the contents of the mug into the sink. She sighed heavily. Everything was against her – even the fucking groceries!

She made herself a cup of black coffee and sipped it morosely, staring sightlessly out of the dirty kitchen window at the railway line. She felt edgy and twitchy. She had to get out of the flat or she'd scream, but with no cash and no cards her options were pretty limited. Walking was free, though, and Richmond Park was only up the road. She decided to take herself there. She threw the dregs of her coffee into the sink and went to pull on jeans, a sweatshirt and a pair of trainers. In less than five minutes she was walking up the road towards the park.

When she reached the main gates of the park she paused and looked at the junction just ahead of her; either she could go along the flat road to the left or up the hill to the right. She decided that the road up the hill looked the more interesting of the two. There was a footpath that ran along through the trees to one side, which she took to avoid the heavy traffic using the park as a convenient short cut between Kingston and Sheen or Richmond. The footpath was nearly as heavily trafficked with pedestrians as the road was with cars, and she noticed with distaste that being so close to a car park and the gates it was also littered with dog turds. Obviously the dog-owners of Kingston regarded this piece of land as the most convenient dog loo available. She decided that as soon as she got further into the park she would leave the beaten track and try and find a bit of space on her own, clear of both people and crap.

As she reached the top of the hill she paused for breath. Time was, she thought, when she could have run up and down a hill like that several times without feeling puffed; now a leisurely stroll made her feel exhausted. God, she was out of condition! Perhaps if she asked Ulysses nicely he'd go for a run with her. Then she decided against that idea. She didn't want him to see how chronically unfit she'd got. That would be too humiliating. She'd have to sort herself out a bit before she went to him, but she wasn't sure she had the motivation any more. After all, she thought, what was the point if she was going to spend the rest of her life behind a desk? It didn't look as if she'd be able to go back to 14 Company again, and she'd missed out on the only bit of real action the Army was likely to see for a decade or so, so what did the future hold? Personnel administration? Staff jobs? An occasional exercise on Hohne Ranges or Salisbury Plain? Whoopee!

Ahead she could see a grassy meadow. She decided to strike off the path, cross it and see where she could get to from there. Still keeping a wary eye out for dog mess she crossed the road and headed deeper into the park. She came to a fence surrounding the large grounds of a private house, skirted that and struck out through bracken, across meadows and over rides; trying to keep away from paths and roads. After a mile or so she came to a clearing in a small wood and sat on a fallen tree to enjoy the peace and quiet. She couldn't hear any cars, and she hadn't seen another soul for ages. The only sign of civilisation was the sound of an aircraft overhead droning on its descent into Heathrow.

Edwina slid off the tree trunk and sat on the dry ground, using the dead oak as a back rest. She sat still. Her training for surveillance jobs meant that she had the discipline to remain motionless for hours if necessary, even in the most uncomfortable of situations. But she didn't need to call on these resources now; her position was perfectly tenable, the temperature was mild, and above her the sun was burning off the early-morning mist and would break through in the next few minutes. She allowed herself to relax and closed her eyes.

It took her a second to orientate herself when she opened them again. She hadn't meant to fall asleep but the peace and warmth and quiet had been irresistibly soporific. She realised almost instantly where she was and resisted the urge to stretch her stiff shoulders, because not three feet from her was a small herd of fallow deer. They were so close she could see the lashes which framed their beautiful dark eyes, see every spot on their dappled coats and hear the sound of their contented munching as they chewed away at the available grazing. Then she became aware of a staccato drumming in the branches above her. Slowly, cautiously, not wishing to disturb the deer, she turned her head. It took her several minutes to spot the woodpecker. She didn't have a clue what sort it was but she was quite surprised to find what a kick she got from seeing it.

Suddenly she realised how high the sun was in the sky and she instinctively glanced at her watch to see exactly what the time was. The movement, tiny though it was, was enough to startle the wildlife, and in a matter of seconds the clearing was empty and Edwina was alone again. She got up and stretched, brushed herself down and began to head back towards the road and Kingston.

Ulysses was livid when she got back.

'Where the hell have you been?' he demanded as soon as she walked through the front door. His attitude made Edwina see red.

'You're not my keeper. I'm a grown-up, remember, and I can come and go as I please. I don't need your permission first.'

'Have you been out getting booze?' said Ulysses suspiciously. He stepped closer to her to smell her breath.

'No, I haven't.' Edwina pushed him away angrily. 'I've been for a walk.'

'You expect me to believe that?'

'Well, it's quite obvious that whatever I say you're going to accuse me of lying.'

'OK. So where have you been walking for all this time? I got back here at nine and it's now nearly one – four hours?'

'I went up to Richmond Park and I fell asleep.'

'Really! You must take me for a moron.'

Edwina was tempted to say that she did, but she didn't want to provoke Ulysses too far. Their relationship had always been rather turbulent, both of them being such strong characters. He'd never hit her but she'd always thought that if she went too far he just might. He'd told her how he'd been in fights with members of his family. Best not to find out if he might use her as a punchbag too.

'Believe what you like, but it's the truth,' she said sulkily. She was angry that his cross-examination had destroyed the pleasure she'd been feeling at seeing all the wildlife in the park. Damn him, she thought.

Ulysses shrugged and dropped the subject.

'What do you want for lunch?' he asked.

'What is there?' Apart from the sour milk, Edwina remembered the fridge as being pretty well empty.

'Bread, eggs, cheese, fruit. I went shopping.'

'Anything. Whatever you're having.'

Ulysses began to make some cheese and pickle sandwiches.

'Is there a library round here?' asked Edwina.

'How should I know?'

'Philistine.'

'Why do you ask?'

'I want to look something up.'

'What?' Ulysses sliced the sandwiches down the middle and put them on to a plate.

'A bird.'

'What sort of bird?'

'I don't know. If I knew I wouldn't have to look it up, would I?' Edwina took a sandwich and ate half of it in one bite.

'Hungry?'

'Famished.'

'It's because you've been walking. It's done you good. You look a lot better than you did.'

'Thanks.' Edwina didn't tell him that she was still longing for a drink, but at least she'd got through the morning without one. Only eight hours more and she could think about going to bed; maybe she might be able to get through the day without one. A day without a drink, it was a start, she thought.

'Anyway, why this sudden interest in birds?'

'I saw one today in the park. Some sort of woodpecker, I think, but I don't know for certain.' She told him about the fallow deer too.

Ulysses suddenly had a brainwave about a possible hobby for Edwina.

'Take a camera with you next time. You might get some good pictures.'

'Haven't got it with me.' She finished off her sandwich. 'It's in my room in Aldershot.'

'Borrow mine then.'

After lunch they walked back to the park so Edwina could get used to using his camera. She took Ulysses to where she'd spent the morning, but the herd of deer had moved on.

'You ought to come up here at night. Try and get some pictures using infra-red.'

'But the park's closed at night.'

'Only to cars. Pedestrians can still get in. Mind you, you may have to be careful. They sometimes have sharpshooters up here to cull the deer – or so I'm told.'

'Dodging snipers. It'd be like being back in Ireland.'

Ulysses didn't have to be back at the gym until four o'clock, so they walked some distance into the park, again getting off the main paths and heading as deep as possible into the wooded areas. Rabbits and squirrels by the dozen skipped out of their way as they progressed through the undergrowth.

'There aren't half a lot of animals,' observed Edwina.

'Only because they're trapped here. There's nowhere else for them to escape to because the park is entirely surrounded by built-up areas and busy roads. So unless they fancy taking their chances in suburbia they have to stay here.'

'If I was to try and get some good shots I'd probably do quite well, then.'

Ulysses was pleased that Edwina seemed keen on the idea of photography. If he could get her to come up here after dusk, she might be sufficiently successful to get even more enthusiastic. The only problem he could see was the several pubs she would have to pass between the park gates and his flat. But it was a start, and if he could ecourage her to take the idea up seriously there was no reason for her not to carry on with it as a hobby. It might be exactly the occupation she needed to keep her mind off booze.

The next day Ulysses came back to the flat with the basics that Edwina would need to develop her shots. The tiny, windowless shower room could serve as a dark room, although it was incredibly cramped to work in. She'd spent two weeks training in photography and developing when she'd been with the Special Forces, so she knew exactly what she was doing and how to achieve the best results, although she was only really happy when using black and white film. After an hour or so of sloshing around in chemical compounds she showed Ulysses the results of her previous day's labours.

He'd been prepared to lie about how good they were in order to boost her confidence, but he didn't have to. Three of the shots, two of a squirrel and one of a rabbit, were extremely good indeed, and there were half a dozen others which would have passed muster by any criteria.

'God, you're a natural! You ought to send them off to a wildlife magazine and see if they can use them,' said Ulysses.

'Don't be stupid. You've probably got to shoot tigers or charging bull elephants to get a picture in one of those things.' She was feeling extremely bad-tempered because all she could think about was her craving – her huge craving – for a gin, and all that was on offer was Coke. Huh!

'It was just an idea.'

But the idea took root in Ulysses' head and the next day, apart from buying yet more film, he also brought home a stack of magazines about photography. He desperately wanted to encourage her in this new-found interest.

'Look through these and see what other people do. I'm sure you could be in their league if you tried.'

Edwina picked one up and began to flick through the pages, not really caring and barely glancing at some of the pictures, but every now and again, almost against her will, something would catch her eye and she'd stop to read a caption or a few lines of text. She not only knew about photography, but she'd also studied composition at art college, and she began to see that, providing she was capable of combining the two skills, producing a top-class picture was not something beyond her remit. She stopped flicking desultorily through the magazine and began to read it properly, with increasing interest. She finished one and picked up another, thoughts of gin temporarily banished.

The weather stayed dry and Edwina spent the next couple of days up in the park. Ulysses didn't own any infra-red equipment so she was restricted to daylight shots, but she decided that when she went back to Aldershot she would try out some night stuff. There was a big badger's sett on a military training area there, and it might be a challenge to get some pictures of its occupants. But she knew that she would have to go back to work in a couple of days and would have all the temptations of mess life on her doorstep again. She'd now done four days without a drink, and although the craving was still appalling at some moments – particularly early evening – it didn't seem to dominate every waking minute in quite the same way it had.

'I don't want to go back to living in the mess,' she said to Ulysses on Saturday night.

'I don't think you can stay here much longer.' He assumed a John Wayne accent. 'This flat ain't big enough for the two of us.'

Which was true. The tiny, poky rooms were OK for a single person, but with two of them in it, living space was almost nonexistent.

'But if I'm in the mess I'll drink again. It's there, in your face, all the time. And everyone else drinks; life revolves around the bar.

'Could you stay with someone else?'

'I suppose I could ask Lizzie.'

'Is that fair?'

'She can always say no.'

'But she wouldn't, would she?'

Edwina thought about it and knew Ulysses was right. Lizzie would always help her friends, no matter how inconvenient it was, or how difficult it made things for her.

'She might be glad of the company. And she hardly drinks herself.'

'Stop trying to justify an arrangement which would primarily benefit you.'

'But where else could I go?'

Ulysses didn't have an answer for that one.

'You could always have a word with Amanda, see what she could suggest.'

'No.'

'Why not?'

'I'm not talking to her. We had a row.'

'Oh, grow up! Do you know that she was so worried about you she managed to track me down to get me to help? She really cares about you and you're carrying on some stupid vendetta over a row.' Ulysses paused and then added, 'I bet you were pissed when you rowed with her. You were, weren't you?'

'Yes,' admitted Edwina sulkily.

Ulysses stretched out his hand for the phone and picked up the receiver. 'Right, you're going to ring her this minute, eat a whole portion of humble pie, apologise and ask for her forgiveness.'

Edwina glowered at him but took the phone. Five minutes later the pair of them were chatting as though the row had never happened. Edwina broached the subject of her future accommodation.

Amanda offered to act as a go-between.

'I'll put it to Lizzie in a roundabout way and see how she feels. She's more likely to be honest with me than you.'

Edwina had no choice but to accept this. In the event Lizzie told Amanda that she would be glad of the company – for a fortnight or so, she didn't think she could face more at the moment – and that it would be nice to have someone to cook for apart from herself.

'I'll go and stay with Ulysses at the weekends,' Edwina promised. 'She'll probably be glad of the space by then. And I promise I'll be good. Honest.'

Aldershot, October 1991

The arrangement was originally just for a couple of weeks, but both Edwina and Lizzie, to their surprise, found that it suited them rather well. To all intents and purposes they lived largely separate lives, but they ate together in the evening, shared the household bills, such as they were, and were able to provide each other with support. Lizzie had never drunk more than the occasional sherry at home, so to give up alcohol in solidarity with Edwina came as no hardship, and having Edwina to talk to made the evenings less lonely. And as Edwina's health improved, as her determination to kick her drink habit hardened still further, she began to look towards her level of fitness again.

'Want to come for a run?' she offered Lizzie one evening. 'I haven't got any more excuses left not to, and I could do with some moral support for the first few times. Of course, if you don't fancy it . . .'

Lizzie thought about it. Why not?

They set off at a fairly easy pace, but even so, after about half a mile Edwina slowed to a walk.

'I don't believe it,' said Lizzie in amazement. 'I'm not going to let you get away with this. When I think how you used to beast Amanda round Sandhurst. Come on. Get moving again!'

Edwina willed herself to jog again and made herself keep going despite the stitch in her side and the ache in her thighs. When they got back to Lizzie's front door she found that her legs were shaking with fatigue.

'When did you last run?' asked Lizzie.

'Not since I got back from Ireland. There didn't seem any point.'

'You'll have to do some serious training if you're going to pass your BFT.'

'Don't worry. I'll get there.'

Autumn turned to winter, Edwina ran every day, and Lizzie helped and supported her and found pleasure in her company. She even found herself laughing on occasions at some of the daft things Edwina said or did. She encouraged Edwina's photography, kept her away from the bottle and listened to her grumbling about her job and her boss. Edwina lost weight and Lizzie gained it. Just prior to Christmas, William and Bob were both posted.

'Do you want to come to the farewell party?' asked Lizzie.

Edwina shook her head. 'I don't think I could cope with being sociable and stay on the wagon. Well, not just yet anyway.'

'How long have you gone without a drink?'

'Ninety-three days. But who's counting?'

'Perhaps in the New Year you may feel you'll be able to join in things a bit more.'

'Maybe.' Edwina changed the subject. 'Have you met your new boss yet?'

'Yes. He seems quite nice, but time will tell. He's not going to be able to change much or do anything until Bob has actually gone. Next week I'll know what he's really like.'

Rather than stay at home while Lizzie went to the party, Edwina decided to go out to the training area called Caesar's Camp to practise her night-time photography skills. She'd made herself a hide in the bushes near the badger's sett but she hadn't used it yet because she'd decided to let the local wildlife get used to the makeshift structure before she began to take photographs from it. But now seemed as good a moment as any to see if she could get some pictures of the badgers entering and leaving their home. However, she was to be disappointed; she stayed there for several hours in vain. She'd read in a natural history book that badgers might lie up for several days at a time in the winter, so perhaps this was one of those moments, but the creatures would get hungry at some stage, and when they came out for food, she'd snap them.

It was late when she got back and it had started to rain. She wondered when Lizzie would return; it wasn't like her to stay out late. Lizzie had joked in the past that she was having a wild time if she stayed up to watch the ten o'clock news. There was a late film on, so

Edwina settled down with a coffee to watch it. It was past midnight when Lizzie came in.

'I didn't expect you to still be up,' she said. She sounded weary and looked downcast.

'Good party?'

'OK. Sad, though, because I'm going to miss Bob and Ginny and William and Sophie. They've been good friends to me and Aldershot won't be the same without them.'

'Poor you.'

'I shouldn't feel sorry for myself.'

'I can't think why you think that. Christ, if anyone has an excuse . . .'

Lizzie sighed heavily. 'I'm going to make myself a hot drink before bed. Do you want one?'

'No, thanks.' Edwina thought that Lizzie didn't sound as if she'd been having a good time. But, as she'd said, she was going to miss her friends.

Lizzie went out into the kitchen and Edwina turned back to catch the last moments of the film.

'I can't think why I watched that,' she muttered to herself as the closing credits rolled. 'Crap!' She picked up her empty cup to take it down to the kitchen to wash up before going to bed.

As she went out of the sitting room and down the stairs into the basement, she was aware of an icy draught whistling past her feet. When she got to the bottom of the stairs she could see that the back door was wide open. Lizzie was standing in the garden in the pitch dark and rain, with no coat on over her skirt and blouse.

'Come back in. You'll catch your death,' said Edwina, running out and putting her arm round her. She could feel that Lizzie was soaked and frozen. 'Come in, Lizzie, I'm getting wet too.'

Lizzie didn't answer.

'I can't leave you out here.' Lizzie shrugged. Edwina took her arm and began to lead her towards the house.

'I'm sorry. I can't go in. I just can't.' The rain streamed down Lizzie's face and mingled with her tears.

'Why? What's so bad about the house?'

'Nothing. But it just seems to be so full of memories tonight. When I came home this evening, and the light was on in the sitting room, I thought for a moment that Richard was here. And as I opened the front door I almost thought I could smell his aftershave.

315

Then I remembered that I was wrong, that it was you sitting with the light on, and I tried to put it out of my mind. But when I came down here to the kitchen it all just got on top of me. I know he's dead. I know he's not suddenly going to walk through the front door and say hello, but almost every day I think I hear him or I think of something I ought to tell him about before I remember that I can't. I still roll over in bed at night and I'm surprised that he isn't there beside me.' She stared at Edwina. 'Sometimes I feel as if I'm going round the bend. Do you think I am?'

Edwina put her arms about Lizzie and gave her a hug. The rain trickled down her neck, making her shiver involuntarily. 'No, of course not. I don't know what it's like to lose someone close, but I should think what you are going through is entirely normal. It only shows how much you loved him.'

'But it's awful, because I know it's only my imagination, and I miss him so badly. Do you know that when it first happened I thought perhaps it was all some sort of test devised by the Army to see how I could cope with this sort of thing? I really believed, for a while, that if I passed, someone would come to the office one day and say, well done, Lizzie, you handled this just fine, so here is your husband back. But of course it wasn't a test; it was for real. Some days I feel so miserable I can't think straight and I can't make any decisions and I know it's affecting my work. And every now and again I feel as though it hasn't really happened and it'll all be better, and then I realise it won't and I seem to feel worse than ever. And when I'm in the house I see where he used to sit, see where he burnt the kitchen table with his soldering iron, and all the hundreds of other things that remind me of him, and it all just keeps telling me that he won't be coming back.' She began to cry huge, painful sobs again, and Edwina held her close. She could feel Lizzie shivering uncontrollably but she didn't know whether it was from grief or cold.

'Come on, poppet. Let's have a hot drink.' This time Lizzie allowed her to walk her into the house. Edwina made the tea and supervised Lizzie drinking it, then ran a hot bath for her.

'Out of those wet things,' she ordered. Lizzie, numb with cold and despair, obeyed wordlessly.

'I'm sorry,' she kept whispering. 'I'm sorry. I should be over it by now. I think that perhaps the wine I drank has made me maudlin.'

Edwina wondered how often Lizzie had felt like this in the past months and had had no one to look after her, to provide a shoulder to cry on and to take care of her. How many lonely, miserable nights had she cried herself to sleep? Perhaps it was a good thing that she was staying at Lizzie's and was here to help. She had planned to move back into the mess after Christmas, but maybe she'd give it a few more weeks.

Kingston-upon-Thames, February 1992

'So your mind is made up? No going back?' said Ulysses as he and Edwina jogged around Richmond Park.

'Nope, I really am going to resign. I enjoyed what I did – well, most of it – and I had a lot of fun, but it's time for me to change direction,' she replied. 'Besides which, I've tried to get back with 14 Company and there's some sort of block on it. They keep telling me it's for the sake of my career, but I just don't believe it. Maybe it's because of Nat – I don't know – but as I can't find out what it is, I can't fight it. I'm not being a loser, just realistic.' She breathed deeply as she ran, enjoying the crisp, cold air of a perfect winter's morning. The frosted grass crackled underfoot and the trees were dusted with white which sparkled in the rays of the low early sun. She'd regained her earlier level of fitness and ran with her customary easy lope that carried her almost effortlessly along over the hard ground. For once the park was almost empty, apart from a few dog-walkers, and they could hear the sound of their feet pounding along the footpaths.

'You don't have any friends in high places who could sneak a peak in your "P" file?'

'No one. And don't think I haven't thought about it. No, I've made my mind up to go and that's that.'

'But you were hardly in the Army any time at all.' Ulysses matched her pace, stride for stride.

'Four and a half years,' she said defensively, 'if you count my time as a cadet.'

'Which is, I expect, the longest you've kept at anything.'

She stuck her tongue out at him and quickened her pace to be out of range of any retribution.

'And then what?' he asked, catching up with her and trying to trip her up. Edwina dodged out of the way.

'Don't know exactly yet. But I've got some ideas and plenty of time to think about it. Lizzie says I can stay at her place until I get myself a job and organise a flat or something. And I've joined a photography club. Don't laugh,' she said as Ulysses grinned. She didn't understand that his smile was not one of derision, but of happiness that his encouragement had paid off. 'I'd like to do something in that line and I need some contacts, that sort of thing. Now I've got into it I realise what a terrific buzz I get out of taking good shots. I'll always be grateful to the Army for teaching me the skills. I really owe them for that.'

Ulysses looked at her with genuine affection. He was truly pleased that she'd found another niche for herself. 'Well, good luck. Right – race you to the gates.'

He sprinted off before Edwina had time to react and had a head start of several yards. Edwina kicked hard and almost caught him up by the finish line.

'Phew,' she panted. 'If you hadn't cheated, I'd have beaten you.'

'No chance. You've got to remember you're only a girlie.'

'Piss off.'

Ulysses looked at her fondly. This was the old Edwina back again, and he was glad of it.

After her weekend with Ulysses, Edwina returned to Lizzie's place to find Amanda's car outside. She was pleased to see that she'd dropped by. As she went in she sniffed appreciatively at the smell of baking that greeted her as she came down the stairs into the kitchen. Sighting the cake that Lizzie had just made, she fell on it.

'Brilliant. Cherry cake, my favourite. It's not for anything special, is it?' Lizzie shook her head and Edwina cut herself a large slice and took a huge bite.

'What have you been doing with yourself over the weekend?' she asked Amanda. But Amanda was faintly evasive about what she'd done where and with whom, so Edwina didn't press her for details. From Amanda's happiness and sparkle she guessed that Bella had probably featured in the weekend's proceedings. However, she'd long since decided that Amanda's private life was exactly that, private. Whatever she did, whatever her sexuality, it didn't affect her performance as an officer, although Edwina knew that the authorities would have to lie down in a darkened room at the knowledge that they were employing a lesbian. Not that Edwina could understand this attitude. She was aware of – and thoroughly disapproved of – the witch-hunts carried out by the Special Investigation Branch to root out gays. Invariably they were heavy-handed, even bullying, and on more than one occasion Edwina had wondered how much more damage they did to the unit they were trying to protect from the terrible gay criminals than their unfortunate victims ever inflicted.

'Six weeks and counting till I'm out of uniform,' she told Amanda cheerfully.

'Six weeks and counting till I have to buy a new one,' replied Amanda.

'Oh, yes. I'd forgotten about the WRAC getting disbanded. Being Royal Signals I haven't really been paying that much attention. Do you think khaki will suit you?' She helped herself to another slice of the rapidly diminishing cake. With no special women's corps there was no excuse for them to have a separate uniform. The new design was to be similar to the men's uniform, except that they would still wear skirts, not trousers.

'No worse than lovat green, I suppose. I just wish I knew what my prospects were before I lay out good money on all this new kit,' said Amanda with a sigh. 'You know that I've got arthritis?'

'No, I didn't,' said Lizzie. 'Oh, Amanda, I am sorry to hear it.'

'Didn't I tell you?' Amanda was puzzled; she could have sworn most of her friends were aware of it, but then Lizzie had had a lot to cope with lately, and taking someone else's problems on board might have been too much to expect. 'Anyway, it could be worse. It's not too painful some of the time, but I failed my BFT last time round and I'm being reviewed medically. I'm doing my promotion exams next week, but if I'm medically down graded I might as well sack any hopes I've got of going to Staff College. They won't accept me if I'm not fully fit.'

'But that's terrible,' said Edwina.

'That's life.'

'When did you find out that you'd got this?' asked Edwina.

'It started out in the Gulf. One lot of vaccinations laid me low and it was like having flu – you know, aching joints, feeling lousy, that sort of thing. After a week or so all the symptoms left except the aching joints. It's been like that ever since, although at the moment it's mostly just my fingers and toes which are affected.' She shrugged. 'Writing is not much fun, so Staff College may not be an option anyway. I'm all right when I can use a word processor but I'm not sure I shall be able to cope with two three-hour exams in one day. All that longhand may prove too much.'

'But surely the Army must make allowances,' said Lizzie. 'I mean, if it all started out in the Gulf, isn't there something they should be doing to help you?'

'There's no proof it's connected. It isn't as if it's some sort of definite injury that anyone can actually pinpoint as happening out there. Their argument will be that I was going to get arthritis anyway – people do. I think it's just something I'll have to accept.'

'Bollocks! If women can sue the MoD for getting thrown out for being pregnant, surely there must be some sort of redress for you,' said Edwina with feeling.

'Yes, but there's loads of women fighting the pregnancy case, and anyway, what have they got to lose? All those women are out of the Army. I'm still in and I think I'd like to stay in. It isn't going to do my career prospects any good if I make waves about something that may or may not be connected with my time in the Gulf. You know how the system is if they find that an individual is getting them a whole load of adverse publicity. No, I'm sorry, but I really can't face the sort of row it would cause.'

Edwina snorted and took another bite of cake.

'I think you're wrong about that. You should look for your own interests and stop being so loyal.'

'But I can't. It's built in now, isn't it?'

Edwina snorted again, but without conviction. If she was honest, she still felt hugely loyal to the Army herself.

'Anyway, enough about me,' said Amanda. 'How's the new boss, Lizzie?'

Lizzie looked uncomfortable. 'All right, I suppose. I just don't get on with him as well as I did Bob. We were a good team, but this bloke is different.'

'How different?' asked Edwina, always happy to dig the dirt.

'I don't know. He's very enthusiastic and bouncy but he's just a bit too good to be true.'

'Smarmy,' supplied Edwina.

'Not exactly. He's quite charming, I suppose. Always got a considerate word for all the office staff, makes the clerks laugh, gives generously to leaving presents . . .'

'Smarmy,' repeated Edwina.

'Well, perhaps,' Lizzie conceded. 'The bottom line is, I don't like him and I really don't know why. It's probably just a personality clash, but frankly, I'm rather hoping I might get posted in the near future. I've nearly done my two years here, so I should be hearing soon.'

'Well, you should be OK. Cathy Roberts hasn't got it in for you.'

'Not that again,' said Amanda with a grimace. 'Honestly, you don't know she screwed things up for you.'

'You're right, I don't know for certain, but all I do know is that since I got back from Ireland, everything I've volunteered for – courses, postings, adventurous training, you name it – I've had every single application refused and no explanation offered. There's something on my file up at postings which puts the mockers on anything I've tried to do, and I bet she put it there, whatever it is.'

'You're paranoid,' said Amanda.

'Who told you that?' retorted Edwina as quick as a flash. Amanda and Lizzie couldn't help but laugh. 'Maybe I am. And now that I'm leaving, no one will ever know for certain, but I'm sure I'm right.'

Lizzie excused herself from the room to go to the loo.

'Good,' said Amanda. 'I'm glad I've got you on your own for a second. How is Lizzie at the moment?'

'Fine. I haven't seen her really low, not since that time just before Christmas that I told you about.'

'You realise that next month it'll be the anniversary of Richard's death?'

'Shit, I'd forgotten.'

'I thought you might have done.' Amanda said this without malice, because Edwina had always been hopeless about birthdays and other significant dates. 'I wanted to remind you so you can make sure you're around.'

'No problems. I haven't much planned over the next few weeks, so I can easily make sure I'm here to provide a shoulder if needed.'

'Good. I was hoping I could rely on you.'

They heard Lizzie on the stairs to the basement.

'Right then,' said Amanda, gathering up her coat and handbag. 'Keep in touch. I'll give you a ring next week, Lizzie. And now I must get back to my own place and stick my head in some books. I'm not going to ruin my chances of passing these exams by not revising, even if I've got other odds stacked against me.'

Lizzie and Edwina watched Amanda drive away, then returned to the kitchen.

'Have you got any plans for that last piece of cake?' asked Edwina hopefully.

'No,' said Lizzie, smiling. 'Oh, by the way, a letter came for you after you'd gone on Saturday. It's over there on the dresser.'

Edwina stuffed the last of the cake in her mouth as she reached for the large manila envelope and looked at it curiously. She didn't recognise the handwriting.

'You won't find out who sent it by looking at it,' Lizzie offered.

'No.' Edwina picked at the corner of the self-sealing flap and pulled it open. She drew out the contents. 'Good grief,' she cried after a moment or two.

'What?'

'I've won a photography competition!'

'No! How? Why? Let me see.'

'Those badgers I staked out have just earned me two hundred and fifty pounds.'

'Congratulations.'

Edwina read the letter further. 'And the magazine which ran the competition will publish the pictures in next month's issue and – blah, blah, blah,' she skimmed further down the page, 'and they want some more stuff to accompany the article. Heavens.' She stared at Lizzie, still stunned by the news.

'I'm so pleased for you. You must be thrilled. You said you wanted to do something with photography once you leave the Army. Surely you won't have a problem getting a job now you can say you're award-winning.'

'Hardly that. It's only a tinpot competition, run by a poxy little magazine.'

'Don't knock it. *Photography World* does not rate as poxy – even I know that. It's bound to do you good.'

'We'll see.' But inside Edwina was delighted. She was good at photography, she knew it, but it was nice to get official recognition too.

Andover, May 1992

Amanda took the foil off the champagne carefully and popped the cork. Instantly golden bubbles frothed down the side of the bottle. She grabbed a glass off the table and held it to catch the foam so as little as possible would be wasted. It spilt over her thumb and she sucked it, giggling. 'I do love champagne.'

'So do I, but I think it's more that I love the occasions you drink it at,' said Bella.

Amanda poured a second glass. 'Anyway, here's to our careers.' She topped up both the glasses and then raised hers.

'Here's to *us* and our careers,' responded Bella. They chinked their glasses together and then both took a sip. Bella wrinkled her nose as the bubbles almost made her sneeze. 'I still can't believe it, though. I mean, both of us passing our promotion exams at staff level. Do you think we'll both get selected to go to Staff College?'

'I don't really mind. It's just great to know that I don't have to sit that wretched exam ever again and whatever happens – assuming my arthritis doesn't get worse – I'll get promoted.'

'I'd have been happy to pass with just enough marks to guarantee promotion, but this is a bonus, I must admit. I mean, even if we don't get selected, it can't do either of us any harm to have got the top grade of pass under our belts.'

'Now we've got to wait to hear who's got selected to go to Staff College.'

'I think they'll tell us in the summer some time.'

The two women sat at the table in Amanda's cosy kitchen and grinned at each other.

'Just fancy.' said Amanda.

'Isn't it great?' said Bella. Then they both giggled again. Amanda topped up their glasses.

'I ought to tell Lizzie and Edwina the good news.'

'Wait till tomorrow,' suggested Bella. 'How about just us knowing tonight?'

'Aren't you going to ring your folks and let them know?'

'Tomorrow, but they won't understand the significance of it. You know what they're like about the Forces.' Amanda did. Bella's father was a vet with a practice near Durham who had been excused National Service because he suffered from mild, but not disabling, curvature of the spine, while her mother was heavily involved in the local WI. Neither of them knew the first thing about the Army, apart from the fact that their daughter, for some unaccountable reason, had decided to join it. Mind you, as Bella had once told Amanda, her reasons for joining the Army wasn't the only thing they didn't know about her – they were also still unaware of her sexuality.

'But why don't you tell them?' Amanda had asked on more than one occasion.

'Because they simply wouldn't understand. They're very sweet but terribly innocent about all that sort of thing. It comes from living in a village in the middle of nowhere. There's no point in upsetting them needlessly.' It had made Amanda wonder about her own wisdom in telling her parents. Too late to go back now, though.

'OK,' Amanda said now. 'But I must tell Edwina and Lizzie tomorrow. They'll be hurt if I don't ring.'

Lizzie was delighted with Amanda's news.

'That's wonderful. I'm *so* pleased for you. It must be such a relief.'

'It's nice to have those exams under my belt. Poor you, you've got it all to look forward to.' Amanda, having joined with a degree to her name and a good bit older than many of her contemporaries, had been put in a fast career stream so that she would hit the rank of major at the right age to allow for further promotion.

'Yes, but being that much younger than you,' said Lizzie, 'I don't have to think about promotion exams for ages yet. Good grief, I'm still only an acting captain; I won't get substantive rank for another two years. Anything could happen between now and then.' Lizzie, having joined straight from school, had to do six years as a subaltern before being promoted to substantive captain, and another six years in that rank before further promotion would be considered. This didn't mean she couldn't be given the next rank up, and the pay that went with it, on a temporary basis, but this acting rank could always be removed if postings or situations changed.

'I don't feel grown-up enough to be a major,' said Amanda. 'Do you remember when we were at Sandhurst and majors seemed so incredibly senior and important?'

'And old,' added Lizzie, laughing.

'Precisely! And I love you too, sweetie.'

'By the way, Edwina's got a job.'

'Brilliant. Doing what?'

'She's been taken on by some local rag up towards Maidenhead – taking pictures of worthies giving cheques to charity and school fêtes and that sort of thing.'

'I can't see that giving Edwina the sort of adrenaline buzz she needs.'

'No. She's not thrilled by it but it's a start, she'll build up some contacts in the press and, of course, there's nothing to stop her trying to get a job on a bigger and better newspaper. She also said that if it doesn't work out she might go freelance. As she pointed out, she was trained to watch people and get pictures of their activities, so catching the rich and famous in compromising positions should be right up her street.'

'But how would she find them?'

'I haven't a clue, but no doubt she will if she needs to.'

'Has she said anything about moving out?'

'She's looking for a place at the moment but I must be honest and say that I'm not looking forward to her leaving. The house will seem very big again when she's gone. She wants to live closer to the job and near good road and rail links to London. She could conceivably commute from here, but it's not a brilliant journey. I've said I'll help her house-hunt.'

'I'd have thought that you've done enough for her. She's the one who owes you all those favours for looking after her.'

'You mustn't forget, Amanda, that it was mutual. She got me through some bad times too.'

Trust Lizzie only to see the good in Edwina, thought Amanda. But then again, perhaps she was being a bit hard in her judgement.

326

'Let me know if she wants a hand when she moves out. I don't mind helping.'

'I expect Ulysses will do it. But what about if I made it into a party? You could come and stay. I've got loads of space.'

'I don't know, I'll have to see.' Amanda couldn't bear the thought of giving up one of her weekends with Bella, and she could hardly suggest that her lover came along too. What would Lizzie say?

Staines, West London,
June 1992

'This is pleasant. I didn't think, after what you told me about the rent being so low, that it would be nearly as nice as this,' said Lizzie, looking round Edwina's flat. She was referring to the general proportions of the light rooms, as Edwina hadn't grown any tidier since she'd left the Army. In fact, if it was possible, she'd got worse. Everywhere clutter and chaos was strewn around; half-read books lay open, face down, on the table, dirty clothes were piled untidily by the kitchen door, there were several dirty coffee cups on the windowsill and everywhere were bits of photographic equipment – lenses, light metres, tripods, monopods, cameras, films and contact prints.

'Have a seat,' offered Edwina. Lizzie cast around for somewhere to sit which didn't involve disturbing Edwina's kit. 'Oh, just push some stuff on to the floor,' said Edwina, realising Lizzie's problem. Lizzie was carefully picking up a pile of glossy periodicals, ready to relocate them somewhere, when she was distracted by Edwina sharing her ideas for the place with her.

'Look, that wall is perfect for shelves, and I'm going to get a cheap sofa-bed for visitors to kip down on, and I'm going to fix some pinboards on these walls,' she told Lizzie, who was still clutching the magazines, 'which should keep me a bit organised. And this,' she threw open the door of a large walk-in cupboard, 'is my dark room.'

'That's great,' enthused Lizzie, peering through the door into the gloom of the windowless cubicle.

'It's what convinced me this was the flat to have.'

Lizzie replaced the journals on the chair and turned her attention to the view from the sitting-room window. She could see across the A30 to a high grassy bank that surrounded one of the main reservoirs for London. Some sheep grazed contentedly on the steep slope, making this suburb seem unexpectedly rural. She became aware of a high-pitched whining roar that grew steadily and rapidly in volume as an approaching aircraft drowned the sound of the stream of traffic on the nearby road. The noise increased until conversation became impossible. The Boeing 757 thundered overhead, the noise so tremendous that Lizzie could feel the floor vibrating under her feet. Out of the window, she could see the sheep munching on, oblivious to the disturbance – this was obviously a regular occurrence. Edwina waited until the din died away again.

'And that explains why the rent is so low,' she said.

'How do people cope with such a racket? It's appalling. I thought that plane was going to take the roof off,' said Lizzie horrified.

'That was nothing,' said Edwina. 'Try imagining what it's like when a fully laden jumbo takes off headed for Australia. With four hundred-odd passengers and fuelled to the brim, you really do need ear defenders.'

'But how do you endure it?'

'Well, they don't fly at night, and when the windows are shut the double-glazing keeps out most of the noise. Honestly.'

Lizzie didn't look convinced. 'I'll take your word for it. Personally I think you have to be some sort of nut to want to live in a place where passing pilots can see what you're wearing in bed.'

'Perhaps it turns me on,' said Edwina with a lascivious leer. Lizzie didn't know if she was referring to the planes or the pilots, but decided that, knowing Edwina as she did, it was probably better not to ask. 'Coffee?' Lizzie nodded and Edwina went into the kitchen, kicking the washing pile towards the washing machine as she went. She filled the kettle and bundled the grubby clothes into the machine. Without them cluttering up the floor, the flat instantly looked much tidier.

Another aircraft thundered towards them, drowning out all conversation again. Lizzie felt that if she lived here she would suffer from a permanent migraine. God, how could Edwina stand this? The kettle boiled and Edwina, speech impossible with the overhead racket, held up the milk bottle with an enquiring look; Lizzie sometimes preferred her coffee black. Lizzie nodded to indicate that, yes, this morning she would like white. As they carried their mugs into the sitting room, the sound diminished to an earth-shaking rumble.

'So what brings you to this neck of the woods?' asked Edwina.

'I thought I should tell you in person; I'm posted.'

'You sound pleased. Is it somewhere nice?'

'Well, apart from being delighted to get away from Major Smarmy, I think it's a job I'm going to like – I'm being sent to PR Branch, up at the MoD.'

'Cor! You must be blue-eyed or what?'

'You always put things so prettily,' said Lizzie with a laugh.

'Well, you know what I mean.' Edwina was impressed, because whoever was in that job had to be guaranteed to present the Army in the best possible light at all times – and they wouldn't trust just any one with that sort of responsibility.

'I do know what you mean.' Lizzie was well aware that it was a real feather in her cap to get this job, but she didn't want to seem too smug about it. 'Anyway, I'm really looking forward to it. I'm hoping it might involve a certain amount of travel, to say nothing about hobnobbing with all those media types.'

'What? Newspaper reporters? You must be joking.'

'And TV presenters. I've seen the ones who report on defence and Northern Ireland, and a couple of them are quite dishy.'

Dishy, my arse, Edwina thought. But she was too pleased at the notion that Lizzie was at last beginning to look at men again to say this out loud.

'So, will you commute every day from Aldershot?'

'That's what I've got to decide. It's perfectly feasible, and I expect there are people who work up in London who commute from further afield, but I can't say that I fancy the prospect in winter. It'll mean leaving and returning home in the dark, and to an empty house. Most of my friends have now moved away from the area and I'm sure there'll be occasions when I'll be required to work till all hours. I'm told that I can have lodging allowance, so what I may do is find a flat for during the week and live back home at weekends.'

'Cool,' said Edwina.

'Actually, I thought I might find someone to share with. I don't like living on my own that much.'

'If I was working in town I'd be happy to oblige – if you could stand the idea, of course.'

'I'd be more than delighted, but I appreciate it's a non-starter.'

'Still, with all these hunky reporters that you're going to be rubbing shoulders with, perhaps you could get me a job on a national paper and then I'll be able to do the honours as a flatmate.'

Lizzie snorted. 'Steady on. I haven't even seen my office yet. How about letting me get settled before I have to start pulling strings?'

Lizzie was spared Edwina's rude retort as the eleven o'clock shuttle to Belfast drowned her comments.

In the peace that followed, and before the next jet could interrupt them, Edwina asked, 'When are you posted?'

'Some time at the end of September – or rather, that's the plan at the moment. You know what these things are like, especially if you're single.' They both knew only too well. Married officers with families to shift, wives to placate, furniture to store and schools to organise tended to get plenty of notice about impending moves and firm posting orders. Single officers could be mucked around much more easily, and often were. 'Still, I don't think there's much doubt about me going to work in PR; it's just the date that may be a little uncertain at this stage. But if they want to bring it forward I'll be more than happy. The sooner I get away from old Smarmy the better.'

'Giving you hassle, is he?'

'I don't know what it is; he's never touched me, he doesn't say anything out of order, but he's always that bit too close to me. What is the ghastly phrase the Yanks have for it – invading one's personal space?' Edwina nodded. 'Well, he does that, and I honestly can't wait to get away from him.'

'You could always punch him in the balls,' said Edwina. 'That'd make him keep his distance.'

Lizzie shook her head, bubbling with laughter. 'It's certainly a solution that would suit you. I think I'd better go for something less hands-on, so to speak.'

'Come on. Let's go out to lunch so we can talk without being interrupted by bloody jumbos.'

'My treat,' offered Lizzie.

'We'll see.'

On Monday Edwina got back into work from an assignment to photograph a vandalised school and found three Post-it stickers on her desk demanding that she phone Lizzie urgently. What the hell could be the matter? Not more bad news, surely? Brushing aside a request to go and see the editor, Edwina picked up the phone and dialled Lizzie's number.

'Hi, it's me,' she said, confident that her voice would be recognised.

'Edwina. At last! Where have you been? Don't you start work at the same time as the rest of the world?'

'I've been out on a story.' Edwina resented the implied criticism that she had been off skiving.

'I'm sorry. Of course you have. I had to phone you to tell you the Staff College selections have been made and Amanda's not on it.'

'Oh, no. Poor old Amanda. She'll be really fed up about that. Have you spoken to her about it yet?'

'I tried to ring her but I keep getting the engaged tone. Either everyone she knows is ringing up to sympathise or she's taken the phone off the hook so they can't.'

'Probably the latter. It's what I'd do.'

'Who *is* on the list?'

'Have you got a fax? I'll send you a copy.'

'Great. Have you got a pen?

A couple of minutes later the fax by the editor's office began to chunter. Edwina read the names to herself as the list emerged.

'Not Charlie Meek, surely?' muttered Edwina under her breath. 'He's as thick as shit.' Then. 'Good God, Archie MacDonald, he'll set the place alight. Oh, look! William Davies – Lizzie will be pleased about that. Well, well, well, Bella de Fresne.'

'What's this you're so riveted by?' asked Gwen, one of the more experienced reporters on the paper. 'I didn't know snappers could read.'

Edwina ignored the insult. Anyway, she quite liked Gwen. 'Just personal stuff,' she replied evasively. She had kept her Army past very quiet and didn't want Gwen – or any other reporter, for that matter – to know about it. All that most of the staff on the paper knew was that she could take good, clear pictures to illustrate the stories, and that was all that was important.

Gwen peered over Edwina's shoulder. 'This looks like it's all about the military.'

'So?'

'So what do you want to know about this lot for?'

'I've got a friend in the Army.' Christ, why was this woman so nosy? The fact that it was Gwen's job to be nosy didn't cross Edwina's mind; it just annoyed her that this inquisitiveness was being directed her way.

332

'What? An officer?' Given Edwina's weird dress sense and her untidiness, Gwen thought it unlikely that she mingled with the officer classes.

'Yes. Is it a big deal?'

Gwen shrugged. Perhaps, perhaps not. It was the sort of information to squirrel away, as it might prove useful in the future. She returned to her desk.

Edwina carried on scanning the list. 'Cathy effing Roberts.' She sighed deeply. How bloody unjust that she'd been picked and not Amanda. Amanda was twice the officer that Cathy would ever be. She returned to her desk and dialled Lizzie's number again.

'How could they have done that?' she shrieked in indignation and without preamble.

'Let me guess. You're talking about Cathy.'

'Of course I am,' spluttered Edwina. 'It's diabolical.'

'Yes, but she did pass the exam.'

'That's got nothing to do with it . . .'

Lizzie laughed at Edwina's unreasonableness. 'It's got *everything* to do with it. Anyway, why should you care?'

'Because if she hadn't been selected, maybe Amanda might have been.'

'I don't think so. She's been medically downgraded, remember.'

'Huh.' Edwina's loyalty to her friends could find no excuse for Cathy being selected in favour of Amanda.

Lizzie calmed her down. 'Still, it's good Bella's going, isn't it? That'll probably cheer Amanda up. They're good friends, aren't they?'

'You could say that,' said Edwina, wondering for the umpteenth time why Lizzie hadn't twigged what the real situation was, especially as Edwina had once pointed it out to her. Just then she caught sight of the editor leaving his office and heading her way. He looked angry, and Edwina remembered guiltily that she'd been told to go and see him ten minutes earlier at least. 'Got to go, call you later,' she said and replaced the receiver, putting thoughts of Staff College and Amanda out of her mind.

The following weekend Ulysses was working. He had some extremely lucrative clients who could only manage to do their fitness training on Saturdays and Sundays, but as Ulysses said, who was he to turn down forty-five pounds an hour? Edwina grumbled, complained that her sex life was virtually nonexistent, and went over to Aldershot to see if Lizzie fancied some company and a girls' night out to go and see a flick.

'Why not?' said Lizzie, who had been contemplating catching up on the ironing and tidying out a couple of cupboards.

'There's *Basic Instinct* or *Howards End*.'

'I've heard about *Basic Instinct* and I'm not going.'

'Spoilsport,' said Edwina, wishing she hadn't offered Lizzie the choice.

'Sorry,' said Lizzie, who wasn't.

'Have you managed to get hold of Amanda yet?'

'Apparently she's taken some leave, gone away for a week. I'll try again then. Fancy a coffee?'

'Please.'

As Lizzie busied herself with kettle and mugs she said, 'I wonder if Bella will find some nice unattached hunks for her and Amanda when she's on the course.'

'I don't think either of them is the marrying kind.'

'You mean like you and Ulysses?'

'You could put it like that.' Edwina suppressed a smile.

'You know, I've never worked out why you two don't make it legal. It's obvious you're made for each other.'

'Piss off,' said Edwina cheerfully. 'Look, I don't mind being on the shelf, I rather like it. I just want to get taken off and given a good dusting on a regular basis.'

Lizzie sipped her coffee. She could fancy being *dusted*, as Edwina had euphemistically put it, but there wasn't much chance of that at the moment. The only man she saw regularly was Major Smarmy, and he would probably jump at the chance, but then he wasn't going to be offered it. Ugh, she thought.

'What about Amanda, do you think she gets dusted? I've always thought that she's so pretty it's odd she never seems to have a regular boyfriend.'

'She's always been busy concentrating on her career. I don't suppose she's had much time for relationships.' Edwina congratulated herself on the evasiveness of her answer.

'It's a crying shame she's ill and it's spoilt things for her.'

'But she can still get promoted, and she may be able to stay in. The arthritis doesn't affect her brain, when all is said and done.

She'll just not get the chance of an overseas posting now she's been downgraded medically.'

'Not that there are many of those left now.'

'Only Hong Kong and Cyprus, and not even Hong Kong in a few years.'

Edwina sipped her coffee and thought about trying to tell Lizzie the truth again about Amanda. The last time had caused an awful row, but surely Lizzie was a lot less naïve now. She must have come across some evidence of lesbians in the Army. But then again, perhaps she hadn't. Lizzie had never been posted to a mainly female unit, so maybe she still thought that everyone in the world was as heterosexual as she was. No, Edwina decided, if Lizzie couldn't work out the obvious answer for herself, then it was probably best that she didn't tell her.

Andover, March 1993

'So come on, tell me what it's like. I'm longing to hear all about it,' said Amanda as she served up curry and rice out of foil containers which Bella had collected from the local takeaway on her way to Amanda's cottage.

'I will, I will. Just make with the food, will you, I'm starving.' The delicious smell of chicken tikka masala wafted up into Bella's nostrils and her stomach rumbled loudly.

'There's a bottle of wine in the fridge. Do the honours with it, would you?' said Amanda, handing her the corkscrew. While Bella dealt with that, Amanda chopped up some tomatoes and cucumber and sprinkled some raisins on to the aromatic chicken mixture. 'Right, tuck in,' she encouraged as the cork came out of the bottle with a satisfactory squeak and a pop. Bella glugged the golden Chardonnay into two elegant glasses and sat down. The candles on the table flickered and danced for a second, and then steadied.

'Yum,' Bella said appreciatively as she contemplated the plate of food in front of her. She took a large forkful and chewed. 'Mmm, heaven. God, I needed this. I missed lunch today because I had so much to do. It's crazy, the workload is appalling.'

Amanda thought that even in the softly flattering candlelight Bella looked pretty tired.

'Is it the same for everyone? It's not just because you're not used to the tactical stuff?'

'Pretty much so. It's things like map-marking and learning mountains of information by heart that take the time. I know we did a lot of that sort of stuff on the Junior Staff Course, but honestly, nothing like on the scale we have to do it now. Everyone is complaining about burning the midnight oil.'

'Poor you.' Amanda, her arthritis worse than usual because of recent damp weather, felt unexpectedly glad that she wasn't being put through this particular mill. She'd been jealous to begin with that she hadn't been selected, but she'd got over that ages ago. She acknowledged now that she wouldn't have been able to cope with what Bella was going through, as she found it increasingly difficult to handle late nights and early starts. 'Tell me, what are the people on the course like?'

'You wouldn't believe some of them. When we were doing the technical bit at Shrivenham, they were mostly pretty quiet.' Bella and the other less scientifically inclined officers had just spent a couple of months at the Royal Military College of Science, being brought up to speed on physics, chemistry, maths and the like so that they could appreciate better the capabilities and limitations of some of the equipment to be found in the modern British Army. 'I think it was because most of them found the maths and science pretty hard and didn't want to make fools of themselves. In fact, some of them seemed to think it was a point in their favour that they were technical idiots. You know – only officers in corps do hands-on stuff with electronics and mechanics; the cavalry and infantry are too busy being proper officers and fighting wars. But now that it's tactics and strategy and all that sort of stuff, well ... Thrusting or what? It doesn't matter what the subject is, what the lecture is about, they just *have* to ask a question at the end. They are so keen to be noticed by the DS it's embarrassing.' Bella scooped up another forkful of curry. 'Then there are the foreigners. I didn't realise so many on the course are overseas students; they make up a third of the total number.'

'I expect we charge their governments a huge amount for the privilege of teaching them.'

'Maybe. There's tremendous rivalry between some of them. The Pakistanis can't stand it if an Indian asks a question or has the last word and vice versa, as for the Germans and the French ... Don't even think of the words *entente cordiale* because they certainly don't apply.'

'It sounds quite fascinating.'

Bella nodded, her mouth full of food.

'What about the building? I've only ever seen it from the outside.'

'Gorgeous. Wonderful. So full of history.' Bella waved her fork around expansively to emphasise her enthusiasm for it.

'I'd like to see it.'

'It'd be worth a visit, you'd enjoy it.'

'Perhaps I could drive up and collect you next weekend. You could give me a guided tour.'

'Why not? By Friday evening most of the livers-in have bugged out, off to see their girlfriends or visit relations, so we'll probably have the place to ourselves, apart from a couple of the foreign officers with nowhere else to go. If anyone asks I can always say you're a cousin or something.'

'Kissing cousin?' enquired Amanda mischievously.

Amanda arrived just after six the following Friday. She flashed her ID card at the cadets on guard at the entrance to the Royal Military Academy, which shared the grounds with the Staff College. She was saluted smartly and the barrier was raised to allow her to pass. As she drove through the gates she thought back over the years to when she'd first made this journey. On that day she'd been awed by the apparent professionalism of the cadets on the gate and wondered how long it would be before she could hope to emulate their turnout and snappy salutes. She'd certainly never expected to end up as a soldier with combat experience of a desert campaign, nor to be senior enough to visit a friend and peer at Staff College. It was nearly six years since she'd first driven through these gates, keen and ambitious, and yet it seemed like only a few months. She swung the car down the right turn that led to the car park for the College. It was almost empty, which confirmed what Bella had said about most single officers going away to friends or girlfriends at the weekends. And if there were a few foreign officers mooching around? They wouldn't know or care who Amanda was.

Bella had been looking out for her and ran to greet her as she got out of the car.

'We'll go in the back way,' she said. 'No one uses the front door much.' The two women walked past some lecture halls and classrooms into the back of the elegant creamy-coloured building, and after passing along a corridor they entered the huge, light entrance hall with its wonderful chequered marble floor. High above their heads, at the top of the sweeping staircase, was a massive skylight. Around them were paintings of past great battles, generals and field marshals; glass cases containing uniforms and medals, swords and lances; and honour boards with the names of past prize-winners and Directing Staff, the great and the good. The décor was designed to encourage the present-day students to follow in the tradition of hard work and excellence.

They wandered into a massive library near the foot of the stairs and stood there, entranced by the wonderful atmosphere of the place.

'Where's the Mills and Boon section?' Amanda whispered impishly.

'I dare you to ask,' replied Bella. 'Come on, I'll show you what else they've got to offer.'

They left the library and crossed the corridor to another magnificent room. This one, placed at the front of the building, had long windows that looked out on to the tennis courts, where two keen women, wrapped in tracksuits, were playing despite the poor light and the chilly weather. On one wall were all the past copies of the Army list, dating back to the year dot.

'These go so far back we can probably look up Julius Caesar and Alexander the Great,' said Bella, fingering the spines of the thick red books. High up were wooden panels with the names of previous notable attendees of the College written in gold paint. One of the more prominent of the names was that of Bernard Montgomery, then a lieutenant colonel.

'I wonder if anyone here at the same time as him guessed what he'd go on to do,' said Amanda, pointing to it.

'I expect so. Apparently there's already a book running on this course as to which officers are going to get promoted first to lieutenant colonel. A couple of them do seem to be noticeably more talented than the rest of us. It's obvious even at this early stage. It shouldn't surprise you to know that one of them is a Green Jacket, of course.'

'And the other is in the Guards?'

'Amazingly not. He's a Gunner, much to the consternation of the Sappers.' Bella didn't have to elaborate on the well-known and deadly rivalry between the Royal Engineers and the Royal Artillery. Both regiments had as their motto the Latin word *'Ubique'* which, depending on your allegiance, either meant 'omnipresent' or 'all over the place'.

Bella went across to the window to look out at the view. 'I'm still having to pinch myself to believe I'm really here,' she said.

'I'm sure you must,' said Amanda joining her. 'I mean, doesn't all this . . .' She waved her arm vaguely to indicate the pictures, the luxuriously deep library armchairs and the general air of antique opulence, so different from the usual run-of-the-mill standard of Army furnishing and interior design. 'Doesn't it all give you a sense of history and tradition? And isn't it exciting being a part of it?'

'It is. I really do feel very privileged. It's a crying shame you're not here too.'

'It's probably for the best. Do you really think we could have kept up the pretence, been totally discreet for nearly a year? Get real.' Amanda spoke with weary fatalism.

'We managed at Guildford.'

'That was different somehow. It was an all-female environment. We were expected to be very friendly with each other, because there was bugger-all as an alternative.'

'You mean that with all these red-blooded males around it would be harder to manage?'

'Even under the guise of female solidarity we'd get found out.'

Bella sighed. 'You're probably right.'

They gazed at each other and shrugged resignedly.

After a short pause Amanda said, 'How's about blowing caution to the winds and letting me see some more of the historic pile?'

'You do mean the building, not the commandant's haemor-rhoids?'

Amanda sniggered and nodded.

'OK, then, I'll show you the rest of the ground floor, then you can see my room. I don't suppose we'll run into anyone who'll be the least bit interested in who you are.'

The two women went out of the room and off down the long corridor which led towards the bar. As they left, Cathy Roberts uncurled herself from one of the deep armchairs at the far end of the room and gazed after them.

'Well, well, well,' she said thoughtfully. She was glad she'd decided to wait until Saturday to travel.

As they approached the bar they could hear the muted hubbub of a dozen or so voices.

'Should we go back?' said Amanda, worried about being seen overtly with Bella.

'Don't worry. It's only some of the blokes. You're a friend going my way and kindly giving me a lift. We're going to have a quick drink before we hit the road. The men share cars and no one suspects them of anything. Relax.'

'OK, you're right, of course.'

In the bar Bella and Amanda found a selection of foreign officers – a Ghanaian, a Jamaican and a Kuwaiti – and half a dozen married British officers who were delaying their return home in the hope of missing the rigours of nursery tea and infant bathtime.

'Hi,' said Bella. 'This is a friend of mine, Amanda.'

'Hello,' said a couple of the men, eyeing up the tall blonde appreciatively.

'What's a nice girl like you doing in a place like this?' asked one, somewhat predictably.

'She's giving me a lift to a party,' answered Bella smoothly. 'She just dropped in to see why everyone makes such a fuss about this place.'

The officers made a space so the girls could get to the bar, and then carried on with their conversation, which seemed to be an explanation of the finer points of the Five Nations rugby championship for the benefit of the overseas students.

Bella ordered a tonic water for Amanda and an orange juice for herself. The barman presented her with the chit to sign just as Cathy walked in. Amanda felt her stomach lurch. God, how could they have been so stupid as to risk being seen together?

'Bugger,' murmured Bella under her breath. 'I could have sworn I heard her say she was going away.' Then aloud and confidently to Cathy, 'My chit is still open. Can I buy you a drink?' Amanda admired her coolness.

'No thanks, Bella. Hello, Amanda. I haven't seen you since commissioning. How have you been getting on?'

'Oh, OK.' Amanda stumbled over the words and felt her face burning. She prayed Cathy wouldn't notice.

'How's the career?' asked Cathy.

'Did you know that Amanda was out in the Gulf, attached to a REME unit?' Bella jumped in, aware that Amanda wasn't up to a coherent answer.

'No, I didn't. We could probably do with some input from you on this course. These men think they know it all. Don't you, boys?' Cathy said louder, to attract their attention. There was a faint mumbling from the men as they acknowledged that they'd been spoken to, but beyond that they made no effort to agree or refute the point. Cathy shrugged. 'Men! Who needs them?' She smiled at the two women.

'They have their uses,' said Amanda noncommittally, mistrusting the smile and trying not to sound as wary of the comment as she felt.

'Still, it must have been great having all those men to yourself in the desert.'

Amanda's shock at running into Cathy now turned to annoyance. She'd had a basinful of this sort of snide remark from the wives when the unit had got back to Germany and had long since got bored with countering it, but she was surprised to hear it from Cathy, a fellow female officer.

'It wasn't really like that,' she replied evenly, keeping her temper well in check. 'For a start I was mostly very busy; secondly, nearly all the men I worked with were married or had steady girlfriends; and thirdly, there may be a time and a place for everything but I would suggest that the desert, in the middle of a war, is neither if you are looking for a casual screw.'

One of the men sniggered quietly and Cathy looked uncomfortable. There were rumours circulating already about her freedom with her favours. She shrugged and tilted her chin defiantly. 'Oh, I don't know. Where there's a will there's a way, as they say.' She stared at Amanda and Bella then added, quite deliberately, 'Or perhaps there wasn't in your case.' The implication seemed unmistakable, and coupled with Cathy's previous comments it suddenly seemed apparent that she knew something.

Amanda suddenly felt her heart pound with fear at the thought that after all these years she and Bella had somehow been rumbled, but she kept her gaze steadily on Cathy's face and prayed that Bella had the guts to do the same. Any exchange of looks between them might confirm to Cathy that her suspicions were correct. Amanda knew she had to bluff this out, and try to convince Cathy that she didn't understand what she was getting at.

Cathy dropped her gaze first and Amanda drained her tonic. 'Right then,' she said brightly. 'I think we'd better get your kit and get going, Bella. We don't want to be late, do we?'

Bella took the hint and put her empty glass on the bar. ''Bye, everyone. See you on Monday.' She led the way out of the bar.

342

In silence, neither girl daring to discuss what had just happened until they reached Bella's room, they climbed the stairs, past the offices where the administration of the course took place, to the top floor which housed some of the student bedrooms. Bella opened the door to reveal a large, well-proportioned room with a big sash window. Still outwardly calm, they both entered and Bella carefully shut the door behind them.

Amanda crossed the room to look at the view while she collected her thoughts and Bella got her overnight things together. She leaned on the windowsill and looked across the tennis courts and lawns towards the lakes, the rhododendrons and the stands of still bare trees that comprised the grounds of the Staff College and the Royal Military Academy. 'Wow!' she whispered to herself as her gaze travelled from the impressive guardroom near the A30 and a glimpse of the town of Camberley beyond, westwards towards the senior officers' houses standing like a row of solid Georgian dolls' houses, then across the lakes towards the colleges of Sandhurst. Reluctantly she tore herself away from the spectacular view and turned to face Bella.

'So what do you think? Has Cathy guessed something, or was that little charade downstairs just a figment of my guilty conscience?'

'I don't know, but I certainly thought the same as you. How can she have, though? I mean, she barely knows me and I certainly haven't discussed my private life with her.' Bella threw a bag of washing things on top of the few clothes in her case and snapped the locks shut.

'Is that everything?' said Amanda hopefully, impatient to get away.

'Good God, no. There's my homework yet.' Bella began to sort through a pile of books and papers, muttering to herself as she did so. 'That can wait, I'd better do this. This needs learning.' She stuffed a sheaf of papers into a briefcase and pushed a large pile of books and military manuals into a holdall. On top of them she placed a number of maps of south-east England.

'Surely that isn't all for this weekend?' said Amanda, horrified.

'It sure is.'

'But it'll take hours to do!'

'I expect so. I'm afraid if you had any plans for a wild social life this weekend you'd better put them on hold.'

'Shit. Perhaps I can help.'

'If you can, you're welcome to.'

Amanda took the briefcase and the overnight bag while Bella lugged the holdall down the stairs. Amanda was dreading running into Cathy again, but they didn't see a soul as they slipped out to the car park. Amanda drove to the supermarket by the A30 where she bought bread, fruit, smoked salmon, salad, fresh pasta and wine. She decided that neither she nor Bella would be able to spare the time to cook an elaborate meal – not if they were going to have any time that weekend which was not to be devoted to military matters.

The shopping done, Amanda drove to the next junction on to the M3, and headed westwards.

'Could she have overheard what we said to each other in the anteroom? You know, about not getting found out at Guildford?' said Amanda, still preoccupied with Cathy's comments.

'But it was empty, wasn't it? I mean, I certainly didn't see her in there.'

'Yes, but we weren't exactly searching for anyone, were we? She may have been behind the curtains, or anywhere.'

'Well, it's a lesson certainly: no more such discussions outside the privacy of your cottage or my room. Let's forget it, shall we? We may well be mistaken, and regardless of that, what's done is done. Anyway, she hasn't a shred of proof, so we can always deny everything.' Despite Bella's brave words both women were worried, but they also knew that talking about it wouldn't make the problem go away.

As the car bombed along at a steady seventy-five, Bella firmly changed the subject and gave Amanda a detailed rundown of the course. Despite the awful nagging worry Amanda tried to seem interested, and as Bella told her more and more about the course, her anxieties, for the moment, receded. It seemed that Bella had been warned, like all the others, that everyone attending the Staff College would find the going phenomenally hard, but it hadn't prepared her for the crushing load that had been heaped upon them every day since they'd arrived. She tried to sound upbeat about it but it was obvious that working until well past midnight, sometimes later, every night was getting her down.

'And it isn't just that. The standard of presentation of our work matters almost as much as the content; the layout of the briefs and appreciations has to be exactly as per the Manual of Service

Writing, and spellings and punctuation have to be checked and double-checked before we submit them for correction by the Directing Staff.'

Amanda made sympathetic clucking noises. 'But surely they can't be that hard on you. Anyway, your English is excellent.'

'You must be joking. Everything is returned covered in red ink, and it's the same for everyone. Well, apart from a couple of people, but there's a rumour that they've got copies of all the pinks from the last course.'

Amanda remembered from her days at Sandhurst that a 'pink' was the textbook answer handed out by the DS along with corrected written work, so called because it was always printed on pink paper.

'That's a bit unfair, isn't it?'

'Only if you haven't got them yourself. The DS try to catch them out by changing some of the details in the exercises but the basic stuff mainly stays the same. I keep telling myself that I'm probably learning more from the course than they are, but when there's a lot of work to be done, it's a depressing thought that some people can take short cuts.'

On top of all the written work, Bella told Amanda that they were expected to learn the exact make-up, in terms of vehicles and personnel, of all the different varieties of units in a division or a brigade. They had to be able to calculate the time it would take to move convoys from one part of a fictional battlefield to another and to make allowances in their mathematics if, for example, the bridge they were using to cross an obstacle should be attacked by the enemy. And in their spare time they had to accurately mark the maps they'd been issued with military map symbols in preparation for the next exercise in tactics.

'Which is why I've brought all mine with me this weekend, because after your time in the Gulf, map-marking is probably second nature to you.'

'It certainly is and I'll be happy to do it.'

'Since I haven't been posted outside south-east England I find it an uphill struggle to remember all the different logos which designate the positions of, say, a unit of amphibious engineers or armoured engineers. I know they're supposed to be logical but I've just got a mental blank about some of them.'

'How do the men treat you?' asked Amanda as she turned off the motorway.

'Oh, it's the standard split. There's a gang of complete chauvinists who think that women shouldn't be allowed shoes, let alone out of the kitchen. There's another group who are great, treat us as equals and accept that women in the Army are here to stay. And then there's the third sort, who think all Army women are either bikes or dykes.'

Amanda began to giggle.

'Have I said something funny?' said Bella, not understanding the joke.

Amanda's giggles turned into laughter, tears began to roll down her face and she slowed the car and pulled into a lay-by. The car came to a standstill and Amanda threw her head back and roared. Her laughter was so infectious that Bella began to join in, although she still didn't get the joke. Finally Amanda got herself under control again and said weakly, 'You don't think that they may have a point?'

'Uh?'

'Well, Cathy's hardly Snow White, is she, if Edwina is to be believed. And as for you ...' Laughter overtook her again. 'If you and Cathy area representative sample ...' but she couldn't end the sentence. Beside her Bella was shaking with paroxysms of mirth as she too saw the funny side of what she'd said.

Bella kept Amanda abreast of her progress at Staff College with nightly phone calls. After the initial shock tactics of giving all the students more to cope with than was tolerable, things began to ease off. It was several weeks later that Bella, incandescent with rage, phoned Amanda with a new complaint.

'You'll never believe what some stupid man said to me today.'

'Amaze me,' said Amanda in a tone that implied she couldn't be amazed by anything that a man said.

'He said that I was only doing well because they're making allowances for my gender.'

'That's bollocks and you know it,' Amanda countered robustly. 'How is Cathy doing, for example?'

'I think she's finding it heavy going.'

'Well then, doesn't that prove that it's your ability which is allowing you to do well?'

'Yes, but I can hardly use that argument, can I? It sounds bitchy.'

346

'True. But hang it, would anybody care? How is dear Cathy anyway? Has she said anything else?'

'No, but there hasn't been much opportunity really. We're in different syndicates for the classroom work and the rest of the time I try and keep out of her way as much as possible because I think it's safer. Actually, there's a rumour that she's swapping extra coaching sessions with some of the brighter men – and some of them are married, apparently – in return for sexual favours.'

'Just as well you're not having to resort to that, eh?'

Bella giggled. 'There's another reason for this call. It's not just so I can beat my gums about some man here. I'm not going to be able to get over to your place this weekend or the next. There's a number of social do's I've been invited to, not to mention a dinner night, and I really can't get out of them. The social side here is quite important and I've been naughty about avoiding it so far.'

'Oh, OK.' Amanda tried to hide her disappointment, as she knew that Bella truly was duty-bound to go to the formal functions. All the same, she didn't relish the prospect of two weekends on her own.

The Ministry of Defence, London, April 1993

Lizzie punched the key code on her office door and let herself in. She switched on the strip-lights, which flickered momentarily before steadying into flat, white, cheerless light. 'Another day, another dollar,' she said to herself as she crossed the small, ill-proportioned office to her desk by the window, eased the chair back and slipped on to it. Her desk faced another; pushed together to fit across the narrow width of the room, leaving little space to manoeuvre into or out of the swivel chair tucked behind it. The grimy, voluminous net curtain that hung across the window had encroached on to her desk and she pushed it off, irritatedly, then switched on the computer terminal in front of her, which bleeped, chuntered and clicked. While she waited for the computer to finish sorting itself out she looked out of the window at the grim courtyard.

Lizzie's office was on the ground floor of the MoD, and above her were a further eight storeys, so neither sunlight nor fresh air filtered into the gloomy depths of the yard outside the window. She had to admit that this was probably the dreariest office she'd ever occupied. Even the flourishing geranium she'd brought in from home to try and cheer things up was looking distinctly droopy. Perhaps she'd better return it to where it had been happier, because it would only be good for compost if it stayed much longer in this environment. Lizzie wondered if she was in danger of becoming wilted and sad like the plant. So much for the glamour job that all her friends had predicted she was taking on when she'd arrived here six months previously.

The computer bleeped at her to indicate it was ready and waiting, and Lizzie keyed in her password and called up the database of fixtures for the next few days. She scanned the list of military exercises, public-relations events, sports matches, equipment displays and the like, to check if there was anything which might generate more than cursory media interest or which might require the involvement of her superiors, of whom there were several – Lizzie had discovered quickly after her arrival at the MoD that grade-three staff officers like herself were so lowly they had no significance at all in the great scheme of Whitehall and politics. Finding that there were no lurking banana skins in the next few days' agenda, Lizzie turned to her in-tray, to see what delights lay in store for her there. She leafed through the faxes and signals that had come in overnight and saw that it was all routine things, mostly stuff to be fed into the various databases which were her responsibility. But that was no surprise, because nearly everything she dealt with was routine. So much for her hopes she'd be rubbing shoulders with media personalities. Sometimes she felt she was no more than a glorified clerk, which was rather depressing after all the responsibilities of her last job.

Lizzie glanced at her watch and saw that there was at least another half-hour before her immediate superior, Major Bruce Villiers, would put in an appearance. That's something to be grateful for, she thought. For if her last boss had given her the creeps, this one was completely repugnant. It worried her that she seemed to have a problem with male colleagues, but being Lizzie she looked for the flaw in herself. No one else she knew had problems with workplace relationships. Before Richard's death she had always got on well with her male colleagues, so she assumed that this problem had more to do with her current circumstances than the personalities she shared the office with. To compensate for what she felt was her irrational dislike of Major Villiers, she tried hard to be pleasant. For, like her last boss, Charles Ward – alias Major Smarmy – Bruce Villiers did nothing which she could possibly construe as improper behaviour.

She remembered their first meeting. She'd been waiting at the reception at the main entrance, the North Door of the Ministry of Defence, wondering what her office would be like, excited about her new post and nervous that she wouldn't manage the job as well as her predecessor. She couldn't go through the main doors to find out for herself because she wasn't yet in possession of a pass. She had been told that the first day of her handover period would largely be spent sorting out that kind of personal admin.

'Captain Airdrie-Stow?' asked a man's voice.

Lizzie spun round. 'Yes. And it's Lizzie, please.'

'Lizzie it is. I'm Bruce Villiers.' He held out his hand and Lizzie shook it. 'Come on then. Let's get you signed in and made legal.'

Bruce led Lizzie over to the desk and asked the security personnel for a temporary pass until her proper one could be issued. As he did this, Lizzie had a chance to size up her new boss. Size up, though, was an unfortunate turn of phrase regarding Bruce Villiers, as he couldn't have been much more than five foot six at his most optimistic. He had curly, rather oily, black hair and a neat moustache. He reminded Lizzie of the sort of man who appeared in nineteen thirties films as the romantic lead. He seemed a bit too good to be true, and she tried to suppress her feelings of instant mistrust. So what if he was the antithesis of Richard? So what if he looked a bit of a smoothy? She really shouldn't judge him just by her first impression. He was obviously quite dapper and took a pride in his clothes, because his rather flamboyant tie had a matching handkerchief, visible in his breast pocket. As he stood at the desk a colleague walked past.

'I see it's National Tasteless Tie Week again, Bruce,' the man said.

Bruce laughed and self-consciously stroked the brightly coloured piece of silk. 'You wouldn't call this tie tasteless if you knew what it cost,' he retorted.

'More money than sense then,' was the parting shot as his adversary left the building.

Bruce laughed heartily. Lizzie decided that if he had a sense of humour and could laugh at himself, at least that was a point in his favour.

The exchange also lulled her into the feeling that perhaps this huge monolithic edifice wasn't quite such an anonymous and faceless place in which to work as she'd feared, although she was still terrified of being in such close proximity to more generals than you could shake a stick at. She tried to calm her apprehensions and misgivings as, paperwork completed, Bruce led her to the main door.

'When you get your proper pass you'll be able to let yourself in through these bulletproof tubes.' He indicated the three banks of narrow, curved glass doors that opened when swiped with a card. He chatted amiably to her as he led her past the escalators sweeping personnel to the upper floors of the Ministry, and through the rest area designated for smokers. Lizzie wondered if there was a way to her office that would allow her to avoid this smoke- and nicotine-laden ghetto. He steered her round the corner and down a succession of dreary corridors until they arrived at the hub of the military's PR machine.

Lizzie recalled that her next impression had been that he obviously had charm in abundance, but then charm was probably a prerequisite for anyone in PR. He'd busily explained the nature of her job, introduced her to all and sundry, made her coffee, been attentive, allayed her fears about her capabilities and swept away any illusions she had that she would be dealing with the world's press. But although he was apparently charming, friendly, funny and relaxed, Lizzie found she couldn't warm to him at all and viewed with horror the news that they were to share an office.

Later, on her way home to the little flat that she'd rented in Kilburn to spare her long train journeys during the week, Lizzie had decided that there was something about him which reminded her of a character in a book. It took a day or two for her to work it out, but she was amused by the aptness of the image when she finally pinned it down. Tigger! Small, bouncy and full of himself, although somehow not as lovable.

As Lizzie returned to the present she was still struck by this image of her boss. She grinned to herself at the thought but then told herself that she couldn't sit and day-dream all day. She eased out from behind her desk and went to the clerks' office to put the kettle on. She'd just made herself a cup of coffee when she was aware of a phone ringing back along the corridor. It sounded as if it was hers.

'Damn,' she swore as, trying to hurry to pick it up before the caller rang off, her coffee slopped into the saucer. She dumped her cup and saucer on the filing cabinet near the door and lunged across the desk to grab the receiver.

'SO3 PR Army,' she said. 'Good morning.'

'Lizzie?'

'Yes, who's speaking?'

'It's me, Amanda.'

'Amanda! How are you? I haven't heard from you for ages.'

'Sorry. I've been busy.'

'Obviously, but then haven't we all?' said Lizzie without malice. 'It's been months since we last spoke. Before Christmas.' It said volumes for the level of their friendship that the girls could pick up its threads at any opportunity and after any length of time.

'I know, I'm sorry. I wanted to let you get settled into your new job and then I just lost track of time. I kept meaning to ring you at the weekends, when you would be back in Aldershot, but things just had a habit of getting in the way and before I'd know it, it'd be Monday morning again and I'd be up to my ears in work.'

'Don't apologise, I've been quite as bad. My excuse is exactly the same as yours, and often, by the time I get home in the evenings, all I really want to do is fall into a hot bath and then go to bed.'

'The reason I'm ringing is that I've got a free weekend coming up and I could do with cheering up. I wondered if you, me and Edwina could get together. What do you think?'

'It sounds brilliant. I haven't seen Edwina for ages either. What a great idea. I'll get hold of her and ring you back. Do you want to come to the house in Aldershot?'

'I was wondering about going to see something cultural and perhaps having a meal together afterwards. Have a girls' weekend out, up in town.'

'An even better idea. If we do that you'd be better off staying with Edwina. My flat is way too small to offer you any sort of accommodation. I'll talk to Edwina and get back to you.'

Lizzie put the phone down feeling thoroughly cheered up at the prospect of seeing the other two again. It had been far too long since they'd been together. She glanced at her watch and decided it was probably too early to catch Edwina at the paper. She decided to wait half an hour or so before phoning.

'Good morning, Lizzie,' said Bruce from the door.

'Morning, Bruce,' replied Lizzie, trying, out of politeness, to sound pleased to see him – and knowing that she'd failed.

'You look well today.'

'Thanks.' In previous working relationships Lizzie would have been happy to enter into a conversation with a fellow worker, but she found that with Bruce, exchanging more than the bare minimum of words was almost too much to bear. It was only when situations necessitated it that she entered into any sort of dialogue that might be called a conversation.

'Well,' he said, disappointed by the lack of response, 'I think I'll get myself a coffee. Would you like another?' he added, seeing the abandoned cup on the filing cabinet.

Lizzie smiled a polite smile but devoid of warmth, shook her head and buried herself in updating one of their computerised databases.

'Right, well then.' He hesitated by her desk momentarily before disappearing out of the door.

352

Lizzie shivered and hoped this would be one of the days when Bruce would be required to do lots of stuff out of the office. Unfortunately, her wishes were not fulfilled, and she decided to wait until Bruce went to the canteen for lunch before trying to get hold of Edwina.

'She's out,' she was told by an unknown voice.

'Can I leave a message, please?'

'If you must.'

'Could you tell her to phone Lizzie as soon as possible.'

'OK. 'Bye.' The line went dead.

Lizzie stared at the receiver and decided that she must have caught this colleague of Edwina's at a bad moment.

Of course, as luck would have it, Edwina not only phoned when Bruce was in the office, but also when he was at a relatively loose end. Lizzie was acutely aware of the fact that he was listening to her end of the phone conversation as she made arrangements for Amanda to stay with Edwina and they discussed what they should go and see.

'Leave it with me,' said Edwina. 'I'll get tickets.'

'Yes, but to something nice and jolly, please. I really can't face the thought of something which is either kitchen sink or utterly terrifying.'

'Wimp.'

'By the way, did I say something wrong when I left a message that I wanted to speak to you?'

'Not really. The editor and one of the senior reporters have got it into their heads that I might be moving on to another paper, so I'm not the most popular person at the moment.'

'Is the rumour true?'

'I'm not sure yet. I'll let you know if things start to develop.'

'OK. Well, I must get back to work. See you at the weekend. 'Bye.'

'Are these Army friends you're planning on seeing?' asked Bruce when Lizzie had finished her call.

'One is, one isn't.'

'And what does the one who isn't do for a living?'

Lizzie didn't think this was any of Bruce's business but she was too well brought up to say so, despite her dislike of him.

'She's a press photographer.'

'Really? Did you meet her through this job?'

'No, she was a cadet with me, but then she took up photography as a hobby and a little while ago decided to make a career out of it. Also she was fed up with the Army.'

'Any particular reason for getting so fed up?'

'A problem with postings, I think.' Lizzie tried to indicate that the conversation was at an end by returning to her computer terminal and continuing her work on the weekly press briefing that the branch issued to all the most senior officers.

'Ah, she got the black spot then, did she?'

Lizzie looked up. 'I beg your pardon.'

'The black spot. Surely, my dear, you've read *Treasure Island*?' Lizzie nodded. 'In which case you'll know that the black spot was the kiss of death. Well, the people up at the postings branches can do that to someone's career if there is a suspicion that all is not well – financial problems, a hint of impropriety, a difficult wife, that sort of thing.'

'Surely they can't?' In spite of her loathing of her boss, Lizzie wanted to know more.

'But they can. All they do is put an asterisk, a little black spot, by someone's name of their computer records. In itself it means nothing, but to everyone involved with postings, it means, at worst, "don't touch this officer with a bargepole", and at best, "exercise extreme caution". The real beauty of the system is that the donor of a black spot is completely untraceable, so there's no chance of any sort of retribution.'

'But that's terrible,' said Lizzie, all thoughts of the weekly press briefing forgotten, and intrigued by the implications of what Bruce was saying.

'Not at all. Everyone's on their honour only to give someone the black spot if they really merit it, and believe me, they always do.'

'But if someone had a grudge against another officer . . .'

'Well, that's rather unlikely, don't you think?'

'No, I don't.'

'I can assure you that only the most trusted officers get posted to Stanmore.'

Lizzie shook her head in disbelief. If that was the case they'd slipped up with Cathy Roberts – if her conduct regarding Edwina at Sandhurst was anything to go by. But she had to check something before she jumped to any conclusions. 'How do you know about all this?'

'I had a spell up at Stanmore myself. A couple of years ago.'

'That would have been when Cathy Roberts was up there.'

'Yes, lovely girl. Always very friendly. In fact, she would have been responsible for your posting here, wouldn't she? Just before she went to Camberley.'

'Yes.' Lizzie thought for a second or two. 'She wouldn't have had anything to do with posting female signals officers, would she?'

'Not officially, of course, that would have been handled entirely by the Royal Corps of Signals postings officer. But it was a very close little community up there. We all knew each other very well, always in and out of each other's offices. The male officers often asked her about the female officers in their corps, especially the junior ones, because she was involved with training a lot of them.'

'Did they now?' said Lizzie thoughtfully.

'Yes. You know how well a platoon commander at Sandhurst gets to know their troops. Her input could be very useful.'

'So the officer in charge of Royal Signals postings would have asked Cathy about the female members of his corps?'

'More than likely; especially, as I said, the junior ones.'

'And if she was privy to anything in their background which might make them unsuitable for some postings . . .'

'Yup, she'd be certain to advise him about that.'

'And presumably she could also recommend somebody as the recipient of a black spot?' Bruce nodded. 'If you heard anything about someone, from one of the other postings officers, say, did you check out the information?'

'Well, it would depend rather on our source. If it came from within our number we could always trust it as being reliable.'

'Hmm,' said Lizzie, wondering if they had been right to do so, especially if Cathy was involved.

London, April 1993

Edwina, Amanda and Lizzie met punctually on Saturday at Waterloo station under the clock, which, due to Army indoctrination, meant that they were all five minutes early. The stares of passers-by were ignored as the three attractive women yelled greetings to each other and fell on each other's necks.

'It's been far too long since we've seen each other,' said Amanda as they linked arms and strolled towards the tube.

'I think it was last year. Just before you took your Staff exam,' said Lizzie.

'Shit. That's ridiculous.'

'I see your language hasn't improved at all, Edwina,' responded Amanda.

'Too fucking right it hasn't.'

'Edwina!' said Amanda and Lizzie simultaneously in horror. But Edwina was completely unrepentant.

'Anyway, look what I've got tickets for.' She pulled three theatre tickets out of her bag with a flourish. Amanda grabbed them.

'*Cats*! Hey, brilliant. I've been meaning to see it for ages. But I thought it was still fully booked till the millennium?'

'Not if you happen to know a theatre critic it isn't.'

'How come? I mean, I don't want to be churlish but I wouldn't have thought that the *Maidenhead Courier* would have much call for a London theatre critic.'

'Don't be so rude, it's a very good local paper. No, it's not one of my contacts, it's one of Ulysses'. He trains this guy, takes him for exercise sessions in some swanky gym in Kingston, and every now and again he gets slipped some tickets.'

'That's brilliant,' said Lizzie enthusiastically.

'Right then,' said Edwina. 'If we want to have time for a quick drink first then I think we should head towards that end of town.' She caught sight of Lizzie and Amanda exchanging glances. 'And don't worry, I haven't fallen off the wagon. I'll be on boring old mineral water.' But she said it with a sense of pride.

As they travelled across the station to the tube, Edwina told them about the delights – which didn't seem to be many – of being a staff photographer on a regional newspaper, Amanda filled them in on the progress of her arthritis, and Lizzie dispelled any illusions that her job had any glamour attached to it whatsoever.

'But you were going to get me contacts with all the top national daily newspaper editors,' complained Edwina. 'I can't stay on the *Maidenhead Courier* for ever. It may pay the bills but it is unbelievably dull.'

'But I thought you said you might be getting head-hunted by another paper,' said Lizzie.

'Really? How exciting,' said Amanda.

'I'm afraid "head-hunted" is hardly the correct word. I want to work for a bigger paper, something that comes out more than once a week. I don't think I've got a chance of being taken on by a national, and anyway they use a lot of stuff from freelancers, but there are a lot of evening papers that might fit the bill. So I sent off a portfolio of pictures to half a dozen possibles –'

'What, like the *Evening Standard*?' asked Lizzie.

'Well, yes, but there's no chance there, it's too big a jump. But there are loads of other ones – Oxford has got an evening paper, so has Shrewsbury, Worcester, Brighton . . . Anyway, to get back to the point, I sent some stuff off and I've had a couple of phone calls back expressing interest. Gwen, the chief reporter, got wind of this and she's not very happy.'

'But surely you're a free agent?'

'Yes, I am, but Gwen and I work well together and I think she's upset that I want to move on so quickly.'

'That must make things a bit difficult,' said Amanda. As she spoke there was a rush of stale air as their tube train approached the station. They paused in their conversation while they waited for passengers to alight before they boarded. The doors swished shut and the train moved off, rattling and swaying into the tunnel, carrying them northwards.

'I think whatever happens I've rather burned my boats. If I don't get an offer I can't refuse I think I'll have to take the plunge and join the paparazzi.'

'Oh, Edwina. Surely not?' cried Lizzie over the racket of the train.

'God, you make it sound as though I'm doing something immoral.'

'But it's spying on people.'

'Yes, and I'm good at that.' The train pulled into the next station on the line.

'By the way,' said Lizzie, 'I've got some information for you.'

'What's that? A hot tip on where I can find the Chief of the General Staff engaged in something so illicit and scandalous I'll be able to get the shot which will make my fortune?'

'No, nothing of so much public interest,' said Lizzie, laughing. 'And I'm not going to tell you till we get to a pub and you are sitting down calmly.'

Edwina paid Lizzie back for making her wait for her information by insisting she ran from Covent Garden tube station to the bistro in the old marketplace where they'd decided to have a drink. But still Lizzie wouldn't say anything until their drinks had been ordered and delivered.

'Now tell me,' demanded Edwina.

Lizzie explained about the black spot.

'Cathy said she'd get me, and I didn't believe her. Well, at least I know how she did it.'

'I don't mean to pour cold water on this theory,' said Amanda, 'but you don't think that your drinking had anything to do with your postings problems?'

Edwina shook her head. 'No, I'm certain of it. Yes, I admit I probably always did drink more than was good for me when I was off duty, but I never let it affect my work. Remember, it was only *after* my career went tits up that I began to go off the rails.'

'Yes, I'd forgotten.'

'She may have been able to tell your postings officer that she had some information which made it appropriate to mark your name,' said Lizzie. 'Alternatively, all she had to do was wait till your postings officer was out of his office, then slip in and stick an asterisk on your file. It's not the sort of thing that anyone would notice for ages –'

'Not until they looked up my records when I was due a move. And when I did need a move, my postings officer had only just taken up the job. He wouldn't ask why my name was marked, he would just assume his predecessor had a good reason. And of course there was that business with Nat – that wouldn't have helped things.'

'No, he'd just accept it and send you to a job where you couldn't do any damage,' said Amanda.

'And where I could be kept an eye on by the fearsome number of senior female officers stationed in Aldershot,' finished Edwina. 'Of course we don't have a shred of proof,' she said as an afterthought. 'But I do know she hated me with a vengeance. She made that perfectly clear when I ran into her in Northern Ireland. She told me in no uncertain terms that she didn't think I should have been commissioned in the first place. Obviously she wanted to see the back of me and couldn't resist the opportunity when it presented itself.'

'I think it's fairly safe to assume that you're almost certainly right. You weren't paranoid, Cathy did screw up your career as revenge for what happened at Sandhurst,' said Lizzie. 'How dreadful of her.'

'What I can't understand is why she should hate me so much.'

'Perhaps it was jealousy,' said Lizzie. 'You were incredibly popular – remember, the whole platoon formed up to defend you when it looked like you were going to be thrown off. Everyone backed you up, which made Cathy look bad. Also, you were very fit; it was you who got us through that appalling endurance run, not Cathy –'

'And you were selected to do something very special,' added Amanda.

'And you've got Ulysses,' finished Lizzie.

'Yes, she saw us together in Ireland, but it wasn't as if we were doing anything other than having a drink together. Well, not just then, at any rate. I can't see that she could really have convinced anyone that I was a danger to the status quo because I met a staff sergeant for a drink. It's not as if we're engaged or anything.' She paused and then added, wickedly, 'He just gives me a good seeing-to now and again.'

'Ssshhh,' said Lizzie, horrified by the stares of some of the people at the adjacent table.

'What's wrong with that?' said Edwina, all innocence. 'I like getting a good seeing-to.' She repeated the phrase even louder.

Amanda dissolved into giggles. 'Please don't ever change, Edwina. The world will be a poorer place if you do.'

Three hours later they staggered out of the New London Theatre, all feeling exhausted by the spectacle they had just seen.

'Not that it was really my sort of thing,' said Edwina.

'Oh? So why were you clapping in time to all the songs like the rest of the audience?' asked Lizzie.

'Well, the songs were catchy, I admit, but there wasn't any violence or gore or chainsaws, and you really can't call it a proper evening's entertainment if there aren't some of those.'

'So what you mean is, you would rather have had Skimbleshanks underneath the wheels of the eleven forty-two and not riding in it?

'Put like that, yes.'

'Philistine,' said Amanda.

They went for a Chinese meal in a nearby restaurant which was a favourite of Lizzie's, and then at about eleven o'clock split up; Lizzie, protesting tiredness, went back to her flat in Kilburn, and the other two headed towards Edwina's place near Staines. They had to run to catch the last train and collapsed, panting, into their seats as it drew out of the station.

'What have you done with Ulysses this weekend?' asked Amanda.

'I told him to make himself scarce. It's not difficult because he often has to work Saturday or Sunday. With clients who pay him as much as his do, they expect poor old Ulysses to be available whenever they want.'

'That's a bit steep.'

'So are his fees.'

It started to rain softly and the two women watched the glistening raindrops slide, first diagonally, then, as the train gathered speed, horizontally, across the windows.

Edwina watched Amanda's reflection in the grimy window. She thought back to her conversation with Ulysses earlier in the week, when she'd told him he would be *persona non grata* over the weekend, and wondered what Amanda's reaction would have been if she'd been present to hear the bombshell that Ulysses had dropped. Edwina would be the first to admit that she was hard to shock, but Ulysses' announcement, that he'd guessed years ago that Amanda was gay, had rocked her to the core. It crossed her mind now that if Ulysses had guessed, then so might others. Perhaps, thought Edwina, it was time to reveal to Amanda that she wasn't being as discreet as she so obviously thought she was. All the same, she wouldn't use the same form of words that Ulysses had chosen a few days ago.

'So I don't get to try to convert her,' he'd said, when Edwina had told him to make himself scarce because Amanda would be staying.

'What do you mean, convert her?' Edwina had asked, not understanding.

'Don't play the innocent with me. You know as well as I do that your best chum is gay.'

Edwina could still vividly recall her stunned surprise at his matter-of-fact statement about such a taboo subject.

'How . . . who . . .?' She'd given up trying to frame a proper question and shrugged.

'I worked it out, stupid.'

'But how? You don't even know her that well.'

'You tell me things: she likes her privacy, she doesn't have a boyfriend, she lives out of the mess –'

'Hang on, all those things apply to Lizzie.'

'Maybe, but I put money on Amanda being a dyke when I first came across her at Sandhurst. There was something about her that instantly told me she wasn't interested in men.'

'Ha! You mean she didn't fall down and swoon at your feet.'

'Get real,' said Ulysses with a note of contempt. 'I never said anything at the time because I might have been wrong, but I'm not, am I? And I guessed you knew because, unlike Lizzie, you never tried to push any of your single male friends in her direction.'

'No, I didn't.' There was silence for a few seconds. 'But please don't say anything to anyone. She's had this steady relationship with another woman for years and she's not doing anything to hurt anyone else.'

'Don't be so fucking melodramatic. Of course I wouldn't. It's no skin off my nose, as long as she doesn't suddenly decide she wants to muscle in on my bit of skirt. But I'm sorry I'm not getting to meet her properly. I wouldn't mind showing her what she's missing.'

Edwina had raised her eyebrows in horror. Ulysses had obviously never heard of political correctness.

'Which is exactly why I don't want you about. God knows what you'll say to her if you get to meet her again.'

'How about, sit on my lap and we'll talk about the first thing that comes up?'

'No,' said Edwina, but she'd been unable to suppress a giggle. 'That's exactly the sort of thing which wouldn't go down well.'

'I bet she goes down well. "No muff's too tough, she dives at five",' quoted Ulysses from his supply of revolting soldiers' sayings.

At this point Edwina had punched him hard on the arm. 'You are disgusting. This is a friend of mine you're talking about here. Now promise me faithfully you won't tell anyone, not a soul, about Amanda.'

'Yeah, yeah. Of course.'

'I mean it. I'll bite your balls off if I find that you've gone back on your word.'

'OK, OK. But I'm most upset that you don't think you can trust me.'

'Because, Andrew Lees, I know what a scheming, devious, lying, cheating and completely untrustworthy bastard you are.'

'And those are just my good points,' he'd said with a grin before they'd ended up on the bed.

Now Edwina glanced guiltily across at Amanda, who was still staring out of the window; Amanda would have been terribly hurt if she'd been a fly on the wall. The tone of their conversation about her had been, in many respects, unforgivable, but Edwina still wondered how many other people had come to the same conclusion as herself and Ulysses. She was worried that Amanda was playing a dangerous game and that both she and Bella were going to wind up losing. It was no good, she was going to have to talk to Amanda tonight. She had to warn her that her deception, her mask, was becoming distinctly see-through.

They got off the train at Staines station and headed along the road to Edwina's flat.

'Drink or a coffee?' offered Edwina as she unlocked the door and switched on the light. 'Don't worry, I keep a bottle of whisky here for Ulysses, so you don't have to stick to orange juice.'

'No, a coffee would be fine.'

At that moment a jet thundered overhead. Amanda stared at Edwina in horror. As the noise died away she said, 'Lizzie didn't exaggerate, did she?'

'Sorry. I honestly hardly hear them now, I've got so used to them.' She looked at her watch. 'That should be one of the last ones. They aren't allowed to fly during the night.'

Edwina went into the kitchen and began to make coffee for

them both. 'It'll have to be instant,' she called through to the sitting room.

'Is there any other sort?' said Amanda, who had put a pile of Edwina's junk on the floor so they would both have somewhere to sit down.

Edwina returned with two steaming mugs. 'There you are,' she said to Amanda, who was standing by a table, examining Edwina's photographic equipment.

Amanda took it. 'I was just admiring your cameras. They must have set you back a bit.'

'The entire gratuity that I got from a grateful government for my four years' commissioned service, and then some. It isn't just the cameras that cost so much; the lenses can set you back well over a thousand pounds a time too.'

Amanda whistled. 'I can only just about cope with an Instamatic for some holiday snaps. If it isn't idiot-proof then I can't handle it.'

'They're not that difficult once you know the basics. I don't use them that much on this job, but if I'm going to go freelance, I've got to be able to compete with the big boys. Of course, having a decent camera doesn't necessarily mean you'll get the picture that'll make your fortune –'

'You mean like the ones of the Duchess getting her toes sucked?'

'Exactly. But having a good camera means that, if you get the chance to take such a shot, you're less likely to screw it up.'

'Yup, I can see that makes sense.'

'So. How are things for you, healthwise?' Edwina had noticed that Amanda's hands seemed to be as stiff as ever.

'I think I'm probably going to be kicked out soon as medically unfit. I can't pass my BFT and in the new lean, keen Army there isn't room for people who can't pull their weight. My health isn't getting worse but it's just not getting any better.

'Is it something to do with the Gulf? There's been a lot of stuff recently about that.'

Amanda sighed. 'I don't know. My symptoms aren't as bad as the people we hear about in the press. And lots of people get arthritis, even young kids. It's probably just a coincidence, and I'm certainly not going to try and blame the Army for it.'

Edwina couldn't help but admire Amanda's loyalty. She didn't think she'd have taken such a stoical approach if it had been her. 'All the same, it's pretty tough if it means you'll lose your job.'

'I'll qualify for a pension.'

'So I should bloody well hope, after what you went through. But it won't be enough to live on, will it?'

Amanda shook her head.

'So what will you do? Go back to teaching?'

'Heaven forfend! I don't quite know yet, but there are plenty of jobs to be had that won't require me to be able to run like a rigger. I'm sure I could do something in sales or personnel management – anywhere that I can put my administrative skills to use. I'm not completely disabled, you know.'

'I know some people who have left and become bursars at public schools. What about something like that?'

'I haven't really given it that much thought yet, but frankly, as long as it pays the bills and keeps me off the streets I don't really care. I'm working on my CV to make it sound as though I'm not completely khaki-brained.'

'And how's your love life?'

'In what way?' asked Amanda warily.

Edwina took a deep breath. It was about time she revealed to Amanda that she knew.

'How's Bella?'

Amanda put her mug down on the floor. 'Bella?'

'Yes, Bella.'

Amanda narrowed her eyes. 'What are you saying?'

Edwina had screwed up her courage to get this far, and she had to go through with it. 'Please don't play games with me, Amanda. I've known for years about you two; ever since that party at Guildford. You've been an item for almost as long as Ulysses and me.' Amanda stood up, white and shaking. Edwina held out a hand towards her, as if she wanted her to take it. 'No, don't go. Please don't go. I'm not judging you; your affair is no business of mine. I'm out of the Army so I don't care. OK?'

'So why are you bringing the subject up?' Amanda's voice was cool and suspicious.

'Sit down, would you. Please. It's taken more than you can imagine for me to say what I have so far. I really do mean it when I say that whatever you do, however you choose to live your life, it is nothing to do with me. Oh, please sit down, Amanda, I'll get a crick in my neck if you don't.' Amanda lowered herself back on to the sofa but sat on the very edge, still poised for flight.

'I've only said something,' continued Edwina, 'because if I know, if I've worked everything out, don't you think others may have guessed?' She wasn't going to mention that Ulysses already had. That would be too much for Amanda to take right now. 'You know how the Army treats anyone they think may be homosexual. I don't want the Special Investigation Branch to turn their attention on you – or Bella, for that matter – but I'm terrified that's what going to happen if others start to put two and two together like I did.'

Amanda sagged suddenly on the sofa. The trapped look left her face and she raised her eyes to look at Edwina. She stared at her friend in silence for a minute, maybe more.

'You know,' she said quietly. 'I think I almost feel relieved that you know. It's as if you've taken a weight off me, like I've had a bloody great albatross around my neck like the poor Ancient Mariner and you've come along and cut the string. It's been dreadful, lying to you for all these years.'

Edwina felt a huge wave of relief that she'd been right to broach the subject. She half wished she'd done it years ago, but then again perhaps it was best that she hadn't.

Amanda rearranged herself on the sofa so she could lean back more comfortably, now that she wasn't planning on running away. She rested her elbow on the arm of the sofa and leant her chin on her palm as she studied Edwina thoughtfully. 'But if you've known since that party – God, that was years ago – why didn't you tell me sooner?'

'I thought it might spoil our friendship. And if anything had happened to you, if the brass had found out while I was still in the Army, you might have thought that I was to blame. I decided that it wasn't that important an issue. OK, other people may feel strongly about the whole subject, but I'm afraid I don't.'

'That's refreshing to hear. I thought that everyone in the Army was completely homophobic.'

'Let's face it, a lot are, and no doubt they have their reasons, all of which they can justify till the cows come home. I suppose, because I went to art school, I got to meet a whole load of people who made it their life's work to break rules, taboos and moral codes. And you know that I've never been that good about obeying all the Army's rules and regulations myself.'

'I seemed to be the opposite. I could do all the kow-towing required; when they said "jump" I didn't ask "why?", I said "how high?". I learned outwardly to be the perfect cadet, but I couldn't

365

suppress everything about the way I was. And knowing myself as I did, I have to admit to feeling extremely guilty when I got awarded the sash of honour. I expected to be struck down by a bolt of lightening on the spot as I reached to accept it.'

Edwina smiled wryly. 'And there was me thinking that your legs were just shaking because you thought you were going to make a prat of yourself in front of all those people.' She stopped as a thought struck her. 'So your parents never made an appearance at the RMA because they didn't agree with your lifestyle?'

'You could put it like that. When I told them that I was gay I was told never to darken their door again. Which didn't seem to be such a problem at first, but when I heard I was being awarded the sash and I knew they would refuse the invitation to Sovereign's Parade, I was terrified that the DS would tumble to the reason. I mean, most parents would walk barefoot over burning coals to see their daughter receive such an accolade. In the end I decided to tell Colonel O'Brien that my mother had psychiatric problems, a mental illness, and that it would be difficult for my father to leave her – a complete lie, of course. But it did have the advantage that it's not the sort of thing people want to seem too curious about. I didn't think the DS would wish to know any details and check out the story.'

'And it worked. The fact that they weren't there was something no one ever really questioned. All the same, didn't it show you how difficult it was going to be to maintain the lie, especially if you ended up in any sort of relationship?'

Amanda told Edwina about the subterfuges she and Bella had employed over the years: never being seen to leave a mess together, booking two hotel rooms if ever they went away together, using their mobile phones to ring each other rather than use the public ones in the mess . . . the list went on and on.

'It's got to the stage where I think I'm looking for an excuse to kick the Army into touch. I've loved the jobs I've had, I've made a whole load of brilliant friends, I've had some fantastic experiences and I've been well paid for the privilege. But I can't go on with this double life for much longer. It's too much of a strain. That's why I don't think I'll fight it if I have to take a medical discharge. You have no idea how hard it is to lead this sort of double life.'

'I dated an Other Rank, remember? The brass didn't exactly condone that either. It was probably one of the levers Cathy Roberts used to get me out.'

'Yes, I know, but even that isn't in quite the same league on the Army's scale of undesirable offences.'

'No, you're right.'

'And there's another thing.'

'What's that?' asked Edwina. Surely Amanda couldn't have any other secrets.

'I don't think you're the only person who has guessed about Bella and me.'

Edwina looked at her quizzically. Lizzie hadn't guessed, surely?

'I think your friend and mine, Cathy Roberts, has rumbled us.' Amanda's voice suddenly sounded very weary.

'You're joking. But how could she have done? You haven't been posted anywhere near her –' Edwina stopped. 'But Bella has. They're at Staff College together.'

Amanda nodded her head. 'Exactly. And I ran into her when I went to visit Bella a while back. She made some comment or other, which might have been innocent but I don't think it was.'

'You did what? You visited Bella at Staff College? After everything you said about being careful for all those years. Really!' finished Edwina in exasperation.

'I know, I know. It was a stupid thing to do; we both know that now. I don't know why we did it. Perhaps after so long we thought we could afford to let our guard slip a little, perhaps it was just over-confidence. Either way, it was a stupid, *stupid* mistake. But were you always entirely discreet when you and Ulysses were both in the Army?'

Edwina remembered Ulysses bluffing his way into the officers' mess at Blandford. 'No, we weren't. We did some crazy things too.'

'Well then. So now we've just got to keep our fingers crossed and pray that she doesn't blow the whistle on us.'

'Good luck,' offered Edwina, thinking that luck was all they could hope for. And now that Cathy was involved, it had probably run out.

The Ministry of Defence, London, September 1993

'I don't believe it,' said Lizzie to herself as she scanned the morning papers. Across the front page of one of the biggest-selling tabloids was yet another story about a senior member of the armed forces who had been caught with his trousers down – literally, judging by the picture. It seemed that almost every day there was another exposé about someone in the military playing away from home. She suspected that it was much the same as the press feeding-frenzy over the recent dangerous dogs issue. Certainly there had been a couple of horrific cases involving small children and large dogs, but it had got to the stage when even a friendly nip on the ankle by a terrier was yet more fuel for the tabloids' campaign to get certain dogs banned. Now, following one peccadillo by an ex-aide to the royal family, a major in the Life Guards with a penchant for rent-boys, the spotlight had been turned on uniformed brass-hats and their private lives. Still, this current story apparently had more than a little substance to it, if the report and picture on the front page were to be believed.

Lizzie refolded the paper and left it on the pile for the Director of Public Relations (Army), Brigadier Mike Wallace, who would no doubt have the more senior members of his staff running around like headless chickens for the rest of the day. First they would have to get hold of the Adjutant General – the man responsible for discipline within the Army – to give a statement on the subject. Then they would have to find out what summary action had already been taken to deal with the miscreant. And lastly they would need to feed back into the press the latest Army policy designed to prevent a repeat of the incident. All in all it was going to be a tough day up at the sharp end, and Lizzie thought that, for once, it probably wasn't too bad to be tied up in purely routine matters. The damage-limitation exercise that was going to have to take place to deal with this latest scandal would have the rest of the office working till God only knew when.

She checked that the pile of that day's newspapers, put ready for the DPR's attention, looked untouched, made herself a cup of coffee and returned to her desk ready to start another day's work in her cell, as she thought of her office.

'Morning, Lizzie,' said Bruce breezily from the door. 'I like your hair. Have you had it cut?'

'Yes,' she replied coolly. It was becoming his latest thing. Every morning he would make some comment or other about her appearance. She suspected that she was supposed to enjoy this flattery, but it had the reverse effect. She knew that Edwina, in her position, would have had a showdown with him by now, but Lizzie just couldn't bring herself to be rude or aggressive to her boss. Being unpleasant, no matter what the provocation, simply wasn't in her nature.

He came over to her desk and pushed a stray tendril behind her ear. Lizzie froze. She said nothing, willing him to go away, to return to his side of the office. He stood beside her for a minute, perhaps more, getting no response. Then the phone on his desk shrilled.

Talk about saved by the bell, thought Lizzie, still unnerved by his action.

She returned to her work, but despite trying to concentrate she couldn't help overhearing his end of the conversation.

'Well, it's damned inconvenient that you can't give me more notice,' he said to the caller, 'but it can't be helped. If you've been short-toured, you've been short-toured . . . Yes . . . Yes, I understand . . . And what about your replacement? Doesn't he want somewhere to live?' There was a pause, then, 'But that'll mean paying double the rent . . . Yes, I know it's nothing to do with me . . . OK then, we'll discuss it this evening. 'Bye.'

He replaced the receiver and, without being prompted by Lizzie, who didn't give a damn about what was obviously a personal matter, said, 'One of the tenants in my house has left me in the lurch.'

Lizzie said nothing. She knew he owned a house somewhere south of the river and that he sublet some rooms to other officers.

'It's hellish inconvenient because I overstretched myself on the mortgage rather, and I need the rent to help with the shortfall.'

'That's tough,' said Lizzie tonelessly.

'You wouldn't want to move in and share this house with me, I suppose?'

'You suppose right. I wouldn't.'

'It's a nice place – in Clapham.'

'I'm happy in Kilburn, thanks.'

'There's another officer who has the third bedroom, Derek Lesser from Procurements.'

'No.' Lizzie said it with finality, and to emphasise the point she got up from her chair and left the office.

Bruce stared after her. 'I'll have you one day, Captain Frigid. So help me I will,' he said in a low voice.

Later on in the day, when she was in the clerks' office collecting some files, he came in behind her and stood overly close. Or perhaps he didn't, perhaps it was only her overactive imagination as a result of his touch that morning. No one else noticed or paid any attention to him, but then everyone was frantically busy. I'm getting paranoid, she muttered to herself as she fled back to her desk.

That evening she phoned Edwina and confided in her.

'So that's it, Lizzie, is it? One touch, one bit of standing too close and a few compliments.'

Put like that it sounded ridiculous. 'Yes, I suppose so.' She felt foolish.

'He's just being friendly. You know, a father/daughter thing.'

'He gives me the creeps, though.'

'So tell him.'

'Oh, Edwina, I'm not like you. You know I can't do that.'

'Then put up with it, it's your choice.' Edwina always saw everything in black and white – never shades of grey.

'He asked me to become a tenant of his, too.'

'I imagine you declined.'

'I did, but he just doesn't seem to get the hint that he makes me squirm. What would you do?'

'Me? I'd knee him in the nuts, but then I don't think he'd have a go at me in the first place.'

'You mean he'd know that you would be more than he could handle?'

'More likely he just wouldn't fancy me,' said Edwina with her customary down-to-earth directness. Lizzie giggled despite her worries. 'Look, my advice is that if what he's doing gets no worse, just grit your teeth. But I do suggest you keep a diary of every little thing that he does. Then, if he graduates to mauling your tits in the lift or shoving his hand up your skirt, you have a whole pile of evidence that you can produce straightaway if you think you need to get really heavy. And if all else fails you can go to the press.'

'I keep telling you, Edwina, I don't know anyone with any influence in that field.'

'You do now.'

'Sorry?'

'I've got a job on the *Standard*. I heard today. They suddenly had a vacancy, the picture editor still had my portfolio, so he rang me up and told me I've got a month's trial. If I don't fuck up I'll get a more permanent contract.'

For a moment or two Lizzie forgot her own problems in her delight at Edwina's news. 'That's wonderful, brilliant! I'm so pleased for you.'

'I may even be able to afford a flat without hot and cold running jumbo jets.'

'There's a room going in Clapham with Bruce.'

Edwina laughed. 'I'll stick with the jumbos. Anyway, I'll be in touch soon, and give my love to Amanda if you speak to her.'

When Lizzie put the phone down her mood had lightened considerably, but then Edwina always had that effect on her. She was always so upbeat, so positive, even if she didn't have good news to impart as she had today. She was glad she'd decided to call her because apart from the cheery news, her common-sense advice made Lizzie feel more relaxed. After all, as Edwina had so succinctly pointed out, the harassment had hardly amounted to much, even if it did upset her. But her advice about keeping a diary was certainly sound, for if she could produce a detailed list of behaviour that had distressed her everyone was bound to be on her side. Lizzie went to her desk, found a small empty notebook and wrote in the date. Underneath she put in the two latest incidents, hoping as she did so that they would be the last.

The next day, Lizzie went to work as usual, but on this occasion she felt less apprehensive than she had of late. Perhaps it was knowing that her little notebook was safely tucked into a pocket of her handbag. Just try it now, buster, she thought.

She settled down into her office with her coffee, having quickly scanned the papers and seen that the colonel and the call girl had been relegated to the bottom of an inside page. Things on that score would start to calm down now as the eyes of the world – even those of tabloid readers – became focused on a handshake between Yasser

Arafat and Yitzhak Rabin in front of the White House. With such momentous world events unfolding across the Atlantic, the MoD's PR department could afford to relax for a minute or two – hopefully. Or at least until the next person couldn't keep their flies buttoned or their hand out of the till.

The day improved in leaps and bounds. Bruce phoned in to say he'd been asked, at short notice, to visit the Command Headquarters in Aldershot; then, in the early afternoon, Lizzie was handed her annual confidential report, which was graded excellent – the highest grading she could get in her rank. Her boss, the brigadier, had been extremely complimentary about her in the written pen picture and Lizzie had felt faintly overwhelmed by the praise. Amongst the phrases that were used were ones like 'always cool', 'level-headed', 'an eye for detail', 'delightful personality', 'a credit to her corps'. Lizzie had to read it twice to make sure she'd taken everything in, and hoped that one of the clerks might allow her to take an illicit photocopy of the report later – copies were, officially, strictly forbidden, but everybody did it if you could get away with it. She thanked the brigadier, signed her report to prove she'd seen it and was about to leave his office when he suddenly said:

'Um, Lizzie?'

'Yes, Brigadier?'

'Have you ever come across an officer in your corps called Bella de Fresne?'

'Bella? Yes, I have, a couple of times. She's a friend of a friend.'

'A female friend?'

'Yes, they were stationed at the WRAC Centre at Guildford together.'

'Ah.' A pause. 'Know her well?'

'Not really, sir. We've only ever met at parties, that kind of thing. Not the sort of occasions where you get to hold an in-depth conversation.' Lizzie was struck by a sudden thought. The PR branch was often amongst the first to know if a member of the armed forces had been involved in a serious or fatal accident. Keeping her fingers crossed that the reason for this interest was entirely trivial, she said, 'Why do you ask? There's nothing wrong with her, is there?'

'No. Nothing at all. Forget I asked.' He was brusque and it was obvious the conversation was at an end.

But Lizzie couldn't forget. If there was nothing wrong with Bella, then why the secrecy? Unless, of course, there was a story breaking, some scandal, which involved her. In her empty office, with little to occupy her except mundane and routine tasks, her mind mulled over the problem. Then, suddenly, she thought she realised the answer and laughed to herself at her stupidity. Of course, Bella was at Staff College and the postings would be announced in the next few days for all the newly fledged high-fliers. Perhaps the brigadier had been offered Bella to go into an SO2 slot. Glad that she'd worked out the answer, Lizzie returned to her desk and tried not to feel too smug about her confidential report and her powers of deduction.

It was after six, and she was on the brink of switching off her computer and clearing her desk, when Bruce appeared.

'I didn't expect to see you today,' said Lizzie, glad she was about to go home if he was going to be working late.

'There's a flap on.'

'God, not another officer who can't control his urges.'

'You could put it like that,' said Bruce grimly.

'So what's your involvement?' Neither Lizzie nor Bruce dealt with major PR problems, since they were both responsible for other areas, of internal PR and the like. Lizzie couldn't understand why Bruce should be having anything to do with this at all.

'I heard a rumour of something unpleasant happening when I was in Aldershot and informed the brigadier *tout de suite*. He told me to report straight to him, with a fuller briefing of what I'd heard, as soon as I got back.'

'And what did you hear?' Her curiosity overcame her dislike of the man.

'It's confidential at the moment. You'll find out about it soon enough, especially as it involves one of your lot.' He dumped his briefcase on his desk and hurried off to see the brigadier.

Slowly and thoughtfully Lizzie switched off her computer, put away her files and tidied her desk. The words *one of your lot* echoed and re-echoed in her mind. Presumably he meant that whoever was involved was a female member of the Army. Curious. She half thought of staying on to get the rest of the griff, but if it was a major flap it could be hours before things calmed down enough for her to get included in the scuttlebutt. Deciding that she wasn't *that* curious, she switched off the light and pulled the door closed behind her.

It wasn't until she was leaving the building that she remembered the brigadier mentioning Bella's name only that afternoon, and Bella was at the Staff College, which was only a few miles from Aldershot.

Surely not? No! Lizzie stopped dead in the middle of the huge portico that formed the entrance to the Ministry. All around her pin-striped civil servants and officers were hurrying down the shallow steps, heading for home, but Lizzie was oblivious to the activity, unaware of how she was impeding the impatient commuters. In her mind she went over her conversation with Bruce. What exactly had she asked him? *Not another officer who can't control his urges?* Yes, that was it, but it was she who'd assumed that the officer in question was a man. Nothing specific had been said. He'd replied, *You could put it like that.* And then he'd said that it involved *one of your lot*, so it had to be a woman. It all seemed to add up. God, Bella must have been knocking off a fellow officer there. Perhaps it had been one of the DS.

Lizzie was transfixed at the thought that someone she knew personally was involved in a scandal. Her friends and acquaintances simply didn't do that sort of thing. But she felt no stronger emotion than curiosity about Bella's part in the next tidying-up exercise that Army PR was about to embark on, for when all was said and done, she barely knew the woman. A couple of casual meetings hardly put her in the role of bosom buddy. But Amanda was much closer to Bella. Should she warn Amanda that a friend of hers might be about to appear in the headlines? As Lizzie stood in Horseguards Avenue, toying with the idea of ringing Amanda, a tall, bespectacled man in a tearing hurry barged past her and nearly sent her flying. She decided that she was not in the most convenient of places to stand and think, and reluctantly continued on towards the tube and Kilburn.

By the time she got home, she knew that if an unpleasant news story was about to break and it involved Bella, the last person she should call was Amanda. She didn't have a single concrete fact she could pass on, and if she was honest, she didn't know for sure that it *was* Bella involved in the issue. It would only worry Amanda senseless to be told half of an unconfirmed story, a story about which Lizzie knew nothing beyond Bella's possible involvement. She gave herself a mental shake for even entertaining the idea in the first place.

Then she thought of Edwina; Camberley and Aldershot were both well within the area covered by the *Standard*. She might have heard something via the paper. She looked at her watch and decided that Edwina should be at home. Quickly she dialled the number and waited impatiently as the phone rang several times. She was on the point of replacing the receiver when she heard Edwina's breathless voice.

'Hi.' A clatter, then, 'Oh, fuck! Hello, hello, are you still there? I dropped the phone.'

'It's me, Lizzie. Sorry, did I get you out of the bath?'

'No. I was in my dark room and my eyes hadn't adjusted properly so I tripped over a pile of books as I picked up the phone.' Lizzie, who knew the mess that always surrounded Edwina, wasn't the least bit surprised. 'Now, what can I do for you? Not more trouble with Bruce, surely?'

'No, nothing like that.' Lizzie told Edwina of the few scant bits of conversation that had led her to suspect that Bella might be in trouble.

'Hmm,' said Edwina at the end.

'You think I'm making a mountain out of a molehill again, don't you?'

'No.'

'But it's not much to go on, I could be wrong.'

'Will you pipe down for a second, I'm thinking.' Lizzie shut up. Then, after a short while, 'Did anyone say anything about any other person being involved?'

'No, I don't think so. The brigadier asked me if I knew Bella and I said she was a friend of a friend. Then he said, "A female friend?" and I said yes.'

'Shit.'

'Sorry?'

'Lizzie, you and I need to talk. I'll come over.'

'But it's late.'

'It's not that late and it's important.'

Lizzie put the phone down feeling rather shaky, and also feeling that she wasn't seeing the same picture as everyone else. What was it she was missing? She went into her minuscule kitchen to make herself a quick snack and a cup of coffee and to catch up on the evening news, trying to suppress the uneasy feeling that things were far from right.

It was well after nine o'clock when Edwina reached her flat.

'The traffic was dreadful. Even on my bike I had problems getting through.'

'Coffee?'

'Brill.'

Lizzie filled the kettle and got out a mug. 'So what is so urgent?'

'You need to be sitting down for this one,' said Edwina flatly. Lizzie shrugged and finished making Edwina's drink.

'OK,' she said as she settled herself in her favourite armchair. 'What the hell is going on?'

Edwina took a deep breath, sipped her coffee and said, 'Bella is a lesbian, and she and Amanda are having an affair, have been for ages.'

Lizzie's eyes widened, then she threw her head back and roared with laughter. 'Not that old chestnut again. Just because Amanda is over thirty and hasn't waltzed up the aisle with anyone, you have her labelled as gay. I thought I'd made you realise you were wrong after that party at Guildford.'

'Lizzie!' Edwina almost shouted. Lizzie's laughter died. 'I'm not joking. I've been right all along. I've spoken to Amanda about it. She confirmed everything only the other day.'

'No. Enough is enough, Edwina. I don't know why you're doing this or what axe you have to grind, but forget it.' Lizzie was trembling with anger.

'Ring her, then. Go on, ask her yourself.'

'Get out,' Lizzie shouted, standing up.

'No. Don't you understand?' Edwina was shouting too now. 'It's their affair that your boss has got wind of, that's why he was asking those questions. Why else would he want to know if you knew her via another woman? Which probably means that right now either Bella or Amanda, or both of them, is being investigated by the SIB, and you know what that means.'

'No.' Lizzie's voice had dropped to a whisper, and her denial now was at the horror of Amanda's current circumstances rather than Edwina's accusation. She sat down abruptly.

'I'm afraid it's true. Amanda told me only the other day that she thought Cathy was on to them.'

'Oh, God. Cathy's at Staff College with Bella.'

'Exactly. One moment of carelessness was all it took.' The two women stared at each other.

Eventually Lizzie said, 'What do you think we should do?'

'Nothing at the moment. At least, not until we're absolutely sure of our facts. We're still only speculating, even though I really think there's no doubt.'

'I'm glad you've told me all this before I heard it from someone else,' said Lizzie.

'How do you feel about it?'

'I don't know. She was my friend –'

'She still is,' cut in Edwina. 'Whatever you now know about her doesn't change who she is, what she did for me at Sandhurst or what she did for you after Richard died.'

'No. I suppose not. It's just . . .' Lizzie stopped and stared at the blank TV screen in the corner of the room. 'We've all been so brainwashed into thinking that homosexuality in the Army will mean the end of civilisation as we know it. But you're right, it doesn't change who she is, does it?'

'Nope, nor does it affect how good she is at her job.'

'But the powers-that-be aren't going to see it like that, are they?'

'No. The system says that if you're homosexual you must leave. There's no leeway to take into account how good you are, how popular, how well respected.'

'It's ridiculous, isn't it?'

'It's the way the system works. It'll take a lot to change it.'

'So all we can hope for now is that whatever's happened involving Bella has nothing to do with her relationship with Amanda.'

'Unlikely, isn't it?'

Lizzie knew that this was a vain hope shortly after she got into work the next morning. Unusually, Bruce was in the office first.

'Good morning, Lizzie,' he said with a smile.

'Morning, Bruce,' she replied as coolly as she could. 'Been here all night?'

'No. I got away shortly after eight.' He was still smiling, which unnerved Lizzie somewhat. She put her briefcase by her desk, switched on her computer terminal and went to make herself a coffee in the clerks' office. As she stood by the chief clerk's desk, flicking through the daily papers, praying that Bella's name wouldn't be in them, she was aware of a presence close, too close, behind her.

'Make me a coffee too,' said Bruce. Lizzie came out in goosepimples as she felt his breath on the back of her neck.

'Looking for your friend Bella? You're out of luck. She hasn't hit the front pages yet. She may be fortunate and stay out of the press altogether. Especially if she uses her head and keeps her mouth shut. But I think it explains a lot of things, don't you? Suddenly, realising who your friends are, I feel as though I know you a whole lot better.'

Although he didn't say it specifically, Lizzie knew that he was referring to her rebuttal of his advances. She was at a complete loss as to how to handle this situation. Boarding school and officer training had done nothing to prepare her for this sort of thing. All she knew was that she wanted to get away from him before he could make any other horrid innuendoes. She couldn't move forward because of the desk in her way, and to one side was a filing cabinet, so she took a side-step to her left, halfturning as she did so, in order to sidle past him. Whether by accident or design she couldn't tell, but he had positioned himself so that to pass him her breast had to brush against his arm.

'Excuse me,' she said through gritted teeth, feeling a wave of nausea sweep over her. She found it hard not to run out of the clerks' office, then, ignoring the boiling kettle, she fled down the corridor to the ladies' loo. She leaned against the basin and looked at her reflection in the mirror. 'Ugh,' she shuddered. She breathed in and out several times to calm herself. You're overreacting, she told herself. A touch or two, the odd compliment, a smutty remark doesn't mean anything, she thought, to try to reassure herself. But as she stared at her face in the mirror, she wasn't so sure.

'You forgot to make the coffee,' said Bruce, when she returned to her office some minutes later. 'So I did it.'

'Thanks,' responded Lizzie without looking at him, and ignoring her drink. She pulled her in-tray towards her and began work.

'You'll be pleased to hear I've found someone to take that empty room of mine,' said Bruce.

'Good,' said Lizzie, not looking up from her computer keyboard.

'Yes. One of the single officers at Staff College is to be posted to Procurement Branch to work with my remaining tenant, Derek Lesser. Derek put us in touch, as she'll need accommodation. I think you know her. Didn't you say Cathy Roberts was a friend of yours?'

Lizzie stopped typing and raised her eyes to look at Bruce. She swallowed hard in order to regain her composure before she replied, trying to keep her voice as steady as possible.

'I know her, certainly, but I wouldn't go as far as to call her a friend.'

'Oh, I thought she was. She seems to know you quite well. We had a long chat about you on the phone last night.'

'Did you?' Lizzie refused to be drawn.

'About you and Amanda Hardwick.'

'Cathy was our platoon commander at Sandhurst.'

'So she said. I didn't realise you knew Amanda before you were married. You, Amanda and Bella.'

'I really don't know what you mean.'

Bruce smiled at her, knowingly. 'I think you do, Lizzie. I think you do.'

Andover, December 1993

Amanda looked at her friends gathered around the pine table in her kitchen. The blinds were down, shutting out the cold, dark December night, and on the radio some carols played softly. The light from twenty tall ivory candles and the warmth of the Aga made the kitchen a haven of peace and comfort, despite the chatter of the three women standing there with her. She was glad they had been able to visit her prior to disappearing for the Christmas holiday. She raised her glass.

'Here's to Civvy Street,' she toasted.

'To Civvy Street,' responded Edwina and Bella. Lizzie hesitated for a second, as she wasn't certain that Bella and Amanda's hurried departure from the ranks of Her Majesty's Armed Forces was a reason to celebrate, but if Bella and Amanda thought so, then what the heck? She raised her glass too.

The four women each took a sip of their drinks. Edwina wrinkled her nose in distaste as the bubbles from her tonic water went up her nose. 'Ugh. I wish I were on the champagne like you lot,' she grumbled.

'Do you want some?' offered Amanda.

'No fear. I'm not risking a relapse after all this time.' She changed the subject. 'Do you think you'll miss the Army?' she asked with her customary directness.

'I think I will. Oh, not all aspects of it, by any means, but there are things about life in the Army which I don't think you find else-where.'

'Give me an example,' demanded Edwina.

'The friendship, or camaraderie, call it what you will.'

'OK,' conceded Edwina. 'What else?'

380

'The pay came in handy. And I liked the ceremonial side of things. I had some brilliant jobs and some even more amazing experiences. But I couldn't have kept up the pretence for much longer.'

'Look, if it's not a rude question, what on earth possessed you to join up in the first place?' asked Edwina. 'You must have known that the odds were stacked against you from the outset.'

'I know, I know. It's a predominantly male environment, so were we putting ourselves through some sort of test, subconsciously denying our sexuality? Or was it that we wanted to seduce young recruits to our perverted life style? I've heard all the arguments countless times. But the order of it, the sense of tradition, the fact that it's full of intelligent, committed adults was exactly what I needed after five years of teaching badly motivated, ill-disciplined children who wanted to be anywhere but in my classroom.'

'And I didn't really understand my sexual orientation until after I was in,' said Bella. 'It came as a bit of a shock to me when I realised that it wasn't just a phase I'd been going through, something I'd grow out of. I tried going to bed with men but it never worked out.'

'I knew before I joined, but I thought I would be able to ignore it,' said Amanda. 'I was in a relationship that was petering out and I thought that I'd be able to stay celibate and concentrate on my career; after all, people do. I hadn't planned on meeting Bella.' Amanda smiled and held out her hand to her lover. Lizzie, watching them, couldn't believe that anyone could condemn a relationship between two people who so obviously adored each other. She remembered how she had felt about Richard and knew that if Amanda and Bella had found just half the happiness she had then they were lucky indeed. It was just such an appalling business that their love was so totally immoral in the eyes of the Army.

'Was it ghastly?' asked Lizzie gently. 'Being found out?'

'You can't begin to understand how grim,' said Bella, putting her glass down and sitting down. It was a signal for them all to sit. Their chairs scraped on the stone flags on the floor as they made themselves comfortable around the table in the warm, cosy kitchen, decorated with holly and ivy from Amanda's garden to make it festive.

'The RMPs came into my room and went through everything; every photograph album, every book, every piece of paper and every letter. Then they interviewed me. There were two men and a woman – I'd never met any of them, but the questions they asked . . .' She shuddered as the horror of it returned. 'They wanted to know every detail of every sexual encounter I'd ever had. I didn't give them the satisfaction of answering them, but I learned more gynaecological terms in those few days than I ever did doing human biology at O level. Looking back, I don't think they were going to be able to prove anything and they were relying entirely on me confessing. And I couldn't do that because of what it would do to Amanda. Eventually I was hauled in front of the commandant and given an ultimatum: either I resigned my commission then and there and there would be no more questions and I would be given a gratuity and a resettlement grant, or the investigation would continue and if they did find anything I would be given a dishonourable discharge. Of course, I knew that if I tried to soldier on regardless, my career was already at an end. I would never get any sort of security vetting with this business on my file and I couldn't think of any jobs available to a Staff College graduate that wouldn't need it. I realised that, in fact, there was no choice in the matter at all.'

Lizzie was aghast. 'Bella, I didn't realise. How dreadful.'

'It wasn't pleasant.'

'Funnily enough,' said Amanda without a trace of humour, 'I was offered a medical discharge the following week. Coincidence or what? But Bella's actions spared me what she was put through. And now it's all over, and despite the fact that money is a little tight, we're very content.'

'I am so glad for you,' said Lizzie, meaning it absolutely.

'Do you know for certain that it was Cathy who tipped the authorities off?' asked Edwina.

'Not for sure,' said Bella. 'Cathy was as jealous as hell because I was doing better than her on the course –'

'Only because you spent your time there working, not lying on your back satisfying the sexual urges of the male officers,' added Amanda, dryly.

'That's as maybe. Like everything else, her promiscuity was only a rumour.'

'A rumour that has followed her from Ireland,' interjected Edwina. 'I think Ulysses' exact words were that she'd had "more rides than Disneyland".'

'Well, I suppose if you've got a reputation you might as well live up to it,' said Bella. They all laughed, more out of politeness than anything else, glad that Bella could still crack a joke.

Amanda rose from the table, poured more champagne, topped

Edwina's glass up with tonic and then busied herself at the sink, peeling potatoes.

'It's stew and mash tonight, OK?'

'Yum,' said Edwina appreciatively. 'My own cooking is so gross it's a wonder I don't starve.'

Lizzie twiddled her glass by the stem thoughtfully and said, 'I just think it's an odd coincidence that, having declared her undying hatred of Edwina, Edwina's career suddenly grinds to a halt, and then Cathy just happens to be around Bella and Amanda when things go wrong for them.'

'You'd better watch your back then, Lizzie,' cut in Edwina. 'She's at the MoD with you now, and it wouldn't surprise me if she didn't have you in her sights. When I met her that time in Northern Ireland, the only other people off our course she was interested in hearing about were you and Amanda.'

'Oh, come off it. You're imagining things,' said Lizzie brightly. But the look on Edwina's face made her wonder. She felt a little frisson of apprehension as she thought of Cathy renting a room from Bruce. What an unholy alliance that could prove to be. If what Edwina had said was to be believed, then this could be a very unhealthy situation. 'Well, I suppose forewarned is forearmed.' She brightened somewhat at the thought that Bruce had been warned for a posting and might not be around much longer; that was something to be grateful for.

'Anyway,' said Edwina, 'let's get away from the gruesome subject of the awful Cathy. What plans have you two got for the future now that you've swelled the ranks of the unemployed?'

'I'm going to work for a wine importer,' said Amanda, half-peeled spud in one hand and knife in the other.

'What a waste,' groaned Edwina. 'What a moment for me to be on the wagon when I have a friend who will have access to some lovely free samples.'

'I doubt it,' laughed Amanda. 'I'm working purely as an administrator. I shall have nothing to do with the liquid assets of the company.'

'What about you, Bella?' asked Lizzie.

'I've got a job at a travel agency. The pay is lousy and the perks are few and far between, but it's quite fun, and after Staff College the pressure is nonexistent, which makes it wonderful.'

'It all sounds cool,' said Edwina with approval.

'That's the potatoes done.' Amanda scooped them out of the sink and into a pot of water bubbling on the hot plate of the Aga. 'Now, who wants to help me get the tree in from the garden so we can decorate it?'

'I will,' said Lizzie. 'I'm so sorry that I can't be here with you on Christmas Day, but I promised Mummy and Daddy ages ago that I'd go out to Germany to be with them.'

'And me,' apologised Edwina, although she knew in her heart that she would really rather be with Ulysses. She'd seen very little of him over the last few months and she was hoping to use the holiday to persuade him to help her look for a new flat, closer to the centre of London but also handy for Kingston. She actually wanted somewhere big enough for him to move in with her, but she was taking that next item on her agenda very slowly indeed.

'Don't worry,' said Amanda, 'it's great having you here tonight. And it's even better knowing that we've got friends who'll stand by us, whatever has happened recently.'

Lizzie raised her glass. 'To friendship, then.'

'Friendship!'

Clapham, March 1994

Lizzie couldn't think for the life of her what had persuaded her to accept Bruce's invitation to his farewell party; inbred good manners, she supposed, could be the only logical answer, coupled possibly with relief that he was finally on his way to a posting to his regiment in Catterick, North Yorkshire. She consoled herself with the notion that there would be safety in numbers, because there were to be over fifty other guests there, if Bruce was to be believed. She peered out of the rain-washed windscreen of her car to read the names of the roads as she crawled along the south side of Clapham Common, looking for the turning to take her to Bruce's house. She spotted the turn, indicated and swung the car to the left. Quickly she glanced at the directions written on a scrap of paper clutched in her left hand. 'Down to the T-junction, right, first left then second left,' she muttered to herself. She drove slowly, not wishing to miss the turns in the dark and realising that with narrow roads and cars parked all along them, doing a U-turn was going to be a problem.

'I wish I hadn't agreed to come,' she chuntered to herself. She thought about sacking the whole thing, turning round and going back home. But it would be so rude, and being rude to people was simply beyond Lizzie. She'd accepted his invitation so she must go. She turned into Bruce's road, which consisted of Victorian terraced villas. The residents parked along either side of the road and their cars, together with the influx of Bruce's friends, meant there wasn't a single space to be had anywhere. Lizzie put the car into first gear and crawled along the road. Then the next one, and the next. Eventually, half a mile away, she found a space into which she was able to squeeze her little car. She grabbed the bottle of wine from the front seat, flung her raincoat over her shoulders, locked the car, put the keys in the pocket of her skirt and began to tramp through the cold drizzle back to Bruce's house. By the time she arrived she was cold and wet and felt not in the least like a party.

The door was open, so she pushed through it and into the crush of people in the hallway. Someone took her coat, muttering about putting it upstairs. Lizzie was surprised to see so many people. I didn't think he could possibly have this many friends, she thought uncharitably. Then, as an afterthought, she thought that perhaps all these people wanted to make sure he was really going. That was even less charitable, she told herself.

Lizzie decided that she would give Bruce the wine, make sure she was seen, and then leave as soon as was decently possible. She didn't think anyone would care, or even notice, if she only stayed for about an hour. She put her weight behind her shoulder and pushed her way along the hall, heading, she hoped, for the kitchen. She recognised a couple of faces as she passed and called out greetings to them. She was just about to make her way into the kitchen when a familiar voice called, 'Hi, Lizzie.' Lizzie turned.

'Hello, Cathy. Bruce said you had moved in here.'

'Yes. I'm lucky as it's so convenient for work. How are you? I was sorry to hear about your husband.'

Lizzie listened to her words, outwardly friendly and caring, and yet all she could think about was that Cathy was probably the person who had destroyed the careers of two of her closest friends. She didn't think she could talk to her without saying something really catty.

'Thank you, but it was a while ago now,' said Lizzie hurriedly. 'I must find Bruce. Please excuse me.' She dived into the kitchen.

Bruce was holding court with a group of half a dozen guests around him. It was obvious he was in the middle of telling a joke.

'. . . so the greengrocer said,' and he held out one hand limply and put the other on his hip to emphasise the punch-line, '"Isn't it obvious that I'm a fruit?"' His audience roared with laughter. Bruce caught sight of the new arrival. 'It's little Lizzie. Now here's someone who knows all about *fruit*, don't you, dear?'

Lizzie clutched the bottle she was holding to stop herself from smacking his face. She quickly decided that the best course of action was to ignore the comment. God, it had been a mistake to come!

'Hello. I brought you this.' She thrust the bottle into his hand but she wasn't quick enough. Bruce grabbed her by her arm and pulled her towards him.

'Why, thank you,' he said as if he'd never been given a bottle of Hungarian Merlot before. Before she had a chance to turn her head away, he had kissed her hard on the mouth. She compensated by keeping her lips firmly pressed together. As soon as he relaxed his grip a fraction Lizzie pushed him away.

'I mustn't monopolise you,' she said, escaping out of the kitchen and into the sitting room. She wiped her mouth on the back of her hand to rid herself of the feel of his lips on hers. He'd obviously been drinking quite heavily, even though it was not yet nine, as his breath had the sour smell and taste of stale red wine.

Lizzie saw some faces she recognised and made her way through the press of people to talk to them. On her way to join them she collected a glass of wine and looked at her watch. She had made up her mind to be away by half past nine at the latest, and was pleased to see that she didn't have much more than forty minutes to kill. It would be past ten before she got home to Kilburn – if she was lucky with the traffic – and she'd never been one for late, boozy parties. She chatted desultorily, waiting for a time when she could make her getaway without appearing to be in indecent haste. Well-trained by Army cocktail parties and dinner nights, she could make endless small talk, as could all the other guests, so the noise grew as people bellowed greetings, jokes and drunken conversation at each other.

Lizzie, conscious that she was driving, eked out her glass of indifferent white wine as she talked, and kept a wary eye out for Bruce and Cathy, but they didn't come near her. When she next looked at her watch she saw with relief that it was almost nine thirty-five. She could go. She put her glass down on the mantelpiece, murmured an excuse about finding a loo and headed back towards the front door. She was about to leave when she remembered her coat. It obviously wasn't in the hall. Perhaps it was upstairs. Tentatively, stepping carefully between couples sitting chatting on each of the treads, she made her way up to the first floor. A dim, unshaded bulb lit the landing, and by it Lizzie could see five doors. Two were open and led to a bathroom and a loo, but the other three were closed.

Lizzie went to the nearest door and turned the handle cautiously. It opened with a mild squeak. Lizzie put her head round it and saw a tidy room with a neatly made bed. It smelt of aftershave. Obviously a man's room, Derek Lesser's or Bruce's, but either way it was devoid of coats. She shut the door again and tried the next one. It was similar, tidy and masculine, but bigger, and there were still no coats. She was just shutting the door again when she felt a violent shove in the small of her back that propelled her forwards. She was about to cry out when a hand was clamped over her mouth and her arms were pinned to her sides. She heard the door being kicked shut and what dim shadows she'd been able to make out were now lost in the pitch darkness. But even though she couldn't see and she couldn't yell, she could smell, and she recognised the smell of the stale red wine she'd detected earlier on Bruce's breath.

Lizzie struggled in rising panic, but despite his diminutive size Bruce was surprisingly strong. He pushed her forwards, half carrying her using his arm around her middle, until they reached the bed, then he forced her to bend over so that her face was buried in the thickness of the duvet. Lizzie found she couldn't breathe, and tried to bite the hand covering her mouth, but he must have realised what she wanted to do and moved it round to the back of her head so he could press her face even harder into the bedding.

Lizzie knew that her heavily muffled cries and yells wouldn't be heard across the room, let alone over the babble of voices that were clearly audible even through the closed door and the bedclothes. She squirmed and struggled but Bruce was too strong for her. She could hear the blood pounding in her ears, and her chest was racked with agonising pain as her lungs tried desperately to draw in air and failed. She was dimly aware that Bruce was now almost lying on top of her and his free hand was groping up her skirt to her knickers. She felt his finger wriggle under the gusset and then roughly penetrate her. With a desperate effort Lizzie tried to kick him, but all she achieved was the removal of his hand. Then she was dealt a swingeing slap across her bare thighs. It was her last effort, for she knew she was losing consciousness; she was suffocating. Oh, God, she thought, why me?

Then her head was lifted clear of the duvet. She sucked in air, gasping, coughing and retching. She couldn't talk or shout as the need for air dominated every function of her being. Her face was held clear of the bed for several seconds, perhaps nearly as much as half a minute, before her tormentor plunged it back into the depths of the bedding.

'Do as I say and I'll let you breathe, OK?' said Bruce, his voice thick and slurred, whether with desire or drink Lizzie didn't know or care. 'Understand?' he asked. Lizzie tried to nod. He must have felt her feeble movement under the hand that was holding her head down. 'Is that a yes?' Lizzie tried to nod again. The pressure on her head eased slightly and she was able to turn it a fraction. She was able to breathe again – just.

'You know you want me really. If you hadn't been so friendly with those fucking perverts you'd have been quite willing. It's all their fault, because I know what you're really like. You pretend to be Little Miss Frigid but you're gagging for it really; it's just they've convinced you not to go with men.' He pinned her down with his weight again, and Lizzie heard the sound of a zip. Again she felt him fumbling up her skirt with his free hand. She drew in a deep breath, preparing to scream, but felt her face forced back into the bed covers again: 'No you don't, you little cow,' and he held her head down hard. Lizzie was beyond panic now; she was convinced he was going to kill her. She couldn't fight him; she didn't have the strength. As her lungs began to ache and scream for air, he released her again, and as he did so she felt her pants being pulled down. His hand was fumbling between her legs, trying to force them apart.

Rape! she wanted to scream, but no one would hear her pathetic whimpers, which was all the noise she could produce.

Suddenly the door opened and light and the noise of the party flooded into the room. Bruce jumped backward, leaving Lizzie's naked buttocks exposed as she lay bent over the bed. She began to sob, 'Thank God, thank God,' over and over. She reached a hand up to her waist and pulled her skirt back down to cover her shame.

'Do you mind?' shouted Bruce, swaying drunkenly.

'Sorry to interrupt,' said Cathy, pretending to notice nothing, 'but you're wanted on the phone.'

Bruce turned his back on Cathy momentarily as he zipped his fly up, and then stormed out of the room.

'Thank you, thank you, Cathy,' sobbed Lizzie. She slithered off the bed and slumped on to the floor, weak, terrified and exhausted.

'Sorry. I didn't mean to interrupt anything.' Cathy's sang-froid was spooky.

'No, you don't understand. He was trying to rape me.'

'Rape you?' Cathy laughed. 'Get real. Bruce wouldn't do a thing like that. He's a big pussycat.'

Lizzie stared at her through her tears. 'But you saw him. He was trying to suffocate me; he was forcing himself on me. Please, I need your help. A witness.'

Cathy stared coolly down at her. 'I'll tell you what I witnessed. I witnessed someone who has been making sheep's eyes at Bruce all evening, who has been throwing herself at him, making any number of improper suggestions as to what you could do together if they got any privacy. So it comes as no surprise that you finally got your way and seduced him. Isn't that the truth? Isn't that what I saw?' She smiled sweetly.

Lizzie pulled herself off the floor and sat on the edge of the bed. She looked at Cathy imploringly, her face tear-stained and stricken. 'Why? You know you're lying. What have I done to hurt you?'

'I'm not lying, sweetie. That's what I saw and that's what I'll tell anyone who asks.'

'You can't. It's not true.' Lizzie couldn't believe that anyone could be so treacherous. It would be her word against Cathy's – and Bruce's.

Cathy shrugged again. 'Tough.'

'But I don't understand.'

Cathy moved forward so she was only a few inches away from the bed, then she bent forward and thrust her face close to Lizzie's. 'I've got a long memory, Lizzie. I remember you and Miss Hardwick and precious Miss Austin making me look a fool after I saw Mr Moore leave your lines. You three nearly wrecked my career while you all went on to be the golden girls of the Army. So, we're quits now, ducky. I think I've called in the debt with each of you. I wouldn't try charging Bruce with attempted rape, because it won't stick. All I can say is, it's just such a shame I came in when I did so he couldn't finish the job properly.' Cathy swept out of the room, leaving Lizzie staring after her in absolute horror.

She remained transfixed for about a minute, unable to believe that anyone could be so vindictive and vengeful. Then it dawned on her that she was still in Bruce's room and he might return. The thought galvanised her. She stood up, her legs trembling like a new-born gazelle's. Her knickers fell round her ankles. She kicked them off and stuffed them in her pocket. Bruce had touched them; she didn't want them near her skin. Tentatively she walked towards the door. Once on the landing, where there was light and noise and people, she felt safer. Quickly she checked that her car keys were still in her pocket and then she picked her way back downstairs, through the press of laughing, chattering guests and out into the cold, miserable, rain-soaked night. Instantly she began to shiver, whether through the shock of what had happened or because of the cold she didn't know, nor did she care. It didn't matter a damn about her raincoat, all she wanted to do now was find her car and get home.

Aldershot, March 1994

'I'm coming right over,' said Edwina. 'I'll be with you in about forty minutes or so.' Lizzie protested that it was late.

'Balls,' said Edwina as she slammed the phone down.

Lizzie sat down at the table in her basement kitchen and cradled the large drink she'd poured herself when she'd got in. She could barely remember the journey home as she'd driven like an automaton, changing gear, braking, indicating without thinking because all her thoughts were occupied with what Bruce and Cathy had done to her. She had been past crying by the time she'd got to her car, and she still didn't feel like tears now. All she felt was numb. Numb and betrayed.

She'd planned to return to her bed-sit in Kilburn because it was so much closer, but somehow she'd found herself on the A3 and realised that her instincts were taking her home. It was with relief that she let herself in through the front door and was greeted by the familiar smell and atmosphere of her house. But as she descended the stairs to the basement, flicking on light switches as she went, she was suddenly overcome by a wave of panic. She tried to be brave, reassuring herself that Bruce didn't know her address here, but regardless of that, she was assailed by irrational thoughts. Despite the stiff whisky and water she poured for herself, the awful images and thoughts still kept crowding in. She looked at the stairs and dreaded the thought of going up them to bed. Supposing someone was hiding at the top? She knew she was being ridiculous, she knew that the house was empty, but she couldn't find the courage to go up there. Lizzie realised that she had to talk to someone about what she'd gone through. It was the advice she would have given to any-one and she knew she ought to take it herself. She tried ringing

Amanda but there was no reply, so she dialled Edwina. She couldn't believe the sense of relief she felt when Edwina answered. She poured out the whole sorry, sordid tale. Predictably, comfortingly Edwina had believed her implicitly and had been appalled. And now she was on her way over.

Lizzie got up from the table and poured herself another drink. Her hand was shaking so much she spilt half of the measure on to the dresser. She went to fetch a cloth to mop up the mess and found that tears blinded her. She grabbed a piece of kitchen towel and blew her nose noisily. She was angry at what had happened, angry that she was so upset, angry at being betrayed, angry at making a mess . . . The tears returned and this time she gave in to them. She sat down at the kitchen table, laid her head on her arms and allowed herself to sob, heart-wrenching, heaving sobs until she had no tears left to flow.

By the time Edwina arrived she felt exhausted but much calmer and was able to recount in detail the events of the evening.

'She said what?' Edwina couldn't believe Cathy's vindictiveness. 'You know, I suspected her, we all did, of having something to do with my problems and Amanda and Bella's dismissal, but I simply can't believe she had it planned all along.'

'It wasn't planned,' said Lizzie wearily. 'She just made use of the opportunities as they presented themselves. It all stemmed from the incident with Jeremy Moore. She obviously got into a lot of trouble over it and she blames us.'

'But that's ridiculous. None of us had anything to do with it. The whole incident was entirely of her own making. If she'd investigated the circumstances of the affair at the time instead of jumping to conclusions she wouldn't have ended up making a complete fool of herself.' Edwina was almost spitting with righteous anger. 'God, it's me that should be bearing a grudge. If she only knew what I went through in that hour that I spent in my room, waiting to be kicked out. Jesus!' She got up and stormed around Lizzie's kitchen. Then she stopped, contrite and apologetic. 'I'm sorry, Lizzie. This isn't helping you at all, is it? I shouldn't be angry about something that happened years ago. I should be helping you.' She went over to Lizzie and gave her a big hug. 'Forgive me?'

'There's nothing to forgive.' Lizzie smiled wanly. 'So what should I do?'

'Apart from telling the bitch what you think of her?'

'Yes, apart from that.'

393

'Do you want to go to the police?'

'Do you think I ought to?'

'It was a serious sexual assault, even if you ignore the fact that he planned to do more than that.'

Lizzie sat still and silent as she thought about it. 'Would I be an awful coward if I didn't?'

'No. It's got to be entirely your decision. But the police can't do anything if you don't make a complaint.'

'But I'll have to go through all the details with them, won't I?'

'Yes.'

'I don't think I could do that.'

'Then don't, if that's how you feel.'

'Do you really mean that?'

'I do. They'll want to examine you, which will be pretty gruesome.' Lizzie shuddered. 'And what evidence is there? Have you got any bruises?'

'I don't know. I thought he was going to suffocate me but he didn't hit me.' A thought struck her. 'Oh yes he did.' She pulled her skirt up to expose her thigh. 'He slapped me hard, here.' Edwina bent down to look, but apart from a faint red mark there was nothing to see.

'What about your arms, if he was holding you down?' But there was nothing on them either. 'I think you're right, sadly. Even if you did make a complaint I don't think anything would come of it. Bruce would probably say it was just a bit of slap and tickle, and as Cathy is the only witness . . .'

Lizzie signed heavily. 'It was just so frightening. I really thought he was going to kill me. I couldn't believe that someone I knew well could do that to me. And then Cathy . . . I thought she was my rescuer but she seemed pleased at what had happened. I couldn't believe it. How could she?' She began to sob again. Edwina pulled her close and gave her a cuddle, rubbing her shoulders and making soothing noises. After a while Lizzie's tears subsided again.

'I'm going upstairs to run you a huge hot bath, and then I'm going to tuck you up in bed with a hot toddy,' said Edwina practically. 'Will you be all right while I do it.' Lizzie nodded. 'I'll call you when it's ready.'

Edwina climbed the stairs to the bathroom. She turned on both taps and it wasn't long before the bath was full of hot water and the air was full of steam. She was just turning to go and call Lizzie when she noticed the bathroom mirror. Faintly visible in the steamy droplets which had condensed on it was the vague outline of a past message; a heart, pierced by an arrow. Underneath was written, 'Lizzie loves Richard' then, in brackets, 'still'. Edwina wondered how recently Lizzie had traced that little message to herself and had to blink back the tears at its poignancy.

Then rage overtook her again. To think that that bastard Bruce thought he could take Lizzie just because he wanted her. And worse, that he was going to get away with his assault because of Cathy. Edwina felt absolutely livid. There had to be something she could do. She didn't know what, not right now. But she was sure she'd think of something.

Edwina spent the night in Lizzie's spare room. She wanted to be on hand if Lizzie had nightmares or if she just needed a shoulder to cry on. But due partly to exhaustion brought on by her ordeal, and partly to the size of the Scotch Edwina gave her as a nightcap, Lizzie didn't stir until after ten o'clock the next morning.

When she came downstairs Edwina was already tucking into toast and marmalade.

'Want some?' she asked.

'But there isn't any food in the house.'

'There is now. I went to the corner shop, first thing.'

'What an angel you are,' said Lizzie.

'How are you?' asked Edwina as she fed more bread into the toaster.

'I'll survive. It's not the worst thing that has ever happened to anyone.'

'No,' said Edwina, thinking of what had happened to Richard. She suspected Lizzie was probably thinking the same. 'What about tomorrow in the office?'

'Bruce has handed over. He's got some gardening leave before he takes up his new post.'

'Well, that's something to be grateful for.'

'If he were going to be in I'd have called in sick. I couldn't have faced him.'

'I don't blame you.' There was silence for a minute, then the toast popped up and Lizzie busied herself with spreading butter and marmalade.

'I just worry about what might happen if he has a go at another woman.'

'He may not try anything like that again.'

'But I would feel so responsible.'

'Don't. Put it out of your mind. Forget it. It's not your problem. Your priority is to get over it, OK?'

'OK.'

Edwina smiled. 'I've got to go back up to town later on today. Ulysses is helping me move into a new flat, so I'd better make sure he does it properly. But I'll come back here again this evening so you're not on your own.'

'Oh, Edwina. I'm sorry that I've been such a nuisance to you. Mollycoddling me must be the last thing you need right now. You should have said.'

Edwina shrugged. 'It's what friends are for.'

Chiswick, March 1994

Edwina put her back against her battered old sofa and shoved it across the carpet, into the corner of the sitting room of her new flat.

'What about here?' she asked Ulysses.

'Nah. I won't be able to see the telly properly from there.'

Edwina flopped down on it in exasperation. The springs twanged ominously.

'Well, where would you put it then?' she said crossly.

'On the council tip.'

'Apart from there.'

'Where you had it before wasn't too bad.'

'Ooh . . .' Words failed her. 'But when I asked you, you said to try it over here.'

'Yeah. But I was wrong.'

'Oh, fuck it. I'm too tired to do any more tonight.' She gazed around the piles of books, half-unpacked boxes, stacks of pictures leaning against the walls and open suitcases spilling imperfectly folded clothes. 'What am I going to do, Ulysses?'

'Get rid of the bloody thing. I told you.'

'No. Not about the sofa, you moron. About Lizzie.'

'Oh, her. It's not your problem.'

'It is. She's my friend.'

'It still doesn't make it your problem.'

'I'd like to give that vile Roberts woman a piece of my mind. Tell her exactly what I think of her.'

'Why on earth? It wasn't her that tried to maul Lizzie.'

'No. But she was the one who really betrayed her. From what Lizzie said, she almost gloated over the whole incident. I simply can't believe it. She must be really sick.'

'If you feel so strongly about it, why don't you go and see her? If nothing else it'll get if off your chest and then you'll stop banging on about it.'

'But don't you care about what happened to Lizzie?'

'Yeah, I do. She's a lovely lady and she's been dealt some rotten cards in the past, but if she isn't going to the police then I don't see why you feel you've got to interfere.'

'Because Cathy Roberts isn't the only one with a score to settle.' Edwina got up from the sofa, picked up her keys and crash helmet and headed for the door.

'Where are you going?' demanded Ulysses.

'I promised Lizzie that I'd spend tonight with her again. I hope this place is sorted out by the time I get back tomorrow.' She quickly opened the front door and dodged the cushion that came flying through the air.

Lizzie was feeling much calmer about her frightening ordeal and had decided that she was quite capable of returning to work the next day. She would then go back to her little bed-sit in Kilburn, as she usually did during the week. Edwina was glad she would be freed from her self-imposed responsibility of looking after Lizzie, although she told Lizzie to ring her at her new flat if she felt the least bit apprehensive.

'I wish there was room for you to come and kip down with me for a couple of nights,' said Edwina, 'but it's such a tiny place there really isn't the space. But I'm only a stone's throw away, so if you need me . . .'

'I won't. I'll be fine now,' Lizzie reassured her. 'And I think going back to work will be the best antidote. If I'm busy I can't brood.' She looked pensive for a second or two. 'After all, it worked after Richard died.' For the second time in as many days Edwina felt her heart go out to Lizzie. She was such a lovely person and yet she'd had a miserable series of events in recent years. And again Edwina felt a spasm of anger that Cathy had done her best to make things worse.

Early the next morning, Edwina returned to London to find everything in her flat much as she'd left it. Irrationally annoyed – after all, it was her flat and her mess – she banged her helmet down, made herself a coffee and then rang into the picture desk for her assignments that day. It was all routine stuff; she was to cover a luncheon at

Critchley's, the current favourite restaurant for the rich and famous who wanted to be seen, then on to Twickenham to get a picture of a child heroine. Finally she was to go back into town to snap the glitterati arriving at a film première. She surveyed the mess that surrounded her and wondered when she'd find time to get things straight, or as straight as they'd ever be in her chaotic life. She made a desultory effort to put away a few clothes. At least if she emptied the suitcases it would clear some of the muddle off the floor. She was putting the now empty cases away on top of the wardrobe when she spotted a scrap of paper tucked into the edge of the mirror screwed to the door.

It read, 'I've got an idea for how we should arrange things. Leave it till I get back. U xxx.'

She noticed how he'd written 'we should arrange things'. She still hadn't broached the subject of him moving in with her, but she'd specifically picked this flat with that in mind. Kingston wasn't a difficult journey from Chiswick, only across Kew Bridge and then through Richmond Park, and it was a breeze for her to get into central London too. It was a perfect location for both of them, but she wasn't going to rush Ulysses into anything, least of all cohabitation.

Feeling cheerful that Ulysses wanted to help her sort out her new home, and had been giving the matter some thought on her behalf, Edwina packed the cameras, lenses and film that she would need for the day into her rucksack, crammed on her helmet and headed down the three flights of stairs to the car park and her bike. The engine fired first time with its customary satisfying throaty roar and Edwina kicked it off its stand with a practised heave, then swung her leg across the saddle. Checking there was a gap in the traffic she pulled out of the car park and on to the road, quickly changing up through the gears and weaving expertly through the other, slower-moving vehicles heading for central London. She had plenty of time before she had to be at the restaurant; it was a sunny day and she took a detour through Hyde Park. It was only eleven forty-five and she didn't have to be at Critchley's, now only half a mile away, until twelve fifteen.

Edwina stopped her bike, took off her helmet and sat on a bench to enjoy the spring sunshine. In the relative tranquillity, her thoughts returned to Lizzie's recent ordeal and the unfairness of it all. She desperately wanted to do something to help, but she knew that all that reasonably could be done had been. And yet she felt strongly that she should do something to put matters right. She thought about the options available, and realised that Ulysses was right: the only thing she could do would be to confront Cathy. To tell her to her face what she thought of her, to tell her about the recent dreadful events that had conspired against Lizzie. Perhaps to try and extract an apology? No, Edwina reckoned, that was probably asking for too much. Perhaps the best she could hope for would be to make Cathy realise what a mean, hurtful and unnecessary thing she had done – to make her squirm. She would have to go and see her. It might not do any good, but she would feel better for doing it.

Feeling more at ease with herself now that she'd made up her mind, Edwina pulled her helmet back on and headed for the swanky and expensive restaurant where her day's work was due to start. It was easy to find, due to the press of other journalists crowding round the door, hoping to get shots of the glamorous arrivals at the launch party for a new charity to raise funds for refugees fleeing the war-torn former Yugoslavia. With the support of two duchesses, three film stars and half a dozen politicians, media coverage was guaranteed. 'As will be the donations,' a reporter from *Hello!* magazine remarked within Edwina's hearing as she snapped away at the great, the good and – more importantly – the filthy rich. Edwina wasn't sure who half the faces were as she moved smoothly round the tables, clicking away, but the *Standard*'s society reporter accompanying her knew, and she pointed Edwina at those who ought to be snapped, and those who expected to be.

After about twenty minutes the press were invited to leave; the reporters clutching bundles of handouts detailing the objectives of the new charity, and the photographers clutching their cameras. Edwina checked her watch. She would have to get a move on if she was going to get the reels of film she'd just taken developed, and then make it to Twickenham for three o'clock. It wasn't far from Belgravia to Kensington High Street, but even on her motorbike Edwina found the going difficult. Dumping her bike outside the newspaper offices, she ran in with her films and handed them to the picture editor.

'Snaps of the society do at Critchley's.'

'OK,' he said, looking up. 'Do you want to get them developed?'

'Can you? The traffic is dreadful and I've got to be in Twickenham soon. Caroline from the society page was with me. She's got all the details of who was there. She'll tell you what she wants when she gets back here, which should be soon, I left her trying to get a taxi. I'll leave it all to you two.'

'Drive carefully,' the picture editor said to Edwina's departing back view. She waved in acknowledgement.

By the time she'd finished at the film premiére, later that evening, Edwina was only too glad to be heading home. The pictures of that event weren't required until the next morning, so she didn't have to go back to Kensington, which was something to be thankful for. She stopped to buy a copy of the *Standard* at a newsagent's so she could admire her work, and after she'd parked her bike, wearily made her way up to her flat, dreading the chaos that would greet her. She really didn't feel like doing any more unpacking, but if she didn't make the effort now, she could see that it was never going to get done. She put the key in the lock and, as she opened the door, was surprised to see that all the cardboard boxes, all the piles of books, all the mess had disappeared.

'*There* you are,' said Ulysses. 'I'd thought you'd left for good.'

Edwina said nothing. She was standing in the middle of the room with her mouth open.

'How about saying "That's bloody brilliant, you hunk. Please use my body to act out all your most depraved fantasies"?'

'It's bloody brilliant,' repeated Edwina, a smile spreading across her face.

'What about "Please use my body . . ."?' prompted Ulysses, hopefully.

'It's not *that* brilliant. But thanks anyway. You didn't have to.'

'I did. I couldn't live in the sort of mess you can. If I'm going to move in with you, I shall have to insist on some standards.'

'Move in with me? You haven't been invited yet.'

'But it's what you want.'

'Don't flatter yourself,' said Edwina, her face covered by a huge smile. Ulysses grabbed her round the middle and began tickling her.

'Stop, stop,' she shrieked. 'Yes, of course you can move in.'

'Good. I'm glad we've got that settled. Right then, wench, where's my supper?'

It was a week before Edwina's schedule allowed her to wait outside Fleet Bank House, the home of the MoD's Procurement Executive, for Cathy to appear at the end of the day's work. Edwina had no idea where she lived, beyond 'somewhere in Clapham'. She'd tried looking it up in the phone book, but Bruce Villiers' number wasn't listed, and although she had considered asking Lizzie, she'd soon decided against it. Lizzie would have been bound to question her as to why she wanted the address, and would have tried to persuade her against her plan. No, much better, she had decided, to use her skills to follow Cathy home and then confront her on her own doorstep. Besides which, it had been a long time since she'd put her old talents into action. It would be interesting to see if she was still as good as she used to be at tailing someone.

Now, however, waiting on the pavement in the chilly, drizzling, dark and dreary March evening, Edwina wasn't quite so sure that she'd gone about things in the best way. She'd been standing here since five o'clock and it was now nearly seven. Cold, wet and fed up, Edwina was on the brink of calling it a day when she saw the familiar figure appear in the doorway. Cathy paused for a moment to put up her umbrella before turning and heading along the pavement away from the tube station – which surprised Edwina. She had assumed the woman would be heading home to Clapham on the underground.

Tailing Cathy was a piece of cake, as her red and navy spotted umbrella could be seen bobbing above the heads of the other pedestrians from thirty yards away. Edwina followed her as she wove her way eastwards along the busy pavements towards the City. After about fifteen minutes of walking, the umbrella paused, was lowered and disappeared. Edwina moved swiftly forward; obviously Cathy was entering one of the premises just there. She got to the place she'd last seen the umbrella and scanned the windows hopefully but discreetly. There, in a smart bistro, she saw Cathy being greeted by a distinguished-looking man of about fifty, perhaps older, whom Edwina thought she recognised. He obviously knew Cathy well, because he kissed her on both cheeks before removing her coat.

Edwina stood outside the wine bar, unsure of what to do next. The way Cathy was acting didn't make it likely that her companion was a relative. She was certainly flirting with him, whilst the way he was holding her hand was far from avuncular. They were handed menus by a deferential waiter, and from their apparently intent study of them, it seemed as though they were planning on eating. Hell, thought Edwina. She wanted to go home. She toyed with the idea of confronting Cathy there and then, but she didn't think a public scene

402

would achieve what she wanted. She had hoped for a quiet talk with Cathy to make her realise the consequences of her mean-spirited actions. Edwina reckoned that she would get nowhere here, except, perhaps, forcible ejection courtesy of the management.

But the face of Cathy's friend niggled her. She was sure she recognised it from somewhere, although she couldn't place it. It's always the same, she thought; if I see someone I know out of context, I can never think of the name right away. She pulled her rucksack off her shoulders, selected a camera, set the aperture and, pressing it against the restaurant window, focused Cathy and her friend in the viewfinder. She'd compensated for not wanting to use flash, and thus draw attention to what she was doing, by using a wide aperture, which meant that the focusing was crucial. She hoped that, as Cathy and her companion were sitting down at a table, they wouldn't move suddenly and ruin things. Click. Edwina lowered her camera, certain that the shot, although it would be unacceptable to the picture editor of the *Standard*, would suit her purposes very well. All she wanted was a record of the man's face so she could study it at her leisure until she remembered his name. In the mean time, she could follow Cathy home another day. After all, there was no particular urgency.

Edwina pinned the photograph up on her wardrobe door when she had developed it.

'Are you going to use it for target practice?' asked Ulysses, intrigued by her actions.

'Nope,' said Edwina, getting a black biro out of her bag and disfiguring Cathy's face with the addition of spots, a moustache and glasses.

'Very grown-up,' said Ulysses sourly. 'So why?'

'I know this man,' said Edwina, drawing a circle round his face.

'Biblically?'

'Piss off. No, I've seen him somewhere before and I can't place him. It'll come to me sooner or later. I want to know who Cathy has got her hooks into this time. It might come in useful.'

'Is he Army?'

'No.' Edwina shook her head. 'I'm almost certain he isn't.'

'Then is he someone you've photographed?'

Edwina shook her head but uncertainly. 'I don't know.'

The light dawned two days later. 'Of course,' she said, sitting up in bed suddenly one morning and almost spilling her tea. 'The charity lunch at Critchley's. He was one of the guests.'

'Who was?'

'The man in the picture, stupid.'

'So you're hardly any nearer finding out who he is. You said there were hundreds of people there.'

'But Caroline from the gossip column will know who he is. She knows everyone.'

'Wolfgang Zeidler,' Caroline said after she'd studied the photo.

'Never heard of him,' answered Edwina, unimpressed.

'You should have done. He's a major manufacturer of optical and electronic equipment and one of the richest men in Germany, if not Europe. His wealth is the subject of a lot of criticism; his factories – though they were then owned by his father – were major beneficiaries from slave labour during the war. He tries to counteract it by getting involved in high-profile charities, the higher the profile the better. He also like women, racing and the opera.'

'How much does he like those?'

'He has a huge racing stables near Hanover, he's a patron of the opera in both Berlin and Covent Garden, and despite his age, his reputation for being seen with young, beautiful women is nearly as big as Peter Stringfellow's.' Which explained why he'd been at Critchley's, but certainly not why he'd met Cathy in some back-street bistro in the City. Even if Edwina had been feeling charitable – which she wasn't – though Cathy might qualify as young, she certainly didn't qualify as beautiful.

Edwina thought she'd better speak to the financial and business reporters to see what she could find out about Zeidler, other than that he liked to be seen giving to charity.

'Are you thinking of investing the surplus from your huge salary in one of his companies?' asked the financial editor, Philip Lang.

'Get real. Do I look like a bloated plutocrat?'

'So why the interest?' Philip looked at her with curiosity. 'Don't you have friends in the Army?' Despite her efforts, rumours about Edwina's connections had followed her from Maidenhead.

'What's that got to do with it?'

'Rumour has it that Zeidler is tendering for MoD contracts. That's why he's over here at the moment.'

'What sort of contracts?'

'I'm not sure. Something like night sights?' Philip wasn't sure of the terminology. Edwina nodded, encouragingly. 'Whatever it is, it's worth big bucks to whoever gets it. And of course, anyone who has got shares in the company will also do well, as the price will rocket once the contract is announced.'

'But isn't that insider dealing?' asked Edwina.

'Only if you know who is going to get the contract beforehand. Otherwise it's just speculation, and that's perfectly legal. It's what everyone on the Stock Exchange does every day.'

'Oh, right,' said Edwina. 'In which case I must tell my stockbroker to buy more shares for my portfolio.' But she left his office thoughtfully.

Did Cathy have anything to do with this contract? Edwina looked at what she knew from every angle and kept coming up against a wall of problems. For a start, the contract had certainly been put out for tender months, if not years, back; long before Cathy got the Procurement Executive job. Secondly, Cathy was unlikely to be involved in the decision-making process; she was far too lowly. Thirdly, if Cathy couldn't influence the decision-making, what on earth was her use to Zeidler? And he couldn't have been telling her that since he was going to get the contract she should buy a few shares, because it hadn't been awarded yet. Anyway, why would he?

None of it made any sense, and yet Edwina knew what she'd seen at the bistro. So why had Cathy been wined and dined by Zeidler, a man who, if Caroline was to be believed, could have the pick of European beauties? Unless Cathy had something very tempting to offer him, he wouldn't look twice at her bland, mousy features. Also, if Zeidler was as wealthy as all that, what he doing in an unknown bistro near the Guildhall? He was a man more used to dining at Rules or the Ritz and, according to Caroline, he liked to be seen out and about. But not that night. It was obvious that the low-key bistro was not somewhere that was regularly staked out by the paparazzi, if at all, thought Edwina.

All day long, while she worked, snapping the pictures required by her editor, she found her mind mulling over the scant information that she had on Cathy and Zeidler. Zeidler was obviously up to something and it required him to keep to a low profile. Edwina had two irrefutable facts to go on, but that was all: he was tendering for an MoD contract; and Cathy worked for Procurements. Something was very fishy, Edwina concluded, but what the hell was it?

When she got home that evening she told Ulysses of her suspicions.

'It's all pretty circumstantial,' he said. 'It may be that her reputation as an available screw has spread as far as Germany and Wolfgang wants to know what it is that she has to offer. After all, if most of the British male population under sixty has seen a piece of the action, don't you think the Germans mightn't want to get their share too?'

'This, of course, is quite likely,' agreed Edwina, 'but I think there's something else she's offering too.'

'What? Deviant sex?'

'Pervert!'

'We could always go and have a snoop round her place,' suggested Ulysses. 'If she's up to no good we might find something out.'

'Unlikely.'

'Got a better idea?'

'No.'

'Where does she live?'

'I don't know yet.'

Ulysses smacked his forehead in disbelief. 'How long have you been interested in this woman?'

Edwina shrugged.

'Leave it to me,' said Ulysses firmly. 'Girlies!'

Two days later Ulysses had chapter and verse on the whereabouts, movements and habits of Cathy Roberts.

'So what are you doing on Monday?' he asked Edwina.

Edwina consulted her diary. 'Apart from working, nothing.'

'Right. I'll meet you at Clapham Junction station at three o'clock.'

'Do you want me to bring anything?'

'Camera, film, the usual sort of stuff.'

'And how are we going to get in?'

'How do you think? You're going to indulge in a bit of breaking and entering, of course.' Edwina looked sceptical. 'Don't worry. I'll do a proper recce before then.'

They met as arranged and travelled on Edwina's bike to the residential road where Bruce's house was. They parked the bike in the next street, locked their crash helmets in the panniers and the bike to a tree and wandered back looking as nonchalant as they could. Edwina pointed out a Neighbourhood Watch sign tied to a lamppost.

406

'I wouldn't worry too much,' said Ulysses. 'There's hardly a soul around at this time. Mums and nannies are collecting kids from school and it'll be a while before anyone who works gets home. I should think we've got half an hour clear at the least, probably a lot more.'

'That should be enough.' They reached the front gate of Bruce's house and opened it boldly, not checking if anyone was watching – the way innocent callers wouldn't. Edwina shut it again carefully. She heard Ulysses ring the doorbell before she joined him in the small tiled porch.

'This is handy,' she said, noting how the porch sheltered them from any curious glances from passers-by or neighbours.

'Stop yakking and get us in,' said Ulysses. Edwina drew a small pouch from her pocket and extracted a couple of long, thin lock-picks. 'You know it's illegal to even possess these things,' she muttered as she inserted them into the Yale lock.

'Stop whining and get on with it,' retorted Ulysses, unsympathetically.

Edwina fiddled and twiddled for about five seconds and then there was a minute click.

'Well done,' said Ulysses as he and Edwina moved swiftly into the hall. Anyone watching would think an occupant had let them in.

'I'll look upstairs,' said Edwina, already halfway to the landing. She could see into the loo and the bathroom, but three doors were shut. She opened the first two, as Lizzie had done a couple of weeks previously, and shut them again; one was empty, the bed stripped and no sign of occupancy, and the second one was obviously a man's room. The third door had to be Cathy's.

Edwina had a quick but methodical look in the drawers and the cupboards before she came across a small pile of computer diskettes. She returned to the top of the stairs.

'Ulysses,' she called softly.

'Yeah?'

'Is there a computer down there?'

'In the dining room, on the table.'

'Good.' Edwina grabbed the four disks and headed downstairs. Quickly she switched on the machine, tapping her fingers impatiently while the computer bleeped and ticked as it geared itself up for action. 'Have you seen any blank disks around?' she asked Ulysses, who had come into the room to see what she was up to.

'No. Why?'

'It'll be quicker to copy these and go through them at our leisure, rather than look at every file now.'

'I'll have a look.' Ulysses began moving around the room, carefully opening and closing drawers and examining their contents.

The phone rang, and they both froze with shock as the shrill bell broke the silence. Then they relaxed as the answering machine cut in. They couldn't hear the outgoing message but listened intently to the caller's words: 'Cathy. Please meet me as usual on Wednesday. Goodbye.'

Ulysses walked over to the machine, picked up the receiver and dialled 1471.

'We do not have the caller's number,' said the oddly jerky female voice that the BT service used.

'Well, it was worth a try,' said Edwina. 'What do you reckon, the same wine bar as before?'

'It could have been anyone. A boyfriend, her father, anyone at all. Still . . .'

Edwina slipped one of the diskettes into the 'A' drive of the computer and looked at what it contained. Not a lot. She flipped it out and tried another. That didn't look as though it had much on it either.

'Look at this,' said Ulysses. He had returned carrying a big lever-arch file. 'I found this under her bed.'

Edwina opened it. The file contained a mass of Cathy's personal papers: old bank statements, copies of her confidential reports, old posting orders, insurance certificates. 'Handy,' murmured Edwina, taking a camera from her pocket and photographing the bank statements and some of the other papers. 'Oh, look at this,' she exclaimed gleefully, snapping another picture.

'What is it?' asked Ulysses.

'Only a share certificate for eight thousand Zeidler Industries shares.'

Ulysses whistled. 'And look at the date, the fifteenth of March 1994.'

Edwina shuffled through the bank statements. 'I think these might have been a gift. There doesn't appear to be a record of her paying that sort of money out.'

'Building society?' asked Ulysses.

'I haven't seen a passbook. Go and see if you can find one.' Edwina returned to the computer and looked at the next of the four disks. She scrolled down the files listed but nothing leapt off the screen as something that she should look at. She ejected it and tried the last one.

'That looks hopeful,' she said to herself.

'What does?' said Ulysses from the doorway.

'This one. "Bids".'

'Check it out.'

Edwina double-clicked on the file and opened it up. 'It's all Greek to me.' She stared at the list of initials and numbers. Ulysses peered over her shoulder. 'What do you make of it?'

'I don't know. It doesn't mean anything to me either.'

Edwina took out a notebook and jotted down half a dozen lines of information. 'I'll think about this later. Any joy with the blank disks or the passbook?'

'No, but I found this.' Ulysses flourished a Yale key.

'The front door?'

'Yup. It was hidden behind the clock on the mantelpiece so I don't suppose anyone will notice if it's missing for a few days.'

'Brill. I'll buy a load of diskettes tomorrow and come back and copy everything. Right. Let's get all this back where it belongs.' The two scurried efficiently around, returning the disks and files. They checked to make sure that nothing looked the least bit out of place and then let themselves out as discreetly as they'd entered.

'Will you follow Cathy on Wednesday?' asked Edwina as they returned to where the bike was parked.

'Can't,' said Ulysses. 'I've got a client that evening.'

'Can't you move the appointment? I've got a job too. I'll have to take time off to come here and copy the computer files and all the disks. I can't do everything.'

'That's your problem. You're the one who's got a bee in your bonnet.'

'Bastard.'

But Edwina didn't have to return to Cathy's house the next day, because the result of the tender for the night sight was announced, and surprisingly – well, not to Edwina – Zeidler's won the bid. In a spare moment Edwina wandered over to the business news desk.

'What have their shares done?' she asked Philip Lang casually.

'Why? Did you invest after all?'

'No, I did not.'

'More fool you. They've just gone up sixty-three pence.'

Edwina took Philip's calculator off his desk and did a quick sum. She whistled. 'Christ,' she exclaimed. 'I know someone who's just made a little over five thousand pounds.'

'I hope for their sake they didn't know anything about the award in advance. The authorities would take a dim view of it if it were proved they did.'

'Oh, I don't think so,' said Edwina.

'Just as well. There's already an almighty stink about Zeidler's getting the contract anyway.'

'Why?'

'Because there were four British firms bidding and they lost.'

'But that's business, isn't it?'

'Not if people get laid off as a result, or British companies go bust.'

'Is that likely to happen?'

'It's a very real possibility for one of the companies,' said Philip gravely.

'So why didn't the MoD take that into account?'

'I don't know. But if the bid from Zeidler's was really much more competitive than the others, the MoD probably felt duty-bound to get as much as they could for their money and to hell with the consequences.' Philip looked at Edwina thoughtfully. 'You aren't half asking a lot of questions for a snapper. Is there something you'd like to share with me?'

'No. Well, not yet, at any rate.' Edwina had a sudden thought. 'You haven't got a list of all the companies who bid, have you?'

'I might have.'

'Let me have a look. Please,' she added as an afterthought.

Half an hour later Philip presented her with a typed list of names, most of which meant nothing to Edwina.

'Now, what's in it for me?' he asked.

'Nothing. Well, something, maybe, I don't know. Look, if I do ever find out what I suspect may have happened, I'll let you know, I promise. But I can't say anything until I've checked out some facts.'

'OK.' Philip returned to his desk, but from the way he kept glancing over at Edwina as she worked with the picture editor, it was obvious that he was trying to figure out what it could be she thought she was on to.

Edwina couldn't wait to return to her flat that day. As soon as she'd let herself in she hauled the list of names that Philip had given her out of her pocket and compared it with the list of initials and figures she'd copied from the information on Cathy's disk. As she'd thought, the initials tallied exactly with the full names of the other companies bidding for the contract. What puzzled Edwina was that Zeidler Industries didn't feature on Cathy's list. When Ulysses arrived home later that evening she made him think about the problem too.

'Got it,' he said. They were watching the evening news, which had the award of the contract as its main story because of the disappointment that it had caused the workers at the four British companies.

'Got what?'

'The answer about Cathy's list. She's been feeding Zeidler details of the other bids so he can undercut them. That's why Zeidler wouldn't feature on the list – because his bid was going to go in after the others and be the lowest –'

'So they would be almost certain to get the contract,' finished Edwina.

'Which could explain why she's got those shares; payment for services rendered.'

'A payment which would increase considerably as and when Zeidler landed the deal.'

'And presumably, if it is Zeidler she's meeting on Wednesday, he's going to give her another backhander.'

'Wow!' whispered Edwina.

'Now what?'

'I'm going to tell the paper. This is a scoop.'

'What about the police?'

'They'll have to be involved at some stage – the paper will know what to do.'

When Edwina went to the editor he listened in silence as she told him the story.

'How did you get hold of the computer disks?' he asked.

'Do you really want to know?' replied Edwina, wishing to dodge the issue.

'Was it legal?'

'Not really.'

'Then I certainly don't want to hear any more.' He pressed his intercom and told his secretary to get Philip Lang into the office.

Philip arrived in under a minute, panting slightly. The editor quickly gave him the gist of Edwina's suspicions.

'She could be right,' Philip agreed. 'We can certainly check out what the exact bids were from the other firms involved. If they tally with Edwina's information then I think we can go further with this one.' Philip thought for a moment. 'Eight thousand shares would have been a bargain-basement price for Zeidler to pay this woman. There must be some other payments he's given her.'

Edwina piped up, 'I didn't see anything like that on her bank statements.'

'I don't want to know,' growled the editor.

Philip made arrangements for one of his staff to contact the dealing register for Zeidler's. 'We'll see who has done all the recent major deals with their shares. It may lead us somewhere.'

'Good,' said the editor.

'And I think she's meeting Zeidler again tonight. I was going to follow her and get another picture.'

'No,' said Philip and the editor simultaneously.

'We'll put another snapper on this one,' continued Philip. 'We don't want her to get the wind up through recognising you. Can you give us a picture of her so the photographer knows who he's looking for?'

Edwina nodded.

'Find out where Zeidler is staying in London and get someone to keep tabs on him. I want to know where else he goes or who goes to see him.'

'Does that mean you think Cathy may only be a small player in this?' asked Edwina, unable to keep the disappointment out of her voice.

'I don't know. But I'm not going to run this story until I'm sure of my facts. I assume you've heard of the word libel? Zeidler has taken bigger papers than this to the cleaners.'

'Yes, I'm sorry,' said Edwina, feeling a little foolish.

The full power of the paper's investigative capabilities was swung into action. At first Edwina was thoroughly annoyed that she was now a bystander watching events and not a main participant. But she was not a journalist and there were any number of employees on the paper who were far better qualified for this than she was; they also knew of any number of ruses to acquire information and angles to make the story more readable once they had the low-down. It took four reporters, working almost flat out, the best part of a week to get all the evidence that was needed. Philip showed Edwina the finished story just before the paper went to bed on Friday morning.

'It's one hell of a story,' he said as Edwina scanned down the front page. On the inside were the pictures of Cathy's meetings with Zeidler, the first taken by Edwina, the second by another of the *Standard*'s staff photographers. The pictures of the second meeting also showed Cathy being handed a small package.

'What was in it?' asked Edwina.

'We don't know, but the police will find out. As soon as this edition hits the streets they are going to move in.'

Edwina thought that she'd better ring Lizzie at work and warn her what was about to happen.

'I'm sorry, I don't understand,' said Lizzie.

'It's simple,' explained Edwina patiently. 'Cathy fed all the bids to Zeidler so he could go lower and secure the contract.'

'But how did you find all this out?'

Edwina had no doubts that she would get a great deal of disapproval from Lizzie if she told her absolutely everything – the fact that she'd indulged in breaking and entering would not go down well with her friend. She opted just to let on about the law-abiding side of her role.

'I was following her and saw her with Zeidler. It didn't take the brains of a nuclear physicist to realise that, if she worked for Procurements and he was after a contract, something extremely fishy was going on.'

There was a pause as Lizzie took the information on board.

'But I don't understand why you were following her in the first place.'

'I wanted to have a go at her about what happened with you and Bruce. I was so angry I was going to find out where she lived and have it out with her.'

'I see,' said Lizzie coolly.

'You don't approve?'

'Not really.'

'Why not?' Edwina was hurt by Lizzie's response.

'I'm not eighteen any more. I don't need you to fight my battles. If I'd wanted something doing I'd have done it myself.'

'Oh.' Edwina couldn't think of anything to say. She was disappointed that Lizzie wasn't grateful.

'And now I feel responsible for what has happened to Cathy.'

'Now you *are* being ridiculous!' Edwina was getting cross. 'Cathy only has herself to blame. It was her choice to get involved with Zeidler. That had nothing to do with you.'

'But if it hadn't been for me, she wouldn't have been found out.'

'Does that make it right?' Edwina's voice was getting shrill as she lost her cool. There was silence at the other end of the line. Edwina realised she ought to back down. 'We mustn't quarrel over her. She's not worth it.'

'No, you're right. I'm sorry. And thanks for telling me. No doubt the editor will be ringing the SO1 – not that we can do anything to stop the story breaking.'

Which indeed they couldn't. The *Standard* devoted three pages to the scoop, and the later editions even had pictures of Cathy being led away from the MoD by the police. Irrationally Edwina, as Lizzie had done, suddenly felt sorry for Cathy. It was one thing wanting to call her a nasty, two-faced, manipulative bitch, but it was another thing entirely seeing her being led away in handcuffs.

She felt even lower when, a few days later, she discovered that she would probably be required to give evidence at the trial.

'I don't know why,' she told Lizzie, 'but I don't want Cathy to find out it was me that got the police on to her.'

'Why on earth not? I'd have thought that was exactly what you wanted – to have a good go at her to get even for all that happened to us.'

'Yes, but there's getting even and getting even. I think this is rather more than I had in mind. A vicious tongue-lashing is one thing; two years in Holloway is something else.'

'Is that what she'll get?'

'Quite likely.'

'Hmm. Well, that's her career profile screwed up, isn't it?'

'Have you heard from Amanda?' asked Edwina, not wishing to dwell on Cathy's future prospects.

'Haven't you spoken to her?'

'No.'

'Why on earth not?'

'Well, you disapproved of my part in it. I didn't want her to feel the same. I was afraid she'd ask me about it if I phoned her and I wouldn't have been able to lie, so I chickened out and kept off the phone.'

'I suppose she wouldn't have seen the *Standard* down where she lives.'

'No.'

'Well, you must tell her all about it. She'll be so hurt if she finds out about all this from someone else.'

Edwina knew this was good, solid advice.

Amanda was comfortingly down-to-earth about it all. 'If it hadn't been you, someone else would have more than likely twigged what was going on. Cathy was never Mensa material; she was bound to get things wrong in the end, even if it was just having too much money to splash around.'

'I don't suppose she'll be doing much of that in the future. She's lost her pension and her job, and the shares that Zeidler gave her will be seized if it turns out she was guilty.'

'And that's not in much doubt.'

'I don't think even a really sharp lawyer will be able to get her off this one.'

'What's going to happen to Zeidler?' asked Amanda.

'I think he'll get done for corruption too – once they catch up with him.'

'You mean he's skipped the country?'

'He flew back to Germany after he met Cathy and has gone to ground. I've no doubt he'll face the music one day; a man like that can't just disappear.'

'Asil Nadir did.'

It was the autumn when Cathy's trial came up. Edwina was glad the prosecution had decided not to use her evidence. They were worried about her stormy relationship with Cathy and her motives for following her; besides which, they had plenty of other material that incriminated her. Edwina was surprised how relieved she felt.

'And if I thought it was going to be an ordeal in the witness box, I suppose I ought to spare a thought for what Cathy is going through,' she said to Ulysses.

'Are you going to the trial anyway?' he said.

'No.'

'Don't you want to get all the juicy details?'

'Not really. Why, do you?'

'I want to find out what Zeidler gave her at the second meeting.'

415

Edwina had forgotten about the little package.

'Well, you go if you want to, but I think it would be out of order for me to be there.'

Ulysses had fewer qualms about the whole business than Edwina and decided to take time off work to go.

The trial was scheduled to last two weeks, but in the end it didn't even last one. The evidence against Cathy was conclusive: she had had access to the bids once they had been submitted, the bids from each of the other firms matched exactly the numbers and initials on her computer disk, she had had two official meetings with Zeidler prior to her clandestine ones, and her shares in the company had been transferred from his name to hers. Her defence was that she'd been overwhelmed by the importance of the industrialist, that she was young and foolish and that she'd lost a great deal more than she'd ever stood to gain – which had been the eight thousand shares, now, most likely, forfeit. The only other gift she'd had from Zeidler was the contents of a small package – a bunch of keys, which mostly proved to be duplicates of ones already in her possession. There were two that didn't seem to open anything, and she maintained she'd forgotten she had them and what they belonged to. Her story was that she'd lost her keys, and Wolfgang Zeidler had found them and was returning them. Whether this should be believed or not was anyone's guess, but it couldn't be proved otherwise.

'What do you think, Ulysses?' Edwina asked him.

'No idea. I can't even tell if she's lying or not.'

'But surely she must have been incredibly stupid to risk everything for just a few thousand shares. There must be more to that bunch of keys than she has said. After all, she knew that if she got caught she'd lose her job, her pension rights, her self-respect . . .'

'I agree, but think of all the soldiers and officers who've been court-martialled for false travel claims and the like – they've lost just as much for even less.'

Edwina had to agree that when it came to fools looking for a quick buck, and who gave no thought to their long-term losses, the Forces probably had more than their fair share.

On the Thursday the jury found Cathy guilty, and on the Friday the judge sentenced her to eighteen months in jail. As she had already been in custody for six months she could look forward to being out by the spring.

As soon as Edwina heard the news she rang Lizzie.

'A year? That's less than you thought.'

'I think the judge thought that Cathy came off worst out of the deal. After all, the bids have been resubmitted for the contract and a British firm got it this time, so the wrong was righted. Zeidler is still free and the only one in the dock was Cathy. And she's hardly an arch-criminal – just a stupid, greedy woman.'

'Still no news of Zeidler?'

'The word is that he's in South America somewhere. On the scale of world crimes it doesn't rate that highly. I don't get the impression anyone is trying too hard to get him brought back here. I expect when it all dies down he'll reappear, but whether anyone can be bothered to prosecute him . . .'

'I wonder what she'll do when she comes out?'

'Knowing Cathy, she'll land on her feet. She'll sell her story to the *Sunday Sport* or something.'

'By the way, talking of falling on my feet, I've got a posting.'

'Where?'

'I'm going to be a platoon commander at Sandhurst.'

'No!' Edwina couldn't think of a person more fitted for the job than Lizzie. 'But that's brilliant.'

'Thank you. You can come and watch Sovereign's Parade with me if you like. That should stir some old memories.'

'Yes, I'd like that,' said Edwina, meaning it.

The Royal Military Academy, Sandhurst, April 1995

Lizzie felt tears of pride and happiness prick her eyes as she watched her platoon, dressed in impeccable navy uniforms with gleaming blancoed cross-belts, march around the square in front of Old College.

'They're a credit to you,' whispered Edwina, surreptitiously wiping away a tear.

'Aren't they wonderful?' agreed Lizzie, bursting with pride. 'They're all going to make such cracking officers.'

'With you as their role model,' said Amanda, 'they can't fail.'

The band played a jaunty regimental march as the ranks of cadets swung past in quick time, first the male platoons and lastly the female one. At the head of the women a tall blonde officer cadet yelled the words of command with gusto.

'You'll never guess what the winner of the Queen's Medal is called this year,' said Lizzie with a grin. The Queen's Medal was awarded to the cadet who gained the highest academic results, whereas the Sword of Honour, now competed for by the girls too, was presented to the best cadet in all fields of achievement. So far a girl hadn't managed to win it, but Edwina and Lizzie were both certain that one day one would.

'Surprise me,' replied Edwina.

'Miss Austin.'

'You're joking,' said Amanda with a grin.

'Straight up.'

Edwina watched as the music changed to 'Auld Lang Syne' and the cadets slow-marched up the steps. She was flooded with memories of how she'd felt when she'd been a part of the parade: the pride, the sense of achievement and the excitement at her future. She wondered if things would have been very different for the three of them but for the intervention of Cathy Roberts. There was an endless stream of *what ifs*, and no telling how things would have panned out, but all in all the three of them were pretty content with their lot. Amanda and Bella were happy and settled in Andover, Lizzie had confided that she was dating a fellow officer at the RMA – 'It's purely platonic,' she insisted – and Edwina couldn't deny that she'd found her niche as a press photographer. She was extremely happy in her work and had no doubt that she owed the Army for finding out what she really liked doing. In fact, thinking about it, she owed the Army for her two best friends, her lover and her new career. But the Army had had its money's worth out of her too. Perhaps honours were even.

As she watched, the Academy adjutant's horse walked through the big double doors, which shut firmly behind it. From where she sat, even with the music playing, Edwina could just hear the roar of triumph from the cadets. She remembered the time she'd been part of that – the elation, the happiness and the sense of relief – and felt a twinge of nostalgia.

'Good luck,' she murmured.

'And just who are you wishing luck, Miss Austin?'

Edwina swung round in her seat in amazement as she recognised the Irish brogue of Lieutenant Colonel O'Brien.

'Good God, ma'am, what are you doing here?'

'I see you haven't lost your natural charm,' said Denise O'Brien. 'And I think,' she added, 'seeing as you are a civilian these days, we can dispense with the *ma'am* bit.'

'OK, ma ... Oops.' Edwina stopped and stared at Denise's epaulettes. 'Good heavens, I mean congratulations. Brigadier O'Brien, wow!'

'I take it that you aren't too upset by my advancement?'

'No. I'm chuffed to bits for you. I was only remembering the other day how you stuck up for me when I was here.'

'Well, I think perhaps that under the circumstances it was called for.'

Neither of them mentioned Cathy. It didn't seem necessary.

The crowd of onlookers began to mill on to the now empty parade square as they waited to be rejoined by the cadets and then escorted to lunch. Edwina noticed that Amanda was hanging back, avoiding the eye of Brigadier O'Brien.

Amanda was keeping a low profile deliberately. She knew that, however much her lifestyle was acceptable outside the Army, it might embarrass many of her former comrades to meet her again if they were aware of the real reason behind her dismissal. Denise O'Brien would certainly have been privy to all the facts regarding her former trainee's hurried departure. Amanda didn't resent it; she knew such a momentous change in attitude would take time. Heaven knew, it had taken forty years after the end of the Second World War for women to cease to be regarded as simply admin fodder and be accepted as capable of holding down a job in the Forces which required anything more than typing and organisational skills. Perhaps the day would come for people like her – but not for a long time.

'It's a shame so few of your platoon are still serving. You were all fine officers,' said the brigadier. 'And who'd have thought that I'd see one of you back here as a platoon commander. I bet none of you ever considered that was possible when you were first cadets here.'

'And I bet she's a brilliant platoon commander,' said Edwina.

'She is,' said Brigadier O'Brien. Lizzie flushed red with embarrassment.

The brigadier nodded farewell and went to talk to other members of the public, and soon the cadets made their way from Old College to escort their guests to the post-Parade luncheon. Edwina and Amanda followed Lizzie as she led them across to the mess at Victory College, where they would be eating with the cadets about to be commissioned in the Adjutant General's Corps.

'I hope you're making a better fist of teaching the poor old cadets in your charge than Cathy Roberts did,' said Edwina as they walked through the grounds to the distant building.

'She didn't do too badly. We all turned out OK,' said Lizzie loyally.

'She's out of nick, you know. She came out a week ago.'

'What's going to happen to her now?' asked Amanda.

'I have no idea, but she seemed quite well set up, with a nice flat near Finsbury Park. How she can afford it is anybody's guess, but Ulysses has a theory that the bunch of keys Zeidler returned to her had a key to some strong box or other with the rest of her payment in it. But that's only his theory; I don't think we'll ever know the truth.'

'I don't suppose when she got commissioned she ever imagined she'd end up in Holloway,' said Lizzie thoughtfully.

'I don't suppose she did, but then I never imagined I'd end up where I am,' said Edwina.

'Nor me,' agreed Amanda.

Edwina looked around at the immaculate uniforms of the cadets escorting proud parents, friends and relations to the commissioning lunch.

'I wonder what will happen to all of them,' she mused to herself. 'I wonder what their hopes and ambitions are, and if they'll achieve them. I wonder how the next generation of sisters in arms will fare.'

Hitched
Zoë Barnes

Hitch number one ... A quick jaunt to the registry office and off to the pub with a few friends to celebrate. That's all Gemma wants for her wedding to Rory. But then the parents hear the news.

Hitch number two ... Suddenly her little wedding is hijacked and turned into a Hollywood-style extravaganza. Before she knows what's hit her, Gemma is stampeded into yards of frothing tulle, fork buffets for five hundred, kilted page boys and an all-inclusive honeymoon in the Maldives ...

Hitch number three ... And while the dress may be a perfect fit, Gemma and Rory's relationship is coming apart at the seams ...

An irresistible look at wedding fever from the bestselling author of *Bumps*.

Praise for *Hitched*

"lively and compulsive" *The Mirror*

"A great book for anyone who likes their romance laced with a healthy dose of real life" *Options*

"An entertaining and light-hearted story" *The Observer*

Hot Property
Zoë Barnes

The new novel from the bestselling author of
Bumps and *Hitched*

When Claire inherits a house out of the blue - she thinks
she's struck it rich!

But while the word 'cottage' inspires images of romantic
idylls and roses round the door – there's nothing remotely
heavenly about Paradise Cottage. It's a tumble-down wreck
in the middle of nowhere – more in need of a demolition
expert than a decorator.

Still, Claire's not one to shirk a challenge. Much to the
amusement of her hunky new neighbour, Aidan, she decides
to renovate the cottage herself. After all problem-solving,
trouble-shooting - it's what Claire does best. She's used to
planning events for thousands of people. She can sort out
one little cottage ... can't she?

Praise for *Bumps*

"an enjoyable and moving read"   *Daily Mail*

"An entertaining and light-hearted story"   *Observer*

The very best of Piatkus fiction is now available in paperback as well as hardcover. Piatkus paperbacks, where *every* book is special.

☐ 0 7499 3088 8	Sisters In Arms	Catherine Jones	£5.99
☐ 0 7499 3008 X	Army Wives	Catherine Jones	£5.99
☐ 0 7499 3111 6	Hot Property	Zoë Barnes	£5.99
☐ 0 7499 3072 1	Hitched	Zoë Barnes	£5.99
☐ 0 7499 3030 6	Bumps	Zoë Barnes	£5.99
☐ 0 7499 3110 8	Catch the Moment	Euanie McDonald	£5.99

The prices shown above were correct at the time of going to press. However, Piatkus Books reserve the right to show new retail prices on covers which may differ from those previously advertised in the text or elsewhere.

Piatkus Books will be available from your bookshop or newsagent, or can be ordered from the following address:
Piatkus Paperbacks, PO Box 11, Falmouth, TR10 9EN
Alternatively you can fax your order to this address on 01326 374 888 or e-mail us at books@barni.avel.co.uk

Payments can be made as follows: Sterling cheque, Eurocheque, postal order (payable to Piatkus Books) or by credit card, Visa/Mastercard. Do not send cash or currency. UK and B.F.P.O. customers should allow £1.00 postage and packing for the first book, 50p for the second and 30p for each additional book ordered to a maximum of £3.00 (7 books plus).

Overseas customers, including Eire, allow £2.00 for postage and packing for the first book, plus £1.00 for the second and 50p for each subsequent title ordered.

NAME (block letters) _____

ADDRESS_____

_____

I enclose my remittance for £ _____

I wish to pay by Visa/Mastercard   Expiry Date:_____
